TH_

FORGOTTEN

BRIDE

*For Denise,
Here comes the bride!*

BY PHILIP ANTHONY SMITH

Philip Anthony Smith

GET A FREE BOOK BY VISITING:
WWW.PHILIPANTHONYSMITH.COM

INSTAGRAM: @PHILIPSMITHFICTION
FACEBOOK: PHILIPSMITHFICTION
COPYRIGHT © 2024 PHILIP ANTHONY SMITH

CONTENTS

PROLOGUE 1
THE NEW HOME 13
THE MISTAKE 21
THE BEGINNING 36
THE DATE 50
THE REUNION 62
THE BEAR 77
THE OTHER WOMAN 89
THE QUESTION................................... 102
THE CIRCUS 115
THE DINNER.. 128
THE LIES.. 144
THE TEST 159
THE REVELATION................................ 173
THE GIFT 189
THE TRUTH 200
THE HUNTERS 210
THE RELEASE 221
THE CELEBRATION 236
THE COVER-UP 247
THE SECOND 256

THE SPIKE	265
THE EGG	277
THE SANDWICH	284
THE VISITOR	295
THE RETURN	307
THE NEEDLE	323
THE LAW	331
THE SEARCH	346
THE JUDGEMENT	355
THE WHITE FLAG	365
THE LETTER	374
THE GOODNIGHT	385
THE LOVE	395
THE NIGHTMARE	403
EPILOGUE	416

PROLOGUE

OLIVIA – 2014

Well, *fuck*, here we go! Who would have thought that little old me, the pale and unapologetically potty-mouthed Brit, would be loitering outside a Californian church in the blistering sun, waiting to get married to the man of my dreams? Certainly not me.

I knew that Nathaniel, my hunky American husband-to-be, was probably a trembling wreck inside, tensely waiting for me to burst through the doors in my thrift-store dress and saunter down the aisle towards him. Unlike him, I didn't feel nervous, not one bit, and I didn't even have a single shred of niggling doubt to hold me back. Every single uncertainty was long ago quashed by the incredible ten years I had already spent with him, and for practical reasons alone, we had put this day off more times than I could count. It wasn't really the wedding of my dreams, but having said that, I never really dreamt of getting married, and we did it all on a shoestring budget for the only reason that truly mattered to either of us: *love*.

Cute, right?

We were a family of tortured artists, and creativity definitely ran in our blood, but unfortunately for us, success didn't. I played the part of the overworked and underpaid writer, constantly peddling my latest novella or short story to prospective publishers and independent bookshops, while my husband-to-be was the struggling artist, trying to flog his most recent oil on canvas to the local motels or cafés. It won't come as a shock that neither career path ever earned us much, but it was a labour of love, and between us, we managed to get by.

When our six-year-old daughter, Aurora, unexpectedly came along, our surprising foray into parenthood strained our finances almost to breaking point, which is mostly why the wedding was perpetually pushed back. Luckily, we never longed for anything materialistic; I would be perfectly content with just writing and watching our daughter play in our garden all day.

For years, we scraped together every spare dollar, and even though the wedding venue was the only thing we could afford, in its own way, it was still completely breathtaking. Straight from a postcard, the tiny white chapel was slap bang in the middle of a delightfully green meadow, and the towering sycamores gently swaying in the wind behind it only added to the majesty. The magnificent morning orchestra of chirpy birdsong that filled the valley was complemented by the occasional refreshing breeze, which brought the heady aromas of flowers and sweet honey along with it, and I closed my eyes and inhaled the pure serenity of it. The wind picked up slightly, which made my dress billow, and I struggled to keep it all together as I wistfully gazed up, trying to spot a single cloud in the sky.

In summary, it was fucking beautiful.

The unhindered sun warmed my ivory face, and although it was unusually clement for this time of year in California, the unwavering heat was still far too intense for my pasty British complexion. I thought after eight years of living here, I would have acclimatised to it, but the obstinate sun was still as relentless as the day I stepped off the plane. Lest I fry like a vampire, I quickly moved into the shade to escape the punishing rays and leaned against the chapel wall, impatiently waiting for the proceedings to begin. I testily tapped the wooden cladding of the chapel with my tatty, borrowed shoes, and although I felt like I wasn't in any state to give an opinion on appearances, I couldn't help but feel there was something fundamentally uncouth about building a house of God out of timber.

Back in England, the churches felt like they had been standing for thousands of years or more, and the damp but dusty smell that hit you when you walked into one would certainly attest to that fact. Churches always gave me the creeps, and my skin used to pugnaciously tingle whenever I stepped foot inside one. My parents were always firm believers, and back when they were still kicking, we used to attend church often. As I continued to stare up at the sky, for a split second, my unwavering atheist mind wondered if they were somehow looking down on me and whether they felt proud of me or not. I also mindlessly asked if *He* was with them, what the big man thought of our venue choice, and if *He* had an opinion on us getting married.

Well, let's see now…

We had sex before marriage *frequently*, so according to the Bible, I'm technically a whore, and having a child out of wedlock likely earned me double sin points. I drank far too much, I was a secret smoker, and there were very few profanities that I wasn't comfortable using, even in polite conversation. Most damning of all, I suppose: I was a non-believer, and I haven't had faith in God for a single second of my life. To add insult to injury, when the priest who was about to marry us asked me if I was a Catholic, I just gleefully smiled and nodded, so that makes me a liar, too. I just hoped *He* wasn't home when I sheepishly walked through those doors and that I didn't spontaneously combust in a ball of smiteful flames as soon as my foot crossed the threshold.

My train of thought was giving me the heebie-jeebies, and as I uselessly patted myself down trying to find the hidden packet of cigarettes that I usually kept for emergencies, the lack of pockets in my dress became painfully apparent, and my search proved fruitless. I heard the church doors ominously creak open, and our beautiful daughter hysterically burst through them in a ball of energy.

"Mummy! You look beautiful!" she excitedly screeched in a high-pitched voice.

"Thank you, Aurora, so do you!" I gushed.

"Are you going to marry Daddy yet, or what?" she sternly asked with her hands on her hips.

"I'm waiting for you to give me the signal to walk in, darling. Do you remember your job?"

"Come and get you, walk down the aisle, and scatter petals. It's not rocket science, Mummy."

"*It's not rocket science?*" I lovingly mocked as I knelt down to her level. "Who taught you that?" I added.

"Uncle Al said it to Daddy when he was tying his tie for him."

"Yeah, he was always useless at that, love."

I heard the distant scraping of a car traversing the gravel driveway towards the church, and as I turned my head to look at it, they flashed their lights at me wildly. I didn't immediately recognise the white vehicle but surmised they were probably a late guest, so I happily waved at them regardless.

"You better go inside and practise again sweetheart," I fondly started as I stood up, "it'll be starting soon."

"I will!" Aurora happily exclaimed as she cheerfully skipped back into the church.

The unknown car stopped in the car park, the driver's side door flew open, and one of my oldest friends from England, Stacey, stepped out in a cheery dance. She still lived back in dreary London, and I hadn't clapped eyes on her for years, so I excitedly ran as quickly as my fluttering dress would allow me to meet her halfway.

"Oh my God, Stace, you look smouldering hot! Are you trying to upstage me on my wedding day? You bitch!" I laughed as I wrapped my arms around her.

"Thank you. I love your dress?" she falsely enthused with an upwards inflexion.

"Oh, come on, this little charity shop number? Don't be catty," I retorted with false disdain as I pulled at my dress.

"Honestly, you look beautiful, Olivia. I can't believe you are getting married! I feel like I've not seen you in forever!"

"Still, true to form, you manage to be fucking late!"

"Oh, come on, flawlessness such as this takes time," she said with a glamourous twirl.

"Worth it," I satirically leched as I sucked my teeth.

"Liv, I've missed you. It's so lonely in London without you," she said while hugging me tightly.

"I've missed you, too."

"I'm so jealous! When are you going to find me a nice yank to spank?" she joked with a quivering bottom lip.

"Never, if you carry on talking like that!"

"Are there any hunky groomsmen that should be on my radar?"

"It's a small wedding. The only single bloke is the best man, Alexander, and he's fair game, I suppose."

"Alexander… I don't remember him. Is he good-looking?"

"He's not my type, but he's a safe pair of hands. Just be gentle with him, okay?" I laughed.

"You know I can't promise that," she uttered as she fixed her hair in the wind, "when's it all kicking off then?"

"Well, according to Aurora, Nath has a problem with his tie, hence the delay."

"Catastrophe! Cancel the whole thing!" Stacey jested.

"Hey, you haven't got a ciggy I can bum, have you?" I cheekily whispered as I leaned in closer.

"*Bum a ciggy?* I thought you would've changed after almost a decade over here."

"It's a special occasion," I said as I framed my dress with my hands and a cheeky grin.

"And I thought you quit for Nath?"

"Like I said: a special occasion."

"Well, don't tell him I'm the one who gave you one," she warned as she rifled through her bag before producing a packet of cigarettes and handing me one, "I know how he feels about it."

"And the lighter?" I said with my hand out.

"Jesus Christ, it's like we're back at uni."

"Wow, go easy on the blasphemy. That's God's house over there."

Stacey handed me the lighter as she judgementally shook her head, and as I heard the church doors slowly creak open behind me again, I clumsily tucked the borrowed smoking paraphernalia into my garter to keep it concealed. I innocently turned around as if nothing had happened, and I nearly burst into laughter when I saw Nathaniel walking towards me with his hands over his eyes, being carefully guided by Alexander.

"What the fuck are you playing at?" I asked through a stifled chuckle.

"It's bad luck to see the bride before the wedding," Nathaniel muttered fearfully.

"Don't be such a knobhead," I laughed as I pulled his hands away from his face, and he reluctantly opened his eyes as his jaw figuratively hit the floor.

"Oh my God, Olivia, you look amazing," Nathaniel said with tears in his eyes.

"Thank you," I smiled.

"Houston, we have a problem," Alexander satirically announced as he pointed to the groom's tie.

"Oh?" I asked.

"My tie is too short! It looks ridiculous," Nathaniel explained as he held it out.

I walked around behind him, quickly undid his tie to redo it to its correct length, and then returned to my previous position in front of him to inspect my work.

"There you go," I began with a smile, "now, can we please get married before I'm burnt to a crisp?"

"Yes. I'll see you inside," Nathaniel said with a smirk as he lovingly kissed me on the cheek, "I love you."

"I love you, too."

As soon as their backs were turned, I stealthily retrieved the cigarette and lighter from my garter and pensively watched on as they all excitedly laughed and joked together on the short walk back to the chapel. Stacey licked her finger and dramatically placed it on Alexander's shoulder whilst she sucked her teeth, miming that he was red hot, and I let out a loud chuckle. Nathaniel heard it and turned around again as he strolled to wave at me with a beaming grin across his face. Once they had made their way through the doors and they shut behind them with a loud thud, I immediately lit the cigarette that Stacey had provided me with and started walking over to the chapel to return to the shade and enjoy my last cigarette as an unmarried woman.

All jokes and gratuitous vulgarities aside, I doggedly adored that amazing man with every fibre of my heart, and although I know that I threw caution to the wind when I wilfully abandoned my old life for him, such huge risk had spectacularly paid off beyond my wildest dreams. I had never wanted something so much or been so sure about a life-changing decision, and putting the birth of our daughter aside, I can honestly say that morning outside the church was the happiest I had ever been. We had our astoundingly beautiful little girl together, our lives were finally clicking into place, and we were at long last finding our feet in the world. I was standing on the very precipice of having everything I ever desired and wanted to savour every delightful moment because I knew that Aurora would come for me at any second now, and I would be finally walking down the aisle.

As I was reflectively taking the final few drags on the borrowed cigarette, I heard unexpected footsteps crushing the gravel slowly behind me. The noise startled me, and I hurriedly removed the cigarette from my lips and quickly discarded it on the floor to turn around and see who it was, but before I could, I felt a gloved hand tightly grip my bare shoulder and violently jerk me backwards.

Whack.

Without warning, I had been hit by something, and whatever it was that struck me at the side of my head was heavy enough to knock me over with ease, causing me to plummet onto the stones below abruptly. The initial blow was enough to lose my sense of orientation completely; there was a piercing ringing in my ears, and blood started to gush from the split on my cheek. As I groggily attempted to push myself up from the ground, another brutal impact was swiftly delivered, knocking me for six while my face was punishingly forced back into the gravel.

In my escalating confusion, the sheathed hands then wildly clasped around my ankles and started violently dragging me around the corner of the chapel as I ineffectively kept flailing my arms and legs to try and escape their grasp. Suddenly, a huge weight was directly on top of me, and one of their hands was unrelentingly forcing the side of my face into the grit whilst the other callously clutched a filthy rag around my gaping mouth. Before I even contemplated batting it away, I couldn't help but breathe in a lungful of whatever chemicals the piece of cloth was doused in, and the damp yet sicky-sweet chemical aroma quickly coated my airways. Although I had no idea what the hell was going on when I started to feel faint, I knew that I was fighting for my life, and I desperately continued to try to shake my assailant's restraining hands off me.

There was a brief opportunity to get help when the chapel doors creaked open once again, and I tried screaming through the sodden rag as stridently as my dwindling physical strength allowed me to, but the muffled noise wasn't nearly as loud enough as to be heard by anyone else other than my ruthless attacker. I convulsed my entire body and clawed at the dirt with what little energy I had left in me to try and emerge from the corner of the building and hopefully become visible to whoever had come out of the doors. My assailant was strong, far more so than me, and in my weakened state, I was dragged even further into the shadows and away from the safety of the sunlight.

"It's time!" I heard Aurora melodically shout from around the corner as my limbs started to tire, my eyelids grew heavier, and I knew I was moments away from succumbing to the foul-smelling substance involuntarily inhaled by my nostrils.

"Mummy?" she distraughtly shouted before I went limp, stopped fighting, and reluctantly slipped into unconsciousness.

1

THE NEW HOME

OLIVIA — 2014

I was abruptly awoken by the mould-ridden dust that I was face down in, and when it caught the back of my throat, I started coughing uncontrollably. The frenzied panic quickly set in when I realised that my shaky hands were loosely bound behind my back and that I had some kind of cloth bag over my head. I feebly writhed around like an ensnared animal trying to release itself, and when I finally managed to slacken the crude rope just enough to liberate my wrists, I immediately ripped the bag off my head. In my haste to free myself, I disturbed the particles within, and the dry cough grew to a hacking one as I desperately attempted to clear my airways to breathe normally again. Once the coughing fit was over, I realised that removing the bag was of little utility because I was surrounded by unfathomable darkness at every angle and, worst of all, I could barely make out the tip of my own nose.

The only sound piercing the silence was the rasp and rattle of my lungs, desperately fighting to fill themselves with the stale air while I fumbled around in the black void, frantically attempting to divine where I was or find anything solid to gather my bearings against. My quaking hands found a cold and damp concrete wall in the shadowy abyss. I quickly turned my back to it to anchor myself and anxiously waited for whatever would happen next.

Suddenly, I was deafened by the droning hum and raucous pop of fluorescent lighting activating overhead, and as I threw my arms over my eyes to shield them from the blinding light, it brought sheer bewilderment and terror with it, and it involuntarily forced me to shuffle myself into the closest filthy corner hysterically. The startling change in illumination triggered a skull-splitting headache that had been lying dormant, and as I gripped my temples to quell the intense throbbing, my dithering fingertips found wet blood still seeping from the headwound where I was struck. The sensation brought the recollection of the events with it. Adrenaline took over, and I screamed at the top of my lungs for help.

"Aurora! Nath!" I shrieked.

There was no reply.

After my voice was hoarse from the persistent yelling, I noticed that my wedding dress had been removed, and instead, I had been clothed in some fetid and stained jumpsuit. I was barefoot, and the granular debris on the floor stuck into my soles as I frantically paced around the small space, trying to work out what the hell was going on. In my frenzy, I saw a huge steel door, which I sprinted over to, and I ferociously pounded my fists against it as hard as I could muster. The reverberating thuds echoed back at me within the tiny room and were only dampened by my blood-curdling screams of absolute terror when I realised that I was well and truly trapped.

"Help! Let me the fuck out of here!" I screeched.

"Language, Olivia," a heavily distorted voice boomed over an intercom.

I stopped my incessant banging and screaming as I turned around to look for the source of the voice and noticed a small crudely wired-up speaker mounted within a protective steel cage, and next to it was a CCTV camera that was following my every move. I walked a few paces into the centre of the room until I was directly facing it, and I heard the small motor within it whir as it ominously angled down and slowly zoomed into my face.

"Even though I walk through the valley of the shadow of death, I will fear no evil," the voice dramatically boomed.

"Who are you?" I asked.

"Call me... Benjamin," he responded.

"Do you have my daughter?" I asked softly.

"No, she is safe, as is Nathaniel, for now. If you want that to continue, it really depends on you and how you behave here."

"Why did you do this to me?"

"That's none of your concern."

I started to look around the room for some way to break out, but before I managed to find anything that looked even remotely promising, the television screen that was behind glass and mounted to the wall underneath the camera started to fire up, and I inquisitively walked over to it. It took a few seconds for it to warm up, but once it did, it was some barely visible and amateurish footage of woodland. I didn't recognise it at first, but once I spotted Nathaniel's beat-up car parked in the driveway, my blood ran cold, and I grimly realised that it was my home. The shaky camera gingerly poked around into the front window, and I could see Nath pacing the room on the phone with Aurora in hysteric tears in the background. The footage abruptly ended after a few seconds, and the television turned itself off.

"That was an hour ago." Benjamin matter-of-factly said.

"You're fucking sick," I woefully muttered.

"Play nice. Do as I say. If you do, no harm will come to them. If you don't, I won't be held responsible."

"You stay away from my fucking family!" I shouted.

"Olivia, you really aren't in any position to make demands."

"How long are you going to keep me in here?"

"That isn't up to me."

"Is this about money? Because if it is, you're barking up the wrong tree, mate. We don't have two cents to rub together," I announced with manic laughter.

"It isn't about money."

"Then why the fuck have you locked me in here?"

"Get comfortable. You'll be waiting here a while."

The background crackle of the intercom faded, and I let out one final earth-shattering scream, which bounced back at me as it echoed against the thick concrete walls. I refused to accept what they told me and started frenziedly riffling through all the items in the room, looking for some means of escape. I compared every item I picked up to the steel door separating me from freedom as the camera followed me around the room, and nothing in there seemed remotely sturdy enough to pry it open. Once I had exhausted every possibility, I spotted the slab of steel mounted to the wall that unfolded into a bed, and I released the mechanism to sit on the edge of it with my head defeatedly in my hands. I took several intentionally deep breaths to try and calm myself down, and it was only when the initial panic faded that I understood the gravity of the situation I had been thrust into.

This wasn't random.

My kidnapping was diligently planned, well thought out, and flawlessly executed. Benjamin, if that was his real name, knew mine, so this was personal, too. I wasn't kidnapped on a whim, and he had gone to ridiculous lengths to put me in this place, but why? I racked my brains, trying to conjure a single name of someone who I had wronged deeply enough to warrant this reaction or who was even capable of doing it. Nonetheless, no one plausible sprung to mind. I knew I was foul-mouthed, and I wasn't known for mincing my words either, but was there something so vile that I said to someone that made them do this to me?

As I continued to look around, I realised that I clearly wasn't there for the short term either; the pantry cupboards were stocked to the gills with shelf-stable food, and the racking beside the bed even housed clothes and spare sheets. I walked over to the shelves and started idly flicking through the clothes, and they were all in my size. He had seemingly thought of everything, and he had left me no choice but to simply comply with his demands for now because I couldn't risk the safety of Nath and Aurora by staging an attempted breakout. The footage they showed me let me know that they could get to them at any moment, and after what he did to me to get me there, they certainly had no qualms about violence.

I returned to my new bed, agitatedly rocking backwards and forwards on the edge of it, trying to get my head around the fact that every single facet of my life from then on would be controlled by the voice I just heard.

"I love you guys so much," I whispered.

THE FORGOTTEN BRIDE

TEN LONG YEARS LATER...

2

THE MISTAKE

OLIVIA – 2024

Ten fucking years. If I hadn't kept a diligent record of how long I had been imprisoned, I would never have believed it. Nevertheless, I counted every single one of the lines I had inscribed into the concrete twice over, and the results were soberingly indisputable: five-hundred-and-twenty gruelling weeks spent locked away in that hellhole. I may have unknowingly lost track a few days here and there, but with only the tiny slither of non-artificial light that glimmered through the single solitary air vent above my head, I came to terms with the fact that it was impossible to be perfectly accurate. The truly depressing thing about my little weekly ritual of marking a line on the wall was that it was a daily routine when I started it off, but after two or three weeks, I decided to count in weeks out of sheer pragmatism when it dawned on me that I would run out of free wall space before anyone could find me.

The milestone anniversary compelled me to torturously play the events of my short-lived wedding day over and over again in my head. I was only mere seconds away from tying the knot when I was abducted, and even after a decade, I couldn't even remember how I had got entangled in that situation, nor did I know very much about the faceless menace that had cast me there. It should have been the happiest day of my life, but it was instead the most horrific thing I could ever have imagined happening to me. He just cold-heartedly chucked me in there as his plaything with no explanation whatsoever and has incongruously kept me alive for over a decade. When he abandoned me in there, I had a thousand and one questions, which over the years boiled down to just one:

Why?

Benjamin never answered. At least that was the name he gave me after he jailed me in here, and although it's what I called him, I was under no illusion that it was conveniently made up. It seemed like a private joke I wasn't privy to, and I heard the slight laughter in his voice whenever I used his pseudonym. Other than his propensity for the Bible and his flair for the sadistic, that was pretty much all I knew about him.

I sorely missed my family. If I had been a little stronger that day and just managed to get away from my abductor, Nathaniel and I would have been celebrating our tenth wedding anniversary that evening over a candle-lit dinner. Our teenage daughter would have been with us too, sharing in the abundant happiness as we swapped stories about how far our little family had come. The privilege of watching Aurora growing up was mercilessly snatched from me that day too, and even if I somehow managed to escape my captivity, I knew it would be something I could never get back. I may have become a distant and foggy memory for them both, long forgotten, probably presumed dead, and I left them with nothing but a handful of photographs to remember me by.

I hadn't forgotten them, though.

I thought about little else whilst I was detained in this hovel. I desperately tried to preserve their memory in whatever way I could; I would sometimes cry myself to sleep thinking about their faces, and it would be the first images I would conjure up in the morning when I opened my eyes. It is true that I wasn't blessed with Nathaniel's artistic talents, but the manic manuscripts I produced during my captivity were littered with sketches and drawings of them to try and keep the vision of them intact. After all the monstrous things that happened to me within these four walls, my family were my anchor, and I wouldn't still be alive if it wasn't for them.

My very own personal penitentiary had all the mod cons, and I had been confined to it for so long that it sickeningly started to feel like home. It was a little bigger than my cramped university flat in London but buried deep underground in an unknown place, initially designed to be some kind of bomb shelter. My bed, if you dared call it so, was simply a slab of steel mounted to the wall on a hinge, coupled with a paper-thin mattress that even a stray dog would refuse to sleep on.

I had a complicated relationship with the shower. After my abduction, I didn't touch it for weeks, not only because it was in full view of the CCTV camera that tracked my every move but also because it only ever produced ice-cold water. Nevertheless, out of necessity, I forced myself to get used to it a few months in, and after a certain incident, I didn't even hang the sheet to cover my body anymore. The toilet, which was a rather grandiose term for the plastic bucket I had access to, gloomily remained in the corner and served as a festering reminder of what little dignity I had left. I refused to use it at first, but as you can imagine, that meagre protest didn't last long.

My little kitchenette was wholly comprised of a portable gas stove that had long since been disconnected as a punishment and a plastic ice box to keep somewhat edible what little fresh food my captor deigned to bequeath to me. Not that I did much cooking in there anyway; the perpetual state of nausea I constantly felt failed to give me the most voracious appetite, forcing me to sustain myself on the bare minimum. I felt like it was a victory for Benjamin whenever I desperately ate something, and I hated giving him the satisfaction of watching me eat like some frightened animal in a cage.

At the back of my cell, there was a heavy steel door that, from what I understood, was locked and unlocked remotely. It led to a small entrance area, which housed another locked door. It served as a kind of airlock, a means of allowing my enigmatic captor to leave the morsels of food for me and swap the full buckets for empty ones. In the decade I was kept there, I only fleetingly saw what was beyond both doors a handful of times, and I never ventured beyond them.

If I were well-behaved and my week in captivity was uneventful, I would be pathetically provided with basic writing supplies along with my weekly food drop. The only thing that kept me even remotely sane was my writing, and I had spent the last decade amassing an enviable collection of novels and memoirs that would put even the most prolific authors to shame. The vast majority of the mad ramblings that were contained in those pages only served as a constant reminder of the dramatic ups and downs of my mental state over the years in captivity, and I didn't even recognise the woman behind those erratic writings anymore.

On the wall beside the ever-vigilant camera was a small speaker that Benjamin used to communicate with me, and only God knows how many hours we spent talking over it. Of course, his voice was heavily distorted to preserve his true identity, and if I ever managed to get out of there, I didn't think I would even recognise it if he walked by me in the street. Oftentimes, the intercom would click, and a little jibe or a bad-humoured insult that was painstakingly selected to slowly break me would follow, but when the mood took him, my kidnapper would use it to sinisterly play his macabre games with me for his own twisted amusement. The fact that he had taken me away from my family wasn't in the least bad enough for him, and he kept rubbing salt into the wounds, so much so that throughout my captivity, I amassed some very painful memories that I would never be rid of.

Last but not least, the television, which was mounted behind thick glass in the centre of the back wall, was the source of the lion's share of my own misery. At the behest of my captor, it sadistically provided me with a carefully curated window into the outside world. For the first few years that I was held in there, it would immediately fill me with cold dread every time it clicked into life, and the light started to emanate from it. Regular programming was usually a shakily produced home movie directed by my cruel kidnapper, gallingly designed to emotionally torture me in some painful way or another. To be honest, I had grown desensitised to them, so they didn't really bother me anymore as I was already immeasurably broken beyond recognition.

The only reflective surface in the entire bunker was the polished surface of that screen, and even though it was virtually impossible to avoid, I tried my hardest not to gaze into it. Whenever I accidentally caught the reflection, I was shocked and appalled by what I saw. The threadbare rags that constituted my clothes were quite literally rotting at the seams and did little to conceal my skeletal body; it was clear to see that I had multiple vitamin and mineral deficiencies. My thinning hair was falling out in clumps, my once ivory skin was almost translucent, and my brittle nails would splinter and snap even under the slightest amount of pressure. The garish dark circles under my eyes were growing even more prominent by the day due to the deprivation of both sleep and sunlight. All in all, I resembled a ghoul more than a human.

Nathaniel always chirpily reminded me to be positive in the face of adversity, and I had managed to survive a long decade of this; that was a cause for celebration, right? I had already tried everything conceivable to escape my captivity, and as the failed attempts racked up, my sombre acceptance of my dire predicament grew without respite. At first, I screamed at the top of my lungs, pretty much constantly, in a forlorn plea for someone to hear me and come running to my rescue. When my voice gave out, I took a leaf from Benjamin's book and partook in manipulation, and as much as it turned my stomach, I even tried befriending him. The endless ragtag collection of schemes and ill-conceived plots was long behind me, and over the years, I had fashioned all manner of failed devices and ineffective tools to facilitate my escape with what little resources I had available. With nothing else left to try, my tactics always reverted to waiting, interminably waiting for a stranger, my husband-to-be, or even the police to smash those doors somehow down and save me.

Hope was a luxury I wasn't afforded, and over the years, it grew incredibly scarce. I came to the grim conclusion that I was only postponing the inevitable; one day, the food deliveries would abruptly stop, the ventilation system would pack in, or the water would stop running, and I would slowly wither away without anyone ever knowing I was there in the first place. For the longest time, I thought that I was utterly powerless in that room, but with little left to lose, the realisation that I had one final trick left up my sleeve began to dawn on me.

I was going to kill myself.

To be perfectly clear, in my mind, it wasn't suicide; it was escape, release and freedom. It wasn't born out of sadness, depression, or even defeat. It was a decision spawned by rage and victory. After a decade of keeping me breathing, his unwitting hostage bleeding out on the floor was the very last thing he wanted to happen, and although I had no idea what his nefarious motives really were, the only real thing I knew about him was that he wanted me alive. I'm sure he had his reasons to keep me as the plaything he could torture at will, and if taking my own life was the only way to take back the power and choose my path, I would do it without giving it a second thought. Anyhow, I knew that I couldn't survive another ten years in such a state, nor did I want to give him the barbarous satisfaction of seeing me erode before his lecherous eyes.

After an incident that took place a few years earlier, he removed all the cutlery from my cave, and he was painstakingly careful not to give me anything that I could use to break out of there. However, since I once turned my nose up at the constant stream of baked beans coming through the doors, my ever-comical captor developed a penchant for providing them. It's remarkable how jagged the lids became when a can opener was as old and overused as mine, and it didn't take much ingenuity to fabricate one into a blade, which I carefully kept stashed beneath my mattress.

I planned to patiently wait for that week's delivery, and when the outer door was locked again, I would slit my wrists. I barely had a scrap of food left, so I knew that the delivery was imminent, and by the time he returned to the sentry box he was monitoring me from, I would finally be free. I had already written my notes, one for Nathaniel, one for Aurora, and another for Stacey. I had so much to say to all of them, and I must have rewritten them a hundred times; in fact, they were written so well that I would probably have been awarded a fucking Pulitzer.

There was a time that I thought I was strong enough to possibly make it through both doors in the split second they were unlocked to slit my abductor's throat, and I fantasised about it day in, day out. Nonetheless, I knew I was perilously outgunned, and even though I tried building my physical strength up in whatever way my predicament allowed, I was so emotionally drained that I barely had enough motivation to get out of bed most days.

I often paced around my personal penitentiary to keep my strength up, yet I couldn't remember the last time I jogged even a few metres. The window of opportunity was so razor-thin that I didn't know how my legs would respond if I were to somehow escape and sprint for my freedom. If I tried to flee and failed once again, I didn't know what I would be subjected to afterwards or what safeguards Benjamin would put in place to prevent it from ever happening again.

The constant clicks and hums of the ventilation filled the silence as I sat for maybe an hour in waiting, and the minute I heard the distant sound of his footsteps forebodingly beyond the doors, I knew it was time. I was far more nervous than I had initially anticipated, and even though my hands were fiercely trembling, my resolve was unwavering, so I wiped the sweat from my brow and remained eager to enact my plan. My eyes were firmly fixed on the indicator panel on the wall and the two pairs of two bulbs it housed. It had one set for each of the doors:

green signified a door was locked, and red was unlocked. The interior bulb went green, the exterior door went red, and I heard the familiar clunk and screech as it opened, then the usual sound of movement in the entrance.

He was there. I could almost hear him breathing.

With only a few inches of steel separating us, the deadened thuds of drinking water and food hitting the floor were almost audible as the interior door remained locked, according to my prediction. As I covertly retrieved the makeshift blade and was poised to carve at my arm the second that the outside door was closed again, the brief window of torturesome opportunity arrived. Both doors were unlocked, and I intently watched the bulb, waiting for it to turn green again.

"I love you both so much," I whispered to myself as I closed my eyes and pressed the blade into my wrist, ready to slice it open without the slightest hesitation.

I just needed the green light.

But they remained tauntingly red.

The eerie silence filled me with fear, and my brain couldn't compute what my eyes were seeing. I had fallen prey to this before; it was probably a loathsome test of compliance from my kidnapper to make sure I was obeying his rules. If I dared flout them, I would be set upon with vicious violence as soon as I tried to open the internal door. After remaining entirely motionless for a fleeting while, I began to worry that I was missing my perfect opportunity to end all this at last, and I touched the handle of the interior door softly to turn it hesitantly.

The food delivery had been abandoned as usual against the wall of the small corridor connecting the two doors, and the exterior door appeared to be locked at first glance, but after so many years without maintenance, the rust in the mechanism had sealed it open. I placed my ear to it in order to try and hear if he was standing on the other side, but I couldn't hear a damn thing beyond my own laboured breaths. As I gripped and pulled the handle, it began to creak open threateningly, and I was met with an ambivalent mixture of stomach-churning panic and the overriding urge to run as fast as my withered legs could carry me. Nonetheless, I stood rooted to the spot for a few seconds, staring up at the concrete steps and waiting for the inevitable trap to snap.

The coast was clear.

I carefully took a single step out of my concrete cage and onto the cold steps beyond it with my eyes almost shut. To my pleasant surprise, nothing happened. Then another step. And another. I cautiously reached the top of the steps, and a thin wooden hatch atop some rusty ladders was the only thing that stood between me and my freedom. I had no idea what danger was lurking above it, and I would be lying if I said that part of me didn't want just to walk back down the stairs rather than face it. Then, I remembered what mattered to me most: my family. I imagined the woeful look in their eyes after finally coming home out of the blue after all these years, and that tender thought was what gave me the strength I needed to make the right call.

"Fuck it," I hysterically whimpered.

If I was determined to put an end to my miserable existence, I was willing to do so while trying to escape, so I took a deep breath, wearily climbed the ladders, and began pushing up into the flimsy sheet of wood as fiercely as I could. As the lock started to give way, and I could feel the timber creaking, I gave one final push, and it flung open with enough force that I nearly fell from the ladders. When I managed to clamber out, I immediately stumbled and fell to the ground on my knees, fully expecting to be bludgeoned on the back of the head or shoved back down the hatch. However, after a few seconds of being totally incapacitated by the fear, I realised that Benjamin wasn't waiting for me, and I cautiously picked myself up. I found myself in an eerily calm and silent forest in the dead of night, and as the cool breeze dried the sweat on my face, I spun my head around, trying to make out a figure waiting for me in the shadows. The access hatch I had just burst through was concealed very well in the undergrowth and covered in moss and ivy, and if I hadn't just emerged from it, I wouldn't even have known it was there.

Without the walls of the bunker surrounding me, I suddenly felt extremely exposed .and frantically driven by panic alone, my legs thankfully remembered how to run, and I hysterically began sprinting down the thin track that led away from the bunker. Even though I could feel my bare feet being slashed to ribbons by the rough path, I ran as quickly as my atrophied legs would allow, but they struggled to keep up with my demands, which led me to trip over and fall constantly. After a few minutes, the fatigue quickly started to set in, so I stopped for a moment to catch my breath and intently look back on the path I had just travelled.

I couldn't believe it. I was free at last.

There was no one chasing me. It wasn't a ruse. I was finally out, and an overwhelming sense of hope and relief suddenly washed over me as I continued to hobble down the path that was surrounded by the seemingly endless, unrecognisable woodland. The beaten trail I was following started to widen and led out onto a road, and I just hoped that I would reach civilisation before my abductor realised that I was missing. I let out a sardonic laugh when I saw the sign pointing down the road reading Hammerdale because I was only five miles away from home and right under my family's noses the entire time. I picked up my pace as quickly as my injured soles and extreme weakness would accept and began making my way towards town.

Barely had I been out on the road for a few minutes when I saw a set of headlights that were speeding towards me in the distance, and I didn't know whether to retreat back into the forest or hysterically wave my hands to get them to stop. In my nervous indecision, I ended up doing neither and stayed completely still in the middle of the road like the proverbial rabbit caught in the headlights as the car came to a screeching halt only a few metres away from me. The intense beam of light emanating from the vehicle was almost burning a hole in my retinas, so I raised my quaking arm to shield them from further damage as the door opened and the driver emerged. He was an elderly man in a plaid shirt and a cowboy hat, and when he started to stroll over to me ominously with his arms outstretched, I instinctively lowered my arm and cowered back slightly like a recaptured prey. It was plain to see that the old man was annoyed because I was walking down the middle of the road. However, when he dropped his glasses and got closer, he looked me up and down, and then the expression on his face turned to one of utter astonishment.

"My God. Olivia Lakewell?" he asked.

3

THE BEGINNING

OLIVIA – 2024

I involuntarily remained cast in stone in the middle of the road as the mysterious man slowly continued to creep towards me with his hands still extended and desperately trying to convey to me that he wasn't a threat. I didn't know whether to believe him or not, and in my mind, I couldn't decide whether this man was my long-awaited saviour or if he was going to drag me back into my cell heartlessly. Every impulse I had was frenziedly screaming for me just to bolt and run away, but a glimmer of hope told me that he could have been my only chance to escape. He knew my name, although instead of comforting me, it only made me more jittery.

"Who the fuck are you?" I spat through gritted teeth.

"My name's Hank," he softly said as he came ever closer.

"Just stay back!" I threatened as I held up the makeshift blade at him and swished it back and forth.

"It's okay. I just want to help. Folks around here have been looking for you for a long time, Olivia."

"How the hell do you know who I am?"

"Your face was on every news channel for months. I'd recognise it anywhere. You're that missing British lady, right?"

Although his calming demeanour seemed genuine to me, and just looking into his eyes made me almost believe that I wasn't in danger anymore, lingering in the back of my mind was the thought that this was all another hoax. I didn't trust him or anyone, and it all seemed too convenient and easy. My scuffed and bloodied knees wobbled as I wearily continued to back away from him, and the light-headedness was beginning to become too much as my ankles almost gave way. There wasn't a snowball's chance in hell I was going to get away from him in my condition, and I couldn't believe how far I had gotten just to be captured within minutes so close to home. The calm acceptance of my fate, whatever it would be, slowly washed over me, and tears began rolling down my grimy cheeks as I pressed the blade into my wrist.

"Are you Benjamin?" I timidly asked as my voice broke. Hank looked down at my hands, saw what I was threatening, and immediately started to back away.

"I don't know a Benjamin; I promise I'm not going to hurt you. I think your husband still lives in town with your daughter. We can go find them," he said warmly.

"Nathaniel and Aurora?"

"Yes, please let me take you to them. Just put the knife down and get in the car."

"No!" I shouted as I lifted the knife again. "It's some kind of trick! You're him!"

The passenger door opened on his car, a little boy clumsily got out whilst holding a blanket, and he shily made his way over to Hank's side. I watched as Hank protectively placed his hand on the little boy's back and lovingly pulled him in close. Upon seeing it, every single one of my over-tensed muscles released, the sensation of pins and needles ran up and down my spine, and I instinctively dropped the knife. I felt like I could finally breathe again; my faltering legs started to weaken further, and I fell to the ground in a heap. He quickly ran over to carefully help me up, and I clutched onto him for balance. Without another word, he slowly helped me to his car, opened the passenger side door, and eased me inside. The child got in the back in silence, and Hank started driving us towards home.

The strained silence persisted for maybe a mile down the road; the tears continued to stream down my face, and I was solemnly filled with quiet gratitude that he wasn't taking me back there. I had fully committed myself to my misguided plan, and the unexpected turn the evening had swiftly taken left me numb and bewildered. I never thought I would taste sweet freedom ever again or even breathe fresh air, and for the longest time, I thought I was doomed to die in that concrete coffin. My rescuer was almost trembling in excitement that he had found me, and he was clearly desperate to start firing questions at me, yet his polite restraint only lasted a few more minutes before he spoke.

"What happened to you out there?" he softly asked.

"I don't want to talk about it," I uttered.

"Sorry. That's fine," he started as he lit a cigarette, "do you want one?"

"No thanks. I quit."

"How about a little music?"

"Sure."

With one eye still on the road, he turned on the radio and some old country tunes played through his tinny speakers as he leant his arm out of the open car window. I pensively gazed through the glass, watching the huge Californian redwoods blur past, and they seemed taller somehow. I was determined to take in every detail of every leaf because I was expecting to wake up at any moment back in my steel bed. The little boy behind me began to fuss, and I looked in the mirror to see him curled up on the backseat, gradually drifting off to sleep.

"Is he your son? What's his name?" I quietly asked.

"That's my boy, Jonah," he replied, "he's taken to only falling asleep in the car, which is why I'm out here so late."

"That's a nice name," I mused.

"Thank you."

"How old is he?"

"Seven this fall."

"That's about how old Aurora was when—"

I stopped myself before I could speak the words, and Hank sighed loudly as he slowly shook his head, took the cigarette from his mouth and tightly gripped the steering wheel.

"Listen, ma'am, I know you said you didn't want to talk about it," he began carefully, "but I'm so sorry for what happened to you."

"Yeah, me too."

"My heart broke for your husband when he was on the news, and we all heard your story."

"Nathaniel was on the news?" I added.

"Every single day," he said, tapping the dashboard with his finger with every word, "and your daughter, too. They were pleading for help to find you."

"I thought they'd forgotten about me."

"Hell no. It was like that for months. After the vigil, the news seemed to lose interest."

"A vigil? That's for dead people."

"Well, no offence, ma'am, but it seemed that way, and we all thought it. Where in tarnation have you been all this time?"

"Trapped in a bomb shelter a few minutes from where you found me."

"For ten years? Damn, that's rough."

"Yep. Congratulations, you are the first person I've made eye contact with in the last ten years," I facetiously enthused.

"Your family are just going to be so thrilled you've been found."

"I hope so."

"I'm going to drop you off at the sheriff's station if that's alright with you. They will be able to get in contact with your husband."

"He was never my husband," I mumbled quietly.

Suddenly, the treeline began to thin, we arrived at the edge of town, and Hank pulled up the vehicle outside the sheriff's station. When he turned the engine off, he exhaled loudly before turning to me with a sympathetic look on his face, and he almost instinctively put his hand on mine before thinking better of it.

"Sheriff Daniels is new around these parts, but he's a good man. You can trust him," he explained.

"Thanks, Hank, you've saved my life," I said sullenly.

"Don't mention it. I'm just glad I found you. Do you want me to walk you inside?"

"No, you better stay with little Jonah. Don't let him out of your sight, you hear?" I said with a half-smile through the tears.

"Not even for a second."

I slowly opened the car door, cautiously stepped outside, and sluggishly made my way towards the polished concrete steps leading up to the sheriff's office. I gripped the handrail tightly to steady myself, and my battered feet stung with every laboured stride as I painfully pulled my body up onto each cold step. Once I eventually reached the closed wooden doors, I turned around to see Hank still waiting for me to go inside, and I gave him a weary wave as he pulled away.

Without the soundscape of Hank's ridiculously loud motor to drown out my intrusive thoughts, you could hear a pin drop in Hammerdale, and the silence allowed my festering anxieties free reign. I hesitated before I walked through those doors because I knew that this wasn't the end but the beginning of something else, and I would be forced to go through every vile and putrid detail of what happened to me. I bitterly wished I could dispense of the inevitable inquisition, forget what had happened to me, and pick my life up where I left off without any further pain. It's pathetic, but the only real desires I had were for a nice cup of tea and to be treated like a human being again.

Instead of going inside, I casually stepped away from the doors, sat down cross-legged on the top step, and buried my head in my hands. I was acutely aware of what I *should* have done; I should have burst through those doors like a bat out of hell, equipped with the inexorable demands to immediately see my family and command that Benjamin should be hunted down and brutally punished. That course of action would require a level of energy and rage, though, both of which I had in strangely scarce supply.

The ferocious flames of unfathomable anger that I initially felt when I was captured were extinguished a long time ago, abandoned to slowly decay in the absence of any intervention from the outside world, and by the time I was free, barely a single ember continued to glow. What crawled out of the ashes was a burnt-out husk, devoid of any genuine emotion or humanity, simply existing from one moment to the next in perpetual confusion. From where I was sitting, the Olivia that my family and I knew died in that bunker, and dead women don't get angry, and they certainly don't get justice.

I was emotionlessly gazing through the looking glass, hoping against hope that someone would be able to click their fingers and send me hurtling back in time with no memory of the nightmare I had endured. As far as I was concerned, I was surviving on borrowed time and way too confounded and numb to even contemplate life beyond the very moment I existed. The adrenaline of my escape had well and truly worn off, and without the primal need for freedom to fuel me, I realised that I had reverted to my quiet and introspective bunker persona. As difficult as it would be, my family deserved answers, and unlike me, they were still human with thoughts and feelings. I realised that from then on, I would have to make a conscious effort to masquerade as one of them too.

Just as I was plucking up the courage to enter, my heart immediately jumped into my throat when I spotted a silhouetted figure standing beneath a streetlight a few hundred metres away from me. No matter how hard I tried, I couldn't take my eyes off him. He had a similar gait and build to Benjamin, and the way he was just standing there, eerily motionless, made me want to vomit. My anxiety peaked when his knees slowly bent as he carefully squatted on the ground like he was ready to pounce, and I tentatively put my weight onto my hands so I could try and run away if needed. Suddenly, the dog he was walking sauntered into the light, and I breathed a sigh of relief when he picked up the mess with a plastic bag and he began casually sauntering towards me, whistling some merry tune.

"Good evening," he enthused as he passed.

"Err... evening," I titteringly responded.

Swiftly feeling very exposed, I took a deep breath and nervously groaned as I picked myself up to walk through the doors of the office. I found the reception unattended, so I leaned on the countertop in exhaustion and reluctantly slammed the bell on top of it. As soon as my forehead resignedly touched the cold polished marble of the desk, I could feel myself quickly succumbing to the fatigue, and for a split second, I nodded off momentarily. All of a sudden, the doors flew open, which startled me awake. As I groggily lifted my head, I saw a tall and handsome man in sheriff's uniform disdainfully looking back at me. He huffed and judgementally put his hands on his hips as I futilely tried to stand up straight.

"Ma'am, do you know it's an offence to be intoxicated in a public place?" he asked sternly.

"I'm not intoxicated. My name is Olivia Lakewell; you've been looking for me," I explained.

"So, there's a warrant out for you? What for?" he asked as he started tapping away on a computer.

"No, I've been missing."

"You've skipped bail?"

"No, you fucking imbecile, I got abducted ten years ago. I'm Olivia Lakewell!" I shouted as I slammed my hand on the counter.

The unexpected outburst caused me to feel faint; the unsteadiness got the better of me, and I collapsed into a bony mound on the floor. The last thing I hazily remembered was the inept sheriff shouting something imperceptible over his radio and rushing over to my side to help me.

I shakily woke up hours later by the relentless morning sunshine beaming directly into my reddened eyes; it was shining through the tiny slither of a window in the jail cell

I must have been carried to in my sleep. The steel door had been left wide open, and I was shrouded in a blanket on the tiny bed I had spent the night. I unsteadily sat up to find a grey sweatsuit that had been left for me, along with a tepid glass of water and an energy bar. The insatiable hunger and thirst consumed me as I ripped open the packet like a feral animal and washed down the contents with the water. Just as I was wiping the excess water and crumbs from my chin, the same incompetent sheriff from the night before frantically rushed into the room with his hands apologetically in the air.

"Miss Lakewell, I'm so sorry, but I had nowhere else to put you, and after learning who you are, I'm so sorry for leaving you here," he explained.

"Ah, *Officer Friendly*, are we in a better mood this morning?" I mocked with a stretch.

"I'm Sheriff Matt Daniels," he corrected, "I'm fairly new here, so I wasn't familiar with your disappearance. We did manage to get in touch with Nathaniel, and he's waiting for you at reception."

"What? He's here?"

"Yes, we thought it best to let you rest, but he's been there all night."

"Is there somewhere I can get a shower first?" I asked as I critically gazed down at the rags I was wearing.

"You don't want to see him first?" he asked bemusedly.

"Yes, but I can't have him see me like this."

"Yes, of course. Follow me," he said with a nervous smile as he picked up the grey sweatsuit that had been left for me.

Daniels slowly led me to the communal showers in a small locker room at the back of the station, and on his way, he grabbed a few towels to place on the shelf outside. Without thinking, I immediately started undressing, which made the sheriff quickly avert his eyes and turn away in embarrassment, and when I realised my innocuous faux pas, I grabbed a towel to cover my body.

"Sorry, I'm not used to people anymore," I said flippantly.

"I'll give you some privacy and mind the door so nobody comes in here," he awkwardly uttered with his hand over his face.

"Thank you," I replied.

I turned on the shower, and the mildly tepid water that came out of the head almost felt as if it was melting my skin, so I quickly turned the temperature down as low as it went, and the icy cascade of water that poured out was far more comfortable. I leaned against the white tiled wall and watched as the clumps of dirt rinsed from my skin swirled in the drain. I stamped down the bigger pieces of debris with my feet so they would disappear down it. I didn't linger; as soon as the water ran clear, I turned the shower off and jumped out to dry myself and get dressed. There was a thin, full-length mirror in the locker room, and I fluffed my wet hair up in a futile attempt to gussy my appearance. The ill-fitting sweatsuit concealed my dramatic weight loss quite well, but I still looked undeniably sickly and gaunt. Even more of my hair fell out when I dried it with the towel. I scraped back what little I had left and took a deep breath before walking outside.

As I sheepishly opened the door and Daniels stepped back from it as I walked through, he gestured down the hall where I could see Nathaniel anxiously standing at the reception desk, tapping his fingers on the top. He noticed me looking at him from a distance, ran around the counter and ploughed into me with a tight embrace.

"I've missed you," I whispered in his ear.

"Oh my God, I can't believe it!" he replied as he gripped me even tighter, which made me groan a little. "Sorry," he said as he pulled away slightly.

"It's okay. I'm just a little sore."

"Olivia, we thought you were dead. We all tried our hardest to find you, but there wasn't even a trace."

"I know you did. But I'm here now."

"Where the hell have you been?"

"I'll tell you everything, but for now, I just want to go home."

I dispiritingly gazed into his face and put my hands on his stubbled cheeks to hold him close. Although he had obviously gotten older, his eyes were almost exactly how I had remembered them when we first met: ocean blue with tiny specks of green and brown. Nevertheless, something was missing. It was something undetectable that I couldn't put my finger on at first, but I realised the spark was missing, and I frowned slightly in confusion as I removed my hands. I could tell he was working up to telling me something I wouldn't like, and I flinched away slightly to await it.

"Listen, it's probably not the right time, but I need to tell you something," he explained with a gulp.

"That you've got a new girlfriend?" I asked matter-of-factly.

"Fiancée, actually," he uttered.

"I know," I began with a sigh, "I watched it happen."

4

THE DATE

OLIVIA – 2004

Stacey promised me that it would be fun, but spending a rainy Friday evening in London painting a buck-naked bloke at a life drawing class wasn't exactly my idea of a good night out. It was okay for her; she actually had some artistic talent, which is why she was studying art in the first place, yet my talents lay elsewhere, and I couldn't help thinking that I should have been drawing in crayon. For some unknown reason, my friend had become increasingly desperate to find a man and was no longer content with visiting our usual London haunts of student union bars, pubs, or nightclubs. Somehow, she had managed to convince me to be her wing-woman and that going to a class like this allowed her to meet someone with similar interests to hers. She vehemently swore that the string of one-night stands that she usually had wasn't her thing anymore, but part of me wondered if she just wanted to ogle a nude man for a few hours and the rest of it was just window dressing.

There were at least twenty doomed souls crammed into that tiny room, all sat in a circle with an easel in front of each of us, and in the centre proudly stood the strapping specimen we were all here to see with a nauseating smirk across his face. I wasn't shy or body conscious, but there was no amount of money in the world that would convince me to parade myself like that, least of all enjoy it like he clearly was. The pompous art tutor who organised the evening strolled around the outside of the circle, diligently inspecting our work, and I shuddered in extreme embarrassment as he made his way past me and analytically glanced over my shoulder.

"I'm so shit at this," I whispered to Stacey beside me.

"You can't be *shit* at art. It's whatever you want it to be," she ostentatiously explained under her breath.

"Okay, fine, I'm all for that, but seriously, you've got to look at it."

"Oh my God!" she shouted through laughter.

"Quiet, please," the tutor sternly scorned before adding a loud shush.

"Sorry," Stacey uttered with an innocent smile.

I caught the eye of the man sitting directly across from me, and he cheekily raised his eyebrows at me while giggling at my blunder. He had deep brown hair that was haphazardly tied up in a messy bun, a jawline so sharp you could sharpen your charcoal with it, and as his smile widened, I caught a glimpse of his perfect, pearly white teeth before he positioned himself behind his sketch.

"Hey, who's that?" I quietly asked Stacey as I pointed.

"Nathaniel," she softly replied in a put-on posh voice, "he's the American on my course."

"Why does it matter if he's American?"

"It's the only thing I know about him."

"Yeah, but it's not his defining trait, surely?"

"Well, this is the quietest I've ever seen him. You can usually hear him laughing from a mile away."

I returned to my failed sketch for a few moments before the dissatisfaction with Stacey's answers got the better of me, and I covertly kicked her lightly to get her attention.

"Have you two… you know?" I asked with a wink.

"God, no. He has a bit of a reputation," she dismissed.

"What kind of a reputation?"

"The *fucks-anything-that-moves* reputation."

"So, why haven't you?" I murmured with a snigger.

"Cheeky bitch!" she exclaimed as she batted at my arm with her hand.

"Shush," the tutor repeated between us.

"Listen," Stacey began softly in my ear, "this is about getting me a bloke; you've never had a problem finding one, so put your eyes back in."

"Okay, who else have you got your roving eye on then?" I asked.

We both moved our eyes around the circle, and without being rude, I had never seen such a gaggle of mostly unattractive people in one place. When our eyes met again, I couldn't help but burst into laughter, which set Stacey off too, and the tutor abruptly came over to chastise us.

"Everyone, I think we are going to call it a night," he announced to the class before turning to Stacey. "I need to talk to you, Stacey, now," he firmly said to her.

"Thanks for that, Liv," Stacey said to me as she followed him to the corner of the room behind us.

The model put a robe on, started drinking from his water bottle, and began strutting around the room as he tried to garner even more attention for himself. The rest of the class dispersed themselves to look at each other's work, and the room was suddenly abuzz with debate and traded constructive criticism. Nathaniel made a beeline for me, and I frantically tried to separate the pages of the sketchbook I had been drawing in order to conceal my creepy creation, but he jokingly put his hand over it before I managed to and leaned in to look at it closely. I took a step back, barely holding it together as he judgementally inspected an illustration that even a chimpanzee would have been embarrassed about.

"That's an interesting interpretation," he mustered.

"Oh, come on, it's a pile of shit," I laughed.

"No, you've got real potential. Really great shading on this part here."

"His cock?" I boldly suggested with a laugh.

"Yes, that part," he said with a snigger and a blush.

"Who happily attends a life drawing class but goes bright red when they hear the word cock?"

"Me, apparently."

"I'm Olivia. Nice to meet you," I abruptly announced to swiftly change the subject.

"Nathaniel," he said, pointing at himself with a shy grin.

"So, you are on the same course as Stacey; what's that like? Is she a nightmare?" I joked.

"I don't think we have ever spoken; she seems nice enough, though."

"Yeah, you clearly don't know her then."

"What about you? Are you studying art?"

"Absolutely not, no. I'm a writer."

"Why are you here if you aren't an artist?"

"Stacey is on the prowl for a bloke, and I'm here to lend my assistance."

"So, is this assisting? Are you just buttering me up for your friend?" he asked flirtatiously.

"No, I don't think you are her type," I said with a smile.

"What are you both up to after this, then?"

"I think we are going for a glass of wine."

"Are you sure about that?" he said as he pointed behind me with a cynical smirk.

I turned around to see her twirling her hair in front of the scantily clad life model and obviously exchanging phone numbers. When her eyes met mine, she shot a wink at me and nodded her head towards the door, which was my cue to leave her to it. She had obviously got off lightly with the tutor and pounced on the only eligible bachelor in the room, and I disapprovingly shook my head at her as I turned back to Nathaniel, who was grinning back at me.

"I think our plans might have changed," I mused.

"Well, I'm not doing anything after this, so I can take her place if you're agreeable. I'd love to hear about your writing," he said invitingly.

"Fine, one glass," I replied sternly with my finger pointed at his face.

Nathaniel and I began meandering our way through the bustling sea of artists and easels when I caught Stacey's eye, but she gave me a threatening look back, so I decided not to cramp her style, and instead, I left without saying goodbye. Once we got outside, it was so perilously cold that I shuddered, to which Nathaniel immediately removed his coat and charmingly placed it around my shoulders.

"Listen, buddy, I'm detecting a covert but domineering tone of romance from you, so before we go any further, I just want you to know that I'm not the kind of British girl who just hops into bed with anyone," I announced jokingly.

"You writers and your big words! I just want a glass of wine and a chinwag, I promise."

"As long as we are clear."

We immediately crossed the road and instinctually ran into the closest pub that was in sight to escape the brutal chill. I spotted a vacant table near the steamed-up window and sat down as Nathaniel made his way straight to the bar. He returned a minute or two later with two glasses of questionable wine and delicately placed one in front of me as he got himself comfortable. I took a sip of the supposed wine; the sheer face-contorting bitterness made me violently wince, and I nearly spilt the whole glass all over the table. Nathaniel stepped into the role of a sommelier, swirling the murky blood-red liquid in the glass before inhaling the scent deeply and, after a satisfied exhale, took a huge boorish gulp. He held the liquid in his mouth for a few seconds before managing to force himself to swallow it and then reproduced the exact same expression I did when I tasted it.

"Wow, sorry, I'm a poor student studying abroad! It was the best I could afford," he said with a smirk.

"I'm sure it will be okay once the initial shock wears off," I joked as I cautiously took another mouthful.

"So, Olivia," he began as he leaned in closer, "what kind of thing do you write?"

"Short stories mainly. I'm still trying to find my genre. What's your speciality? Sketching barely clothed men?"

"Oh yeah, big time," he laughed, "I like painting, and the plan was to just do a semester over here before I head back to the States."

"So, you aren't planning on sticking around?"

"I haven't decided yet. It depends on whether I have something to stay for," he pondered provocatively.

"My friend told me that word around campus is that you are a bit of a philanderer."

"Again, with the big words, what does that mean?"

"A player."

"Be honest, is it the man bun?" he grinned.

"Yes, the hair isn't doing you any favours," I teased.

"To set the record straight, no, I'm not a philanthropist."

"Philanderer," I corrected.

"That either. I'm just an American in London who loves painting and wants to get better at it."

"That's fine then."

We spent the rest of the evening discussing art and literature, swapping stories, and sipping the disgusting wine. Although we were from opposite sides of the pond, we had a remarkable number of interests and passions in common, and Stacey's words of warning quickly waned into insignificance. We seemed to share the same outlook on life; we were both desperate to avoid the rough and tumble of the rat race, and we simply wanted to spend our lives creating beauty, whether it was by pen or brush.

There was definitely something about him that drew me in. Whatever that precisely was remained a mystery to me, but I was eager to find out. God, he was good-looking too, and if it weren't for that constructed bird's nest sitting atop his head, he would have been my type to the letter. Although the conversation had seemingly dried up, we found ourselves rejoicing in an unexpectedly lovey-dovey silence as we smilingly gazed into each other's eyes, and I was glad that Stacey was able to persuade me into coming along with her after all.

The barmaid abruptly rang the bell for last orders, which startled us out of our wordless reverie. When I stood up, I realised that the vinegar we had been drinking was far stronger than I had bargained for. I was feeling incredibly tipsy, and Nathaniel offered out his arm for me to hold on to as we made our way back out onto the wintry street.

"Here," I said, holding Nathaniel's coat out to him, "you better take this back."

"I was hoping you'd forget. It's an excuse to call you," he smirked.

"You don't need an excuse."

"It's frightfully cold; why don't you come back to mine?"

"To repeat, using the American vernacular, I don't screw on the first date, bucko," I said in my best Texan accent.

"What about a little kiss then?" he asked.

"That depends. Do you think you deserve one?"

"I did pay for the fine wine," he reasoned with a shrug.

"I suppose it's only fair then," I said with a smile.

Nathaniel amorously leaned in and softly pressed his full lips to mine; I was expecting him to go gung-ho and all guns blazing, but he was pleasingly respectful and desirously tender. I found myself immediately wanting more, and I gently put my hands behind his neck and lightly pulled him in tighter. His hands started to wander down my spine towards my backside, but just as he was firmly putting his hands on to squeeze it, I ran my hand up the back of his head and removed the bobble holding his man-bun together. His laughable hairdo collapsed like a house of cards, the mess of curly brown hair dropped to his shoulders, and I childishly stepped back to admire my handiwork.

"There you go, much better," I teased.

"You prefer it like this?" he asked.

"Much better. Less *player* energy."

"Then I'll keep it like this. How was that for you?"

"The kiss?"

"Yeah."

"It was alright. I've had worse."

It was more than alright.

I hadn't been kissed like that ever; the butterflies were still fluttering away in my stomach, and I felt myself fiercely battling the urge to drag him into a taxi right there and then. The compulsion to staunchly remain true to my word wasn't as powerful, but combined with the pleasure I felt seeing him squirm, it was enough to resist. On top of all that, I knew that he would have seen it as some sort of victory, and if Stacey's warning were indeed warranted, I would rather give the opportunity a miss and wake up with some self-respect the morning after.

He truly had no idea what was going on in my head and remained smiling at me expectantly until something caught his eye behind me. The flirtatious smirk that had exclusively resided on his face was wiped clean, and instead, he frowned as he moved his head around to see behind me more clearly. I bobbed my head from side to side to catch his attention again, and when I turned to look over my shoulder, I saw the outline of the hooded figure he was staring at, standing in the shadows of a closed shop doorway across the road.

"You've got to be kidding me," he uttered quietly under his breath, "what are they doing here?"

"Who is it? A friend of yours?" I asked.

"No, honestly, it's no one. I'll get you a ride," he nervously dismissed as he abruptly flagged down a passing black cab.

"Seriously, Nath, is everything okay?"

"Yes, it's fine, just someone who can't take a hint."

The taxi pulled up and Nathaniel all but shoved me inside as soon as it was stationary. My head was on a swivel, trying to work out what Nathaniel's issue was, as his eyes were still fixed on the silhouetted person loitering on the other side of the street.

"Just drive, cabby. She'll give you her address in a minute," he said to the driver before turning to me, "I'm sorry, but I must deal with this. I'll call you."

Before I even had a chance to say goodbye, he shut the door and patted the back of the taxi, signalling to the driver to set off immediately. The driver obliged, and as I turned around to look through the back window, I saw Nath confrontationally making his way over to the figure with his arms aggressively outstretched. The unknown person backed even further into the shadows before Nathaniel confronted them, and before we turned the first corner, I could hear Nathaniel shouting at the top of his voice, although I was unable to make out the words as the taxi driver sped away from there.

I was bursting with questions on the entire journey home. Were they an ex-partner of his? Or someone he has beef with on his course? I felt quite disheartened because even though we had just met, it seemed like there could have been something special between us, and that whole scenario had sullied that.

Maybe Stacey was right about him after all.

5

THE REUNION

OLIVIA – 2024

My unexplained words hung in the air like a foul stench, and I had no intention of cutting Nathaniel the slack of enlightenment, at least for the moment. I suppose that when I dropped the bombshell that I watched him get engaged, it was a cruel thing to say without an immediate explanation, but it was my subconscious way of protecting what little self-respect I had left by announcing I knew about it before he could confess it. The atmosphere was palpable, and I found myself nastily savouring every micro-expression of confusion and bewilderment from him as I saw the cogs turning behind his eyes and rapidly trying to fathom how I could possibly know. Perhaps for the first time ever since I met Nathaniel, it actually felt awkward between us.

Even Sheriff Daniels was starting to look uncomfortable in the prolonged silence; he was awkwardly leafing through some papers on the reception desk until the unease got too much for him, and he raised his finger, cleared his throat, and stepped between us slightly.

"Olivia, I know you want to go home, but I'd like to get some details from you whilst it's still fresh in your mind. Are you ready to talk about what happened to you?" Daniels asked gingerly.

"We may as well get it over with," I replied to him with my eyes still scornfully locked on Nathaniel.

"If you both want to follow me, we have somewhere more comfortable," Daniels said as he gestured down the hall.

I barely took notice of where I was walking. I was far too busy playing spot the difference in my head between the image I had of my fiancé and the cheating scumbag who was walking beside me. That being said, he wasn't my intended anymore; he was someone else's, and even though I thought I had come to terms with it, I clearly hadn't. Technically, I had been cheated on, and although logic would dictate that neither party were truly responsible for the infidelity, surely, I can be afforded some scorn given the circumstances. For the first time ever, I was bizarrely thankful for Benjamin's sadistic proclivity for psychological torture because I would otherwise have been none the wiser about the happy couple, and my return to freedom would have been laden with one horrific shock after another.

When my kidnapper first excitedly showed me on the television screen inside my cell the shoddy footage of Nathaniel and the hot blonde that he had been cavorting with, it was a turning point for me. With each movie night after that, the blade was maliciously turned as I watched their relationship grow and blossom, just like ours once did. Whilst I was trapped in that box, there wasn't a damn thing I could do to stop it other than sit down, watch, and try to accept what I was seeing. After the years he had patiently waited before moving on, I realised that finding someone else would be inevitable, but witnessing it with my own eyes on a TV monitor was an entirely different beast. The footage was so grainy and poor quality that I thought it to be a trick of the camera at first, and I firmly denied the truth. My subjugator swiftly ushered me through the stages of grief, and by that point in the sheriff's office, I was far beyond acceptance. Nevertheless, the bubbling broth of jealousy still simmered within me, and I, maybe mistakenly, felt wronged and that I at least deserved some kind of explanation.

My ex-husband-to-be had no idea what contemptible things I had endured, all whilst he was flippantly flitting around with his new fancy woman. To reiterate and be crystal clear, deep down, I didn't blame him even in the slightest for finding someone else, and I knew that he had waited a hell of a long time before moving on with his life. I loved that man for long enough to know that for him to move on like that, he must have truly thought I was lost forever.

Maybe I should have stayed that way.

We were led into the interview room, and the stark contrast between the rest of the station made me feel instantly nauseous. The plush sofas and mundane floral wallpaper superficially screamed calm and reassurance, and it was all designed to make victims like me malleable enough to spill their guts. Almost immediately upon entering the room, Daniels' facial expression subconsciously turned to one of feigned sympathy, and he sat down on one of the sofas as Nathaniel and I sat on the other. I felt the heat emanating from Nathaniel's leg on mine, and I inched myself away as far as possible to create some space between us.

"Whenever you are ready, Olivia, just tell us what happened in your own words," Daniels said with a pen poised to capture every detail.

I initially planned on addressing the sheriff directly, although I quickly realised that I should probably be speaking to Nathaniel, so I turned around in the seat to face him. I had rehearsed this moment a thousand times in my head over the years. I knew exactly which parts I wanted to share with him and the huge chunks that I would rather forget forever. I carefully sifted through the memories, stripping my account to its bare bones, only giving away the details that would hopefully allow the sheriff to catch the man responsible. I didn't anticipate the pure emotion of the situation, though, and I could already feel my voice breaking before I even tried using it, so I elected to look into space instead and avoid all their judgemental eyes.

"So," I softly began as I cleared my throat, "after you all went back into the church on our wedding day, someone jumped me outside and knocked me out."

"That's awful," Nathaniel said.

"When I woke up, I was locked in some kind of bomb shelter, or something, in the woods. That's where I've been this entire time."

"Do you remember where it is?" Daniels interjected.

"Roughly, it's about five miles out of town. I can probably trace where I ran when I got out and show you on a map."

"Give me a second."

Daniels briskly left the room, abandoning Nathaniel and me in the most discomforted silence I had ever endured. We were both bleakly staring into space until I subtly looked over my shoulder at him, and it was clear to me that he was ruminating on what little I had already said and bracing himself for the rest. The sheriff returned a few moments later with a foldaway map and a pen, and he unfolded it on the coffee table in front of me.

"Can you please mark out where you think the area was?" he asked.

"Here," I began as I pointed out the location, "that's where I emerged onto the road. If you follow that trail, you'll find a wooden hatch buried beneath some undergrowth. It's quite well hidden, but the bunker is below that."

"That's fantastic. Please continue."

"I didn't step outside of there for ten years. Whoever did this didn't want me dead. He kept me alive."

"Did you have any contact with him?"

"Physically? Only a few times, but I never saw his face. He communicated with me through an intercom and showed me things on a television screen mounted on the wall."

"What did he say to you? And show you?"

"Well, that's how I knew you had a new girlfriend," I said to Nathaniel before turning back to Daniels, "mostly, it was just grainy footage of Nathaniel and Aurora. He must have been following them for years with a camera."

"Mostly? What else was shown to you?"

"It was—" I stuttered as I nervously picked at the grime still underneath my nails. Suddenly, my mouth went incredibly dry, and the back of my neck broke into a profuse sweat. I leaned forward to grab a glass of water that had been left there for me and took a few sips before placing it back down. Both of them were intently staring at me, and the pressure I felt to tell them everything was phenomenal. Nevertheless, I literally couldn't form the words, so I sternly shook my head.

"No, sorry, I'm not ready for this yet," I whispered.

"I understand, Miss Lakewell, but the more information you give us, the better chance we will have of finding him," Daniels softly explained.

I watched in the corner of my eye as Nathaniel's hand slowly snaked across the couch, his little finger just touching mine lightly, and the basic human contact made me immediately break out in goosebumps. I was confused for a moment, as the warmth of his touch should have been comforting, but quickly, the sensation started to intensify. In a split second, I felt as if my entire arm was set ablaze, and I jarringly shook off his painful grasp.

"Don't fucking touch me!" I sharply exclaimed.

"Shit, sorry!" Nathaniel immediately blurted out.

The flash of madness that I released had left his jaw agape with his hands awkwardly suspended in the air, and I felt immediately embarrassed of my volatile reaction. Nonetheless, even the simple warmth of another person's touch was such an alien concept that it made me incredibly uncomfortable.

"No, I'm sorry. That was clearly an overreaction," I solemnly whispered.

"Are you okay to continue?" Daniels interjected.

I nodded.

"Did he ever tell you his name?"

"Benjamin," I uttered with disdain.

"Is there anything else you can tell me about him?"

"He's religious. He used to quote the Bible all the time."

"This is good. Anything else?"

"I wasn't his first victim. There were others."

"How do you know? Did he tell you that?"

"He fucking *showed* me," I sobbed through incongruous laughter.

"Okay, I don't want to push too much, and I think we have enough to go on for now. We should meet again in a few days after we've done a thorough search of the location you've provided. You should go home and get some rest and probably get checked over by a doctor."

"Home?" I asked quietly.

I looked at Nathaniel, who was looking increasingly awkward as the pressure was mounting for him to offer a place to stay. Daniels looked at him anxiously as he tapped his pen on the pad he was holding, and just enough time elapsed that he missed the perfect opportunity to extend an invitation.

"You are more than welcome to stay with us, obviously," Nathaniel disingenuously suggested.

"I don't need your pity. No, thanks," I dismissed.

"You really shouldn't be on your own, Olivia, not at a time like this. Have you got any other family you can contact?" Daniels added.

"Yeah, in England. I'm obviously alone here."

"You aren't alone," Nathaniel softly said.

"I'll get a motel, Nath. I'll be fine," I insistently said as I stood from the couch and abruptly started making my way to the door. Nathaniel and Daniels quickly followed as I stormed out of the room and walked beyond reception to leave immediately.

"Olivia, wait," Nathaniel shouted.

"What?" I snapped.

"I *want* you to stay with us. It's just a uniquely shit and confusing situation, and I'm not sure what to do for the best."

"Don't worry about it. I wouldn't want to be a third wheel."

"What about Aurora?" he abruptly asked as I opened the door to leave. "What about your daughter?" he softly added when I froze on the spot.

"How is she?" I uttered dispiritingly.

"Well, she's a typical teenager and quite a handful at times, but I'm sure she will be ecstatic when she finds out you're back."

As much as I was unyieldingly desperate for everything to go back to how it was before I was taken, the thought of a little family reunion made me feel sick to my stomach. Everything had changed in my absence; I had missed so much that I didn't know if she would even recognise me, and it would break me in two if she didn't. At sixteen years old, she was becoming her own woman and just learning to find her place in the world. The last thing she needed was her barely sane victim of a mother rocking up for her to deal with on top of everything else teenagers have to go through. I had no earthly idea what damage my sudden disappearance had inflicted on her, and I felt more guilty about that than anything else.

I lightly bumped my head against the open door in frustration. Even though I awkwardly shrugged his olive branch off, I remained stationary in the hope that he would make a further plea to invite me back into his life. Nathaniel cautiously walked over to shyly put his hand on my arm but thought better of it and gawkily took the weight of the door from me instead.

"Come and see Aurora, and at least pick up some clothes. We still have some of your things at the house, and of course, if you feel up to it, you're welcome to stay," he offered tenderly.

My resurrection was every bit as complicated as I knew it would be, and as horrendous and implausible as it sounds, at that moment, I yearned for the illusion of safety that the bunker had provided me with for so many years. The simplicity of survival alone without having to worry about everyone else was actually attractive, as I had barely made a decision beyond what to have for dinner in the past decade, and all the little hurdles of normal life that I would have hopped over without a second thought were suddenly monumental.

I knew I wasn't welcome. I was probably every bit as deranged as they all thought I was. Who in their right mind would want me in their home? Putting my own perplexing feelings to one side, twenty-four hours before, he was starting a new family without me, and just as suddenly as I left his life, I had just burst back into it. The vestigial sense of duty he felt to make sure I was okay was seriously misplaced, as he had no legal obligation to me anymore, and certainly not a romantic one. I couldn't help but think I was a massive burden that nobody wanted, and I expected to be treated simply as the estranged mother of his child. That being said, he willingly extended a hand to help, and I suppose that had to count for something.

"Okay," I mumbled as quietly as a mouse.

Nathaniel sprang into action and raised a hand at Daniels as he awkwardly pushed the door open for me, clumsily offering me to walk through it first, then following as soon as I was clear of it. The intense Californian sunshine blinded me as soon as I got outside, and I raised my arm to shield my eyes from it as Nathaniel handed me the pair of sunglasses that were hanging from his shirt pocket. I put them on, and he led me to his car: a brand-new ice-white SUV. Nath gracelessly opened the door for me and then jogged around the other side to the driver's seat and got in. The car seemed more like a spaceship to me, and as Nathaniel noticed my diligent inspection of the screens and technology around me, he started the engine.

"This is a lot nicer than the clapped-out jalopy we had," he remarked.

"Doing well for yourself then?" I asked.

"Yeah, the art really took off a few years ago. This was a little treat for me," he gushed.

"That's good. I'm happy for you," I flatly enthused.

"Shit, sorry, Liv. I didn't mean to—"

"Don't be sorry," I interrupted, "honestly, you deserve it."

He nervously began driving, and I pensively gazed out of the window as we went through the town that I thought I knew so well, but I barely recognised any of it. The quirky small businesses that used to make up the town had mostly vanished and were replaced by franchised big businesses sporting flashy new shop frontages. I suddenly felt extremely out of place, like I was lost out of time, and I was far too transfixed on the alien land we were traversing to even muster any uncomfortable small talk with him. When he seemingly missed the turning to home, I promptly turned to him with a puzzled expression on my face and pointed down the road he passed.

"You've missed the turning," I bemusedly said.

"Oh, sorry, we moved years ago. We live up on North Ridge now," he explained.

"Near our old hiking trail?"

"It's houses now, it's nice, you'll see."

"Why did you move?"

"Well, the art was going well, and it just made sense. We got an amazing deal on the place we have now."

"Very astute of you."

"That was a lie," Nathaniel started with a huff, "it's what I used to tell people. The truth is, we couldn't bear to be there anymore after you were gone."

I remained silent.

"Anyway, I think our old house got condemned a while back," he joked with a smile.

"It was a bit of a tear-down."

"You'll like the new house. It's much more your style."

The discordant small talk gladly only lasted for a few more minutes before he pulled up in front of a brand-new house in an area that used to all be woodland. I occasionally used to take Aurora there for hikes because it afforded a beautiful view of the whole town through the treeline, although in my absence, the trees had long since been chopped down, and now it was just another soulless collection of decadent mansions and swimming pools blighting the landscape.

"This is us," Nathaniel announced before hesitantly climbing out of the vehicle.

Although the home was certainly an architectural masterpiece and modular in nature, it was also unassuming and tucked away in between the towering trees effortlessly surrounding it. It was clad in a mixture of warm, oaky wooden strips and blackened steel sheets that oozed modernity and sophistication, so I wasn't sure why Nath thought it would be more my style. One thing was for sure: it was a stark contrast to where we used to live, and the memory of the rotting timbers and peeling paint of our old house made it feel like they were from entirely different worlds.

I realised I was about to see my daughter, and my hands were uncontrollably quaking with the nerves, so I remained seated for a few seconds to take a deep breath to regain some composure. As I maniacally tried to line up a few sentences that I would say to her in my head, Nathaniel had managed to get out of the car without my notice, and he was waiting for me outside the passenger door, tapping on the glass.

As I nervously exited the vehicle, my heart nearly stopped when I heard the front doors to his house burst open, and I quickly removed the borrowed sunglasses as I agitatedly followed him up the driveway. The sun was bouncing off the façade of the house as I sheepishly looked around Nathaniel to see who had emerged, and I quickly realised it wasn't Aurora like I had hoped, but Nath's betrothed.

The footage I had seen from the bunker didn't even begin to do her justice. Even at a distance, and with the sun beaming into my eyes, her beauty was staggering. She was classically pretty, impossibly slim, and her long, flowing golden locks swayed effortlessly in the wind beside her bronzed shoulders as we approached. The expensive-looking exercise clothes she was wearing were so ridiculously tight that I could see every single striking curvature of her absurdly fit body, and she was so immaculately preened that it looked like she had just stepped out of a beauty salon rather than a gymnasium.

Her pearly-white grin was visible until she caught a glimpse of me, the ragged cave dweller who was gracelessly stumbling up the driveway towards her. Her smile slipped, and she dramatically put her hands on her hips. Nathaniel threw his hands up apologetically as he crept up the concrete driveway a few metres ahead of me and looked back with a worried expression for a split second before he reached the porch.

"What's going on?" she asked.

"Sorry. I can explain, but don't freak out," he shakily replied.

As I stepped out of the influence of the sun and into the shade of the house, I saw all the colour immediately drain from her face as she recoiled into the house in shock. I had seen her many times before; she was featured prominently in Benjamin's amateur flicks, but I never got a good look at her face. As I sheepishly made my way closer to her with the warmest smile I could summon, I was taken into her dark eyes. A light bulb turned on inside my head, and I let out a single, crazed laugh.

"Stephanie?" I uttered.

I fucking *knew* her.

6

THE BEAR

OLIVIA – 2005

With every time-wasting and useless lecture that I felt compelled to attend, it became increasingly clear to me that I had made a terrible mistake in picking my degree. The clue was in the name: creative writing. In my opinion, it wasn't something that could be taught. You either had it in you, or you didn't, and I was big-headed enough to count myself amongst the lucky few who did have it. To be honest, I was in the minority, and my course was filled with aspiring authors who didn't. Although most of their writing was technically proficient, you could just tell they were never going to make it. I believed in writing from the heart and was constantly pulled up on my grammar or the so-called rules, but regardless, I was still immensely proud of everything I had written.

As soon as I wandered into that musty lecture hall, I instantly realised I had made an error, especially when I saw the words 'iambic pentameter' on the huge screen at the front. That specific lecture was plainly about poetry, something in which I had precisely zero interest, so I realised there and then that I had clearly got my days mixed up. Given that the lecturer was already in attendance and was staring directly at me with a beaming smile when I entered the hall, it felt incredibly rude to turn round and walk straight out, so to avoid societal embarrassment, I started eagerly looking for a seat.

As a matter of course, I would rush in with only seconds to find an empty seat, but at that time, I largely had my pick of the entire hall because it was essentially devoid of life, bar a few die-hard poetry enthusiasts. I quickly shuffled to one of the empty seats at the back of the hall and put my bag down, hoping that the lack of proximity from the front would at least allow me to be out of the firing line of the lecturer. I slumped in the chair and began to accept that I would have to sit it out for at least an hour, during which I was likely to learn nothing valuable in exchange for my precious time. I stealthily checked my phone underneath the small desk in front of me, and there was a text message waiting from Nathaniel.

> *I miss you. What are you doing?*

Even just a year on from our first date, we seemed to have a blossoming romance, and that innocuous text made me embarrassingly grin like a loved-up schoolgirl. We had been hesitant to put a label on our relationship, and I had convinced myself it was a friends-with-benefits type deal to protect my own sensibilities. Despite coming from very different backgrounds, we had a tremendous amount in common with each other, and the kiss we shared that night alone was enough to leave me wanting more.

After the admittedly weird ending of our first date, I was hesitant to allow it to grow into more, largely because of Stacey's warning that he was rumoured to be a womaniser, and I didn't want to get involved in whatever shenanigans he was embroiled in at the time. I grilled him about the mysterious figure he had the altercation with, but it seemed to make him incredibly uncomfortable, so out of respect, I ended up just forgetting all about it. The curious part of me always wondered whether it was a scorned ex-lover or even a friend he had such a raucous argument with, but he didn't owe me the explanation for it, so I left it at that. Nothing else untoward had happened since; the red flags faded, and I started to find myself having feelings for him. There was no denying that we had a connection, and it would have been foolish to refuse to explore that.

About ten minutes into the most boring lecture that I had ever had the displeasure of enduring, the hall doors opened again, and another female victim apologetically snuck in, hurriedly picking a seat in the row behind me. I turned my head to look at her with an awkward smile, and I couldn't help thinking if I had been asked to describe a typical poetry student, I would undoubtedly have picked her out. She was slightly overweight, with greasy reddish-blonde hair and a spotty complexion, sporting a black turtleneck jumper with a stars and stripes brooch proudly pinned to it. She unnervingly grinned back at me, exposing the braces on her teeth, and I gawkily threw my head back and exhaled through my nose before unwillingly returning my attention to the speaker who kept blabbering on about the tedious iambic pentameter and the importance of it in English poetry and verse drama.

Now that I had an observer from behind, I put my phone away and reached into my bag to place a notepad in front of me for appearance's sake, with a pen poised in my hand to diligently take notes. Like a teenager, I idly wrote my name and Nathaniel's in the corner of the page in a crude love heart before looking back up at the speaker with the most engaging and enthralled face I could feign. I decided that I was stuck there, and whether or not I was interested in poetry, I should really give this poetic nonsense a go, so I set about writing my very first poem:

> There was once a professor who claimed,
> That poetry was a grand sort of game,

> But try as she might,
> They all sounded shite,
> And drove all her students insane.

When I finished the last line, I heard a suppressed chuckle behind me, and I spun around to find the girl behind me, peering over my shoulder at my notepad and incredibly amused by my hastily written limerick. Her outburst gave me a sense of camaraderie, and I sensed that she had also blundered badly when she chose to attend the lecture that was boring the two of us to tears.

"Hey, don't grass me up," I whispered facetiously.

"It's funny, much more entertaining than this lecture," she uttered back in an American accent.

"Do you have any idea how long they usually go on for?"

"The last one was a few hours."

"A few hours?" I gasped in astonishment. "No, I can't stick it out that long," I disdainfully added with a head shake.

The thought of being trapped there for longer than an hour filled me with terror, so I silently collected all of my things, bundled them into my bag and covertly navigated the room to the exit whilst the speaker's back was turned. As I looked around the room before I pushed the doors open to make my escape, I gave a wry shrug to the girl I had just spoken to and rushed out of the doors. I immediately pulled out my mobile phone and called Nathaniel to see if he fancied meeting up, but he didn't answer and just as the call rang out, I saw the girl from the lecture exiting the room too, and she impishly giggled when she saw me standing in the corridor.

"I'm sorry, but I couldn't bear another minute in there. You gave me the inspiration to follow my dreams and leave," I said in jest.

"I don't blame you. When you upped and left, it gave me the motivation to do the same," she replied jokingly.

"Is that not your thing either, then? Poetry?"

"I'm not sure, to be honest. I'm wondering if I like writing at all. I kind of got forced into this by my parents."

"I know that feeling."

"You're Olivia, right?"

"Yeah, sorry, I don't think we've met before."

"I'm the outcast who normally sits at the back, so you probably haven't noticed me. I'm Stephanie," she replied.

"Nice to meet you. I thought I knew all the Americans on campus. You're not friends with Nath Anderson, are you?"

"No," she pondered with her face scrunched up, "I don't think so."

"I have no idea why I even asked that. It's not like you know absolutely everyone from the States, is it?"

"I don't know many people over here, to be honest," Stephanie said with a self-deprecating laugh, "I'm a bit of a loner."

Stephanie's abrupt and effacing overshare made me feel very uncomfortable, and I just remained standing in front of her with a clumsy smile. She quickly realised her gaffe, but there was something in the way that she sorrowfully looked down at her feet, which made me feel incredibly sorry for her. She was clearly alone and studying abroad, and I couldn't imagine how isolated she must have felt away from her friends and family, so I felt guilty for rushing to pass judgment shortly after introducing ourselves to each other. The pressure I was feeling to alleviate the awkward silence grew, and I ham-fistedly gave her a jovial tap on the arm.

"Listen, I could murder a watered-down beer. Do you fancy being an accomplice?" I enthusiastically asked.

"Sure! I'd love that!" she gushed.

"I know just the place; it tastes like horse piss, but at least the glasses are clean."

"It sounds delightful."

Stephanie began following me out of the building when I noticed the little grizzly bear pin attached to her bag. In the absence of conversation, I flicked it with my finger, and she looked down at it.

"Are you from Cali? My boyfriend is from there."

"Sunshine State born and bred. Haven't you ever heard of not poking the bear?" she cheekily said.

"Very good," I mused, "are you sure you haven't met Nath? Tall guy? Painter? Ridiculous man-bun?"

"Pretty sure."

We made it onto the street, and I showed my new acquaintance to my local boozer, "The Slippery Pig," and much to my amusement, I caught her wince at the sign before she trepidatiously followed me inside. It was your typical London pub, decrepit, filled with layabouts, and had a floor so sticky that you felt compelled to wipe your feet on the way out to keep the street clean. The off-putting smell of last night's stale beer hung in the air, and when I looked back at Stephanie, she was taking short and rapid breaths in response, like she had been poisoned by it. Even as a student, she looked out of place in an establishment like that, and the apprehensive grin was still nailed to her face as we snaked our way through the hustle and bustle of the lunchtime crowd to get to the bar. The barmaid eagerly arrived, and I keenly nodded my head at Stephanie so she could order first.

"Hello. Do you have a wine list?" Stephanie asked.

The barmaid's shocked expression said it all, and it identically mirrored my own, so I immediately intervened.

"No. Forget that," I interrupted, "just two pints of lager, please," I requested as the barmaid silently selected two glasses and walked to the pumps.

"Did I say something wrong?" Stephanie asked.

"*Never* drink the wine in a place like this. For a start, no one else does, so you don't know how long the bottle has been open. I've learned that the hard way."

"Sorry, I don't normally go to places like this."

"Where's your usual haunt then?"

"The library, mostly," she laughed dryly.

"Is that a bar?" I asked.

"No, it's—"

"I'm kidding. I do occasionally study, you know."

"Do you know where the bathroom is?"

"Bathroom? Yeah, sure, just at the back there through those doors, but before you go, here's another piece of unsolicited advice: hover."

"Thanks?" she uttered with an upward inflexion.

"All will become clear," I laughed.

As the drinks arrived, I took out my phone to try Nathaniel again, and before it could even ring, I felt a pair of hands slide around my hips. I quickly turned around to find him inexplicably standing there, and he had clearly had a skinful because his eyes were redder than a baboon's backside.

"Jesus Christ, look at the state of you! How long have you been in here?" I sternly questioned.

"A while, my lecture got cancelled, and Al and I have been celebrating," he managed to say in between hiccups.

"Celebrating what?"

"I sold a piece! It was only for twenty quid, but it's a start."

"Nath! That's amazing! Well done to you! Who bought it?"

"Me," a deep voice said as Alexander emerged from behind Nathaniel, clumsily holding a wrapped canvas.

"You two are dickheads," I merrily chastised.

"We are just heading somewhere else. Are you coming?" Alexander asked.

"I'm with someone from my course, and she's just nipped to the loo."

"She can come with us."

"I'll ask her. Here she is," I said as I pointed behind the boys.

As they turned around to look at her, Stephanie nervously pushed through the raucous crowd, closely guarding her handbag with her eyes glued to the ground. The instant she arrived at the bar where we were all standing, she looked up and gasped when she realised who I was with, and I looked at Nathaniel, who appeared as if he had just seen a ghost.

"Steph? We've spoken about this. What are you doing here?" Nathaniel asked.

Without a single word in response, she quickly scurried out of the bar and back out onto the street, leading me to look at Nathaniel and Alexander, who were just weirdly staring at each other.

"You two know each other?" I asked.

"Yeah, from high school back in Cali," Nathaniel replied, looking instantaneously sobered by the brief exchange.

"She's on my course. I implicitly asked if she knew you, and she said she didn't."

"She doesn't even study over here."

"What?"

"Stephanie Ward is a complete psycho," Alex added, "has she still been incessantly calling you?"

"Not for a while," Nathaniel dismissively said as he shot Alexander a look to keep quiet.

"Calling you? Is she stalking you or something?" I asked.

"No, it's not that bad. She just calls every now and again. I haven't seen her in a while."

"Our first date? Was she the one in the shadows?"

Nathaniel and Alexander looked at each other weirdly again and, in unison, sipped the pints they were holding rather than answering.

"What's going on, Nath?" I firmly asked.

"There's nothing going on, I promise. Like Al said, she is just a psycho who won't take no for an answer."

"Why didn't you say anything before?"

"I didn't want to worry you," he said defeatedly.

"I'll sort this out," I sternly announced.

"Please don't. It will make her worse," he protested.

Ignoring his plea, I immediately stormed outside and made it just in time to see her about to climb into the back of a black cab.

"Oi, Stephanie!" I shouted.

She simply smiled at me, got inside the cab, and as it began driving, she pressed her middle finger against the glass. I responded in kind as I remained standing outside the pub as menacingly as I could and watched the taxi disappear into the sea of heavy London traffic.

Not once had Nathaniel as much as uttered her name to me, and the fact that he had been keeping this alleged stalking a secret made me feel grimy. My first thought didn't immediately point to infidelity; I was more concerned about why he felt as if he couldn't tell me what was going on, and the idea of her sniffing around him like that made me feel nauseous. Whatever misguided scheme she had hatched in trying to befriend me was foiled almost immediately, but what kind of person would even attempt something like that? She was clearly unhinged, and I had fallen for her sympathetic loner performance spectacularly.

Worst of all, I even felt sorry for the bitch.

7

THE OTHER WOMAN

OLIVIA – 2024

Many people wear their hearts on their sleeves, but I tended to wear mine across my face, and even though Nathaniel hadn't seen my crumpled-up look of intense disdain and unbridled fury for over ten years, I could sense the trepidation radiating from him. He clearly had a type because his new flame was donning the exact same expression, and we remained in a hostile staring contest, neither of us wanting to turn away first. I actually felt for him at that moment, as all his chickens had come home to roost, and they were poised to scratch each other's eyes out viciously.

"We thought you were dead," she said fearfully.

"There's a lot of that going around," I satirically replied, "you finally dropped the excess weight. Congratulations."

"You too," she venomously smirked as she looked me up and down.

"Listen, Olivia is going to stay with us for a few days so she can get back on her feet," Nathaniel announced with pseudo-bravery.

"What?" Stephanie scornfully snapped.

"Let's talk about it inside," he softly said as he brushed his way past her.

Stephanie gave me the single most chilling look I have ever been on the receiving end of, and I tauntingly gave her a cutesy wave in reply. I smirked as I watched them both storm straight through the hallway and into the kitchen, with Nathaniel pulling the door to behind them. After a few seconds of hesitance, I timidly stepped over the threshold to idly mooch around their home and try to eavesdrop on their heated conversation. However, the slightly ajar door provided just enough privacy that I couldn't fully make out the words, bar the odd volatile expletive followed by my name. I remained idle, waiting for them to hash it out until my attention was drawn to a small table beside the front door, which proudly displayed a stomach-churning picture of the happy couple enjoying a meal at some fancy restaurant, and I pettily slammed it face down so hard that I thought it would crack.

"Bitch," I whispered under my breath.

I thought that I had come to terms with Nathaniel moving on. Besides, given the number of years that I had spent bitterly chewing it over, I almost felt prepared for the level of emotion that seeing them together would bring. Nonetheless, I was convinced that he had met someone by chance, and the fact it was *her* made me feel sick to my stomach. One thing had to be said, though: Stephanie had undergone quite the transformation over the years, and the obvious aesthetic contrast between us was painful. Not only had she shed the puppy fat, but her skin had also magically cleared up in the Californian sun, and the new set of plastic tits and porcelain teeth were the cherries on the cake. I was disappointed in Nath's stereotypical male gaze more than anything else, and the fact that my husband-to-be overlooked how crazy she was because she had bleached her hair and been kicked through a plastic surgery clinic left a very sour taste in my mouth. He knew that I despised her with a passion, for good reason, and if Alexander was anything to go off, I wasn't the only person in his life who felt that way.

I gazed into the mirror in the hallway and almost smashed it off the wall in a jealous rage as the gaunt shadow of the woman I used to be was looking back at me. I was paler than ever, and the dark circles hanging under my sunken eyes almost protruded beyond my jutting cheekbones. As I pushed my lank hair out of my face and ran a single finger over my lips, I felt that they were so cracked and rough that it felt as if I was touching sandpaper. I dared look any further down my body; the instinctual urge to compare myself to her would only have ended in tears.

Just going off looks alone, it wasn't a mystery why Nathaniel eventually conceded to Stephanie's obsessive attempts at romance. However, the big questions remained unanswered, and I was desperate to get them from him. How exactly did that diffident little psychopath somehow snake her way into my family? And after everything she had done to us, why the hell would he pick her? Most unforgivably of all, after those years of mania from Stephanie, he deplorably let her near our daughter, and who knows what untold damage her presence in our family had caused.

I had to have a quiet word with myself to remind me of what was important; my little girl was probably up the stairs behind me, and she had no idea that I was about to drop back into her life. My palms started sweating as I gripped the bannister and searchingly gazed up the steps, hoping for her to appear suddenly after all the commotion.

"Aurora?" I breathily rasped up the stairs.

I couldn't hear any movement apart from the muffled argument escalating in the kitchen, so I began to quietly creep up the steps. The wall beside the staircase was littered with family-style photos and keepsakes, and over the last decade, it seemed like Nath's work had taken them all over the country. From where I was standing, my fears were confirmed that I had missed her entire childhood, and I barely recognised the young woman she was growing into as I continued to climb the steps tentatively.

When I reached the top, I gingerly poked my head through an open door to find Aurora's room to be taken aback by the sheer number of posters featuring unrecognisable bands that dominated the walls. The teenage angst was immediately apparent; she had firmly entered her rebellious era, and all of her icons were sporting crazy hairstyles, piercings and tattoos. Creativity evidently ran through her blood too. Any space not occupied by the images of gritty-looking guitarists and vocalists was filled with haunting sketches and paintings. My attention was drawn to a large corkboard mounted on the wall, which was crowded with ticket stubs and instant-print photos of Aurora and her friends. I randomly plucked one from the board as I sat on the edge of her unmade bed.

It was a moody shot of her on a skateboard going down a ramp, and as inane as the photograph was, I instantly broke down in tears that flooded down my cheeks and soaked into my borrowed tracksuit trousers. I missed her first day of middle school, I didn't get to wave her off to high school, and I never helped her get ready for prom; I was nowhere to be seen for every single defining moment in my young daughter's life, and the guilt I felt was literally horrendous. Those experiences should have been a moment of pride for any parent, and not only were they taken from me, but they were spitefully enjoyed by someone who should have been nowhere near my family.

She wasn't my little girl anymore.

I barely recognised her, and the image that I vehemently guarded and preserved all those years in the bunker was proven to be a lie. The murmuring voice of logic told me that I wasn't to blame and that I couldn't prevent my absence, but my heart was filled with bitter regret and shame. Benjamin had so much to answer for. Blood flowed to parts of my brain that had laid dormant for years, and I realised that, more than anything, I needed him to pay for what he had taken away from me. The anger rose within me to a fever pitch, and it was only when I was confronted with the extent of what I had lost that I gained some semblance of a normal reaction to what had happened. I yearned for justice, regardless of the way it was dispensed, against the person who callously threw me in that cell to begin with and even against Stephanie for being so hard-faced to take advantage of the situation. Between them, they had literally taken *everything* from me. Why should they get to lead their lives as if nothing had happened when I was sentenced to live in the rubble of mine?

"She doesn't miss you," a distorted voice said from behind me.

In a sudden panic, I quickly turned around to find the source of the voice, and I swear that the dusty television in the corner of the room flashed almost imperceptibly as I looked at it.

"You are a horrible mother," the television crackled.

"Leave me alone," I uttered.

"It's true. She didn't need you anyway. Look at how far she has come without you."

"Get out of my fucking head," I mumbled as I squeezed my temples together with a single hand.

I heard the stairs creaking, and the screen suddenly became lifeless again. I quickly wiped the tears from my cheeks as the door opened, and Nathaniel cautiously crept into the room to observe me from the doorway.

"Who are you talking to?" he softly asked.

"No one," I dismissed. "Where's Aurora?"

"She's staying at a friend's house for a few days," Nathaniel tenderly murmured.

"I want to see her. Now," I announced.

"I know you do, but we need to be delicate."

"What the fuck does that mean, Nath? She's my daughter too."

"She's a teenager who hasn't seen her mother since she was six years old. I don't know what this will do to her."

"I *need* to see her."

"I know that you do, and I promise we'll make that happen soon enough. Just give me a few days to work everything out first."

"What about me? I have been through hell and back, and no one around here seems to give a shit."

"Of course we do, and I hate what happened to you," Nathaniel sympathised as he sat on the edge of the bed next to me.

"I should have been here. I've missed everything," I angrily said as I gestured around the room.

"I know, and I'm so sorry Olivia."

"I bet she hates me. You do too, probably."

"We don't hate you, not one bit. We just thought we'd lost you forever."

"Maybe I should have stayed lost. It would have been simpler for everyone."

"Please don't say that. It's going to be an adjustment, but we can get through this; we just need to give it time."

I knew that he was right, of course, but I still huffed and threw the photograph down on the bed beside me. I could feel myself welling up again, so I rubbed my eyes with my sleeves to stop the tears from taking root. He responded only with a look of sheer bewilderment; he clearly didn't understand that I should have been the one featured in all those photos leading up the stairs and that my face was supposed to be in all of Aurora's memories of her growing up. I wasn't naive enough to think that my escape would have a fairy tale ending, but I never anticipated how far the shockwaves of what Benjamin did to me would reach.

"Fine," I started with a snuffle and a numbed shrug, "you're right."

An awkward silence ensued, and I could tell by his face that he was anxiously seeking some words of comfort for me that didn't plausibly exist. The silence was broken by Stephanie stamping around downstairs, followed by the sound of the front door slamming behind her. He let out a prolonged exhale and dropped his shoulders into a hunch.

"Sorry, Nath, I've got to ask. *Stephanie? Really?*" I asked.

"It just kind of happened," he began with a shrug, "I know it's not easy to hear. Or accept."

"Nath, I was gone, and for the record, I don't blame you for moving on, but seriously, why her? She stalked you for years. She's a psychopath," I said matter-of-factly.

Nathaniel suddenly became animated and stood up from the bed to start pacing the room. I could tell by his uneasy demeanour he was getting quickly annoyed by my line of questioning, and I leaned back slightly on my hands to await the inevitable argument that would follow.

"Liv, you're tired and upset. This isn't the time. You need to rest and see a doctor or something."

"No. I think it's the perfect time to talk this out, and I'm done holding my tongue; I've done that for far too long."

"If you want to do this now, then fine, but you have to realise that she was there for me when—"

"When I wasn't?" I interrupted.

"When you were missing, yes," Nathaniel conceded.

"Oh, well, I'm so sorry for being fucking kidnapped. What a huge fucking inconvenience for you," I mockingly shouted.

"We all went through the wringer."

"The *wringer*? I was kidnapped, Nath, not stuck in traffic. I've come home, or whatever you fucking call this place. It's as if I never existed."

"It didn't just happen to you, you know?" he snapped.

"The difference is that I *actually* went through it though, and all you care about now is preserving your pathetic relationship with that spineless wretch."

"For Christ's sake, Olivia, what did you want me to do? Wait for you all these years? Even though I had no idea if you were coming back or not?"

"I waited for you. I had no other choice," I uttered sullenly with my eyes fixed on the floor.

"We thought you were dead. Everybody did. We tried absolutely everything we possibly could to find you, and Stephanie was there for me when I needed it the most."

I let out a single incredulous laugh and threw my hands in the air, which provoked a prolonged eye roll from Nath and for him to stare off into the distance.

"So, let me get this straight: in your grief, you found a warm shoulder to cry on, and it just so happens it belonged to your sicko-stalker-ex? Have I got that right?"

"I was fucking lonely, okay?" he shouted, "I thought you were gone, Aurora was in bits, and Steph helped put us all back together."

"She stole my fucking life, Nath, how can you not see that? All those photographs leading up the stairs should have been me. That freak got exactly what she wanted, didn't she?"

"Listen, I understand that you're angry, and I get it, I really do, but none of this is anyone's fault other than the man who did this to you," he meekly reasoned.

"You don't understand a thing that happened to me down there," I screamed with my finger pointed in his face.

"You know what, you are right, but you don't know what we went through up here either."

Nathaniel's words lingered in the blue air like a malodorous smell whilst both of us tried to catch our breaths after the spat. A single tear rolled down his cheek and soaked into his beard as he solemnly sat back down on the bed with his head in his hands.

"Do you love her?" I timidly asked.

"Yes," he said under his breath.

"Do you still love me?" I muttered with a broken voice.

"I don't know," he replied after a second, "what the hell are we going to do?"

"No idea," I sighed as I laid back on Aurora's bed, "you don't fancy running away with me to sunny Mexico, do you?"

"What?" Nath asked as he turned his head to look at me.

"I'm kidding."

"Steph is going to stay at her parents' house for a few days while we can sort everything out and get you back on your feet, so you don't have to worry about bumping into her."

"Thank you," I whispered.

"Wait there a second, I want to show you something."

Nath left the room for a few minutes and returned with a battered leather-bound journal that he placed on the bed beside my head.

"We never forgot about you," he proclaimed.

"What's this?" I asked.

"If you want to know what it was like for us when you were missing, it's all in there. Well, the first few years or so."

"You kept a diary?"

"Yeah, it sounds ridiculous now, but I didn't want you to miss anything when we finally found you, so I took to writing it all down."

"I've never known you to keep a journal."

"I know, but it seemed the right thing to do. There's newspaper clippings and photos in there too."

"I'll give it a read."

"If you need me, I'll be downstairs. You should get some rest."

"Thanks a lot, and Nath?"

"Yeah?"

"I know how difficult this must be for you. I'm sorry."

"It's okay. Get some rest, Liv," he uttered as he crept out of the room.

I could already feel my swollen eyelids closing under the weight, but I grabbed the journal and started idly flicking through it. As I skimmed it, I realised that he had kept a diligent record of everything, and the enclosed newspaper articles fell out as I leafed through. I randomly stopped on a page where there was a photograph of Nath and me taped to it. I instantly recognised it as the front door to my university accommodation back in London. It was a blurry and faded instant print photo that Nathaniel insisted on taking to mark the occasion, and I remembered it being one of the happiest times of my life. The beaming smile on Nath's face and the stupendous grin on mine was almost unrecognisable from where I was lying.

It seemed like a lifetime ago, and in many ways, it certainly was, yet the conflicting emotions of that day instantly came flooding back in droves. What genuinely astounded me was that a simple yes or no could take a life in a completely different direction, and although I had never once regretted my decision that day, I couldn't help but wonder what would have happened if my life had taken a different course.

8

THE QUESTION

OLIVIA – 2007

It's a wrap. My time at university was finally over, and the streets of London were buzzing with students happily drinking their way into oblivion to celebrate. Stacey and I barely managed to find one of our usual haunts that weren't packed to the rafters with rampant revellers, and in lieu of a better option, we were condemned to a seedy cocktail bar down a back alley. The lights were intentionally so dim that no one could barely see one another, let alone detect the sheer grime of the place, but the soles of my shoes told a different story as I tried to pry them from the sticky tiled floor. Stacey was determined to partake in the tradition of getting bladdered in the name of earning a degree, and I half-heartedly agreed to come along, albeit quite predictably, she had left me alone at the table and was surveying the dimly lit bar for some talent up for grabs.

Unbeknownst to her, I had other reasons to desire a stiff drink, and they certainly weren't celebratory. As I sat there pensively swirling my tepid daiquiri, I couldn't think about anything else other than Nath and what graduating meant for us. He and I were good, too good in fact, and the end of university life symbolised something far more final for us because his justification for staying in London had abruptly come to an end. We were unthinkingly floating into uncharted waters, neither of us wanting to discuss what would actually happen once we finally crossed that bridge, with the result that we had a weird atmosphere every day we saw each other. We both willingly started the relationship on the tacit understanding that it had a clock ticking away on it, and although we had chosen to ignore it most of the time, the final few months were rough, especially for me.

I found myself at a crossroads, half of me paradoxically in self-preservation mode, searching for any lame excuse just to break the relationship off, and the other half wanting to jump into it with both feet and fight for what the two of us had romantically built up. He was so guarded about his own feelings, and whenever I tried to bring up the elephant in the room, he seemed just to shrug it off.

"Come on, Olivia, crack a smile. It's finally over," Stacey said as she drunkenly plonked herself in front of me.

"Sorry, I'm not really feeling up to it," I coldly replied.

"Is it Nath?"

"Yeah, I'm just not sure if we are right together, and he'll be going back to the States soon. I'm seriously thinking about breaking it off."

"Good idea, you can do better."

"Stace, it's nothing to do with him, really. It's the whole long-distance thing that makes me feel sick."

"Are you worried he won't be able to keep it in his pants? I did warn you about that."

"Not at all. He isn't like that."

"He absolutely is."

"Seriously, what's your problem with him?"

She never liked him. It always irked me that she vehemently proclaimed he was a prolific womaniser because she was my oldest friend, and from what I had seen, her perception of him was utterly untrue. It was starting to piss me off royally, to be honest, and we were long overdue for a bitter argument on the subject. Under my scornful eye, Stacey clumsily leaned back in her seat, guzzled some of her multicoloured cocktail for a jolt of Dutch courage, and then immediately sat forward again with unnerving solemnity. Even though her glazed eyes were almost pointing in different directions, thanks to the amount of alcohol she had gulped down, I could see the deep-seated anxiety in them, and she was working herself up to give me her answer.

"Well?" I impatiently asked.

"I don't know how to tell you this, so I'm just going to say it."

"Stace, what are you yammering on about?"

"He's cheating on you with his ex."

"No, he isn't," I firmly rejected as I pushed the table to rise from my seat. "You're just drunk," I blurted out.

"Wait, I've overheard him speaking on the phone."

"You're spying on him?" I asked as I sat back down.

"No, but he's just so obnoxiously American and loud, it's hard to ignore."

"I'm out of here."

"Fine, live in denial," she dismissively said.

"Okay, I'll bite. Who was he on the phone with?"

"I don't know, but I heard him shout that they were his ex for a reason."

One person sprang to mind: Stephanie. My mind immediately accused him of stupidity rather than infidelity; Nathaniel assured me that the whole mess surrounding her was dead and buried and that there had been no contact since that night at the pub when the three of us cornered her. I had my fair share of clingy exes in the past. I understood the predicament he was in, and to be totally honest, after meeting her, I didn't think he would look twice at her either. All that being said, the gnawing paranoia subtly grew within me, and I wondered if there was a slither of truth in what Stacey was offloading onto me.

"Where was this?"

"Outside a lecture. Whatever it was they were on about, it seemed quite passionate if you ask me."

"An argument?"

"It sounded more like a lover's tiff to me, and as soon as he noticed I was trying to eavesdrop, he ended the call."

"So, he didn't actually *do* anything? No more details?"

"Well, no."

"What the fuck Stace? You nearly gave me a heart attack."

"Still, it's dodgy, isn't it? I'm just looking out for you."

"When did this even happen?"

"A few weeks ago."

"So why did you leave it a few weeks before choosing to spill the beans about it?"

"I don't know," Stacey started as she finished her drink, "you just seemed so in love that I didn't want to be the bearer of bad news and ruin that."

Even in her inebriated state, Stacey was right: it was very dodgy. Especially considering he told me the contact between them had ceased, although, from the sounds of it, he hadn't physically cheated on me. The fact he kept it from me was a betrayal in itself, and there was definitely something going on between them, but what that looked like, I had no idea. The thought of them even sharing the same air made me feel queasy, and suddenly, the lake of thawed daiquiri in front of me lost all its appeal.

Everyone is innocent until proven guilty, right? And even though I trusted Stacey with my life, she was lousy when it came to relationships and admittedly a keen gossip. I knew that she wouldn't bring it to my attention without being dogmatically sure, though, and she had clearly been struggling to tell me. Whether or not there had been some infidelity remained to be seen, and I would have to get it from the horse's mouth. "I'm going to take off. I need to speak to Nath," I announced.

"Aw no, Liv, I wish I hadn't said anything now," Stacey said with false sympathy.

"You aren't kidding anyone: you got what you wanted," I quipped with an incredulous smile.

"Yeah, you're right. Bin him right off."

"Good night, mate, and thanks for telling me," I said as I left the table and trudged through the front door.

I hadn't realised how long we had been in the cocktail bar until I made my way onto the street, and I saw the soused mess of newly ex-students stumbling their way home. I took out my phone to call Nathaniel; he was likely in a similar state to the rest of the merrymakers, and it probably wasn't the best time to have a serious talk, but I deserved answers, and he had earned the right to defend himself.

"Liv! Where you at?" he answered joyously.

"On my way home. Listen, I need to have a word with you. Can you meet me there?" I sternly asked.

"Sure, is everything okay?"

"Yeah. Fine. I'll talk to you when I see you."

"Okay," he said bemusedly, "give me thirty minutes, and I'll be there."

"See you then," I replied with jarring formality.

I already knew what his explanation would be; he was trying to spare me the upset and anguish by not telling me, and although it was misguided, I understood his rationale. I thought the probability of him confessing to a long-standing affair with the girl was very slim indeed, and I wasn't even worried about that. I was more concerned about what my own response to whatever he had to say would be and if, in the heat of the moment, I would use it as a plausible excuse to prematurely end things between us.

Disregarding the severity of his blunder, it still felt a little cheap and flimsy to use it as a reason. Nevertheless, I knew that it would be kinder to us both if I just ended it there and then, and what was the alternative? Seeing each other on the odd stolen weekend and desperately trying to feign some semblance of a normal relationship in between flights to and from the States? No thanks, definitely not for me. Even considering breaking it off told me that we weren't strong enough to weather the stress a long-distance relationship would impose on us both, and it would be far more painful watching our blossoming romance wither away and die a slow death. There was no way he wouldn't accept my brutal realism wilfully, and he would want to give it a go despite the obvious complications coming down the line.

My walk home was a sullen and sobering one, and the whole thing made me feel incredibly sad because, in many ways, I felt like I was falling for him, and given different circumstances, we could have been really happy together. I knew Nath loved me, and I could see it palpably on his face every time he locked eyes on me. The thought of that filled me with a sudden influx of remorse. I knew that logically, it was the right thing to do, and I was definitely thinking with my head and not my heart, yet that realisation didn't make it any easier.

On approaching my flat, I could already see Nath waiting for me outside of it whilst getting soaking wet in the pouring rain. My heart plummeted to the pit of my stomach when I saw him, and suddenly, the enormity of the task ahead dawned on me. I didn't know if I could bear to see him upset, as he had always been this happy-go-lucky character around campus, and the thought of wronging him in some way or another felt inherently wrong. I had gone through plenty of break-ups from both sides of the fence, and I clearly had no problem speaking my mind, but this felt altogether different, almost as if I was telling my golden retriever I didn't love him anymore. As I drew closer, I saw the intense trepidation on his face, and his metaphorical tail was twitching nervously. "Olivia, what's wrong?" he asked anxiously.

"I thought you said thirty minutes; how did you get here so quickly?"

"I cabbed it. I didn't like the sound of your voice on the phone and was worried about what you had to say."

"I know about her," I abruptly announced.

"Who?" he bemusedly asked.

"Stephanie."

"Liv, I haven't spoken to her since the weird night at The Slippery Pig."

I let out a deep, breathy sigh as I rolled my eyes almost into the back of my skull, placed my hands judgementally on my hips, and tilted my head at him slightly.

"Honestly, Nath, don't lie. It's just going to make things worse," I wearily said.

"I'm serious. I'm not lying."

"So what's this I'm hearing about you two lovebirds chatting on the phone outside a lecture?" I sternly quizzed.

Nath's eyes widened; he started to look like he had been caught out, and I instinctually stepped closer over to him to keep the pressure on. I could see him internally flapping around for some kind of retort, but the guilt on his face was conspicuously palpable.

"Christ, we aren't lovebirds. She just randomly called me as she usually does," he mustered.

"As usual? I thought you said you hadn't spoken to her."

"You know what I mean."

"Why didn't you tell me then? Let me guess, you didn't want to upset me."

"Well, yeah. She's just a nutter, there's nothing going on with her, I swear it."

I sat down on the little wall beside my accommodation's front door with a prolonged exhale as I looked up into the rainy night sky. It was crunch time, and I had already heard enough to be able to make up my mind.

"It's getting old, mate," I began to explain, "I think we should just call it a day. It's inevitable that it's going to end when you go back home anyway."

"What? You're dumping me just like that?" Nath asked worriedly.

"Don't be a child. You'll be toddling back off to California any day now, and I'm sure Steph will dotingly follow you. You can finally be with her like you've always wanted."

"Seriously, Liv, I'm not at all interested in her."

"It doesn't matter. There will be five thousand miles between us. This is the logical decision."

"No, that's bullshit, we have something special, and you know it."

"What do you want to do then? Scrape together what little money we have and squander it on flights so we can spend a few hours together once a month? It's not going to work."

"It will if you come with me," Nath abruptly said in obvious desperation as he stepped underneath the canopy in front of me.

"What? You don't really want that. You're just clutching at straws."

"Oh, come on, you can write anywhere, and London is shit anyway, you've said so yourself. And this," he said as he pointed to the torrential rainfall, "we don't get it back in Cali."

"I'm not going to just forget about her and uproot my life just like that. I've got plans for the future."

"I'm your future. It can be a fresh start for both of us," he declared as he knelt down on the sodden ground and grabbed my hand.

As I sat there staring into his puppy-dog eyes, I realised I was in a pivotal moment in our relationship, and what I would say next would shape our entire future. My resolve had wavered slightly, and just the expression on his face made my heart ache. However, I knew I was making the right decision; I was certain of it, and my lips slightly parted as I prepared to give him my final answer.

"No," I uttered without conviction.

I saw all the hope and expectation evaporate from his face as I coldly shook away the grip he had on my hand and crossed my legs. My body language took him back slightly, and he awkwardly fumbled in his pocket only to produce a small velvet ring box, which he opened, presenting an impressive diamond-encrusted engagement ring. My jaw dropped, and the sudden surge of adrenaline and nerves silenced every voice of reason and logic I had within me as my attention was shared between staring at the ring and dumbfoundedly looking down at Nathaniel.

"What am I going to do with this, then?" he asked wryly.

"Are you fucking proposing?" I exclaimed in disbelief.

"Yes, and I'm on two knees, so it's twice as romantic."

My first thought was how long he had that ring box in his pocket because that was the perfect time for him to produce it. I assumed that his sudden urge for me to move to America with him was born out of the desperation he felt to keep things going between us, but he had clearly been planning this for a long time. It dawned on me that I had been actively looking for motives to break it off and ignoring the reasons to continue. Maybe everything would eventually work out between us, and perhaps an act of commitment like his proposal would be enough for us to weather the upcoming storm and battle through until we could finally be together.

"Well?" he asked.

"Fuck it," I started with a smile, "yes."

"Oh my God, really?"

"Yes! Now get up off the floor, you idiot."

He slid the ring on my finger, we both stood up, and he kissed me passionately on the lips. I could almost feel his metaphorical tail wagging again as he reached into his bag and pulled out a camera to take a photograph of us both, but as the sensation continued, I realised it was his phone vibrating. I decided to ignore it, and like the massive cliché I was, I displayed my new engagement ring into the lens as the flash went off.

9

THE CIRCUS

OLIVIA – 2024

Under Nathaniel's advice, or more accurately, constant nagging, I decided to visit the town's doctor to get checked up. It wasn't his insistence on a full psychological evaluation that I found irritating but the prospect of spending a week handcuffed to a hospital bed somewhere. The doctor's appointment was just what I needed: to be prodded and poked by a perfect stranger. The thought of needing to go to a doctor had always filled me with dread, and I always felt more like a slab of meat being inspected for damage rather than an actual person. That being said, the doctor's surgeries were far nicer in the States than back in Britain; I always put it down to the fact that you had to pay a fortune just to get an appointment in the first place. Strangely, the smell was exactly the same, though, an unnaturally chemical stench that was somewhere in between undiluted bleach and air freshener that seemed to coat your skin as soon as you stepped foot in the building.

The unyielding hiss and pop of the inflating blood pressure monitor made me wince as it unpleasantly wrapped itself around my dithering arm. The machine beeped, signifying that it had embarrassingly failed to get a clear reading once again, and the flummoxed doctor scratched his head before producing a cuff designed for a child, which fit my withered bicep far more snugly.

Forty-eight hours had passed since my argument with Nath, and I felt no freer than when I was stuck in that hole. I was no longer detained in a prison of concrete and steel, but in my own mind, and the longer I spent on the outside, the more isolated I felt. Most of all by him, as he had spent the time constantly asking me if I was okay, like it wasn't absurdly obvious that I was not. In secret, I had read through the journal he had provided me with; I knew that his intention was to give me some insight into what he went through, and it did, but as a byproduct of that, I felt incredibly guilty more than anything else. The past decade was difficult for both of us in massively different ways, and I realised we were every bit as broken as each other.

The only person who sounded genuinely happy to hear that I was alive was Stacey, and when I called her with the news, she almost fainted on the phone. Whilst I was frozen in time, she got married and had a daughter of her own, and although I was happy for her, I realised the dynamic between us had changed, and I was the chaotic friend for once. It took me over an hour to convince her not to drop everything and get on a plane, and I'm glad I eventually did because she was the last person I wanted to see in this state. In the end, I only managed to get her off the line by promising her I would visit her in London once everything calmed down.

My mind felt as if it were being mercilessly ripped apart like wet tissue paper. Nathaniel was gripping onto one of the corners, making me wonder if there was anything left between us and if there was a possibility that we could somehow rekindle what we once had. Aurora's infantile hand tugged at another, asking me why I hadn't immediately come to see her and apologise for everything that I had missed. Stephanie's false nails clawed into the third corner, leaving me eternally paranoid and fearful of what her next move would be and how she would try and get rid of me for good. The last pair of gloved hands were Benjamin's, reaching out from the shadows, simply maintaining the tension and observing the rest of the participants do the dirty work for him.

I felt like I was barely holding it all together, not knowing where my priorities should lie and knowing that even the slightest inconvenience would tip me over the edge and send me spiralling into the abyss. I still hadn't seen my daughter, and I couldn't help but think a reunion was what I needed to snap me out of it, but I understood Nathaniel's point of view, and I continued to respect his opinion. She was supposedly staying at a friend's house for a few days, totally unaware that her mother had essentially come back from the dead. He rightfully didn't want to inflict any more psychological damage on her, but the thought of her not knowing that I was alive was gnawing away at me, and every fibre of my being was desperate to see her.

True to her word, Stephanie had stayed away from the house. However, the incessant buzzing of Nathaniel's phone told me a different story and that she was keeping constant tabs on him. To be honest, it made me smile whenever I heard it because the shoe was on the other foot, and I imagined that every single vibration was a pang of anxiety and paranoia from her that we were somehow getting back together. Not taking her obsessive nature into account, and as a woman, I suppose I had some empathy for her situation too, and if the roles were reversed, I would have been nervous too.

It must have been a shock to her when she saw me tottering up the driveway like a zombie, and just my very existence had put her fairy-tale future in jeopardy. It didn't give her permission to be such a bitch about it, though, and the years of disdain I felt for her were hard to forget. As far as I was concerned, what she took from me when I was at my most vulnerable was unforgivable, and although I knew that I just needed *someone* to blame for what happened, I could think of no better candidate for that than her. She had been clearly skulking in the shadows throughout our entire relationship like some scavenger waiting for scraps to fall off the table until suddenly, after my disappearance, she was politely invited to take a seat and handed a knife and fork.

If I had to describe my relationship with my ex-husband-to-be in that moment, and I were feeling uncharacteristically kind, I would say it was frosty at best. He was still clearly ruminating on what I had said to him, the insanity of the events that had transpired, and how we could all move forward from this without destroying everything even further. My temper had calmed since the argument out of respect for the predicament he had found himself in more than anything else, and I could finally see that he was just trying to do right by everybody. Nevertheless, he was yet to realise it was an impossible task, and at some point, it was all going to come to a head violently.

"Miss Lakewell?" the doctor asked.

"Sorry, I was miles away," I responded distractedly.

"As I said, your blood pressure is incredibly erratic. I think it's most likely due to a combination of stress, dehydration, and malnourishment."

"Are there some tablets for that?"

"Yes, but it's imperative you avoid stressful situations where you can, as it will exasperate the condition."

"Will do," I sarcastically responded.

"All the other tests have come back remarkably satisfactory considering what you've been through, although you do need to work on gaining weight."

"No stress and plenty of chocolate. Got it."

The doctor leaned back in his seat with a sigh as he tapped a pen on his desk and looked at me wearily. My defence mechanism was always humour, and it didn't always go down well in situations such as this, but long ago, I had abandoned giving a toss about what people thought of me.

"How are you feeling, mentally?" he asked searchingly.

"Fine," I dismissed with a smile.

"I can recommend an excellent therapist. If that's what you want, of course."

"I don't. Everything is just peachy, honestly."

"Right..." the doctor began with another sigh, "Miss Lakewell, you should really speak to someone about what befell you. It can be difficult to process what happened to you alone. Psychological issues can often manifest themselves physically too; it's just as important as the tablets and the tests."

"I couldn't agree more," I began with pseudo-enthusiasm, "but I'm good."

"Okay," he said defeatedly, "you are staying with your husband, yes?"

"I'm not really sure what to call him, but yes, I'm staying with Nathaniel."

"Good, it's important not to be alone after something like this. We should see each other again in a few weeks, but if you have any more health concerns in the meantime, please don't hesitate to get in touch," he explained as he handed me a prescription longer than a laundry list.

"I will, thanks, doctor," I hastily said as I joylessly left his office and went back into the reception room to see Nathaniel leaving his seat to escort me outside.

"How did it go?" he asked nervously.

"I've got two weeks to live. It's a tragedy. I've got so much left to give," I joked.

"Seriously, what did he say?"

"I'm deficient in the whole alphabet, my blood pressure is more up and down than a pogo stick, and I've been prescribed a full pizza for every meal until I no longer look like a walking skeleton."

"So, you're a picture of health from the sounds of it," he said with a dry smirk, "did he recommend therapy?"

"He did."

"Are you going to go?"

"Not sure."

"You definitely need to speak to someone; did he at least give you a recommendation?"

"No, I declined it."

"Liv, why?" he asked naggingly.

"Because I'm fine, Nath. I just want to see my daughter," I huffed as I pushed past him to exit the office onto the street.

"The new sheriff should have ensured you were immediately referred to a physical and mental evaluation. He clearly doesn't have a fucking clue what he's doing."

"Thank God for his incompetence! The last thing I want is to be manhandled into a straitjacket and thrown in a padded cell somewhere."

"I can ask Aurora's therapist if he has any space for a new client?" Nath meekly suggested as he followed me out.

"Wait, Aurora has a therapist? Why?" I sternly asked as I stopped dead in the street.

"Calm down, every kid in California has a therapist, and we just wanted her to get all the help she needed after... you know what happened."

"*We*," I mockingly uttered under my breath.

"Sorry, what did you say?"

"Nothing," I said dismissively, "when can I see her? It's been two days, Nath. I'm losing my mind here."

"Maybe we take the doctor's advice and explain everything to her tonight over a mountain of pizza."

"Seriously?" I said as I stopped in my tracks.

"Sure, we have to do it sooner or later. And you are right, it's been days, she deserves to know."

For the first time since all this began, an anxious yet genuine smile started to creep across my face as we approached Nathaniel's car, and after we had both got inside, I grew excited when I realised that, in many ways, this was going to be the first time I would ever meet her. My mind was suddenly awash with irrelevant and ridiculous questions like what I was going to wear, and when the happy tears started rolling down my cheeks, Nath gave me a knowing smile as he started the car and began driving us back. My hands were trembling with unadulterated excitement, and for a brief moment, I actually began to feel like my old self again.

"Do you think she will be happy to see me?" I agitatedly asked.

"Yeah, of course," he nodded knowingly.

"Oh God, Nath, I'm so excited to see her. It's been so long. What do you think about—"

I was interrupted by the sound of Nath's phone ringing and Alexander's picture coming up on the screen inside his vehicle. He hesitantly hovered his finger over the green answer button for a few seconds before turning to me.

"Sorry, one second," Nathaniel said as he pressed the button, "Al, what's up?"

"Nath? Don't go home," Alexander said.

"What?"

"I just stopped by to see how you are all getting on, and your street is packed with news vans."

"News vans? What for?"

"Someone must have leaked to the press that Olivia is back. It's crawling with reporters."

"We have to go back for Aurora," I said insistently.

"Sorry, Olivia, I had no idea you were there," Alexander said.

"I'll speak to you later, Al. Thanks for the heads up," Nathaniel said before hanging up the call.

"I'm serious. We have to go back. They have to let you in your home, right?" I reasoned.

"You didn't see what it was like when you went missing: it was crazy. They were outside our old place pretty much constantly."

"Why?"

"They were keeping an eye on the prime suspect."

"You?"

"It's always the husband, they said."

"That's terrible."

"Uh-huh. Eventually, I was cleared, and they started looking for other suspects. Obviously, they never found one."

"Well, they can get lost. If Aurora's coming home, I need to be there when she does."

"Maybe we should postpone it. I really don't want to overwhelm her."

"Nath? No. She's coming home. I need this."

"Fine, but I don't think you are ready for this."

We turned the corner, and the street was visible. Instead of the usually vacant and quiet street, it was chock-a-block with vans sporting news logos parked bumper to bumper. Nath carefully navigated through the stragglers making their way towards the house and attempted to turn into his own driveway, only to find a blockade of reporters and photographers in his path. He aggressively beeped the horn, and the sea of malingerers begrudgingly parted as they held their cameras up to the glass and randomly snapped pictures of us inside.

"Put this over your head," he suggested as he tossed me a hoodie that was on the back seat and got out of the car to try to herd the crowd back off his property. I did as he suggested, quickly making my way to the front door as Nath followed me to unlock it. The constant blinding flashes and high-pitched screaming filled me with anxiety as the horde of detail-hungry journalists clambered over one another to try and be first in line for comment. The chorus of what seemed like a hundred people discordantly chanting my name almost became deafening as he finally got the door unlocked, and we both rushed inside. I paced in the entrance with my hands over my ears as Nathaniel hurriedly locked the door behind him and slid down it with his back onto the floor.

"What the fuck? That's insane," I shouted.

"They are like rabid animals. If we don't give them anything, they should leave," he anxiously said.

"I really don't need this right now."

"I'm going to ring the sheriff; they should at least stay beyond the property line."

Before we could regain our composure, we both heard the sound of glass smashing at the rear of the property, and we both instinctually ran through to the kitchen to investigate the noise. The middle pane of the bi-fold doors had been put through, and in the centre of the pile of smashed glass, there was a rock with something tied around it with string. Nath got there first, picked it up, and started untying the twine that surrounded it to release the thin piece of paper that was fastened to it. He placed the rock on the kitchen counter and flattened out the attached note as I approached to read it.

"Let him without sin cast the first stone. Come home, Olivia. We aren't done playing yet," I shakily read out loud.

"It's the fucking press playing mind games," he said.

Nathaniel immediately sprang into action and hopped through the new opening at the back of his house to see if he could chase down the perpetrator, leaving me entirely motionless at the kitchen counter. I touched the curled-up note with my shaking hands, and the texture felt bizarrely thin and plasticky, so I turned it around to look at the back. Barely had I flipped it over when I realised it was written on something I would recognise anywhere; it was the label from the exact same tin of baked beans that Benjamin had grown so fond of feeding me.

My heart dropped, and if I had eaten anything that day, I probably would have been hurling it up in the kitchen sink beside me. My knees went incredibly weak to the point where they couldn't support my weight any longer, and I dropped to the floor in a hysterical heap. I had barely thought about Benjamin since I regained my freedom; it was largely a conscious decision that I forced myself into because if I let my thoughts dwell on him for even a moment, the fear would have consumed me. Despite that, I wrongly assumed he was well and truly in the wind. I wrongly thought that he would be terrified of being found out by the law and would at least be several states away or even in another country. His grim little note shattered that perception; any semblance of security I had was instantly obliterated, and emotionally, I was thrown back to day one of the worst decades of my life.

Benjamin was close.

And he wanted me back.

10

THE DINNER

OLIVIA — 2014

I always hated flying. Nevertheless, I told myself that I would have to get used to it because Nathaniel had already moved back to California, and if I ever wanted to see my fiancé, catching a flight would be the only way. I had scraped together every spare penny just to be able to afford the plane ticket, which, to my dismay, was a return one. Practically, we were just not in a position for me to be able to move there just yet, despite the fact our relationship had evolved into the one thing I was terrified of it becoming: long-distance.

I'm not sure why I asked Stacey to come with me. At the time, I felt utterly daunted by the prospect of flying to America on my own, but since she had been begging me to go on a girl's holiday for years, I decided to kill two birds with one stone. As Nathaniel didn't seem to mind her intrusion, I chose to invite her against my better judgement. The regret I felt was palpable when I realised that I hadn't been trapped in an enclosed space with her for so long before, and her nauseating, chirpy demeanour in the face of my aerophobia soon began to get on my nerves.

"Excuse me!" Stacey shouted after the stewardess.

"Yes?" she asked.

"Two more vodkas, please, and do you have any napkins? I've spilled the last one," she loudly requested.

"Sorry, ma'am, we will be landing soon," the stewardess disdainfully explained.

"Well, you're a killjoy," Stacey remarked as the stewardess walked down the aisle. "That's annoying, isn't it?" she asked as she turned to me.

"Uh-huh," I uttered with a deep breath.

"What's the matter? Are you worried about the landing?"

"A little," I said through gritted teeth.

"Did you know that when planes land, they're travelling at over one-hundred-and-fifty miles an hour? That's mad, isn't it?" she gasped.

"No, I didn't know that," I said matter-of-factly.

"I'm glad you are in the window seat. I hate looking out of the window and seeing the wings wobble. That can't be safe, right?"

I glanced out of the window, saw the very thing she was talking about, and tightly shut my eyes as I turned away.

"Stacey?" I softly asked with my eyes still shut.

"Yes?"

"Can you shut the fuck up? Pretty please?"

"Jesus, sorry. I was just trying to take your mind off it."

"Attention cabin crew, please prepare for landing," the pilot announced over the intercom.

"Thank God for that," I whispered to myself.

When the plane started to descend through the turbulent clouds, I gripped onto the armrest for dear life, trying to make light of my fear of flying in favour of the main reason I had decided to fly there in the first place. Nathaniel had already met all the members of the Lakewell family, given I was the only living member, and after popping the question, he wanted me to meet his parents. They wanted to be introduced to the Brit who had stolen their son's heart, and I was quite excited about it, to be honest. In fact, I was always good with parents; I found that just the right mix of humour and respect was a surefire recipe for success. I was eager to find out more about Nathaniel's history, too, and hopefully get my hands on some embarrassing childhood photographs for good measure.

I knew very little about Nathaniel's family tree, but from what he had said, he belonged to a well-to-do clan. You wouldn't think it to look at him simply because he made a point of earning his own money. To be honest, the fact that he wanted to make his own way in the world was not only one of the things I most respected about him, but it was also a principle I identified myself with, not least because I was forced to do the same after the death of my parents.

After a few tense minutes, the wheels finally hit the runway, and the jet engines on either side of us furiously roared to slow us down on our approach to the terminal. I fearfully winced the entire time until we came to a dead stop, and to my embarrassment, Stacey started incessantly clapping in celebration.

"See, told you it will be fine, *Miss Grumpy Boots*," she remarked as she retrieved her case from the overhead locker.

With a loud sigh, I awkwardly shunted myself over the seats, stood up to stretch my back and then retrieved my carry-on luggage from the overhead compartment too. After disembarking from the plane in one piece and patiently passing through the immigration and customs checkpoints, we tried to make our way out of the terminal to meet Nathaniel, who promised he would wait for us in the arrivals lounge. I hadn't seen him in months, and I was desperate to.

"Do you ever think you'll move here?" Stacey asked.

"That's the plan, eventually," I distractedly replied.

"It's not safe over here, though. Everybody and their mother has got a gun, and they have serial killers."

"I think that's an overgeneralisation," I commented.

"No, it's true. Do you not read the news?"

"Not if I can help it," I dismissed, "did we miss a sign? I thought it said the exit was this way."

"Aww, my little Olivia's in love!" she infantilely teased.

"Well, we are getting married. Which is more than you can say about yourself," I hit back.

"Ouch. Below the belt, Liv."

"So you've finally accepted he isn't a player?"

"I'll admit that initially, I had my reservations about him, but the difference in you is night and day. And you're so cute together."

When the automatic doors opened, and we finally made it out of the terminal, I desperately tried to spot Nathaniel in the scrabbling mass of people either standing in the arrivals lounge or busily rushing through it. I stopped dead as I peered through the crowd until I noticed someone holding aloft a hand-painted sign with my name on it surrounded by love hearts. I heartily smiled as I pushed through the gaggle of arriving travellers until I finally managed to lock eyes with him. Then he excitedly ran over to us to give me a passionate kiss and relieve us of our suitcases.

"Guys, we're in public," Stacey dryly taunted.

"Shut up," I jovially ordered.

"How was the flight?" Nath asked.

"Well, this one was shaking in her grumpy boots the entire time," Stacey joked.

"At least I'm not terrified of a serial killer taking me," I snappily responded.

"You are about to lock horns with far worse than a serial killer because we are having dinner with my parents tonight," Nathaniel announced.

"I thought we were doing dinner tomorrow?" I asked.

"Yes, that was the plan, but they had a prior engagement scheduled for tomorrow, apparently. Some charity ball at the country club."

"Country club? Ooh-la-la, I didn't know you were so posh, Nath," Stacey exclaimed.

"I'm not; they are," he smiled.

"Is the car outside?" I asked.

"Your chariot awaits," he dramatically declared.

"It's so cute he's this excited," Stacey whispered in my ear as Nath led us out of the arrivals lounge.

We got outside to his car as the midday sun was beating down on us, and excitedly loaded the suitcases inside, as Stacey fanned herself with her passport. We all got in as he set up the satnav, and Stacey leaned over from the back seat to turn the radio up.

"How long's the drive?" I asked.

"Only about five hours," he muttered.

"Five fucking hours?" Stacey exclaimed.

"Yes?"

"Wake me up when we get there then, and turn that radio down, please," Stacey instructed as she pulled down the eye mask that was resting on her head.

"She has been a nightmare," I silently mouthed at Nath, who giggled as he started the car and began driving.

We caught up on the way, and Nathaniel was busy telling me about all the odd jobs he had been doing so we could save up enough money for me to move over there. However, my job search hadn't gone as well as his, and I was still living off the remaining scraps of my student loan. I tried to forget about all the mundanities of our long-term plan, live in the moment, and just enjoy the stolen weekend we had together. It felt nice taking a real American road trip together, and it was a little glimpse of what life would be like when I finally made it over there.

True to his word, we arrived five hours later. Although, the term 'house' didn't exactly do it justice, as it was a huge, gated property in hyper-affluent Los Altos Hills. The mansion we were driving towards would have been far more suited to a rockstar rather than the family of an aspiring painter. Out of nowhere, I was incredibly nervous. I had a very specific image of what I was walking into, based on Nathaniel's description of them, but suddenly, I felt like a fish out of water. The kind of people who lived in a magnificent place such as that weren't going to laugh at my shit jokes about the tube, and the formula I thought

I had perfected to win parents over rapidly felt juvenile. As Nath leaned over to press the button so the electric gates would open, I furiously tapped him on the shoulder.

"Erm, Nath?" I anxiously said.

"What's the matter?" he replied.

"What the fuck?" I said as I pointed to the house.

"Oh, sorry, welcome," he confusedly mustered.

"It's huge."

"So?"

"Well, you said they were well-off, not stupendously rich beyond my wildest dreams. Look at the state of what I'm wearing!" I said.

"Hey, you look fine! What's wrong with what you're wearing?" he exclaimed.

"Sure, fine to be trudging around an airport! I had no idea they were this wealthy. They're going to think I'm a tramp."

"Don't be silly. You're going to do amazing, and they'll love you."

Without a care in the world, Nathaniel got out to grab the suitcases but was quickly intercepted by his mother and father, who suddenly walked down the steps of their ostentatious home to meet him. After a few seconds, they began peering through the glass to try and get a look at me, which made me awkwardly shuffle in my seat to get Stacey's attention, who was soundly snoring away like a hog in the back seat.

"Stace! Wake up!" I said as I reached round to shake her leg.

"Are we there yet?" she groggily asked as she removed her eye mask.

"Yes, and you need to be on your best behaviour."

"Why?" she sleepily started before spotting the water fountain outside the front door. "Oh shit, is this their house?" she added in shock.

Before I could prepare Stacey any further, Nathaniel excitedly bounded over to open the car door for me, and I was compelled to exit the vehicle with a beaming smile. His wealthy parents remained stationary on the driveway, silently judging me from head to toe as expected. I made my way over there with my arm outstretched for a nervous handshake and the warmest smile I could gather.

"Hello, I'm Olivia. It's lovely to meet you both," I carefully enunciated in my best posh accent.

"Nice to meet you. I'm Ernest, and this is my wife, Gloria," Nathaniel's father said as he shook my hand.

"Charmed," Gloria pretentiously gushed.

Feeling so far out of my element that it was frightening, I winced as I heard the car door slam behind me, knowing that Stacey was rumbling towards us. I quickly gave her a dirty look as she confusedly looked back at me on her way to meet Nath's parents, who looked incredibly perplexed by her sudden appearance.

"I'm Stacey, Olivia's oldest friend," she announced.

"Nice to meet you. I must apologise; we weren't expecting anyone else for dinner. Nathaniel, please run ahead and alert the kitchen to prepare another place setting."

"I will do," Nathaniel responded and pulled a funny face at me as soon as he was out of his dad's eyeline.

"Please, come in," Ernest welcomingly said.

"I do hope you ladies have packed an appetite. Dinner is about to be served," Gloria added.

With an anxiety-ridden gulp, I was slowly led up the marble steps and through the double doors with Stacey in tow and into Nathaniel's childhood home. The walls were tastefully adorned with extravagant-looking fine art and littered with beautifully ornate sculptures. In the centre of the grand lobby was a stunningly majestic staircase leading to the upper floors, and my head was on a swivel as I took it all in on our way to the dining room.

The elegant mahogany table inside was larger than some flats I have lived in, and as we were politely escorted to our seats by white-gloved staff, I started to feel even more uncomfortable. Nathaniel joined us a few seconds later from the kitchen door to take his place facing me, but before we got a chance to speak, course after course of decadent food came out of the kitchen and was placed in front of us.

To my surprise, dinner actually went really well. Despite the odd occasion that Stacey was chewing with her mouth open, I have to say she acted with some modicum of grace throughout. I desperately tried to remember which utensil was for each course, as I grew increasingly paranoid that Nathaniel's parents were silently scrutinising my every move.

After desert, Ernest politely dabbed the corner of his mouth with his serviette as he cleared his throat and looked at me strangely. I knew that he had already formed his first impression of me, and the inevitable parental inquisition was about to commence. Nath saw it too, and I saw his hands begin to fidget as he nervously wondered what his parents would want to know about me.

"So, our son tells us that you are a writer," Ernest started.

"Yes, I've just finished my degree, just trying to work out what genre I want to work in," I explained.

"Does it pay well?"

"Dad!" Nathaniel softly threatened.

"Sorry, are questions of that nature deemed uncouth at the dinner table?"

"No, not at all," I smiled, "it depends if you're any good, I suppose."

"And are you?"

"Sorry, am I what?"

"Any good?"

"Well," I chucked nervously, "I suppose that remains to be seen."

"So, am I to understand that you haven't had anything published, as of yet?"

"Not yet, no," I replied with my best false smile.

"Ahh, the folly of youth. Our son wants nothing more than to be an artist rather than follow in my footsteps in investments. We have tried convincing him, but he is very stubborn in that way."

"Well, he's very talented. Are you both avid collectors? I noticed all the pieces in the lobby; they are beautiful," I remarked.

"Yes, *real* art, though. Not the angry paint splatters that Nathaniel produces, that's for sure," he shamelessly taunted.

Ernest's abruptly harsh criticism lingered on in the air like a bad smell for a moment, and I remained silently stunned as I waited for any of the other dinner guests to correct his faux pas. I shot a glance at my fiancé, who was doing his best to ignore what was being said and was concentrating on drinking deeply from his wine glass instead.

"Sorry, I don't understand. It *is* real art that Nathaniel makes. Some of his pieces – wow – they are out of this world. His style is very highly regarded, in London at least."

"That's nice of you to say," Gloria heartily replied with a condescending smile.

"No, I'm not just being polite. That's actually what I think."

"Interesting," Ernest pensively began, "what do your parents do?"

"Nothing much, considering they have been dead for three years. My mother was a seamstress, and my father was a copywriter." I sardonically stated.

"Dad! I told you that! You are now being deliberately confrontational," Nathaniel sternly said.

"I'm just testing the young lady's mettle. Calm down, son," Ernest dismissively said.

"Oh? I thought we were just having a nice dinner, and I was here to get to know my fiancé's family," I added facetiously.

"I'm only having a bit of fun," he scornfully said.

"Well, let's quit the bullshit, shall we?" I heatedly declared.

Gloria gasped at my unexpected vulgarity as if the very word had caused her immense pain, whilst Ernest actually cracked a slight smile in the face of my sudden outburst.

"What did you have in mind?" Ernest calmly asked.

"You two already seem to have a problem with me being with your son. You clearly don't mince your words, so why not just come out with the reason why?"

"Okay then. I think you're a bad influence on our son. He is already dead set on pursuing this pipedream of becoming a famous painter rather than doing something of substance, and you seem to be supporting him in that endeavour."

"He should be free to do whatever he wants," I remarked.

"I agree. Given that it is worthwhile and worthy of our name."

"Is that all?" I challenged as I sipped my wine.

"Well, I find your intentions unsettling, also. You are the orphaned daughter of the working class, clearly trying to better her standing by marrying into wealth rather than working for it herself. I am concerned my son is marrying beneath himself."

Nathaniel was avoiding eye contact with everyone at the table, and I stared at him, hoping that he would leap to my defence, but he remained stalwartly mute.

"Nath?" I angrily prompted.

He just embarrassedly shrugged back at me.

"Olivia, you don't have to listen to this shit," Stacey provokingly chipped in as I tearfully looked at her. "Come on, let's get out of here," she added.

"Thanks for the backup," I scorned at Nath as Stacey pretty much dragged me out of the dining room.

I shook her grasp once the door closed behind us to eavesdrop on what was being said inside, and I could see Nathaniel getting increasingly agitated by what he had just witnessed, and he forcefully slammed his glass down on the table before furiously standing up.

"Now look what you've done!" he shouted.

"Son, I've done you a favour," his father explained.

"I *love* her, and you spoke to her like she was a piece of shit on your shoe."

"Nathaniel!" Gloria exclaimed.

"I will talk with her how I see fit. It is my house, after all," Ernest agitatedly replied.

"I don't care about family names, wealth, or any of this shit."

"Your father just doesn't want you to make more mistakes with your life, that's all," Gloria interjected.

"That's a lie. He's been this exact way with every single girl I ever brought home. Even in high school."

"That's not true. What was that young lady's name that came by the house that time?" Ernest asked his wife.

"Stephanie," she smiled.

"Ahh, yes, Stephanie. You are much better suited to her. She was just delightful, wasn't she?" Ernest gushed.

"Wait, Stephanie has been to the house? When did this happen?" Nathaniel anxiously asked.

"Come on, Olivia," Stacey uttered in my ear.

I sternly shushed her and continued listening.

"She just stopped by on the off-chance of catching you home, that's all. She's a pleasant and very polite young lady, and the Wards are a very prestigious family indeed. She was telling us that with her father's help, she is looking to open her own dental practice."

"She certainly had her head screwed on," Gloria commented.

"Listen," Nathaniel began seriously, "I'm marrying Olivia, and we don't need your help, or your blessing, for that matter. It's my life, and I make the decisions."

Nathaniel finished his glass of wine and, in a huff, stomped towards the door I was peering through.

"Where are you going?" Gloria asked.

"I'm going after her to see if she's okay and to beg her to forgive me for what you two have just said," he announced.

I stepped back from the door before it flew open, and as Nathaniel realised I was still standing there, I threw my arms around him.

"Do you know any dive bars we can all go to and get a drink at?" I quietly asked him.

"I know just the place," he replied with a smirk.

11

THE LIES

OLIVIA — 2024

The alternating blue and red of Sheriff Daniels' silenced cruiser siren danced across my face through the open blinds as I remained in a fear-induced trance, totally numb to his questions and Nath's hand squeezing my own to coax a response. I was foolish to think for one second that it would be over once I escaped; the nightmare was only just beginning to unfold. Whatever twisted game Benjamin started all those years ago was still in play, and I felt more vulnerable than ever. One thing was crystal clear: he would stop at nothing to get me back into that bunker. His message proved it, and the disturbing thought of my captor not caring about getting caught either did send shivers down my spine. It was a bold move to do what he did in front of every news crew in the state, and it definitely marked an escalation.

Benjamin had clearly been watching me from the start, and his boundless control over me never wavered, even for a second. I was still firmly under his spell; he diligently kept on guiding me in every waking moment, and even though I had escaped his prison of concrete and steel, it didn't weaken the hold he had over me by one iota. Every muscle I moved was with his permission, and each word I spoke, I said willingly with his blessing. Every bitter and perverse emotion that I tried to leave behind had caught up with me all at once, and I became a trembling wreck, unable to think about anything else other than what he might be planning to do next.

I didn't understand if it was a touch of Stockholm syndrome, garden-variety fear, or just the sheer exhaustion I felt, but before I read that note, I honestly had no intention of trying to find out his true identity. I just wanted to reform the tatters of my life in peace, without reliving the past, and somehow drag myself to some semblance of normality. However, in the wake of what happened that night and after how harshly I had been snapped back into reality, I realised my injudicious aim was utterly ridiculous. In order to be able to move on, I needed to prioritise his capture above all else; I inexplicably managed to escape that cell physically, but my mind would only truly be free when the monster responsible was unmasked, arrested, prosecuted and jailed in the same underground bunker he kept me locked up against my will for ten interminable years.

"Miss Lakewell," Daniels prompted.

"Sorry, what was the question again?" I dazedly asked.

"Did you think of anyone who would want to harm you?" he repeated.

"No."

"He used a biblical quote there, insinuating that you have done something wrong or sinful. Do you have any idea what that might be?"

"I told you, that's his thing. He loves the Bible."

"So, he mentioned God and religion often when you had your conversations with him?"

"I've gone over this," I combatively snapped as I shrugged at Nathaniel.

"I know Olivia, and I'm sorry, but we just need as much information as possible if you want us to find him."

"Are we safe, officer?" Nath sharply interrupted.

"You have a hundred reporters with cameras outside. I'm quite sure you are all quite safe," Daniels said facetiously.

"He did this *with* the fucking news crews outside. He doesn't give a single shit about getting caught," I shouted through the tears.

"Sorry, if you are concerned, we'll leave a car overnight to keep an eye on the place."

"How can you be sure it wasn't one of those scumbag reporters who threw the rock? Trying to provoke a statement from us?" Nath asked.

"We haven't released any information to the media, and the context of the message demonstrates they have insider information about the crime. It can only be the perpetrator or someone close to him," Daniels explained.

"Well, someone leaked something to those vultures, or else they wouldn't be circling outside our home, would they?" Nath pointed out.

"I suppose not," the sheriff conceded.

"Can you at least interview a few of them? And keep them off our property?"

"It's all in hand. For now, keep your windows and doors locked, and if you see anything suspicious, give us a call straight away."

"Thanks," I uttered.

"Both of you try to get some sleep," he said as he stood up, "we'll get him, don't worry."

"I'll see you out," Nath said as he followed him.

Nath was far too preoccupied with his personal vendetta against the press to see the message for what it was or even begin to grasp the looming danger we were all in. I understood why; the press had persistently hounded him for years after my disappearance, and he undoubtedly had more reason to hate them than most. It was also easier to blame the media rather than accept the truth: the suffering was far from over, and he was still skulking in the shadows out there.

Daniels was wasting his time; there wouldn't be a single shred of evidence on that note or the rock that propelled it, and all the futile law-enforcement enquiries would eventually draw a blank. It was all part of his plan; everyone would obsess over the religious angle, get precisely nowhere following it, and chaos would ensue. Did they not realise they were being manipulated? Even though I knew that my snatcher wouldn't allow something as trifling as jail time to get in the way of his fun, the risk of it was certainly something he would enjoy.

My tormentor was manically obsessive, meticulously careful, and had a discerning eye for detail like no other; it was those personality traits that kept me hidden for so many years and allowed him to successfully execute the kidnapping in the first place. The deputy's misguided advice to lock the doors and windows was laughable, and even a police cruiser parked outside all night wouldn't deter him in the slightest. I was under no illusions; if he really wanted me back in internment, nothing would stop him. The acceptance of that realisation really provided me with some modicum of comfort, with which I started to feel better as soon as I relinquished responsibility for my own safety and fate. We simply existed as pawns for his malicious enjoyment, impatiently waiting for the next move, and there wasn't a damn thing we could do to prevent any of it.

Once I began to calm down, I realised that as the lone recipient of the note, I was the only person who was even capable of understanding the true meaning behind it. The cryptic words may have been entirely irrelevant, but they helped him achieve his purpose: letting me know it was from him and confusing the law. Benjamin was flagrantly asserting his dominance over me at any cost, and the fact that the driveway was filled with prying eyes only made it even more irresistible to him. It was more of the same twisted and juvenile mind games from when I was under lock and key.

If it wasn't abhorrently harrowing in the most sinister way, it would almost be funny because I barely knew anything about my captor, but on the other hand, I knew him better than anyone else. I had spent a huge part of my life in his thrall, and no matter how careful he was not to reveal his identity, I had an unwanted connection to him that was impossible to break.

I heard chatter in the hallway, and a few seconds later, Nath came back into the room with Alexander, who was holding a bottle of scotch. I feigned a half-smile at him and a sleepy nod as he placed the bottle on the table and sat down.

"Are you guys okay? What happened?" Alexander asked.

"Someone threw a rock with a crazy note attached," Nath began as he pointed behind him to the newly boarded-up door, "I think it's the press messing with us."

"It's not the fucking press, Nath. It's him. It has to be," I scathingly corrected, which led to a few seconds of awkward silence.

"I'll put a pot of coffee on," Nath timidly said as he left the room.

"How are you coping with everything, Olivia? I'm sorry I haven't been around to see you. I was trying to give you some space," Alexander asked.

"None of them realises how much danger we are in. And he was right *here*; it's terrifying."

"Still, the street is crawling with police, so he won't try anything tonight."

"How do you even know what happened to me?"

"Nath filled me in, and I just want you to know I think it's disgusting what happened to you," he said as he leaned forward in his seat, "I hope they get the bastard."

"Me too."

"I don't know if Nath has mentioned it, but I'm actually a grief counsellor now, and I'm here if you need to talk."

"Alexander, are you seriously touting for work right now?" I asked with an incredulous smile.

"All pro-bono, obviously," he gawkily began with his hands in the air, "and call me Alex. Only mom calls me Alexander."

"I'll have a think about it."

"Please do, it can really help. Nath was in bits when it happened; I hope I helped him in some small way through some very dark days."

"Well, he has his new fiancée now," I cynically mused.

"Between you and me, I never liked her. There's something about her that gives me the creeps," he whispered.

I liked Alex; I always did. Granted, he was a bit abrasive at times, but so was I. He always seemed to steer Nathaniel in the right direction, especially when we were younger, and from what little I had heard, he had been there for my family when they needed it the most. Even if he had been vocal about her in the past, I wasn't sure whether he was just telling me what I wanted to hear regarding Stephanie or if he actually shared my opinion. Either way, it was nice to listen to it confirmed out loud that someone else felt the same way about her.

"Seriously, what the fuck was he thinking with her?" I asked under my breath.

"Well, to be fair to him, he waited years, and true to form, she was very persistent. Looking back, I think he was just incredibly lonely, and she just wore him down over time," Alex softly muttered.

"Persistent is putting it politely."

"Uh-huh," he mumbled with a knowing smile.

"When did she lose all the weight? And get those ridiculous silicone tits put in?"

"I can't say I've noticed. Are you insinuating that her transformation was the only reason he finally caved in?" he asked with a smile.

"God no," I exclaimed with fake shock, "but was it?"

"She showed up back in his life around a year after you went missing looking like that. She has a very successful cosmetic dental practice in Sacramento, hence her ludicrous veneers too."

"What's she like with Aurora?"

"From what I've seen, they merely tolerate each other, but Steph has been really supportive after what she's been going through recently, I suppose."

"What has she been going through?"

Nath burst back into the room before I had a chance to get Alex to elaborate, placing a tray filled with mugs of coffee onto the table in front of me, and I instinctively picked one up just to cradle and warm my hands.

"When's Aurora due back, Nath?" Alex asked.

"Tonight, but, and I'm sorry, Liv, I've told her not to come back," Nath responded.

"You've what?" I exclaimed.

"She can't do that now, can she? With all the press outside and potential kidnappers skulking in the garden? It isn't safe for her."

"I need to see her!"

"Is Rejuvenate alright with her staying another night?"

Nath sternly shot Alex a bitingly frosty look over the top of his coffee cup as my head swivelled backwards and forwards between them, and I immediately realised something else was going on.

"Rejuvenate? What's that? What's happening?"

"Please don't overreact," Nathaniel softly said as he returned his cup to the table.

"What the fuck is going on?" I frantically shouted.

"Aurora has had some problems, and we're dealing with them, but we thought it was best she got some professional help for a few days. It was all arranged before you came back; that's why she hasn't been in the house."

"What problems?" I sternly interrogated.

"It started off small. She got in trouble for shoplifting from a store in town. She assured us it was a mistake, and we believed her. Then I found the empty whiskey bottles in her room."

"So, she's in fucking rehab? Aurora is sixteen years old, Nath. How could you let this happen?" I scolded.

"Yes, but there's more," he started with a sigh. "A few months back, she got suspended from school when she was caught smoking pot. Apparently, she managed to get into Steph's medicinal supply and stole a few packets. Lately, it's gotten worse, and when she started going missing for days at a time, that's when we made the call."

"I knew she would be involved. That fucking bitch."

"It wasn't Stephanie's fault, Liv. You don't know what Aurora is like, and she can be really conniving sometimes."

"You are right, I don't. I *do* know that if I had been here, it never would have happened. At least one parent would have been actually looking after her!" I shouted.

"Plenty of kids experiment with drugs, and we're dealing with it. She has the best help available."

"Stop saying *we,* I'm Aurora's mother, not her," I venomously rebuked.

My sweet little girl. The moment I laid eyes on her after she was born, I promised myself and the universe that I would never let any harm befall her. Regardless of the context, the results spoke for themselves. I had betrayed my vow, and I was foolish to console myself with the thought that Nath could handle parenthood on his own. If the wild events of that night taught me anything, it was that I had to get my head in the game and become an active participant in my own family. Everything was falling apart around me, and I was just mindlessly staring into the abyss, patiently waiting for it to all come crumbling down.

I will concede that it was wrong to question Nath's parenting skills, and deep down, I knew that he would have tried his best with her, but I was inconsolably furious and had no choice but to vent my anger and frustration on someone; otherwise, I would explode. Aurora's father was too enamoured with his sociopathic girlfriend to actually notice the path his daughter was on, and the fact that it was her drugs was just the tip of the iceberg for me. I wouldn't have been surprised if the whole thing had been manufactured just to spite me and that Stephanie had maliciously given Aurora the drugs herself in the first place.

"Is there anything else you need to tell me?" I disdainfully said with self-imposed calm.

"No," Nath said as he shook his head.

"Why didn't you tell me sooner?"

"You had enough on your plate," Nath defeatedly admitted with his head in his hands.

"I'm not sitting on the sidelines any longer. We're going to get her. Right now."

"Oh, Liv, I don't think that's a good idea," Alex interrupted as he pointed outside.

"I don't give a shit. If neither of you wishes to come along with me, fine, I'll get her myself, so just give me the address."

"If you are so intent on going, I'll drive you there," Alex offered.

"I'll come too," Nath added.

"No. You've done enough," I said to Nath before turning to Alex, "come on then," I ordered.

After leaving Nath in a depressive silence, Alex and I strode out of the house, hurriedly navigated the police cordon and got into his car. Alex started fiddling with the satnav until he began driving, having to meander through the crowds of media still swarming around the street. Once we were clear of them, he turned the radio down and looked at me empathetically.

"Shit, Olivia, I'm sorry. I thought he'd told you," he said.

"It's fine; at least someone is looking out for me. Who knows when Nath would've grown a backbone to finally tell me about it," I derisively said.

"I'm not defending his decision; he may not have known how to tell you."

"He didn't have to lie to me, though; he told me she was staying at a friend's house so she wouldn't get overwhelmed by my return. It made me feel insane."

"Yeah, that isn't right," he admitted.

I let out a deep sigh, gritted my teeth, and gripped the handle inside the door pensively.

"Why did he have to pick Steph? He could literally have chosen any other woman in the world, and I wouldn't have batted an eye, but he knew all along what it would do to me."

"Yeah, I never fully understood that decision either. Can I tell you something in confidence?"

"Yes, please," I intently nodded.

"I don't want you to go blabbing to Nath, though."

"Alex, spit it out. I won't tell a soul."

"There's something not right about her."

"That's hardly a revelation."

"No, listen," he began, "when they finally got together, Nath changed. I used to go round his place all the time, but suddenly, he was too busy, or they couldn't have me over.

We didn't speak for about a year until he turned up on my doorstep in the middle of the night with a packed bag."

"They had an argument?"

"Yeah, she scoured the house for any photographs with you in them and burned them in the backyard."

"What did Nath say?"

"He was mortified. There was even talk of them splitting up, but in the end, they managed to patch things up because Steph convinced him she was trying to help him move on."

"That's vile. Who even does that?"

"There's more."

"What?"

"He kept all your old clothes in the garage. I think he couldn't bear to get rid of them. When he finally went back home after he stayed at my place for a few days, she'd dyed her hair brown and was standing in the kitchen wearing one of your dresses."

"Oh my God. She really is a psychopath."

"Uh-huh. For all the years since we were in London, I thought she had been obsessed with Nath. Now, I think it was actually you who she was aiming for the entire time."

Suddenly, everything clicked into place, as if I was handed the final piece of a puzzle I had been staring at for a decade. All those years, I regarded her as a niggling thorn in our side, a minor inconvenience that would resurface and annoy us for a while before disappearing into the ether once again, yet the truth was far more damning. I regarded her as insane, but her evident cowardice always made me think she was largely harmless and that it would never escalate beyond annoyance.

Although I couldn't explain the specifics, I realised that the shoe fitted perfectly, and every shitty thing that had happened to me in the last decade, and the decade before it for that matter, could be explained by her presence in our lives. Stephanie once vehemently promised me that she would take Nath away from me, and it was only when Alex shared more of her past exploits with me that I finally understood she had made good on that past promise.

It was *her*.

She was behind it all. She had to be.

12

THE TEST

OLIVIA – 2008

That year was rough. Just as I predicted, we forcefully sandwiched fleeting moments of our jet-lagged relationship between the laborious plane journeys and substituted a healthy relationship with constant texts and phone calls. It was strained, barely holding on by a thread, and only the distant thought of us being able to end up together was stopping it from breaking. When I agreed to his invitation to move to the States, I hadn't envisioned it taking this long for us to make it happen, and I had no idea if our connection was strong enough to weather the constant curveballs that would be thrown our way. He had already defied his parents' wishes by continuing our relationship, and I wasn't sure if we could survive another bump in the road like that.

Money was so perilously tight that on a number of occasions, I almost sold the ring on my finger to put some more of it in the kitty. We were both painfully aware that every stolen weekend we spent together would push the eventual move date back even further, so austerity ruled, and we rationed our romance as much as our fragile relationship could handle. I hadn't penned a single word since my departure from education, and instead of pursuing my childhood dream of writing, I found myself doing whatever it took to scrape up enough coppers to get me to California.

Needless to say, grand ambitions must run in Nath's wealthy family because he harboured them at first. He was obsessed with the idea that he was going to become a famous artist overnight and that everything was going to work itself out as a result. My fiancé was so sure that he was going to make the grade that we even looked at a few houses over there, and although the price tags were inordinately expensive, Nath chirpily arranged the viewings like he had already had the money in the bank. However, after the passage of time had unyieldingly eroded his determination, he came back down to earth with a bump, and like me, he decided to knuckle down so we could reach the arbitrary dollar target that neither of us had the courage to set.

Showing an obvious reluctance to fall back on the deep pockets of his filthy rich parents, Nath took his creative hands to anything that paid and spent most of his time jumping from one dead-end job to another to keep the money rolling in, whereas I managed to snag a few shifts at a busy café in London. The owner, Steve, was good to me and tried to accommodate my time off requests whenever he could. I had absolutely no experience waiting on tables, and he really took a chance on me, so I tried to suppress my personality as much as possible when I was at work. Nevertheless, I still had my moments and felt like I was one crossed word from getting the sack. It had been over a month since I had seen Nath, and I was taking out that frustration on the messy tabletop that I was scrubbing half to death before another set of ravenous patrons sat at it.

"Olivia, you are taking off the varnish," Steve informed me with a tap on the shoulder.

"Sorry, I'm just in a terrible mood," I uttered as I started to reset the table.

"Loverboy again?"

"I don't know. Yeah, probably."

"Long-distance is a tough gig, and you wouldn't catch me doing that back in the day."

"Thank you so much for the kind words of encouragement! What do I owe you for this session?" I sarcastically retorted.

"Customer," he prompted as he pointed to the door.

Steve was a true stickler for the level of service that supposedly made his café apparently so successful, so I quickly batted the residual crumbs from my tabard, finished setting the table, and grabbed some menus on my way to greet them. It was only when I was standing directly in front of her that I realised who it was.

It was Stephanie, and she was nauseatingly waiting for the penny to drop as she happily chewed on a piece of gum with a sickening smirk. Since the bizarre evening in the pub when we all realised how maddened she truly was, I hadn't seen hide nor hair of her, and after the night of Nath's proposal, he changed his phone number, and she apparently hadn't managed to contact him since. We thought we were rid of that little conniving weasel, and I never would have thought she would have the stones to confront me after everything that had happened. Nonetheless, there she was, as glibly hard-faced as ever, and I desperately hoped she was about to order a knuckle sandwich so I could wipe the self-assured expression clean off her face.

"Long time no see," she said in between chews.

"What are you doing here?" I scornfully asked under my breath.

"Hey, I'm hungry! Is that any way to speak to a paying customer?"

"Sod off, Stephanie, I'm not in the mood. Are you sure you don't have a bunny to boil?"

"I've heard English food is horrendous, but no boiled bunny for me, thanks," she contemptuously remarked as she pushed past me and seated herself at the table I had just cleaned, "I'm watching my figure," she added with a wink.

"Seriously, get the fuck out of here," I warned.

"Excuse me? Sir?" Stephanie shouted at Steve, who was witnessing the exchange from behind the counter at the opposite end of the café.

"Is there a problem here?" Steve bemusedly asked as he approached the table.

"I'm not sure, but your employee here seems to have a problem with me supporting your small business."

"Olivia, what's going on?" Steve asked.

Nothing would give me more pleasure than to give her the dressing down that she deserved and a swift punch to her wired-up gnashers for good measure. Nevertheless, as I pictured screaming into her face and dragging her out of the café by her hair, I remembered that I desperately needed that job, and if I lost it, mine and Nath's plan would be dead in the water. My teeth ground against each other until my jaw ached, and I only managed to reluctantly pry my lips apart for a brief second to let out a single bitter-tasting word in response.

"Nothing," I begrudgingly replied.

"Well? What are you waiting for? Give her a menu."

Steve disgruntledly trudged away as I hesitantly handed Stephanie a menu, which she whipped from my hand, and her victorious grin only widened as she pretended to peruse the options with a melodramatic hum and a single finger on her lips. She had carefully picked the one place where I couldn't react volatilely, and the meagre protection that it offered left her feeling safe from my full fury.

"Oh, wow! There are so many options! They all sound delightful," she beamed falsely.

"I can highly recommend the cheese omelette. It's quick. You can throw it down your neck and then piss off back to whatever filthy gutter you slid out of," I emotionlessly recommended.

"I don't fancy that. Tell me, waitress, what are the specials? Come on, entice me. Let's see those sales skills in action." she provoked.

"Honestly, what do you want?" I disdainfully asked.

"I haven't made up my mind yet. Do you have a gluten-free menu?"

"I mean with me and Nath. Are you crazy coming in here? What were you even thinking?"

"Well, when I heard you were working here, I just had to see it for myself. Also, I heard that you and Nath aren't in a good place, so I wanted to check how my old friend was taking it," she explained with a feigned sad face.

"We are fine, I'm not your friend, and our relationship has fuck all to do with you."

"Oh? When did you last see him?"

"Recently," I mustered.

"Recently," she mockingly scoffed, "we actually had dinner a few nights ago," she flippantly added.

"Bullshit," I bitterly snapped.

"Oh God, Liv, nothing like that happened, despite what you think; I'm not some kind of homewrecker," she facetiously said while snapping her menu shut, "then again, does it even count as cheating if he is thousands of miles away?"

"Are you serious?" I softly asked.

"Jesus, Liv, I'm joking! You're engaged to be married!" she heartily laughed. "Like that is going to happen any time soon," she added under her breath.

"Honestly, mate, there is something really wrong with you. You're insane."

"Perhaps. But maybe crazy is what he needs," she retorted with a slimy wink.

"He literally had to change his phone number to stop you pestering him, and I thought that message would've been received clearly, even by you."

"Oh my God, is that what he told you? I could call that number right now and prove you wrong," she said, holding her phone in the air.

"You're totally deranged! What exactly have you flown to London to do? Stalk the fiancée of your victim? Talk shit in a café? What?"

"I'm sorry," she solemnly began, "I came here to do the right thing and apologise to you face to face for stealing your betrothed, but once I saw you in that greasy tabard, I just couldn't help myself," she said whilst stifling laughter.

"He wouldn't look twice at you."

"Wouldn't he?" she remarked with a taunting grin.

"Listen to me very closely, you spiteful waste of skin. This preposterous game of yours is over. There is no way a man like Nath would ever go for an obsessive, manic bitch like you. Or any man, for that matter. So please, order your food, and kindly fuck right off."

Stephanie had obviously exhausted all her acting talent. Her performance was finally over, and the bolted-on smile immediately fell from her face as she leaned in towards me with gritted teeth. Her deadened eyes widened as she slowly beckoned me closer to listen to whatever ludicrous musings would leave her mouth next.

"All joking aside, we both know how famously weak-willed Nathaniel is," she uttered almost in a whisper. "Deep down, you know that I'll wear him down eventually, and when I do, you'll be here, where you belong, scraping beans off a plate and too far away to stop it."

"That's not true," I said with the tears of anger welling up in my eyes, "no one is that desperate."

"I tell you what, let's put it to the test. I'll leave here, get on a plane back to Cali, and when I arrive, I'll go straight to Nath's apartment. If he somehow manages to resist me when I turn up at his door, scantily clad and with a bottle of his favourite bourbon in my hands, we'll know you were right."

I couldn't take it anymore. I didn't give a toss about who would witness it or what the repercussions would be, whether it made me unemployed or even if I ended up in cuffs. I launched myself at her, gripped a fist full of her frizzy strawberry-blonde hair as hard as I could, and violently yanked her backwards from the seat. She was howling like a wounded banshee and flailing her arms as I continued to drag her towards the entrance, and when I reached it, I kicked it open and hurled her clean through it. She gracelessly thudded onto the filthy tarmac outside on her hands and knees as she fearfully looked back at me over her shoulder, fully expecting to receive a brutal beating to remember me by. I would gladly have obliged if it hadn't been for Steve suddenly holding my shoulders back from behind, and I wrestled with his grasp as Stephanie managed to get back onto her feet.

The smile had sickeningly returned to her face when she began aimlessly pawing at her hair, and as she diligently inspected each clump that she removed from the dishevelled mess, her grin only became broader. She flattened her clothes and dusted off her knees before taking a step forward, which led me to viciously struggle against Steve's hold in a desperate attempt to finish what I had started.

"Bitch," she goadingly challenged.

"You stay away from me, do you hear?" I screamed.

"Oh, I will, just as soon Nath realises what he's missing, and he's forgotten all about you."

Looking satisfied with her final words, she turned around and held her arm out for a taxi. Once she had put some distance between us, Steve released my shoulders, and we watched as she climbed into a cab and childishly displayed her middle finger out of the window. I watched it merge into the London traffic, and I breathlessly bent over to put my hands on my knees and recover some fragment of composure.

"Take the rest of the week off," Steve ordered.

"I can't. I need the money."

"I don't want to see you until Monday. Have a bath, a bottle of wine, or whatever you need to do to chill out. I know how important this job is to you; otherwise, you wouldn't be coming back at all. Think yourself lucky."

"It wasn't my fault, and I can explain—"

"I don't want to hear it. It doesn't even matter why. This is a place of business, not a boxing ring."

"I'm so sorry, Steve, I just—"

"Monday. We won't speak of this again."

"Okay. Fine."

Steve returned to the café, where all the patrons were pressed up against the glass trying to witness what had just happened, and I slowly untied my apron and folded it up as I began defeatedly trudging away towards my flat. In a moment of paranoia, I took out my phone and called Nathaniel's old number, and I was filled with relief when the call wouldn't connect.

Stephanie had successfully burrowed herself securely under my skin like a fattened tick. It was likely the whole purpose of her misguided visit, and I suddenly felt a raft of emotions in the wake of what had happened. I was ashamed I allowed myself to react like I did, and I regretted not letting my biting words do the fighting for me. The image of me dragging her by the hair in a blind range out of the café would stick with me forever, and I tried to put it out of my head as I pounded the pavement in embarrassment. I kept telling myself that every venomous word that left her steel-ridden mouth was a flagrant lie, carefully chosen to rile me up enough to react in the way I did, and I vehemently tried to hold onto the weakening belief I had of my own, that Nath wouldn't look twice at her.

The threat of Stephanie skulking in the shadows, waiting for my relationship to fail, gave me a renewed sense of urgency. What troubled me most was that I only knew my own feelings; I was clearly struggling to cope with the long-distance nature of our relationship more than I realised, yet Nathaniel seemed fairly content with the slow pace at which it was moving. I returned to my dingy flat and rushed into the bathroom to scrub the residual build-up of shame, paranoia and disgust from my skin. I turned the water on as hot as it went and stripped off as I waited for it to heat up.

Instinctively, I avoided looking at the windowsill because I knew exactly what I had left there that morning. I realised that it was the nuclear option, and I knew that as soon as I shared it with Nathaniel, it would simultaneously ruin our plans completely and give us everything that we wanted at the same time. I was putting off dealing with the sheer emotions surrounding that unoffensive piece of plastic, and I was definitely reluctant to share it with him because I was terrified the news would derail everything. My trembling hand picked it up, and even though I abandoned it in the sun, the two lines were unfaded and bold as brass. I intuitively touched my stomach as I gazed into the rest of my life that I held in my trembling hand.

When I realised that I was pregnant out of wedlock, with the father living over five thousand miles away, predictably, I fell into a fraught panic. It was hard enough being essentially forced into a casual relationship when we both wanted so much more, and I had no idea what would happen if you threw a baby into that dynamic. I felt like we were too young to start a family, and my ultimate worry was that he would decide it was too much for him, and given the distance between us, he would leave me to raise the child on my own. I planned to leave it as long as I could before telling him, in the desperate hope that we would be living together by the time I was forced to share the news.

My inward monologue was interrupted by the sound of my phone vibrating in the heap of clothes at my feet, and as I bent down to retrieve it, I saw that it was Nath calling. I did think about not answering it, but he thought I was at work, and my heart dropped when I realised that he could have gotten wind of what happened at the café. I trepidatiously accepted the call and gingerly put it to my ear.

"Hello?" I said sheepishly.

"Liv, where are you?" he anxiously asked with uncharacteristic seriousness.

"Just got home from work. What's happened?"

"I need to tell you something."

"Oh God, what is it?" I asked as I turned the running shower off and sat on the edge of the bath.

"Are you sitting down?"

"Yes, Christ, Nath, just tell me."

I heard him awkwardly fumbling around without uttering a single word, and the introduction to 'Living in America' started tinnily playing in the background.

"Do you know what this song is?" he excitedly asked with palpable enthusiasm.

"Is that James Brown?" I bemusedly asked.

"We did it! I've finally sold a piece, and it's enough for a deposit. It's finally happening!" he beamed.

"Nath?" I softly said.

"When can you fly out? How much notice do you have to give at the café? You better start packing."

"Nath?" I repeated a little louder.

"Actually, I should really come to London to help you pack. You don't have to bring much, just some clothes really. Or, actually, scratch that. Can Stacey help you?"

"Nath!" I shouted.

"What?"

"Turn the music off."

"What is it?" he asked as the music was silenced.

"I'm pregnant," I nervously uttered.

13

THE REVELATION

OLIVIA – 2024

Stephanie was Benjamin. As much as it didn't make any sense whatsoever, everything fit perfectly, and all of a sudden, I went both freezing cold and blisteringly hot at the exact same time. The sweat started to pour out of my forehead and palms, and I was wrestling my own stomach to stop it from expelling its contents into the footwell of the car. Alex's attention was divided between the road in front of us and staring at me, waiting for me to speak, but I could barely grasp the notion myself, let alone share it with him.

Nath had fallen for her ruse hook, line, and sinker. It may have taken years to convince him to turn a blind eye to all her red flags and cataclysmic character defects, but Alex and I always remained dubious, and we saw her for what she was: inherently dangerous. It felt good to have it confirmed that I wasn't crazy, yet I already knew what Nathaniel's reaction would be if I shared my admittedly wild theories with him. I ruminated on every encounter we ever had with her, and as I mentally handled each piece, they all snuggly fit together.

Between the weirdness surrounding our first date, her attempt to befriend me, Stacey witnessing the heated phone call, and the café incident, I was almost certain that she was the woman behind the curtain that started all this. What I had already, albeit entirely circumstantial, was damning, and there were even more unexplained incidents in our past that I could have easily attributed to her nonsense. I kicked myself for not seeing it earlier; her obsession with my and Nath's relationship spanned two decades, and when she realised that she wasn't going to win, that sociopath must have orchestrated my kidnapping to take what she desired by force. Nevertheless, she didn't possess the necessary mettle to finish the job and stupidly kept me alive instead, which is why her half-baked plan ended in failure.

Alex was right. It was never about Nath. Then again, I didn't think it was about me either. She coveted the very essence of my life, and when she finally understood that her petty games wouldn't break our relationship like she so desperately wanted, it exasperated her mania, and she aimed to replace me directly instead. Putting the glaringly obvious mental illness to one side, I couldn't even imagine how Stephanie managed to pull it off logistically; she was splitting her time between keeping me barely alive in that dungeon and, unbeknownst to everyone else, cuckooing my family.

Did she spend hours on end psychologically torturing me in that cell, only to return in time to read my daughter a bedtime story? Were the same hands that callously dragged me to my pit of despair then subsequently used to delicately brush my little girl's hair? I was already feeling uneasy about her being around Aurora for all those years unchecked, but my latest revelations sent the discomfort into overdrive. The introspective image alone of that solipsistic witch laying a finger on Aurora was the nauseating catalyst I was trying to avoid, and I frantically started looking for a container to bury my head into.

"Pull over," I frantically ordered.

"What's the matter?" he inquired.

"Fucking pull over, now," I gulped as I held my mouth shut with my trembling hands.

Alex bemusedly obliged, quickly taking the car onto a scrap of empty land beside the road and slamming on the brakes. As soon as we were barely stationary, I hastily jumped out of the car, sprinted towards the bushes, and scarcely got there before I felt the acid rising up my throat.

I could barely hold it in until I heard indecipherable whispers coming from the undergrowth in front of me. It sounded like a chorus of different voices, none more prominent than the other, but I could almost detect Stephanie's self-assured twang piercing through the noise. As I gazed into the gloom, the shadowed outline of a person seemed to materialise before me, and I disdainfully stared directly into where their eyes should have been.

"I bet you think you are so clever," the voice whispered.

"You are going to pay for what you've done to me and my family," I spat venomously.

"Maybe. You'll have to prove it first," the voice stated matter-of-factly before fizzling away into the darkness.

I immediately started to expel the contents of my stomach as Alex abandoned the vehicle with all the doors open and the engine running. He sprinted over to hold my hair back, and when there was nothing left to come up, I inelegantly wiped the remnants from my chin. I stopped heaving and fell backwards onto the dusty ground as Alex handed me a handkerchief that he had quickly produced from his pocket.

"It was fucking her." I breathlessly gasped as I pointed into space with a splutter.

"I'm not following."

"Stephanie. She's the person who took me."

"I thought Nath said it was a man called Benjamin?"

"She used a voice changer or something, I don't know. But it had to be her."

"How do you know?"

"She definitely had the means to pull it off, and as you said, she's been obsessed with Nath and me from the get-go: there's your motive. She probably couldn't bear the thought of us getting married, so she took her last opportunity on our wedding day."

"I don't know, Olivia… sorry, but it's a bit of a stretch, is it not?" he said with his face scrunched up.

"Are you kidding me right now? You, of all people, know how troubled she is and what she's capable of."

"Have you got any evidence? Anything?"

"Not yet, just a feeling," I admitted meekly.

"Listen, I'm the first to admit that she's crazy, but kidnapping? Torture? If you accuse her and she's innocent, it could totally ruin her life."

"She isn't as clever as she thinks. There's got to be a smoking gun somewhere."

"It won't take much to convince me, but Nath? And the police? That's a different story. You need hard evidence."

"I know, and you're going to help me find it."

"Me? Olivia, I'm a small-town therapist. I wouldn't even know where to start."

"Who better than a therapist to delve into the festering mind of a sociopath like her? You could write books about this for years; it'll make your career."

I could tell that I piqued his interest.

"What are you proposing exactly?" he asked.

"Help me prove Benjamin is her. You know her, and you're the only one who would even entertain the theory."

"Fine," he began as he kicked the dirt, "but as soon as we find anything concrete, we have to go straight to Nath and the sheriff, agreed?"

"Agreed," I said as I held my hand out, and he pulled me up from the dirt.

"What now? Are we still collecting Aurora?"

"Fuck yes, I need to know she's safe. After that, we're going to nail this bitch to the wall."

"Okay, fine," Alex unenthusiastically agreed whilst looking incredibly awkward, "it's only a few more miles to the centre."

"Let's get going then."

Suddenly, I didn't feel so alone. When we both got back in the car, Alex fumbled around in the back seat to hand me a bottle of water, which I downed in seconds. As we continued our journey, I tried to concisely explain to him how past events led me to my grim conclusion, and by the end of my ramblings, he seemed a more fervent believer of her guilt than I. Alex had an unbreakable bond with Nathaniel, and not only did he want justice for me, but also for his best friend.

For the first time in ten years, I felt the persistent anxiety and lingering dread fizzle away, and those feelings were immediately replaced with the adrenaline rush of determined purpose. The renewed sense of direction focused the fury and lust for revenge within me, and I began to remember slowly but surely what it was like to be my old self again. On the night that I snatched my freedom back, I was forced to emerge from that hatch a broken victim, and that burden has dictated every single thought, feeling and action ever since. I declined to carry the encumbrance of it any longer; I symbolically tossed it through the open car window and watched it plunge into the dirt like a dead weight.

We were hurtling towards Aurora, and I was no longer dwelling on how she would feel when she met me or if she blamed me for my absence. I was purely fixated on keeping her safe. The huge part of my brain that was trying to process the unrelenting cascade of enduring fear and bitter regret was finally clear. My priorities had aligned themselves, and at the top of the list was my daughter. She had spent far too long under the influence of her depraved stepmother, and I wouldn't have been surprised if it was Stephanie's idea to lock my little girl away like a pariah in some rehab facility in the first place. Like my own mounting problems, all of Aurora's could be traced right back to Stephanie too, and neither of us deserved what happened.

The tables had turned, and a huge part of me was desperate to let Stephanie tauntingly know that I was coming from her. I had an intrinsic need to reflect every single pang of abject fear and pure hopelessness that she had inflicted on me over the years right back at her and for her to feel exactly how I did when she was watching me like a rat trying to negotiate an endless maze. That maniac had clearly derived much pleasure from my unremitting misery and still was. I had to be the one who outed her, and it had to be me who showed the world what kind of calculating monster she truly was. No one had caught a glimpse of her for days, and she could have been up to anything. Sure, she made a big song and dance about me returning and reluctantly agreed to give me some space and stay with her parents for a while, but I knew that it was all manipulation. In reality, she just wanted to avoid being near me, realising that the truth would come out in the wash and that she would be unmasked as the freak responsible for everything if she stayed.

"Are you okay?" Alex asked.

"I just want to see my daughter and make sure she's safe," I uttered.

"She will be. It won't be long now."

"What do I even say to her? Hi, I'm your mum, we haven't seen each other in ten years. Shall we go get takeout and braid each other's hair?"

"Just be honest with her. She'll respond to it."

"How is she even going to begin to understand everything that's happened?"

"Aurora is a lot more mature than you expect. She's had to do some fast growing up after what happened."

"She's still a kid, though. She shouldn't have to deal with this stuff."

"If I can give you one piece of advice: don't mention the Stephanie thing to Aurora."

"What? Why?"

"They've built up a relationship over the years, and it's only going to alienate her if you discuss your theory with her."

"I don't care about that; my daughter isn't safe near that psycho! What if something happens to her?"

"We'll keep a close eye on Aurora while we investigate. She isn't in any immediate danger."

"You don't know what she did to me in there," I uttered.

"I know. I'm sorry."

I balled my fist and slammed it against the car door in frustration. I knew what the smart thing to do was; I should keep my enemies close and all that, keep my theories in the shadows until I had irrefutable evidence, and then hit Stephanie with it all at once when she had nowhere left to run. That being said, I was already fantasising about wrapping my hands around her throat and squeezing, so when I saw her in the flesh, I didn't know how I would react.

"Mark my words, when I get my hands on that fucking psychopath, she'll regret ever meeting me."

My sudden outburst had left Alex uncomfortably stunned, and we remained in silence for the remainder of the brief journey. When we arrived at the modern-looking rehab centre a few minutes later, Alex pulled up directly outside the front door and turned the engine off, giving us a full view of the facility. I never had cause to visit one before, and I wasn't sure what I was expecting, but that place certainly wasn't it. To me, it looked more akin to a spa hotel than somewhere that dealt with childhood addiction. The quiet was only broken by a grand fountain in the centre of the car park gushing water into an illuminated pool below it, and as the eerie light bounced off our faces, the gravity of what was about to happen finally hit me. With a nervous sigh, I finally prepared to exit the vehicle to meet my daughter again, but Alex could sense my trepidation and reassuringly put his hand on my knee, which stopped me in my tracks.

"Go get her," Alex said with a smile.

"I appreciate you listening to what I had to say," I replied.

"Don't mention it. Take your time. I'll be out here waiting for you both."

"Thanks," I mumbled.

"And Liv?" he shouted after me.

"Yeah?"

"For what it's worth, I believe you."

As I slowly climbed out of the car and nervously walked towards the entrance, I dried the palms of my hands on the back of my jeans and took a deep breath before reaching the automatically opening doors. I could detect the calming melodies playing through the speakers inside, and the scent of lavender oil billowed out of the open doors as I cautiously made my way through them.

The room directly inside was a luxurious reception area, warmly clad in timber and delicately lit but totally devoid of life, spare a young woman sitting behind the desk who rose to her feet as I approached. She greeted me with a radiant smile, yet I remained stony-faced as I advanced towards her and twitchingly swivelled my head left and right in an attempt to spot Aurora down the many corridors that branched off from the lobby.

"Welcome to Rejuvenate. Can I help?" she beamed.

"I'm here for Aurora. I'm her mother," I announced.

"Ah, yes, Aurora's father rang ahead. She's just packing her things and will be with us in a moment. Nathaniel did bring us up to speed with what has happened to you and your family, and I find it highly unusual that you aren't being accompanied by a caseworker of some description."

"I don't need a caseworker. I'm fine."

"I've just told your husband that, in these situations, we usually handle things quite delicately. Are you sure you don't want to reschedule for the morning? We can have staff on hand to help you both through this?"

"Absolutely not. I need to see my daughter now," I began firmly, "and he's not my husband," I added.

"Oh, sorry, my mistake," she clumsily said. "This is a private facility, and legally, we can't stop you from picking up your daughter. I was just offering you some advice, that's all."

"Well, I thank you for the unsolicited advice, but I'd like to see Aurora now."

"Take a seat. She will be down shortly," she uttered defeatedly.

Leaving the receptionist a particularly dirty look, I turned around to perch on the edge of one of the many leather couches that littered the lobby. I leant forward with my shoulders hunched, my legs bouncing up and down uncontrollably due to the anticipation of her arrival. After a few excruciating minutes, I heard the lift ping at the end of one of the hallways and obsessively locked my eyes on it until the doors slid open. A man dressed in uniform and holding several bags was the first to disembark, and as he walked down the corridor, I saw my daughter, for the first time in ten years, lagging behind him, texting on her phone.

I let out a hushed, mordant laugh and immediately rose to my feet with tears in my eyes as I carefully watched her approach. She left the lift with her attention unwaveringly fixed on the phone in her hand, and as she mindlessly tapped away at the screen, she was totally unaware of the life-defining moment that she was idly strolling towards. I began unconsciously walking towards them to meet them in the middle of the lobby, and when she looked up for a split second, we briefly made eye contact before she continued texting. Even at a distance, I could see the cogs turning in her head, and she stopped dead about ten metres away from me when the realisation finally hit her.

She looked as if she had seen a ghost. I started to doubt if it was a good idea or not, and I wondered if I was right to callously dismiss the receptionist's concerns so readily. I was just so frantically eager to see my little girl again that I hadn't considered how powerful this moment would be for both of us. The tears started flooding down my cheeks as I warily held my hands out, hoping against hope that she would drop everything she was carrying and run straight into my outstretched arms.

She did.

Aurora ploughed into me with so much force that she nearly knocked me clean off my feet. She burrowed her head beneath mine and held me so tightly that I could barely speak, let alone breathe. I was totally overpowered by the intense emotion of the reunion, and suddenly, everything else took a back seat. It was just me and her alone in the world; I had everything that ever mattered clutched in my arms, and I silently renewed my promise never to let any harm ever befall her again. I tried to conjure up some inspirational words or something to whisper to her, but I didn't want to sully the moment or cut it short after awaiting and dreaming about this emotionally charged encounter for ten long years. I could feel her jolting up and down as she silently wailed into my shoulder, and as we both remained embraced in our shared hysterics, the man carrying her luggage dropped it by our feet, stepped back, and gave me a knowing smile.

"Mom!" she sobbed over my shoulder.

"Aurora, I love you so much," I whimpered.

I tightened my grip on her momentarily before I loosened it and gently pushed her away slightly so I could look at her face. The thick mascara and eyeliner that she had applied were streaming down her cheeks, and as I grabbed them with both hands to wipe the makeup away with my thumbs, we each let out a delirious chuckle. She looked so different to how I remembered, but the bright blue doe eyes staring back at mine were undeniably my daughter's, and I could see the mounting questions racking up in them, so I took a deep inhale to prepare for the barrage.

"Mom, what happened to you? We thought you were dead!" she frantically asked.

No amount of parenting courses or self-help books could have ever prepared me for that heartbreaking moment. Aurora had spent the last decade thinking I was dead, and the monstrous world that I had abandoned her in when I was taken was viciously swallowing her up once again. I desperately wanted to tell her every detail, softly explain to her that none of it was her fault, and vow that I would never leave her again. The truth was that I felt every bit as broken and bewildered as her, and I could barely stop my lips quivering long enough to form an actual coherent sentence. I only did what I felt was right; I smiled, pulled her back in close, and squeezed her like my life depended on it.

"I was taken. It's not a nice story, but I'll explain everything to you when we get home, I promise," I said with a sniffle.

"Did you miss us?"

"Oh my God, yes," I began firmly, "every single minute of every day."

"Where's Dad? And Steph?"

I managed to maintain my smile through gritted teeth.

"It's been a bit weird since I got back, and we didn't want to overwhelm you, so we decided it was best if I came on my own. Uncle Alex is waiting in the car outside."

"Overwhelmed," she repeated with an eye roll, "I'm not a kid anymore. I don't need to be coddled."

"Yeah, I know, I can see that," I said with a proud smile.

"Also, I don't know what Dad told you, but it was a massive overreaction sending me here. It was just a bit of pot."

"I don't care about any of that. Honestly, I'm just glad to see you again and that you're safe."

My eyes were drawn to a silver necklace that she was wearing because it didn't really match the rest of her moody ensemble. As I gently lifted it from her chest and rolled my thumb over the engraved image, my blood ran cold, and my hand started to shake when I realised exactly where I had seen it before.

"Where did you get this?" I assertively asked.

"It's a Saint Christopher necklace. Steph gave it to me for my birthday one year, and I promised I would wear it," she replied innocently.

"Stephanie got this for you?"

"Yes," she nodded.

"Are you sure?"

"Mom, what is it? You're scaring me."

Whether it was sheer stupidity, indomitable bravado, or just another one of Stephanie's stupid games, it didn't matter. What did matter, though, was that only moments after discussing it with Alex, I held the smoking gun tentatively between my fingertips, and whoever hung that necklace around my daughter's neck was responsible for everything that had happened. I calmly reached behind Aurora, unclipped the necklace from her neck, and balled it up in my fist. Although it had ruined a tender moment, I had Stephanie bang to rights.

14

THE GIFT

OLIVIA – 2009

I couldn't believe I was finally there and that everything that we dreamt of for so long had finally come to fruition. The day I told Nath I was pregnant felt like a lifetime ago, but at the same time, the seven months that proceeded seemed to pass in the blink of an eye. All our sacrifices and hard work had finally paid off; we reached our goal, and I finally had the keys to our very first home together firmly in my grasp. When Nath first heard about the place in Hammerdale, he cautiously tempered my reaction by describing it as a 'fixer-upper' but remained wholly adamant that the location was well worth the effort to make it liveable, and I should at least try to see past the obvious shortcomings.

Okay, first impression? Not great.

The Californian sun had relentlessly punished the facade for decades unchecked, and every square inch of the timber that cladded the house was riddled with flaking paint or rot. In the previous owner's absence, Mother Nature had well and truly reclaimed the garden, and it was massively overgrown with stinging nettles and thorny bushes. The ancient insect screen that covered the front door was half-hanging off the wall, and the vintage front door behind it squealed and scraped when forced to open or shut. The original advert boasted that it was carpeted throughout, which I suppose was accurate, although it failed to mention that they were clearly fitted in a previous century and coated in thick dust. The dingy bathroom was plagued with voracious black mould, and my fragile lungs could only bear to be in there for a few seconds before I had to make a quick exit. The kitchen was incredibly dated, not looked after, and all of the appliances made me constantly terrified that they would spontaneously explode at a moment's notice.

Just as Nath suggested, I looked past all the glaringly evident issues, and instead, I saw the unbridled potential that was surprisingly in abundance. I imagined the hysteric laughter of our daughter as we mercilessly chased her through the halls and dotingly pictured her learning to paint with her father in the spare bedroom that we would eventually convert into a beautiful home studio. I saw her lovingly watching me write in the garden in the cooling shade of the mature trees that grew there, with a glass of fresh lemonade, and I wondered where all the little trails into the woods would lead, knowing that over the years, we would explore them all. More than anything, I excitedly visualised all the precious everlasting memories that we would make there together.

It was perfect, and we put an offer in on the spot.

The happy news that we were expecting really put a crimp on our budget, although, to be honest, the long months of endless sofa-surfing would have made even a decaying woodshed seem like a decadent palace. Furthermore, as my obvious bump became even more pronounced, the list of Nathaniel's friends who were willing to take us in for a few nights grew inexplicably shorter, and we grew even more desperate to find a place to call our own. There was no denying that it was a sharp fall from grace, and Nath was sore about the lack of a pool, but time was well and truly against us, and we had to lower our expectations significantly to get our feet on the ladder.

There was some brief talk of me staying in England until I had given birth, largely due to boring financial reasons, but I couldn't handle the stress of knowing that it could happen when Nath was thousands of miles away. I was also adamant that our daughter should be born on American soil because it felt like a new chapter for all of us, and I was incredibly keen to put all the weirdness behind us in order to become a fully-fledged family. Stephanie had seemingly vanished without a trace since her visit to the café, and I was fervently hoping that the pending child would be enough to put paid to her vexing shenanigans for good. She must have heard through the grapevine that we were expecting, and although I firmly hated that she knew something about our lives, part of me relished in the victory, and I was sure she had already moved on to her next sorry victim.

Nath not only roped Alexander in to assist with the house move but also to help with the initial renovations to make it habitable. Given that I was eight months pregnant, it fortuitously precluded me from most of the heavy lifting, and I happily took on a more supervisory role. The three of us had managed to pack a moving truck to capacity and were crammed in the cabin like sardines as we drove to our new home. At the request of Nath, Alexander was at the wheel, and given my condition, I was given first refusal on the passenger seat. Nathaniel was hilariously packed into the middle seat, being violently jostled by every imperfection of the rough road leading up to the house, and I couldn't help but quietly giggle at his meagre temporary discomfort in the face of my own.

"Come on, Alex, slow down. You're going to induce me at this rate, and nobody wants that," I jokingly said.

"Sorry, Olivia, but I'm trying my best here," Alex uttered as he was getting increasingly flustered.

"Seriously, buddy, slow down. I think I'm going to be sick," Nath said.

Alex lifted his foot off the accelerator and slowed down slightly.

"Don't be a wimp. You aren't the one with an actual human kicking the life out of your stomach," I remarked.

As miserable as it sounded, the kicking had grown old for me, and at that point, I just wanted it to be all over so I could get back to feeling myself again. Nath, however, was absolutely amazed by every minuscule movement our little girl made and would cradle me with some kind of scientific curiosity every time it happened.

"Is she kicking again?" Nath enthused.

"She hasn't stopped the entire journey. Either she's going to be a tap dancer, or she's excited to be almost home."

"Guys, directions, please! Is it a right here?" Alex asked.

"Yeah, just here," Nath replied.

"Great, more potholes," Alex muttered under his breath.

Our new house slid into view at the very top of the hill, and as the overloaded van struggled to negotiate the rocky road up to it, Nath and I lifted from our seats slightly to get a better look at it. I wasn't feeling particularly daunted by the mammoth task ahead of us. On the contrary, I was incredibly eager to start transforming the derelict shell we had purchased into the loving home I had been daydreaming of. Alex clumsily put the truck into reverse gear, and it went in with an excruciating clunk. He backed up as close as he could to the property to make our constant trips in and out easier, and as the truck finally came to a halt, he immediately killed the engine with a loud huff, and the passengers enthusiastically clapped.

"Well done, Alex," I congratulated.

"Yeah, thanks mate, we appreciate it," Nath added.

"It's not over yet. We have yet to empty the thing," Alex wearily said.

"Are you sure about helping us, Alex? You've already done so much for us."

"Of course, I love you, guys," he said as he climbed out of the truck, "and I want you off my couch," he quietly added.

"Do you want to do the honours, Liv? We'll start unloading," Nath said with a smile.

"Sure," I groaned as I struggled to step out of the truck.

I waddled over to the porch, violently yanked the insect screen open, which screeched far louder than I remembered, and unlocked the door to our house. As I sheepishly walked inside, it felt imperceptibly different somehow. Instead of being appalled by the dire amount of back-breaking work ahead of us, I smiled as I sauntered in and out of the rooms, imagining what it would look like when it was finally finished. I felt a sharp kick from the bump and excitedly rushed to the room we had picked out to be the nursery, just to show her symbolically where she would be sleeping.

"Let's see your room!" I gushed as I eagerly opened the door, almost in a little dance, and rushed inside with my eyes firmly fixed on my bump.

Upon entering the room, I immediately had a strange sensation on my skin. At first, I thought it was a copious amount of dust in the air that I was walking through, but as I quickly flicked the light switch on, I realised it was infested with tiny flies. The musty air was thick with them, and I held my breath as I threw open the curtains and flung the window open to release them outside. After a few seconds of constantly batting them towards the opening with an old magazine I found lying around, I realised the source: a hideously rotting fruit basket that had been dumped on an old chest of drawers in the corner. I continued wafting the magazine around my face as I slowly made my way through to the centre of the swarm, and atop the decaying produce was an immaculately wrapped gift and a card. I removed them from the mouldy sludge it was sitting in, quickly made my way outside of the room, and slammed the door behind me.

"Nath?" I shouted.

I could hear him rumbling down the hallway as I perplexedly inspected the soiled gifts that had been left, and when he arrived, he greeted me and the presents with a confuddled expression across his face.

"This has been left for us; maybe it was from the previous owners?" I asked.

"What's that it's coated in? Slime?" Nath asked with a disgusted expression on his face.

"The rest of the gift: a fruit basket that's been putrefying in there for God knows how long."

"Gross, why would they leave that for so long?"

"It's absolutely full of flies in there now too. I've cracked a window open."

"Should I call an exterminator?"

"No, they should clear out once we've cleaned up."

"Yet another thing we have to sort out," Nath began with a sigh, "I'll get Al to move it. He isn't squeamish."

"Hey, it's the thought that counts," I joked.

"I wonder what's inside."

"Shall I open it?" I asked as I turned it around in my hand.

"Go on then."

I untied the bright white bow and started ravenously tearing into the hot-pink wrapping paper. It was a small jewellery box, and as I flipped it open, a tiny piece of folded paper fell out, revealing a small silver pendant on a delicate chain. I struggled to reach it from the floor, dropping the card in the process, but Nath beat me to it and picked them up.

"What is this? Some kind of necklace?" I asked as I lifted it up for Nath to see.

"It looks like a Saint Christopher. My mom had one. He's the patron saint of travellers, and it's meant to protect the wearer."

"Bit of a creepy house-warming gift," I began with an uneasy smile, "what does the note say?"

"The fruit of the womb is his reward," Nath read from the unfolded hand-written note in bafflement.

"Psalms, it's from the bible," I pointed out.

"I didn't know you were religious."

"I'm not. It looks like all those years being indoctrinated at Sunday school finally paid off, though."

"What does it mean?" he perplexedly asked.

"Probably a reference to that pile of sludge in there that was once a fruit basket and the obvious," I said as I pointed to my bump.

"Yeah, that is really creepy," he nervously said.

"What about the card? Does it say who it's from?"

Nath ripped open the card, and I saw the front as he opened it, which simply said, "Congratulations on your new home," accompanied by a watercolour print of a house. I saw the colour quickly drain from his face as he read the contents, and he quickly folded it back up and clutched it to his chest. I held out my hand expectantly, and after a few seconds of hesitation and a sigh, he handed it back to me with an unsteady hand.

"To my undying love," I nauseatingly began out loud as I cleared my throat, "this is for you. Please wear it always, it will protect you from harm. I know in my heart that we'll be together one day, and I'll wait for you until then."

Nath remained silent.

"Oh, for fuck's sake, this is from her, isn't it?" I disdainfully uttered as I ripped it into pieces.

"Maybe it's just a prank," he mustered with a shrug.

"Nath, it's been drowned in cheap perfume, and it's signed with a big kiss," I scornfully replied.

"How does she even know about this place?"

"I don't know. How does she know?"

"What are you trying to say?"

"Nath, I swear, if you've been in contact with her—"

"I haven't," he sharply interrupted.

The air suddenly became so thick that I felt like I could barely breathe, so to catch my breath, I angrily stormed out of the house with the necklace still in my hand. When the porch door slammed behind me, Alex's diligent unloading was interrupted, and he called out after me. As I turned around to face him while still in motion, I saw Nathaniel angrily showing him the pieces of the card I had just read. I decided that they could work it out between themselves, so I continued to furiously waddle down the rocky road we had just come from in an attempt to regain my self-control.

Stephanie was proving to be relentless, malicious, and increasingly self-aware enough to cover her tracks. We didn't have any legal recourse because the county sheriff's office would laugh us out of the building if we walked in with something as seemingly innocuous as the gift she had left, and we didn't have the remotest idea where she was living, so I couldn't confront her directly even if I wanted to. Would we have to look over our shoulders for the rest of our lives, waiting for the next creepy stunt to take us by surprise? I was annoyed at myself for reacting how I did because deep down, I knew that it was all designed just to irk me, and if she was in some way or another watching this unfold, she would have been laughing her psycho head off.

She had already proven to me that she was totally unperturbed by our engagement, and even the imminent birth of our child didn't make her resolve waver one jot. She was never going away, and I didn't know what to do about it.

15

THE TRUTH

OLIVIA – 2024

In a mad fury, I fiercely exited through the automatic doors of the rehab facility, with Aurora bemusedly trailing a few metres behind me and the orderly from the rehab centre, lugging the bags a few metres behind her.

"Mom, what is it?" she frantically asked.

"Just get in the car," I coldly ordered.

Alex was still in the same spot that I left him with the engine running, leaning back in his seat with his hands resting on his chest and listening to the radio with his eyes half closed. I reached the car and wildly banged on the window, which gave him the fright of his life, but when he recovered, he quickly unlocked the doors. I decisively flung the boot wide open, and the orderly quickly deposited the bags in there before I shut it and got in the car, leaving him stunned and tipless at the roadside.

"What's happening?" Alex asked.

"Just drive and get us home as fast as you can," I sternly ordered as I pointed forward.

Instead of instantly peeling out of the empty car park as I had imagined, Alex calmly turned the engine off, undid his seatbelt, and slowly turned to me inquisitively. I impatiently shrugged and slapped the dashboard petulantly, but he remained entirely motionless.

"Hi, Aurora," he calmly said before turning to me. "We aren't moving a single inch until you've told me what's going on and you calm yourself," he softly added.

"I've got it!" I breathlessly stated.

"Got what exactly?"

"The smoking gun."

"Just calm down and tell me what's happened."

"The day we moved in, do you remember it?"

"Of course I do. I still have the scars of the blisters."

"Someone left a weird gift for us? With some creepy biblical quote enclosed with it? Ring any bells?"

"Yeah, I remember, but I'm not following."

"It was this necklace," I said as I held it up and jingled it in his face.

"Where did you find it?"

"Around Aurora's neck."

"Did Steph get that for you?" he asked Aurora.

"Yes, it was a birthday present," she nervously mumbled from the back seat.

"Olivia, you can get one of those from just about anywhere. It's hardly any evidence, and it could just as easily be a coincidence."

"Oh, I agree, but it came with a creepy quote from the Bible. What else came with a creepy biblical quote tonight?"

"The rock that was thrown through the window," Alex conceded as he turned the key in the ignition.

"Exactly, now fucking drive."

Alex, finally understanding the gravity of the situation, put his foot down, and the tyres squealed as we exited the car park. I glanced in the rearview mirror at Aurora, who looked incredibly tearful. As she was jostling around in the back seat, I realised she must have thought I was totally insane by the way I had reacted.

"Listen, love, I know you're confused, and this is the short version," I softly began with a broken voice. "On our wedding day, someone knocked me out and then locked me away for a very long time. Whoever it was tried to break me, starve me, and humiliate me, but I survived and eventually escaped. I thought it was all over until a few hours ago when someone threw a rock through the patio doors with a cryptic note attached."

"What did it say?"

"That doesn't matter. They were just trying to scare us."

"Who is it?"

I took a long, deep breath, and not for one moment did I ever contemplate withholding the truth from her.

"It's Stephanie," I firmly stated as Alex subtly shot me a sideways glance.

"Mom, there's just no way," Aurora reasoned in disbelief.

"I know you aren't going to want to hear this, but Stephanie has been messing with us for years, long before you were even born. She's obsessed with me; it was her, and now I have the proof."

"But... how? Why?" Aurora stuttered.

"Darling, I swear I will tell you everything, but right now, we need to get back to your dad and make sure he's safe."

"Okay," Aurora perplexedly conceded.

"Alex, can I borrow your phone?" I asked.

"Sure, are you calling Nath?" he said as he handed it to me.

"Yes," I uttered as I began dialling Nath's number. After a prolonged ring, he didn't answer, and in a huff, I dropped the phone in the console.

"No answer?" he asked.

"No," I muttered.

"Nath can look after himself, and not to mention he's surrounded by half of the sheriff's office."

"Just put your foot down."

I tightly gripped the necklace in my trembling fist for the entire rest of the journey. I was holding it so firmly that I almost broke the skin on my right hand. The thought of Stephanie quietly seething in the background of our lives filled me with fear; it had initially escaped my notice that she had been slowly escalating her attempts to capture our attention, becoming more and more dangerous in the process, and after almost two decades in the making, there was no one that terrified me more than her on this planet. There wasn't a soul that truly knew what she was capable of, and after I left her painstakingly thought-out plans in tatters when I managed to escape, it was only a matter of time before her diseased mind dreamt up an appropriately psychopathic response.

We arrived back at the house to find that the herd of reporters had thinned out with only a few stragglers who stopped loitering around to whip up into a frenzy as soon as they spotted Alex's car approaching. The sheriffs had set up a loose cordon, and Alex carefully negotiated our way through it and back onto the driveway. Before the vehicle even came to a full stop, I bounded out of it and stormed straight into the house, leaving Alex and Aurora in the dust. I immediately walked into the living room, expecting to see Nath still waiting there, and sure enough, there he was. However, he wasn't alone; he was nauseatingly resting his head in Stephanie's lap on the sofa, and she was soothing him by running her absurdly long false nails through his hair and over his scalp. She was the first to notice my arrival, greeting me with a repulsive smirk, and she didn't alter her position on the couch even slightly.

"What the fuck are you doing here?" I abruptly demanded, leading Nath to shoot up in his seat.

"What kind of future wife would I be if, hearing about what happened tonight, I failed to rush to comfort my poor traumatised husband straight away?" Stephanie facetiously asked.

"I'm glad you're here, actually. Explain this," I instructed as I violently threw the necklace directly at her sniggering face. She managed to catch it in her hands as it fell whilst I closely monitored every single micro-expression on her face, looking for any minute signs of guilt. Instead of any indication of remorse, she just looked at Nath with a bemused expression on her face, and he took the necklace from her to inspect it.

"What even is this?" he asked.

"Aurora was wearing it when we picked her up. It's the same weird necklace from the vile housewarming gift she left for us," I said matter-of-factly.

"Olivia, honey, it was a birthday present for Aurora. I have no idea about any gift that I supposedly left you," Stephanie stated in between impetuous giggles.

"I'm not getting the connection here either," Nath said.

"You would've gotten away with it if you hadn't tied that nonsensical bible quote to the rock before you launched it through the window tonight."

"Olivia, enough!" Nath gasped in shock.

"You have clearly gone insane, honey. Why would I do either of those things?"

"Because it was you. You're the one who took me." I coldly accused.

"We don't have to listen to this drivel, do we?" Stephanie said as she stood up, "I think you should leave."

"I'm not going anywhere until I see you carted off in cuffs. Nathaniel, get the sheriffs in here."

Nathaniel remained defiantly seated.

"Sweetheart," Stephanie started as she delicately placed her hand on my arm, "I think all those years locked away made you crazy. Waste no time and get some help."

I looked down at the patch of my goosebump-ridden skin that was in contact with her fingertips. My entire body started to vibrate in a blind rage, and I firmly gripped her wrist with the sole intention of sternly removing it from my arm. However, when our eyes locked for a single fleeting moment, and her impossibly white teeth became slightly visible as her face cracked into an almost imperceptible arrogant grin, something snapped within me.

Without a care for the repercussions, I aggressively bent her arm behind her back, leading her to scream out melodramatically, and I started forcibly marching her out of the house. I was too angry to feel the sensation of Nath pawing at my shoulders as he tried desperately to stop me or even hear him when he was pleading with me to stop because I was far too consumed with wrath to process anything else. Not for the first time, I coldly ejected her through the door and happily watched as Stephanie plummeted to the ground in a heap of grazed limbs.

I bit my lip; it wasn't enough to appease my fury.

I immediately pounced on top of her and aggressively batted her arms out of the way as I placed every modicum of strength that I had left behind every punch. I managed to get a good few hits in before I was inevitably dragged off her by the waiting sheriff deputies, cuffed, and without the freedom to continue, I venomously spat at her cowering form from a distance.

"You did this to me! You are going to rot in jail for what you've done!" I screamed.

"Psycho," she whispered as she wiped the drips of blood emanating from her nose with her thumb.

The flashes of the reporter's cameras were what returned my faltering sanity to me, and I bitterly realised I had played into her hands once again. Her intentions were suddenly so obvious and ham-fisted: she was trying to bait me into action and to paint me as the bad guy in front of my own family, law enforcement, and anyone who would see the photos that had just been snapped of me. Her plan worked spectacularly, and the press were already admiring their handiwork as I was being dragged to the deputy's cruiser and fought against every step.

Nath barely noticed me being escorted away because he was far too busy consoling Stephanie, who was putting on the performance of a lifetime. That being said, by the time the cruiser's door was slammed in my face, she was bleeding profusely from her nose. The last haunting face I saw before the car took me to the sheriff's office was Aurora's, and to my shame, I realised my daughter had ringside seats for the whole thing. She had seen it massively out of context and was fearfully clinging onto Alex's right arm. I would never forget the timid expression on her face as the car took me away.

She must have been petrified of me.

Worst of all, I had gone all in when I impulsively confronted Stephanie; she readily called my bluff, and I was left holding the bag. I missed my ideal opportunity to get Nath and Aurora on my side, and I wasn't even sure if Alex would still support my theory after what he witnessed.

"You looked mad back there," Benjamin's twisted voice whispered in my ear.

I remained silent.

"In front of all those cameras too. You're a real class act, Olivia," he added.

"Get out of my head," I mumbled.

"None of them will believe a word you say now. You have really fucked this up," he laughed manically.

"Leave me alone!" I shouted.

The deputy driving me away looked at me in the rearview mirror as I embarrassingly sunk back into my seat. Not a single one of them knew the depths of intense violence and depravity Stephanie was willing to sink to, and if they did, my meagre display of aggression that night would have paled in comparison. She was perverse, cruel, and something far worse that even law enforcement didn't know.

She was a murderer.

16

THE HUNTERS

OLIVIA – 2015

Tick, tock. Tick, tock. The soul-shattering feeling of the world spinning without me in it was surreal, and it occupied my every waking moment. I resided in my own personal purgatory, crushed by the unfathomable boredom that came with it, and I became increasingly self-aware that there was only so much more I could take. As twisted as it may sound, I actually found myself looking forward to Benjamin's daily bulletins just because they broke the monotony more than anything else.

"Piece of shit," I uttered to myself as the plastic knife I was using to make an indent on the wall snapped.

I stepped back from my do-it-yourself calendar and quickly started counting the scratches on the wall. By my own rudimentary calculations, almost a full year had dissolved into the ether since I was cruelly imprisoned in that place, and it's safe to say I wasn't exactly living my best life. At first, each one of those gouges in the concrete represented another week of survival to me, but as the legion grew in number, my mind instead focused on how many more I would be forced to make before I was finally free. It's funny because I used to fly off the handle if Aurora ever drew on the walls, yet there I was, intentionally taking huge chunks out of mine with flimsy cutlery.

From day one, I needed to convince myself that I chose to do this to protect my family, like I had a choice at all, because pretending it was my decision to continue made my endless misery somewhat more palatable. I constantly reminded myself of Benjamin's golden rule: if I played nice, my family would remain unharmed. He wasn't content with just locking me away; he seemed to have a habitual need to brutalise me continuously at every opportunity, and every interaction was carefully manufactured to break me psychologically. I was steadfastly adamant that I wouldn't let him destroy me like he so badly desired, and I tried to see his badly thrown-together flicks as a chance to catch a glimpse of Nathaniel and Aurora living their lives, regardless of the menacing context behind it.

It goes without saying that I missed my family immensely, and every second I could feel passing without them felt like something precious that I had lost. Even in the relatively short space of time, it was plain to see that Aurora had already grown up so much. Every time I caught sight of her on screen, she had this deadened, faraway look in her eyes, like the child in her had died. My innocent little girl had been inhumanely forced to grow up in order to have the emotional maturity she would need to deal with the horrific thing that happened to our family, and I spent countless hours wondering how she felt about it all. I was desperate to put the record straight and somehow let her know that I was alive, but it was yet another unattainable luxury I wasn't afforded in that hellhole.

Nathaniel was clearly in bits too, and he looked absolutely distraught on every snippet of the television appeals that I was required to watch. I tried looking away at times or even simply closing my eyes, but my tormentor was always watching, and I would be punished without mercy if I didn't give it my undivided attention. At first, the media were sympathetic, and they accurately portrayed Nathaniel exactly how he was: the unconsolable grieving partner who had tragically lost his wife-to-be, who was desperately trying to hold everything together long enough for her to return. After a while without any solid leads or suspects, they predictably turned on him, and suddenly, he was the sole villain of the piece. Every broadcast kept repeating that old adage that 'it's always the husband,' and even the feckless district attorney seemed to concur, as he publicly named Nath in every scathing interview. Out of desperation, the police even dug our garden up, presumably looking for my remains or the fictional murder weapon with Nath's greasy prints on, all with Nath and Aurora gloomily looking on from the sidelines as their lives were quite literally torn apart.

After a year of banging their heads against the wall, the investigation seemed to slow to a standstill, and the thrown-together clips of the news pertaining to me were far more sporadic. Instead, Benjamin filled the schedule with long-lens shots of Aurora at school or Nath crying in our living room, and it was a constant reminder to behave and not even contemplate escape. Under the ever-watchful eye of the CCTV camera that obsessively tracked my every breath, it was almost impossible to find a weakness to exploit. He was incredibly careful, and with an obvious escape plan not immediately apparent, it was clear to me that I had to bide my time even longer and wait for my chance.

With an extended sigh, I bent down with the old dustpan and brush to clear up the mess I had made after my weekly ritual, and as I was just about to rise to my feet again, I heard the ominous hiss and pop of the intercom connecting.

"Quiet," Benjamin ordered.

"I was just cleaning up," I reasoned.

"Just stay quiet," he boomed.

As I remained on my knees, I scrunched up my face in confusion, and that's when I heard the distant rumbling noise getting closer. I quickly returned to my feet and stepped over to the small air vent that was in the ceiling, dragged the chair beneath it, and climbed on top of it to get closer to the noise.

"Get down from there," he scathingly threatened.

I ignored his request; instead, I focused all my attention on identifying the noise above. I couldn't make it out at first, but as it got even closer, I realised it was motorbikes overhead, and the low warble they produced rattled the room until it abruptly ceased. They sounded like they were parked up directly above the air vent I was trying to press my face into, and the euphoria washed over me when I realised this was the opportunity I had been waiting for.

"Don't. I mean it," he menacingly uttered.

As I began to laugh manically, I was plunged into darkness when the lights in the room were switched off, with only the narrow beams of light coming through the vent directly lighting up my face. It was barely audible, but I heard low, muffled voices coming through the tube, so I gripped the vent with both hands, took a deep breath, and prepared to shriek as if my life depended on it.

"Help!" I screamed.

"Did you hear that?" a confused voice said from above.

"It sounded like it was coming out of that pipe," another voice added.

"Help! I'm down here!" I shouted at the top of my lungs.

"Olivia, be quiet," Benjamin quietly demanded.

"I've been fucking kidnapped; they've locked me down here!" I shouted as I shook the vent as hard as I could.

"Hey Jack, there's someone down there," the voice said.

"Yes!" I gleefully yelled.

"There's some kind of hatch here. Try and get it open with the tyre iron on the quadbike," Jack said.

The next glorious sound I heard was splintering wood, a delightfully sharp snap, and then the thrilling creak of a door opening. Before I knew it, there was pounding on the exterior steel door, and I fumbled my way through the darkness to get to the airlock, barely arriving before Benjamin remotely revoked my access. As soon as I arrived at the door, I started unyieldingly pummelling my fists against it with all my might, and I heard the sound of metal on metal as the two unknown heroes on the other side tried to pry it open.

"I'm in here!" I shouted.

"Who are you?" Jack asked.

"My name's Olivia Lakewell. I got taken a year ago."

"That missing English lady from the news?"

"Yes! Just get me out of here, please!"

"This is a mighty heavy door, ma'am; I'm trying my best."

"You have to keep trying and be quick. He's coming," I begged.

"Waylon, get the twelve gauge from the bike and ring the sheriffs! I don't think I'll get this open with what we have," Jack shouted.

"No! You have to! Please, hurry."

"Ma'am, relax, you're safe. I don't know anyone who is a better shot with a twelve gauge than my boy Waylon."

No more than half a second after Jack finished trying to reassure me, we both heard the ear-splitting bang echoing above us, and his attempt to open the door immediately stopped. It was eerily quiet for a moment, and my heart was pumping so hard in my chest that I could hear it bouncing against the steel of the door I was leaning on.

"Waylon?" he shouted.

"He's here," I softly said through the door, "can you hear what I'm saying?"

"Waylon?" he repeated quieter.

"Jack!" I snapped.

"What is it?" he uttered.

"Don't try and fight him. You need to get on your quadbike and go straight to Hammerdale sheriff's office."

"I need to go check on my buddy; that sounded like a gunshot up there."

"Listen, I'm so sorry you both got involved in this, but he's dead, Jack and you're next. Then me if you don't go and get help," I stated matter-of-factly with tears in my eyes.

"Okay," he meekly replied.

"If you make it there, let my daughter know I'm alive, please." I sobbed.

"I will," he whispered.

I pressed my ear as hard as I could against the door, and I heard Jack's footsteps fade into the distance. In a single fleeting second, I prayed to any God that would listen, and I begged them to let him escape Benjamin's clutches so he could free me forever. I dropped to my knees in the airlock with my forehead on the floor, waiting for the quadbike to start or for a second gunshot to shatter my only hope.

"Please," I mouthed silently.

Bang.

My face remained firmly pressed against the cold indifference of the concrete as a tsunami of bitter tears crashed into the stone. My cries were too distraught to make a noise at first until I began grudgingly pounding the floor with my hands, and I began to howl painfully. I wept every speck of hope I still had and watched it soak into the dry concrete beneath me as I pictured the disappointment on my family's faces that I almost made it out of there, but I failed. The lights in the bunker ominously flickered back into life, and I remained down on the ground until the intercom kicked into life again.

"Close the interior door behind you and stand by your bed," Benjamin calmly insisted.

"Why did you have to kill them? They were just trying to help." I frantically bellowed from the airlock.

"Bed. Now."

I defeatedly rose to my feet, walked into the room, and shut the interior door behind me as instructed. I reluctantly walked over to the side of the bed, still uncontrollably weeping, and buried my head in my quivering hands. I heard the interior door lock shut, the exterior one open, and as I searched myself for what little bravery was lurking within me, I wiped the tears from my eyes and apprehensively awaited my punishment. I was shaking from head to toe when there was a single violent thud against the door, followed by a second one a few minutes later, and I attentively watched as the indicator bulbs swapped colours, giving me access to the airlock again. The intercom came back to life a few minutes later, and I eagerly awaited my fate.

"That was a very stupid thing you've just done," he angrily snarled.

"What have you done with them?" I softly asked.

"See for yourself."

He didn't have to say anything else. I cautiously walked over to the airlock to inspect what had been left, and as my shaking hand rested on the handle, I knew what I would find on the other side.

"Open it," he scorned.

As I slowly turned the handle, the weight of what was on the other side forced the door open, which knocked me off balance, and I fell to the ground as it ominously creaked open of its own accord. I sheepishly looked through the open doorway to see two dead men in hunting gear, painted from head to toe in their own blood, thoughtlessly discarded like inanimate trash in a messy heap. I instinctively knew that the man closest to me was Jack, and his disturbingly constricted expression of pure fear would be immortalised in my mind forever.

"He will wipe every tear from their eyes. There will be no more death, mourning, crying, or pain, for the old order of things has passed away," Benjamin sullenly recited.

"Why did you do this?" I uttered.

"Me?" he laughed before sinisterly dropping his tone. "No. You did this. If you would have kept your mouth shut like I asked, they would still be breathing," he spitefully added.

"They were just trying to help," I quietly mumbled.

"This is on you. My hands are clean," he boomed.

"You're a monster."

"I know. Sleep well, Olivia," the voice said before the intercom crackle faded.

"You're not going to just fucking leave them here? What am I supposed to do? Hello?" I shouted.

After a minute or two of eerie silence, I realised what my punishment was. I pushed myself from the ground to get on my hands and knees and moved a little closer to the bodies, absolutely petrified of the thought of what I had to do. I delicately took Waylon's hands as courteously as I could, and although he wasn't a big man, he was far heavier than I anticipated. I was trying to be as delicate and respectful as I could be, but the level of exertion I had to reach to shift his weight made it impossible. I heaved him to the back of the airlock so he was clear of the door, carefully crossed his arms over his chest, and sensitively closed his eyelids to hide the terror beneath them. Jack was next, and I sullenly repeated the macabre process so they were both lying together and at peace.

"I'm sorry," I whispered.

Benjamin was right. He may have pulled the trigger that ended both of their lives, yet the blood was definitely on my hands. As I stared down at them, I couldn't help but picture Nathaniel and Aurora lying there in their place, and suddenly, the grim lesson that Benjamin was trying to teach me was painfully clear. I couldn't take it anymore, slammed the door shut, and immediately ran over to the sink to scrub my crimson-stained hands in the sink.

It was my final warning.

17

THE RELEASE

OLIVIA – 2024

I was becoming a frequent resident at Hammerdale sheriff's office, but owing to the events of the previous night, this time, the door was well and truly locked. I had the time to carefully ruminate on what I had done, and although I didn't explicitly regret the rash decision, I was ashamed that my daughter had witnessed it and a little embarrassed that I had let Stephanie get under my skin. I had woefully spent my night pleading for the deputies to go and arrest Stephanie or, at the very least, look at the new evidence I had. Nevertheless, none of them would even entertain the idea in the slightest. They simply passed the buck to Sheriff Daniels, assuring me he would pick it up in the morning because he was supposedly the one who was solely dealing with my case.

I barely slept a wink all night. I was far too terrified about that conniving monster being near my family and desperately trying to calculate what her next move would be. She knew that I knew and that I was coming for her, but I had no idea how she would react when she was backed into a corner. The image of her self-assured smile plagued me, and I couldn't believe she gallingly remained cool as a cucumber in the face of almost being exposed. Whatever the long game was, I wanted no part in it, and I was determined to derail her plans and unmask her as Benjamin before her mania took anything even further.

I hadn't heard a squeak about my case since I first spoke with Daniels, and I was beginning to think he wasn't taking me seriously. Even after every atrocious act that Stephanie had wilfully committed, laughably, she was still free as a bird and, therefore, given free rein to continue tormenting me as she had done for years. I understood that the evidence I had found so far was largely circumstantial, but when you added it to the growing list of wacky things she'd had a hand in over the years, it proved her guilt with certainty to me. I knowingly held back key details of my captor's exploits in my first interview, largely out of respect for Nathaniel's delicate sensibilities, but the gloves were off, and I was planning to sing like a canary.

I heard the door open to the cell block, and the long-awaited Sheriff Daniels casually sauntered around the corner with a steaming coffee in each hand, carefully balancing one of them on the strip of steel connecting the bars separating us as he nonchalantly took a sip off his own. We made eye contact, and he stepped back a few paces with a sigh, flashing me a cynical smile like I was some mischievous tearaway.

"Rough night?" he asked.

"I've had worse," I replied sarcastically.

"I thought you could do with some coffee," he said as he pointed at the cup.

"Not thirsty. Has Stephanie been arrested yet?" I abruptly quizzed.

"What for? Having the shit kicked out of her by you?"

"Let me see... kidnapping? False imprisonment?"

"There's not one scrap of evidence she was involved," he stated.

"Then you aren't looking hard enough," I said as I tightly gripped the bars in frustration.

"We'll move on to the investigation shortly, but I want to straighten out what happened last night first."

"Of course you do," I facetiously replied with a grimace.

Daniels calmly took out the battered notebook from his top pocket and started flicking through it until he found the correct page. His eyes widened as he began reading from it.

"So, you had an object thrown through the window with a message attached, which led you to pick up your daughter from the drunk tank—"

"It's called a rehab facility," I interjected.

"—from the rehab facility," Daniels corrected himself, "and you spotted she was wearing a necklace that was anonymously gifted to you when you first moved to the States?"

"Yes, and it had a similar message attached that was tied to the rock thrown through the patio doors."

"The quote from the good book?"

"The Bible, yes."

"After that, you confronted her, and because she denied your claims, you proceeded to attack her?"

"No," I began with a dramatic sigh, "I proceeded to attack her because I didn't like the look she gave me," I added dismissively.

"This is serious. She might press charges."

"Good. If it goes to court, maybe someone will deign to listen to me."

"Hey, I'm listening. The problem is: I'm not hearing anything even remotely credible."

"It's her, I know it is."

"You know that I can't arrest her on a hunch. Especially the hunch of a woman who, let's be honest, is clearly having some kind of mental breakdown."

"I beg your pardon?" I irreverently laughed.

"Olivia, you beat up a woman in front of your daughter and half the State's press. It wasn't your finest hour."

Accepting his statement's accuracy, I defeatedly grabbed the coffee cup and paced around my cell.

"So, what, is she pressing charges?" I worriedly asked.

"Not yet," Daniels began as he set his cup down, "I've convinced her not to press charges, but you aren't going to like how."

"What is it?"

"You have to speak to someone."

"Who?"

"A therapist."

"Jesus Christ," I bitterly exclaimed as I turned my back on him and continued to walk the cell.

"It's for your own good, Olivia. You need to talk through what happened to you, and it has the added bonus of keeping you out of jail."

"She's still trying to control me; you have to see that?"

"It was my suggestion, and for the record, I think you are barking up the wrong tree as to her being your kidnapper."

"Well, when you actually start investigating my case, I'll start respecting your opinion, okay?" I said sarcastically.

"We have been investigating. We were at the bunker yesterday."

"You were there? Did you find anything?" I excitedly quizzed as I raced over to the bars again.

"*Nada.* The whole place had been emptied and cleaned."

"No blood?" I flippantly asked.

"Who's blood, yours?"

"No. Two men called Jack and Waylon."

"Olivia, why exactly would we find their blood there?"

"She shot them when they tried helping me escape."

"Why didn't you mention this in your first interview?"

"I wasn't in the right frame of mind," I mustered.

"Not in the right frame of mind then, or now?"

"Then," I emphasised, "and they weren't the only victims of hers."

"Okay, Olivia," Daniels wearily began as he shut his notebook with a sigh, "you do see how this looks, right? You're casually accusing someone of multiple murders the night after you assaulted them."

"It's true."

"No, it's desperate. Just apologise to her and move on."

"Check missing persons. There can't be that many missing Waylons around these parts."

"Okay, I'll check, but you need to stay out of this now."

"I need to go back to the bunker. You might have missed something."

"Absolutely not. Miss Lakewell, you need to let us do our jobs. And if you remember something, you need to come straight to us and do not take matters into your own hands. Am I making myself crystal clear?"

"Okay, I'll stay out of it if you at least look into Stephanie and the missing men?"

"I will. Like I said, I'm new in town, and I don't owe anybody anything. We've already taken the necklace into evidence, and hopefully, something will come back from it. The rock and the note that was thrown through the window will be going down to the lab too. Let's pray they got sloppy and left a print."

"You mean *she* got sloppy."

"Whoever threw it, yes."

"Okay, I'll behave. Can you let me out of here now?"

"Yes, and don't waste that coffee," Daniels joked as he selected the key to the cell from his keyring.

He indifferently unlocked the cell door to slide it open, allowing me outside of it, and he ushered me down the corridor. To my surprise, he seemed like he was on top of things, which made me feel a little better. If he had no allegiances to anyone in Hammerdale, then he would probably have been the perfect person to investigate what happened.

"Is there still a deputy watching over the house?" I asked as we walked.

"Yes, mostly because your little brawl whipped the media into a frenzy, and they've come out in force today."

"At least there are eyes on the house."

"You actually knocked one of her teeth out, you know?"

"Really?" I asked with a gloating smile as we reached the reception desk. "It's a good job that she's a dentist."

"Here," Daniels began as he handed me the morning newspaper, "you have a hell of a right hook on you."

I took the crumpled paper from him and unfolded it to find a picture of me punching the lights out of Stephanie on the front page. If I had seen it without an officer of the law standing a few feet away, I would have probably let out a satisfied laugh, but instead, I stifled the giggles and concealed my smile until I saw the headline.

"The bride from the bunker?" I incredulously asked.

"That's what they are calling you," he replied with an uneasy smirk.

"It's utterly ridiculous."

"That's the press for you."

I folded the paper back up and handed it back, and an awkward few seconds followed when I wasn't sure if I could just walk out of the front doors or not.

"Am I free to go then?" I gingerly asked.

"You are. Your therapist is waiting outside," he stated.

"What? You are joking, right?" I impetuously asked.

"It's non-negotiable if you want to stay out of jail."

"Let me know the instant you find anything."

"I will. Stay out of trouble," Daniels remarked.

I walked through the double doors to find Alex wearing shades and leaning against his parked car with a bag of fast food next to him. Owing to my lack of sleep, it took a few seconds for me to put two and two together. I realised that he was the therapist I had to see, and I started violently shaking my head with cynical laughter.

"Hungry?" he asked.

"Not really. How the hell did Daniels rope you into this?"

"It's not difficult to work out. I'm one of the only qualified therapists in town and certainly the cheapest."

"Is Aurora okay? And Nath?"

"Both fine, a bit shaken up."

"I can't believe I did that in front of her."

"Me neither. Nonetheless, you were angry, and you've more of a right to be than most. It's easily done."

"I bet she thinks I'm a psychopath."

"Maybe a little," he began with an upward inflexion and a cautious wince, "but she'll understand why when she finds out what you've been through."

"I hope so."

"I don't have to tell you that it was a mistake, do I?"

"No. Lesson learned."

"Good."

"What did the bitch have to say for herself when I got carted off? Gloating, I assume?"

"Nothing of note. She was too busy playing the victim as predicted."

"*Playing*? So, you're coming around to my way of thinking, then?"

"I think there's definitely something to what you said. It's hardly concrete though, certainly not to the police, and your little stunt will have set you back significantly."

"Regardless of her guilt, she deserved a wallop."

"Come on," he said with a smile, "let's get going."

Alex excitedly grabbed the food from the bonnet, jogged round to the driver's seat, and jumped inside. I wearily followed suit and got in the car too, and the radio started blaring upbeat rock music as soon as he turned the key in the ignition. He quickly turned it down and offered me a spare pair of sunglasses that I politely refused, and he began driving whilst whistling along to the tune.

"Someone's in a good mood," I remarked.

"Sorry, it's probably a little bit inappropriate given what's happened. I guess I just got out of the right side of the bed this morning," Alex explained.

"Sounds nice. I've forgotten what that feels like."

"Listen, about this therapy, I know Daniels wants me to play it by the book, but if you don't want to talk about what happened, we can just take our time with it."

"Hang on, I thought this was just a ruse? A quick sign on the dotted line and I'm free to do as I please?"

"It will be good for you, Liv. You can't carry on your own what happened to you."

"I just don't know if I can talk about it just yet."

"Like I said, we'll take it slow."

The thought of unleashing everything that had happened to me was simultaneously horrifying and extremely attractive. I urgently needed the weight off my shoulders, and the pragmatic side of me thought it would help with the investigation too. As Alex continued to drive, I pensively stared out of the window and practised mouthing the words I would say when I finally opened up about it. My worry was that I would open the emotional floodgates, all hell would be unleashed, and I would alienate the only friend I had left.

"By the way, it goes without saying that you should give Nath's place a wide berth for the next few days while it all calms down," Alex postulated.

"Great, so on top of everything, I'm fucking homeless."

"Was it still worth it to knock one of her teeth out?"

"Every day of the week," I laughed without hesitation.

"I know it's a little weird," he began awkwardly, "but you are more than welcome to stay at mine for a few days."

"Shacking up with my therapist? Freud would have a field day," I joked.

"It's only temporary. You're an old friend who needs a little help, and I have loads of room."

"You haven't got a crazy fiancée too, have you?"

"I had a perfectly sane fiancée, but that was a long time ago now."

"What happened?"

"She died. I'll tell you about it over a beer one day."

Suddenly, everything about Alex made sense. He was clearly carrying a lot of trauma of his own, and his chosen career path made sense too, given what he had been through. Even though I had technically known him for years, I barely knew anything about him below the surface, and his almost casual admission of his own demons made me feel more comfortable unearthing mine.

"Shit, Alex, I'm sorry," I hastily exclaimed.

"Honestly, don't worry about it," Alex sullenly dismissed. "So, what do you think? Do you fancy being roomies? There is a motel in town, but I can't speak for its cleanliness," he humorously added.

"Okay then, only if you're sure?"

"I am. I'll swing by Nath's later and collect your things."

We took a sharp left, and Alex pulled into the driveway of his home. It was nowhere near as impressive as Nath's house, but for a small-town therapist, he had clearly done quite well for himself. It was an idyllic Californian family home, clad in dark grey stones and beige render, and it even had a white picket fence surrounding the spacious front garden. A beautifully large oak tree grew there, swaying peacefully in the breeze, and the house itself sat in the shade of it. After seeing it, Alex's flippant comment about having lots of room felt sadder somehow.

"Nice house," I remarked.

"It was my parents' house. I couldn't bear to sell it. Too many memories in there."

"I'm nervous about this," I admitted.

"Come on, I'll get a pot of coffee on, and we can start when you're ready," Alex reassuringly suggested.

I meekly followed him inside, and although it was a gorgeous home, it barely felt lived in. The interior was perfectly immaculate, totally devoid of clutter, and he didn't have a single photograph on the walls. The floors were spotless as he led me through the kitchen and into a small annexe at the back, which served as his office.

"I did have an office in town, but the rent was getting difficult to justify, so I ended up moving my workplace, lock, stock, and barrel to this humble abode. Most clients actually prefer the home setting," Alex explained.

"It's nice... very cosy," I clumsily commented.

"Take a seat, and I'll get that coffee brewed."

I took a seat on one of the leather couches and began looking around the room aimlessly. The walls were filled with floor-to-ceiling bookshelves crammed to capacity, and everything was impossibly neat and aligned as they had never been used. Directly behind the sofa across from me was a huge painting that I immediately recognised to be Nathaniel's work, and although his style had evolved since I went missing, it was undoubtedly his. Alex returned a few minutes later with some clean glasses and a cafetiere, set them down on the table between the seats, and sat down opposite me.

"Is that one of Nath's paintings?" I asked as I pointed to the wall-mounted artwork behind him.

"It certainly is. I commissioned him to paint a piece for the office, so naturally, it had to come with me in the move," he said as he cautiously pushed the plunger of the cafetiere down.

"He is good, isn't he?"

"Very good. He really came into his own in the last ten years."

"Maybe it was me holding him back," I sarcastically remarked.

"No, it wasn't—"

"I'm joking," I interrupted.

"Well, to be honest, there is some truth in it. After all the unpleasantness of the investigation was over with, he became somewhat of a local celebrity. The emotion he used to paint his pieces became rawer, and I think that's why he ended up getting noticed."

"I didn't peg you as an art critic."

"I'm really not," he laughed, "just trying to support my friend."

As I leaned forward to grab a cup of coffee, I felt the atmosphere change slightly, and I realised that Alex was now in therapist mode. He leaned back, grabbed a lined pad and a pen from behind him, and tapped at it as he made direct eye contact with me. The strange shift in mood made me feel incredibly uneasy, so much so that he could tell how uncomfortable I was, so he warmly smiled as he put the pad back down.

"We don't have to do this now," he announced.

"No," I uttered, "I want to."

"Great," he quietly enthused.

"Do I just… start?"

"The first thing that springs to mind. You talk; I'll listen. If you feel up to it, we can work through the emotions afterwards."

My eyes were aimlessly drawn to the painting behind Alex once again, and as I silently examined it, a dark memory forced itself into focus. Suddenly, I could feel the rage and sorrow in every brush stroke, the shame and dehumanisation in every rogue paint splatter, and the bitter regret in each imperfection on the surface of the canvas. Grief filled me from head to toe, and as I reached bursting point, I looked back at Alex, who was waiting to collect the onslaught of emotion that I was ready to unleash.

I shakily took a deep breath and let it loose.

18

THE CELEBRATION

OLIVIA — 2016

As I was meditatively sitting on the edge of my makeshift bed, the indicator lights that displayed if the doors were locked or not suddenly changed colour, and I heard the dull sound of footsteps in the airlock. After a few seconds, the lights returned to their prior position, and I tentatively stood up to open the door to look at what had been left for me.

It wasn't a usual delivery. Instead, a small canvas bag had been left there with only a few loose items inside. There was an unwritten birthday card, a cheap plastic pen, a flattened party hat, and a small cake with a solitary unlit candle sticking out of it. I bemusedly picked the items up and brought them to the small table inside the bunker, and perplexedly set them down. As I was confusedly scratching my head at the selection, I heard the familiar hiss and pop of the intercom connecting, and I turned my head towards the small speaker in the corner of the room.

"For by me, your days will be multiplied, and years will be added to your life," Benjamin announced.

"Very nice. What the hell is all this?" I asked.

"Put the party hat on," he boomed.

"What's the occasion?" I anxiously inquired.

"Olivia, exactly what kind of a mother are you? It's your daughter's birthday."

The television fired up, and blurry footage of Aurora in her pyjamas opening presents was displayed on the screen. Nathaniel lovingly leaned in to help her untie the bow that surrounded it, and when she finally got it open, she excitedly hugged him and started unboxing what looked like a brand-new art set. It had been covertly shot at a distance from outside our living room window, and both Aurora and Nath were clearly oblivious to the fact that they were being filmed. The tears started forming in my eyes, and as I knelt down in front of the screen to look at it more closely, it was torturously turned off.

"Play it again, please," I urged.

"Your hat, Olivia," he reminded.

I reached into the canvas bag and quickly pulled out the party hat, and when I unfolded it, I saw that he had crudely written 'world's worst mother' on it in marker pen. I reluctantly put it on my head and carefully tied the strap underneath my chin, and the video immediately continued. It was the first time that when I saw them, they actually looked happy. Nath had the proudest smirk spanning from ear to ear as he watched our daughter enthusiastically tip the contents of the art set onto the dining table, and she immediately began trying to paint something. He walked over behind her to guide her hand, and I let out a bittersweet sob when the footage stopped.

"Congratulations, Mom, you missed your daughter's eighth birthday," Benjamin chastised.

"You've already locked me away in here. Why do you have to torment me like this?" I frantically shouted.

"Oh, come on, Olivia, cheer up! It's a birthday party! We need to turn that frown upside down," his voice sinisterly bellowed with false glee.

"Seriously, fuck off," I said as I disdainfully removed the party hat and threw it at the camera.

"Hey, I know what will put a smile on your face. How about some fun party games?"

"No," I firmly said as I defiantly climbed onto the bed and put my hands over my ears.

"You're really going to want to play this game, Olivia…"

I remained silent.

"Get up!" he screamed.

I tightly closed my eyes and clenched my fists. I already knew enough about him to see that it was likely a sinister trick or some sick game to make me hate myself, and I wanted no part in it. That being said, I knew that my act of flagrant rebellion would be quickly responded to with some kind of merciless punishment, so I reluctantly stood up again and belligerently looked into the camera with utter contempt.

"You really are a stick in the mud, aren't you? Seriously, you need to lighten up," Benjamin snickered.

"One game," I announced.

"How about truth or dare?"

I remained silent, the pugnacious expression on my face only becoming more pronounced.

"We have fantastic prizes available..." he persuaded.

"Fine. What prizes?" I uttered defeatedly.

"Olivia, you are going to love this," he enthused.

"Just spit it out."

"If you win, you can write whatever you want on that birthday card, and I'll make sure your daughter gets it."

Benjamin had quickly piqued my interest, yet it sounded way too good to be true, and I wondered where the inevitable catch was. I wasn't naive enough to think that I could put *anything* in that card, but I could, at the very least, let my family know I was alive. It might even reignite the investigation, and if I was lucky, it could even lead them to where I was being held. Was this the opportunity I had been waiting for?

"Seriously?" I disbelievingly asked.

"Dead serious. Let's have fun! It's a party!" he roared with feigned enthusiasm.

"What are the rules?"

"You really are a stickler, aren't you?"

"I just want to make sure it's fair."

"I ask you truth or dare, and if you complete it to my satisfaction, say… three times in a row, you win."

"Okay then. Truth." I said determinedly.

"Beware, I require total honesty. If you lie, I'll know, and I won't like that."

"Truth," I repeated.

"What do you hate about Nathaniel?"

"He always leaves the toilet seat up," I said without missing a beat.

"Come on, Olivia. Total honesty."

I knew what he was looking for, and I paused searchingly. There was plenty to love about Nathaniel, and I could spend hours listing the reasons, but in reality, there was plenty to dislike too. I wouldn't go as far as to say he was immature, although his approach to life was the polar opposite of my own. I was aware that I made jokes and said heavily inappropriate things, but at my core, I always had our family's best interests at heart. There were many times when I wished he would grow up just a little bit, join me in the real world, and maybe spend longer than a few seconds thinking about the impact of his flippant decisions.

"Okay. I hate how he lives exclusively in the moment and doesn't even contemplate the consequences of his actions," I explained matter-of-factly.

"Deep. Okay, I'll accept that. Round one done."

"Truth."

"Olivia! You're really getting into the spirit of this game. I'm so happy right now."

"Truth!" I repeated.

"Where's the most disgusting place you've ever had sex? You look like you've been around the block a few times."

"Easy," I began with a smile, "a public toilet back in London."

"Was it with Nathaniel?"

"Nope."

"Wow, you really are nasty, I never would've—"

"Last question. Truth," I interrupted dismissively.

"Now, now, Olivia, we need at least one dare. It's no wonder a killjoy like you didn't get invited to Aurora's birthday party."

There it was: the punchline, the inevitable twist, and the sinister end to that ridiculous game. I quickly tried to think of the worst thing they could possibly ask me to do, and given that I was locked in a concrete box, the list I came up with was very short. They clearly had something very specific in mind, conceived of long before I agreed to play the game in the first place, and my heart was pounding through my chest trying to imagine what it was. The prize being dangled a few inches away from my face was enough for me to submit, and I took a deep breath before giving my response.

"Okay then. Dare. Do your worst," I ordered.

"Take off your clothes," he sinisterly whispered.

"What?"

"You asked for a dare, and I dared you. Strip."

"No," I anxiously replied.

"Come on, it's nothing I haven't seen before. Even if you hang a sheet over the shower, you do know I can see everything, right?"

"Not that. Dare me to do something else."

"No," he sternly shouted, "you either do this, or the game is over, and what happens after that will be even worse."

Benjamin just wanted to know what depths of depravity I would plunge into for the sake of my family and if he had broken me enough that I would literally do anything without question. The thought of removing my clothes for his twisted sexual gratification made me want to be sick right there on the spot, and I knew that the feeling of being deeply humiliated like that would stick with me forever, but was it worth it? The niggling voice that told me that the supposed prize could actually be real grew louder, and I decided to ignore my better judgement and comply with his demands. I remembered Jack and Waylon's lifeless bodies in the airlock; Benjamin had a track record of not suffering disappointment well.

I looked down at my body as I turned away from the camera; I was wearing the tatty jumpsuit he left for me, and I heard the CCTV camera moving as I hesitantly unzipped it. It slid off my body onto the floor, and I inelegantly stepped out of it. As I started to dither with anxiety, I sheepishly turned back around to the camera, placing one arm across my chest and the other covering my groin. I had left my underwear on, but I already knew what he was going to say next.

"Everything, Olivia," he ordered.

My half-naked body began violently shaking as I turned back around and unhooked my bra. The tears were already streaming down my face as I threw it on the bed next to me before removing my panties and kicking them to one side. My breathing became increasingly shallow and laboured, and I closed my eyes to await further instructions.

"Turn around," he commanded.

"There you go, I did your sick dare," I announced with false bravado as I turned around and exposed all with a challenging shrug.

"Pull a chair up to the camera and sit down."

Desperate not to appear weak or humiliated, I complied. The chair screeched against the concrete floor as I dragged it in front of the CCTV camera, and I sat down on it, trying to preserve my modesty the best I could.

"Good. Now spread your legs," Benjamin directed.

"Fuck off, sicko," I venomously challenged.

"Do you remember those men you killed?" he asked.

"I killed?" I mocked.

"Maybe I'll leave Aurora in the airlock for you next time," he balefully mused.

"You stay away from her!" I threatened.

"Then do as I say," he sinisterly charged.

I was defeated. My legs violently shook as I moved them, and with every inch they stoically pried apart, I barely had the capacity to take breath in between the distraught sobbing. What morsels of dignity remained crumbled to dust as the eerie silence was only broken by Benjamin's heavy breathing rattling down the intercom. I averted my eyes from the camera as much as my position would allow, and after a few seconds, the rasp of his rhythmic inhalation ceased, and it was replaced with stifled laughter.

"Are you enjoying yourself?" I shakily asked.

"Not like you think. What do you take me for?" he laughed.

"Are we done here?" I demanded.

"We're done. You've won, congratulations. Write your shitty little card, and put some clothes on before I'm sick."

I immediately scrabbled to collect my clothes and went into the shower cubicle, where I continued to convince myself that I had at least some privacy to get dressed again. I stayed in there for a minute or two while I attempted to get a hold of myself because I refused to give them the pleasure of seeing me humiliated even further.

"Let marriage be held in honour among all, and let the marriage bed be undefiled, for God will judge the sexually immoral and adulterous," he joylessly recited.

I sheepishly emerged with two blood-red puffy eyes, walked over to the empty birthday card in the bag, and picked up the pen that had been left. My hands were violently trembling, and I could barely keep a hold of the pen, let alone write. The whir of the camera was still audible as it followed my every move as I wiped my nose with my sleeve. I took a deep breath, unfolded the card, and began thinking of what to write to my daughter.

Aurora,

Happy birthday, sweetie.

I want you to know I love you more than anything, and I'm so proud of you. You and your father mean everything to me, and I'm so sorry I can't be there, but I'm trying my best to get back to you both.

Mum x

19

THE COVER-UP

OLIVIA – 2024

I felt lighter somehow. Just knowing that there was another person on this planet who knew about what happened that day didn't fill me with the deep-seated shame that I thought it would; it was a release. Alex tried to keep a neutral expression throughout my story, but just seeing the slight wince was enough to vindicate my feelings on the whole matter. He didn't judge, smirk, or laugh like my paranoia expected him to. His entire demeanour told me that my new therapist shared my opinion that it was an abhorrent thing that happened to me in the long line of truly disturbing events that made up that horrific experience. He leaned forward from his seat to pass me a box of tissues, which I accepted gladly, and I began wiping away the tears from my cheeks.

"How did all that make you feel?" he asked.

"Humiliated. Angry. Hopeless," I listed between sniffles.

"That's a perfectly valid response, but that day doesn't define who you are. You don't have to carry around shame about that. You did what you had to do."

"I know. Do you know if she ever received the card, by any chance?"

"Sorry, Liv, I have no idea. When it was in the news, all kinds of weirdos started sending stuff to their house; it might have gotten lost in it."

"Nath never told me that."

"In the grand scheme of things, it probably wasn't that important enough to mention."

"I never did thank you," I remarked as I blew my nose.

"For what?"

"Looking after them when I wasn't there. So, thank you."

"I just did what any good friend would do."

"No, you didn't. You went above and beyond, mate."

"You're welcome."

My abrupt tenderness seemed to throw Alex off guard a bit, and he started going over his notes to detract from the tension. After a few seconds, he closed his notepad and placed it back on the side.

"So, to take off my therapist hat, you think Stephanie did those things to you?"

"I *know* she did."

"This is highly unprofessional, but it's remarkable you only knocked one tooth out," he smiled.

"True," I said with indecorous laughter.

"I think we should take a break there," he began as he put his notepad in a drawer, "make yourself at home; there's plenty of food in the fridge."

"Thanks for all this, Alex, seriously."

"You're welcome. If you need me, I'll be in the den making a few calls."

Alex left the room and quietly shut the door behind him, leaving me alone to think about what I had just told him. Although I had a perfect memory of what had happened, actually saying it out loud breathed more life into it than I initially realised it would. I always thought that day was just the product of boredom and a perverse mind, and it didn't go any deeper than that. Nevertheless, now that I was certain it was Stephanie's voice over the intercom, it seemed less like a twisted game and profoundly personal. I didn't wish to ruminate on it any longer. I had just released the painful memory out into the world, and I had no intention of welcoming it back in. There was a small television in the corner of the room, and when I spotted the remote, I turned it on to try and take my mind off things.

As I idly flicked through the channels, my heart sank when I spotted the photograph that had been featured in the morning paper, and it sunk even further when I realised there was a whole news segment devoted to it. I quickly turned the volume up on the remote and set it down beside me; I had caught it partway through the piece.

"We can only speculate on what horrors she has been through, Diane, as details about her imprisonment haven't been made public by the sheriff's office just yet," the reporter said.

"Thank you, Jim, and if you're just joining us on KAVG, we're giving you the latest on the sensational 'bride from the bunker' story, and we're about to go live from the victim's house with Javier Castillo. Javier, what's going on down there?" Diane announced before it cut to a live feed.

"Thanks, Diane," Javier began, "I'm here in Hammerdale, where this tragic story began ten years ago. In the aftermath of the vicious fight we saw last night, I have the other woman in the story with me right now, who doesn't want to be named for her own privacy."

As the camera dramatically panned out, my jaw dropped when I saw Stephanie sporting an empathy-inducing neck brace and preparing to speak as she looked directly into the camera. She had inexplicably gotten her tooth fixed and was almost smirking directly into the lens as if she knew I would be watching.

"Thank you, Javier," she beamed.

"So, you were at the other end of the beating last night. How did that come about?"

"Well, being her ex-boyfriend's new partner, there's obviously been some tension between us, but that being said, I have no idea what was going on in her mind last night. She just stormed into the house and pounced on me like a wild animal! It was a totally unprovoked attack!" she falsely exclaimed.

"Liar!" I shouted at the screen.

"A lot of our viewers will remember Nathaniel from our coverage of the disappearance a decade ago. Do you think Olivia expected him to wait for her?" Javier asked.

"I'm not sure, but I do know that jealousy makes people do some crazy things sometimes," she said with a shrug.

"From what little we've heard, she must have gone through terrible things. Don't you think she should be afforded some compassion and understanding for her erratic behaviour?"

"To be honest, Javier, I'm not sure how much I believe in her story. It seems a little far-fetched to me."

"How so?"

"If I know Olivia as well as I think I do, she faked the whole thing for attention. It was never publicised in the media, but she's well known for it."

"What the fuck?" I whispered.

"That is an astounding allegation. Do you have any evidence of this?" Javier responded.

"Nothing concrete, but then again, from what I've heard, there's no evidence she was ever in that bunker in the first place."

I was aggressively gripping my own thigh so forcefully that I could feel my fingernails digging into the skin. The purpose behind her interview wasn't to protect her own hide or throw law enforcement off the scent. As a matter of fact, she was thoroughly *enjoying* every minute of it. Deep down, I knew that she was trying to goad me into action once again, but even knowing that I was still reeling from utter disbelief when it changed to an explosive rage. I was terrified of making a television appearance, by accident or otherwise, yet she seemed to take to it like a duck to water. I didn't know what her devious plan was, but the one thing I was certain of was that she was two steps ahead of me in every direction. The sheer confidence she was exuding in her own barefaced lies allowed her to control the narrative, and I suddenly understood how Nathaniel had been so easily brainwashed by her.

"If you could say something to Olivia, what would it be?" Javier asked.

"Olivia, I forgive you, but you need to come clean to Nath, your daughter, and yourself. It just isn't healthy to keep lying about it," she stated directly to the camera.

"We've tried contacting her for comment multiple times. When do you think she will give an interview?"

"Get comfortable. You'll be waiting here a while," she said with a sickly sweet smirk.

The television abruptly turned off, and I realised that Alex had been standing behind me the whole time with the remote in his hand. As I tried to pluck it from him, he easily evaded my grasp and took a step back.

"Turn it back on," I ordered.

"No, you shouldn't be listening to that drivel. It isn't good for you," Alex calmly replied.

"Did you hear what she fucking said? That last line?"

"You'll be waiting here a while?"

"That is a verbatim quote that she said to me the first day I was captured."

"I know it's difficult, but you need to ignore it. She's just trying to goad you."

"What if she spews those lies out to Aurora, though? And worst of all, what if she falls for them? I could lose my daughter forever; I've barely got her back."

Alex knelt down in front of me with a sigh, grabbed both of my hands that were resting in my lap, and slowly leaned in empathetically. He looked into my eyes for a few seconds, just long enough for me to feel slightly uncomfortable, and then let go as he began to speak.

"I want you to know that I believe you," he softly said, "but you need to trust me."

"How can I? You just don't understand," I uttered.

"I understand better than you think," he said as he pulled his wallet out of his back pocket and took out a passport-sized photograph which he kept in his hand.

"She was going to be my wife," he said with a solemn smile as he quickly flashed the picture at me before pensively looking at it again.

"What happened to her?" I asked.

"Car accident," he began with a gloomy smile, "she lost control and ended up skidding through the barrier over North Ridge. It was almost seven years ago now, and there's not a single day that goes by that I don't miss her."

"I'm so sorry, Alex."

"I try not to get upset about it. She'd want me to remember the happy times."

"Is she the reason you do this?"

"Do what?"

"Therapy, the grief counselling, whatever this is."

"In a way, yes, I suppose. I learned first-hand how difficult it was to cope with something like loss, and I wanted to help others."

"Thanks," he wearily smiled, "here, this is her," he added before handing me the photograph.

It was a typical photo-booth print of Alex and his wife both smiling into the camera. They were clearly happy. The way they had their arms around each other reminded me of the beginning of my relationship with Nath.

"You both look happy," I remarked.

"We were. Nicole was everything to me."

"Nicole?" I whispered before returning to inspect the picture further, and as I held it closer to my eyes, it dawned on me that I had seen that woman before. In my shock, I immediately dropped it on the floor, let out a scream, and recoiled up the sofa as far as I could. Alex quickly retrieved it, looking incredibly puzzled by my knee-jerk reaction. Between my hysterical breaths, I managed to utter one sentence to him that magnified the look of confusion on his face tenfold.

"Nicole didn't die in a car accident," I declared without a shadow of a doubt.

20

THE SECOND

OLIVIA – 2017

Drip. Drip. Drip. It was slowly driving me clinically insane. Falling asleep in that place was already difficult enough, especially when Benjamin perpetually left the lights on, but the sound of water dropping tinnily onto the stainless-steel air vent tested my sanity to new levels. At first, the constant rhythm of the noise was so predictable that I even grew accustomed to it, but at the exact moment it became white noise, it would change in frequency or intensity, which used to startle me awake. I felt like I hadn't slept in days.

Despite my desperate efforts to drown out the impacts by placing my paper-thin pillow around my ears, I could still hear it; I came to think that the dripping had contaminated my very skull. In a mad haze, I noisily dragged the foldaway chair underneath it and tried banging on the vent to stop it, inexplicably hoping that if I struck it with enough force, the noise would somehow stop. At that point, I would have gladly forgone oxygen and happily blocked the vent up entirely if I had enjoyed some peace and quiet in return.

Since I played the game of truth or dare with Benjamin, life in the bunker had been relatively uneventful. Even though his intrusions into my little world had grown scarce, and his voice was always incredibly distorted, I noticed something had changed. I could tell that he wasn't deriving nearly as much pleasure out of my misery as he once was, and I started to feel like a chore. His show-and-tell sessions on the television were less frequent, the ominous threat of violence against me or my family had begun to fade, and I started to question his overall competence as a kidnapper. As sick and twisted as this whole endeavour of his was, it was almost amusing to me when I comprehended that, in a way, he was a creative as much me, and just like any act of creativity, it was propelled by the necessity for inspiration.

I knew exactly what his problem was.

He had *tormentor's block*.

Benjamin's psychological torture had peaked at the murder of two men in front of me and when he forced me to debase myself for his own pleasure. That's the problem with perpetual escalation: once you have done the worst things imaginable, where do you even go from there? I knew where: likely manufacturing a pathetic drip in the ventilation system so your victim couldn't get any sleep. He had gone from abject terror to minor annoyance, and when that dawned on me, I realised that the whole thing was smoke and mirrors, and I was far more in control of that situation than I initially thought.

"Oi!" I shouted. "Are you hearing this, Benny boy?"

It only took a few seconds before I heard the hiss and pop of the intercom connecting, and I smugly smiled.

"What are you talking about, Olivia?" he agitatedly said with a sigh.

"That dripping noise. Is that you?" I asked with a smile as I pointed to the vent.

"What dripping noise?"

"Water hitting the air vent. Is that your latest attempt to wind me up? It isn't working."

"It's not all about you, Olivia."

"Yeah, right," I started disbelievingly. "I have to say, it's low, even for you. What's the matter? Do you have some performance anxiety?"

"Excuse me?"

"Torturing me isn't getting it up for you anymore?" I laughed.

"You better shut your fucking mouth," he roared.

"How about you come down here and make me? If you're man enough," I coldly suggested.

"You'll regret—"

"Blah, blah, blah. We both know you aren't going to come down here because you're a fucking coward," I said matter-of-factly.

"Those two men buried in a shallow grave would disagree with you," he argued.

"Old news, pal. Why don't you just open the door and let me out of here? Your heart clearly isn't in this anymore."

"Shut up!" he snapped.

"Have I touched a nerve there?" I giggled.

The intercom clicked off, and eerily, the dripping noise became the only sound I could hear. The feeling of bravado continued, and as menacing as the silence was, I was satisfied that what I said was true, so I climbed back into bed with a renewed sense of victory and a beaming grin. Benjamin didn't want me dead and clearly wasn't going to do anything to my family either, for he would have done it by now if he had wanted to. Sure, I was trapped in that room, doomed to perpetual misery, but it didn't mean I couldn't enjoy myself when the opportunity came along and knocked at my door.

That feeling of triumph remained until I fell asleep from mental boredom rather than physical tiredness, only to be awakened some twenty minutes later by the sound of an engine rumbling overhead. My heart sank when I realised Benjamin had clearly called my bluff, and all my bluster quickly dissolved when I suddenly became aware that there was a very real possibility that he was coming to make good on his threats. My lack of imagination may have failed me earlier, but now it was running wild, and I began to mentally list all the horrific things he could do to me that would far surpass what he had already done. The engine fell silent, and then the dripping was accompanied by the metallic clunking of someone messing with the air vent above, and I got out of bed to stand underneath it. As quickly as it came, the panic dissolved, and I laughed so hard when I realised that he was only coming to fix the problem as I had demanded. I was cackling so loudly that it must have reverberated up the steel chute and was audible to Benjamin standing above.

"Coward!" I shouted.

The clunking stopped, and I waited underneath with bated breath, expecting some kind of response, but none came. Instead, a faint hissing sound began travelling down the vent, followed by a faint mist which brought the pungently sweet smell of solvents. I immediately recoiled from the vent and ran into the corner, grabbing a towel to place over my face in a futile attempt not to inhale any of the gas that was wafting down into the bunker. Nonetheless, it was already too late; my eyes were already beginning to water, and I rapidly fell unconscious seconds later.

When I groggily woke up, I was shaking uncontrollably. Such a terrible wave of nausea swept over me that I thought I was going to slip under again. Besides, I had a splitting headache whose intensity made the entire room spin around me. I fell forward from the chair that I had been propped up against and crawled on my hands and knees to reach one of the few bottles of water lying on the floor on the other side of the bunker, but to my surprise, all of them had been intentionally emptied out. As I was running my hands through the puddle they had been left in, the intercom kicked in, and I closed my eyes to prepare for what would happen next.

"Do I have your attention now, Olivia?" his voice furiously crackled.

"What happened?" I wearily asked.

"Watch," he ordered.

I hesitantly opened my eyes and turned my head towards the screen just as it came to life, but instead of the usual video footage of my family that I was expecting, it was black and white footage from the bunker's own CCTV camera. My reddened eyes were straining to focus on it, and I crawled a further few metres to get closer to the screen for a better look. The scanlines on the footage made it difficult to make out what it was, but when I spotted the woman in the film, stark naked and face down in the middle of the floor, sheer panic ripped through me. The surge of adrenaline made me bolt upright so as to step closer and desperately try to decipher who it was on screen and what was going on. It instantly occurred to me that the woman lying helpless on the ground could easily be me because I couldn't recollect anything after being knocked out by the gaseous mist descending from the vent.

The only movement perceptible made by the figure was the drowsy clawing at the concrete floor as she tried to drag herself away from something off-camera. My eyes darted around the frame, trying to spot what she was attempting to get away from, until, suddenly, the footage zoomed in to the back of the woman's head, and she stopped moving. As she turned around onto her back to show her face, I almost breathed a sigh of relief when I realised it wasn't me after all, but nonetheless, the truth was far more menacing: she was another victim.

I was immediately frozen on the spot, my eyes glued to the screen as I watched that poor woman writhing on the floor in unspeakable agony. I couldn't tell what was unfolding at first, but even though the footage was greyscale, I could tell that her lips were going blue. She began to desperately claw at her neck as she struggled to draw every breath, and the muted film did little to stop me imagining the airless rattle of her throat as she slowly suffocated. For a single poignant moment, her pained eyes locked directly with the camera, as if she somehow knew

I was witnessing it, and only then did I truly sense what genuine fear feels like.

The struggle suddenly stopped.

The camera zoomed out slightly and paused, preserving her excruciating expression of unadulterated suffering forever, and I dropped to my knees in front of it, frantically trying to decipher the exact spot where she lost her life. Instead of getting riled up or igniting some fire that would reinvigorate my burning desire for escape, my mind fell silent, and a calm wave of acceptance washed over me. I had been foolish to challenge Benjamin; he had ultimate power in that room, and although the snuff film I had been forced to watch was harrowing in its own right, it was even more terrifying when I understood it could be a window into my own future.

"He will wipe away every tear from their eyes, and death shall be no more, neither shall there be mourning, nor crying, nor pain anymore, for the former things have passed away," he solemnly recited.

"Who was she?" I quietly sobbed.

"You aren't special, Olivia. There were many before you, and there will be many after you," he softly announced.

"What was her name?"

"Nicole. She was like you in many ways. A real troublemaker."

"She didn't deserve to die like that," I numbly uttered.

"You don't know what she did, and she did plenty," he angrily shouted.

"Is that what you're going to do to me?" I fretfully asked.

I heard Benjamin sigh down the intercom and readjust the microphone he was talking into as I powerlessly stared into the CCTV camera.

"You once asked me why I did this to you, and if you'd like, I'll give you the answer."

"Why?" I whispered.

"Because you fucking deserve it."

The background noise of the intercom ceased, and I knew that the conversation was over. I distraughtly perched on the edge of my bed, still staring at the exact spot where Nicole had taken her last breath, knowing in my bones that I would eventually share the same resting place.

I was never getting out of there.

21

THE SPIKE

OLIVIA – 2024

Alex quickly placed Nicole's photograph on the armrest and tightly gripped my shoulders as he blankly stared into my eyes, desperate to find out how I knew her. Nevertheless, I was trapped in a trance, numbly gazing into space, and he began to shake me lightly, which still failed to snap me out of it. As his turmoil became unbearable, he began to well up in frustration and released my shoulders, sending me to crash back into the couch I was sitting on. How could I possibly even begin to explain what happened to his wife-to-be?

The untimely death of his fiancée seemed to have defined his life, and even though he was sure it was an accident, it was clear to see that he still blamed himself. If I were to have told him the truth there and then, that she had been likely tortured, asphyxiated, and then discarded like waste, it would have broken him beyond belief.

"What do you mean she didn't die in a car accident?" he frantically asked.

"She was in my bunker," I sullenly mumbled.

"Did you speak to her?"

"No. I didn't get a chance to."

Alex pulled a menacing expression, and I saw a flash of anger in his eyes, which actually scared me.

"Are you messing with me?"

"No, I promise I'm not messing with you."

"Then out with it. What happened to her?" he ordered with quiet fury.

"It was roughly seven years ago. Stephanie released some kind of gas into the ventilation system, and it knocked me unconscious. It must have been anaesthetic from her dental surgery."

"What's that got to do with Nicole?"

"I'm getting to it. When I woke up, they showed me footage of some other woman in the bunker. It was Nicole."

"What was she doing?"

"Dying," I fearfully uttered.

"How?"

"Oh, Alex. I don't think I can say it. I'm so sorry," I sobbed.

"Just tell me!" he shouted.

"They suffocated her," I announced abruptly.

My words cut into Alex deeply, and he immediately fell back onto the couch as he stared into space. I could see the whites of his knuckles and his fists shaking as the news slowly sunk in.

"I thought it happened before I was taken there. They must have moved me out of there temporarily or something. I had no idea you knew her. I'm so sorry," I frantically reasoned.

"No, that can't be true. I buried her," he murmured.

"She must have staged the crash to cover her tracks."

"No, it was an accident," he distraughtly whispered.

I rose from my seat and went over to comfort Alex, who barely moved a muscle when I started hugging him, and I could feel the tension of his body ragefully shaking against mine. I knew the feeling well. There wasn't a single combination of words out of millions that I could string together to pull him out of that state, so I just did what I desperately wanted someone to do for me. I remained silent, present, and waited for him to speak again.

I physically felt the pressure within Alex exceed the breaking point, and suddenly, he carelessly shoved me out of the way. He stormed over to his desk in the room, opened a drawer, and produced a small handgun, which he frantically stuffed in his waistband. I immediately jumped back to my feet to block the doorway, and as he stopped just short of me, I saw the rabid frenzy firing up in his eyes.

"Get out of the way," he ordered.

"Where are you off to?"

"I'm going to fucking kill her."

"Alex, no."

"Olivia, get out of the way," he insistently repeated.

"You were right. We have to play this out carefully."

"If you're telling me that Stephanie killed my Nicole, I have to do this."

"She did. But this isn't what justice should look like. She deserves to rot in hell for what she's done."

"I loved my Nicole, though," Alex sobbed.

"I know you did, and she'll pay for everything she's done, I promise, but you can't take the law into your own hands unless you want to end up paying too."

I instinctually felt his resolve waver.

"Okay," he shakily agreed.

"Give me the gun," I softly instructed.

I cautiously removed the pistol from his quaking palm, and I gingerly checked the safety before calmly putting it back in his desk drawer. Part of me immediately regretted stopping him from leaving the room because the thought of siccing him on Stephanie was an attractive one, but everything I said was right. She didn't deserve a quick ending to her story. She needed to inhabit the life she forced on me and Nicole. As disgustingly self-absorbed as it was, I realised that it gave him the incentive he needed to bring her to justice, and I finally had someone on my side I could count on to help me expose her for what she really was. Alex, clearly shaken by my admissions, joined me at the desk, erratically poured himself a glass of whisky from the crystal decanter he kept there, downed it in one gulp, and then poured us both one.

"We need to speak to Daniels," I declared before knocking back the amber liquid.

"I'll give him a call," Alex said after swallowing another measure, "we need to tell Nathaniel too."

"No," I dismissed, "he is too close to her to believe us; I learned that the hard way. We need proof."

"What proof? There isn't a shred of evidence."

"All that footage she showed me doesn't just disappear. It must have been transmitted somewhere."

"Do you think there are tapes?"

"Definitely. I bet the psycho even kept them so she could watch it back later to satisfy her sadistic pleasure."

"Maybe they are at the house?"

"No. She isn't that stupid."

"Her office in Sacramento?"

"She was always close to the bunker. At the very most, she was a twenty-minute drive away. Sacramento's too far."

We were interrupted by the sound of the doorbell, and I followed Alex through the hall so he could answer it. He opened the door to find Nathaniel standing there, initially looking quite agitated. However, once Nath saw us both with empty whiskey glasses in hand, he looked more discombobulated than anything else.

"What's going on here then?" he asked.

"I've finally started therapy," I proclaimed with a joyous raise of my glass.

"Can I have a word, Al?" he asked.

"What's up?" Alex answered.

"It's Aurora," Nath mumbled.

"What's wrong with her?" I frantically asked as I pushed past Alex.

"She's missing again."

"Again?"

"I told you: she does this, and it's nothing to worry about. I just wondered if you'd seen her?"

"Not since last night," Alex replied.

"We need to find her, especially with that psychopath running around," I quietly reminded him.

"You're the fucking psycho!" Nath exclaimed as he pointed.

"I'm sorry, I just saw red. I admit I overreacted."

"*Overreacted?*" he mockingly boomed. "You knocked one of her teeth out over a cheap necklace. Who knows how far you would have gone if you hadn't been stopped."

"She's guilty, Nath. She did this to us."

"You're out of your God-damned mind. She had nothing to do with it."

"How did you let Aurora go missing again?" I scorned.

"I was a little preoccupied with cleaning up after you!"

"Guys, can you please have your domestic later? On your own time? We need to focus and find Aurora. Agreed?" Alex shouted as he came in between us.

"You're right," I mumbled.

"Fine by me," Nath uttered.

"We need to check all the usual suspects: school, friend's houses, the skatepark, and probably the mall," Alex explained.

"School already called me. She hasn't been there all day," Nath mumbled.

"Okay, good. I'll drive up to the mall," Alex announced.

"I'll take the skatepark. It's within easy walking distance," I said.

"No, I'll take the skatepark," Nath disputed.

"Well, I honestly don't know who her fucking friends are, Nath. Don't you think it would be better if you took that one?" I condescendingly remarked.

"Do what you want. You will anyway," Nath muttered.

"Okay, it's settled. Call if you see her," Alex said as he grabbed his keys.

I jadedly smiled at Alex as I walked past him, totally blanking Nathaniel, and began making my way towards the skatepark. I kept thinking about Nathaniel's expression when he called me a psycho, and I could tell that he definitely meant it. As a matter of fact, psychopaths are unaware they are psychopaths. In my case, though, I was fully aware that there was a screw loose somewhere in my head, but I also understood that it wasn't entirely my fault, and even if he had only spent a week in my shoes, he would have crawled out of that hole with some mental health problems, too.

Even back before I was taken, the skatepark had a bit of a reputation for alluring unsavoury characters to it. There really wasn't much to do in sleepy Hammerdale for anyone, let alone the younger end of the spectrum. Unlike Nathaniel, I didn't overtly have a problem with Aurora smoking a bit of pot every once in a while, as long as it didn't get in the way of her studies. I appreciated the appeal, and in my youth, I would often take myself away from my overbearing family for a few hours just to let my hair down. I barely had anything to contend with when I was younger, especially not the kind of pressure that Aurora had on her shoulders, and I couldn't imagine how she even dealt with it day in and day out.

"Psst," I heard as I stopped dead, spinning my head around to locate who was trying to get my attention.

"Do you really think she wants to see you? After what you did?" Benjamin's twisted voice whispered behind me.

With a heavy sigh, I tried to ignore it and carried on walking in silence.

"She saw you beat up her stepmother like you were a feral animal. You're the last person she wants to see," he goaded.

"Not now. I'm busy," I dismissively said under my breath as I jarringly shook my head.

"Hey! I'm just looking out for you. I don't want you to get upset when she tells you to get lost. I know how fragile you are."

"Listen, you piece of—" I started, but quickly paused as I passed a stranger in the street with a feigned smile in their direction. "You're just in my head. You aren't real."

"Save yourself the embarrassment, turn back and come home."

"Get fucked, Benjamin," I uttered as I eventually arrived at the skatepark. His voice was immediately silenced when I spotted a group of moody teenagers who appeared to be of the same ilk as Aurora, and I breathed a sigh of relief. I smiled to myself when I spotted my daughter messing around on a skateboard, which left me feeling quite smug to be the one who found her. After realising that she was safe, I did debate whether to watch her from a distance or stereotypically stride over to where she was and demand answers, but when I saw one of the older kids hand her a joint, I felt compelled to intervene. On my approach, the teens noticed me walking towards Aurora and instinctively formed a circle around my daughter, who didn't move an inch.

"Hey! It's that fighting chick from the news!" one of the kids with ludicrously spiky hair blurted out to the group.

"What are you doing here?" Aurora disdainfully asked from the back of the group.

"School called, so I'm just checking to see if you're okay," I said.

"I was until you showed up," she uttered with palpable contempt.

"Wait, that crazy bitch from the news is your mom?" spiky hair asked with raucous laughter.

"Yes, that's me," I sarcastically smiled, "are you coming home or not?"

"I'm not going anywhere with you."

"Why not?"

"Because you're a lunatic. Everyone has seen on the news what you did. So embarrassing."

"You don't know her."

"I know her better than you do. Unlike you, she was there for me."

"Aurora, come on, we can talk about this after."

"No chance."

The rest of the teenagers started to threateningly crowd around me, and I held my ground until they were so close to me that I could taste the marijuana on their breath.

"She said no, lady. Get out of here," spiky hair threatened.

"You tell her, Spike," another kid goaded.

"Wait, *Spike*?" I heartily mocked. "Is that because of the hair? Very original."

Spike got so close that his forehead was almost on mine, and even though he was still a child, I was feeling incredibly intimidated, but I was eager not to let it show.

"Do it, kid. See what happens."

"Olivia, please just go!" Aurora shouted.

"I'm your mum. You can't talk to me like that," I scorned.

"No, you aren't. You're that crazy bitch from the news."

The look in my daughter's eyes summed up everything that I was worried about when I came home. She was looking at me like everybody else did, like I was insane. I hesitantly opened my mouth to speak, not having a single clue what to say, but no sound came out, and I backed away from the mob, losing my footing next to one of the ramps. The gaggle of intimidating teenagers burst into a chorus of laughter, and as the tears started forming in my eyes, I slowly made my way out of the skatepark with my tail between my legs.

Maybe she was right about me being crazy. The footage shown on every news channel definitely corroborated that claim. I tried to put myself in her shoes, and if that had happened to me when I was younger, I would have died from embarrassment. It was totally unintentional, but no matter what I tried to do, I was still wrecking her life from every angle. I just wanted to form a bond with her or a connection, even as friends, if a maternal one was out of the question. Nevertheless, our lives had diverged so much at that point that it was literally impossible to see how we would ever get there.

When everyone around you begins to vehemently claim you are insane, you start to believe it. Aurora, Nath, Stephanie, and even Sherrif Daniels all thought it. As much as Alex's professionalism hid it, I saw the accusatory look in his eyes too.

They all thought I was mad.

I started to agree with them.

22

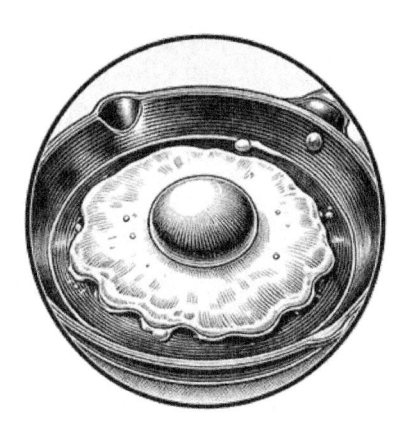

THE EGG

OLIVIA – 2019

It was just another day in the bunker, indiscernible from the days, weeks and months before it, and as usual, I was spending my morning - or at least I thought it was morning - frying a few eggs for my breakfast. It was usually a mindless task, but there was something in the way that the egg was cooking in the pan that immediately captured my undivided attention, and what I witnessed made all the hairs on the back of my neck stand promptly on end.

I wasn't sure whether it was the flawlessly centred position of the yolk floating on the white, the aesthetically pleasing degree of browning along the egg's edge, or the immaculately cooked yolk that glimmered in the overhead fluorescent lighting that sparked the feeling, but it was clearly visible. I felt as if I had witnessed a divine miracle, and I let out a single manic laugh as I moved my face so close to the pan that the spitting oil was burning my skin. In the five years I had spent in that place, I had never seen something so unquestionably extraordinary, and I couldn't believe it was created by my hands.

"It's perfect, it's perfect," I quietly repeated on a loop as I began pacing the room, not taking my eyes off the spectacle for a second.

I was suddenly overtaken by a frantic need to document this momentous occasion, and I rifled through the untidy stacks of notes and half-written books to find a scrap piece of paper to sketch what I had seen. I quickly drew what I thought was a precise likeness of my breakfast, carefully removed it from the oil with a spatula, and delicately placed it on the cleanest plate I had. I took a step back in awe of what I had produced and almost had tears in my eyes when I sat back on the bed to catch my breath.

"Are you there? You have to see this!" I shouted.

My keeper remained silent.

When I watched Nicole lose her life in that bunker, I accepted my fate, and suddenly, everything became much easier. It was only when I let go of any ridiculous notion of escape that I finally realised I wasn't a prisoner at all, far from it. Benjamin only ever locked me in here to keep me safe from the outside world. My faceless guardian lovingly provided me with everything I would ever need, and all he asked for in return was a little obedience and some faith. Even though he hadn't uttered a word to me since Nicole, I knew that deep down, he still cared about me, and the weekly food drops proved it. To my delight, he even started providing me with writing materials in the supply runs as a special treat for being so well-behaved, and for the first time since I had been imprisoned there, I felt somewhat content. My only problem was his silence and every time I heard Benjamin in the airlock, I would slam my fists in the door while begging him to talk to me again. Nonetheless, I understood that his reserve was a punishment that he meted out for my insubordination and a devious way of letting me know that I had to complete my penance.

For the longest time, I misguidedly convinced myself that he was this menacing aggressor that should be feared and a huge threat to me, but finally, everything made sense. All the so-called abhorrent acts he committed were so easily explained away when I realised that he truly cared about me, and he obviously carried out all of them for my own good.

Benjamin killed the two hillbillies that tried abducting me from my home, and I was so grateful that he did, as who knows what those rednecks would have done to me had they succeeded in their attempt to rescue me. Looking back, I knew that my guardian angel was forced to end their lives to defend mine, and I wouldn't still be here if he hadn't reacted the way he did. I thought the silly game of truth or dare was a gross act of humiliation, and I was plagued by nightmares of it for a while, but once I realised that my benevolent warden's intentions were undeniably good, I saw it for what it was. Benjamin just wanted a strong commitment from me and to know that I was ready to bear all to him and accept his love with all my heart. I was so glad that I eventually saw the light. I struggled to justify Nicole's death, and although it was incredibly tragic, I understood that my caretaker wasn't infallible, and who was I to question his motives?

As I continued to ponder every altruistic thing he had done for me, the more ludicrous I felt thinking a fried egg would impress him enough to welcome me back into his embrace. He had selflessly provided me with so many gifts, and with my limited resources, I just wanted to give something back and naively hoped it was enough for him to break his vow of silence. After I so flagrantly defiled his trust, I needed to prove to him I was worthy of his affection and apologise for each of my missteps, but at that point I no longer knew if he was still listening.

I couldn't take the silence; I stumbled over to the centre of the room, submissively got down on my hands and knees, and began hysterically weeping. I must have remained in that position for at least ten minutes, rocking backwards and forwards, anxiously hoping it would be the day he finally noticed me again.

"Please, just talk to me," I sobbed.

Instead of a reply, a deafening, high-pitched siren started ringing, and as I lifted my head up to locate the source, I noticed I had left the frying pan on the stove. The oil had begun smouldering, which set off the smoke alarm. As the room filled with a cloud of thick smog, my instant reaction was to go and take it off the ring, but instead, I restrained myself and silently observed it as the oil set ablaze. I could barely hear the intercom kick in over the sound of the alarm, although when I did, the relief washed over me, and I respectfully rose to my feet to greet him.

"Olivia, take it off the ring," Benjamin frantically shouted.

"You're back! You haven't spoken for months," I enthused.

"Take it off the ring! You're going to burn the whole place down," he sternly ordered.

"Not until you promise you've forgiven me for what I did," I shouted defiantly.

"For Christ's sake, I forgive you. Just put the fire out."

In a state of total euphoria, I hastily sprinted over to the hob and immediately turned the ring off. The flames continued to rise, so I calmly moistened a cloth to suffocate the blaze with it. As soon as the inferno was quelled, I returned to the spot in the middle of the room, the lingering fumes still making me choke, and I proceeded to cough in between the self-deprecating laughs.

"That was a close one!" I fatuously mused.

Before he replied, I heard the doors unlock behind me, and I anxiously looked over my shoulder to catch a glimpse of him behind me.

"Can I trust you, Olivia?" he asked.

"Of course!" I quickly replied in between coughs.

"Open the doors then. We need to air the place out."

"Okay," I replied as I opened both the doors, and for the first time since I was imprisoned there, I witnessed the steps leading up to my freedom.

"Come and sit down," he softly suggested.

I complied, restlessly sitting down on the chair, and as my knees were involuntarily bouncing, I couldn't take my eyes off the exit.

"Have you missed our little chats?" he gently asked.

"Yes. So much. See! I've learned my lesson," I replied.

"What lesson is that?"

"I won't try and escape again. In fact, I think I quite like it here. And I appreciate everything you do for me."

"If we confess our sins, he is faithful and just and will forgive us our sins and purify us from all unrighteousness," he poignantly recited.

"That's beautiful," I gushed as I sat down cross-legged. "Can you read some more?" I asked.

Everything was right in the world again. I could listen to his teachings until the end of time and not get bored with them. Benjamin continued to read his favourite passages from the Bible for what felt like hours, and I hung onto his every word. The steady draught brought fresh air into the bunker for the first time in years. I was overcome with a sense of peace, and all my concerns dissolved into nothing.

"Hey, can we play a game?" I gingerly asked.

23

THE SANDWICH

OLIVIA — 2024

When I arrived back at Alex's home, the absence of a vehicle in the driveway told me he hadn't returned from the mall yet. I pulled out the old phone that I borrowed from Nath and tried calling Alex, but he didn't answer. In desperation, I walked through the side gate, hoping that he had left a door open so I could go inside and depressively wallow in defeat about my encounter with Aurora, but much to my annoyance, everything was locked up tight. Begrudgingly and with a heavy sigh, I tried dialling Nathaniel, who quickly answered the phone in a frenzy.

"Have you found her?" he asked frantically.

"Yes. She was at the skatepark," I said.

"That's a relief."

"She has fallen in with a really strange crowd. That 'Spike' character is a menace,"

"That's teenagers for you. At least we know where she is, so we can call off the dogs. She wasn't smoking again, was she?"

"No," I lied, "just messing around on a skateboard."

"Thank God. Maybe rehab finally worked this time. Thanks for finding her; I'll have a word with her when she gets home."

A few seconds of awkward silence followed, and I could tell the desperate urge I had to clear the air was mirrored by him. We sighed at the exact same time and spoke over each other, leading us both to stop talking again.

"Go on, what were you going to say?" Nathaniel asked.

"I want to apologise. Can we meet?"

"I suppose we should. I'm just about to head to my studio to finish up a few bits before my next show. I can meet you there if you'd like?"

"Sounds good. Text me the address."

"Will do," Nath said before hanging up.

Shortly after the message had popped up on my phone screen, I started the long trek towards Main Street to find his studio. Due to the tremendous amount of guilt that I was carrying around with me, I felt out of sorts, and my feet were rather slothful and heavy on my way there. I had to keep reminding myself that Nath and Aurora were the true innocents in this situation, and despite the fact that they had both done things to upset me since my return, the rational side of me could fully comprehend why. I make no bones about it, but what happened to me was horrific. Nevertheless, I was becoming increasingly aware that I was using it as an excuse for my own erratic behaviour, and I needed to start taking responsibility for my own words and actions.

If Nathaniel hadn't given me the address of his studio, I never would have found it. It was on the top floor of a nondescript building, shared with multiple other businesses and offices. I strained my eyes to see all the handwritten names on all the intercom buttons until I saw Nath's name at the top and held onto it. The speaker crackled and popped as Nathaniel answered the call.

"Come up, Liv," he uttered as the door buzzed.

To the dismay of my lethargic legs, the lift was out of order, so I hiked up the steps to reach the studio on the top floor. When the endless stairs relented, I was confronted with a single door sporting a small enamel paintbrush nailed to it. I knocked, but he didn't come to greet me, so I gingerly tried the handle and found the door unlocked.

"Hello?" I searchingly shouted as I tip-toed through what looked like a small storeroom filled with large canvases that were packaged up and ready to be shipped. As I slowly made my way through them, I detected the distant scraping of paint brushes against the canvas, and I was immediately thrown back into a state of nostalgia. I quietly went through the next door and spotted him inside, where he was, as usual, totally engrossed in his craft.

It reminded me of the early days when I would cautiously creep into our makeshift home studio to bring him a coffee, not wanting to distract him from his work. He was useless at talking about his feelings, and after a few years of confusion on my part, I realised that painting was how he really communicated his emotions. Back when we first moved to California, the subjects of his paintings were largely happy ones, so warm and colourful they made me instantly smile, but if his latest work was anything to go by, he was in as dark a place as I was. The impassioned oil painting that he was currently working on was dominated by furious reds on top of depressive blacks, and instead of delicately applying the paint with each stroke, he was almost throwing it against the canvas haphazardly. I remained at the doorway for a few minutes, just watching his chaotic yet artistic elegance unfold, until I produced a small cough to get his attention, and he clumsily and expressionlessly turned around to greet me.

"Sorry, I didn't hear you come in," he said.

"It's good," I remarked, pointing at the abstract canvas.

"Thanks."

"What does it mean?"

"What does any of it mean?" he facetiously asked.

"It looks angry. And dark."

"It does indeed," he pensively agreed as he glanced at the painting, "give me five. I just need to get washed up."

As he left the room, I slowly made my way over to the domineering painting he had left me alone with, which is when I saw the others around the corner. Ten oil paintings were proudly hung on the walls, each more harrowing and enraged than the last, all depicting the same silhouetted figure: me. The year they were painted was scrawled in the bottom corners in minute writing, and I quickly realised that he must have painted one for every year that I was missing. As I got closer to the first in the series, I realised he had almost imperceptibly written the word 'hope' over and over again in a slightly darker paint than the background, but as I moved along the series, the words got even fainter, and by the tenth, I could barely make them out.

"What do you think?" Nath asked behind me, wiping his hands on a towel.

"Is it me?" I asked as I turned to him.

He solemnly nodded.

"Why, though?" I mumbled as I turned back to view the paintings again.

"I was in pain, and I missed you. It made me feel a little bit better pouring it all out onto the canvas."

"I missed you too," I uttered as I touched the canvas with my fingertips.

"Listen, Liv, I'm sorry. I know you've been through hell, and I should be more understanding," he softly explained as he placed his hand on my shoulder.

"No, I'm sorry. You don't need to worry about me."

"It's just all this shit with Stephanie, it's only getting worse."

"You will be pleased to know that I'm having second thoughts about her anyway."

"How so?"

"I don't know. Maybe I was wrong about her. I still think she's not right in the head, but I admit that, perhaps, she isn't capable of what I accused her of."

Nath remained silent as I glanced back at the paintings behind me, and I realised that some of them were finished long after he was lured by Stephanie's charms in the first place. I looked back at him and saw the suggestion of tears forming in his eyes, and I came to a realisation with an earnest smile. He still had feelings for me. Over the ten years that I had been ripped away from him, the connection between us may have been twisted and warped, but it was still there, lying dormant beneath the surface and just waiting for the right moment to spring back into life.

"Do you still love me?" I tearfully asked.

Just as I could see his lips parting to respond, we both heard the excruciatingly piercing sound of the intercom buzzing, whereupon we both looked at the screen only to see that Stephanie was standing outside.

"Well, that was bad timing," I uncomfortably joked, "there's no fire exit I can slip out of, is there?"

"Unfortunately, not," he began, "she's probably bringing me lunch. She's bound to get pissed if she sees you here with me."

"Just keep her at the front door. I'll wait here and slip out when you've both gone."

"You don't have to do that, Liv."

"Honestly, I just haven't got the energy to deal with her shenanigans today. It's more for my own sake than yours, really."

"No," he firmly said as he pushed the button to let her up, "we aren't doing anything wrong."

"Hey, it's your funeral, not mine," I cynically whispered.

We both walked to the entrance and awkwardly stood there on tenterhooks as we waited for Stephanie to stride into the room. Part of me was almost excited to witness her reaction when she saw us both alone in there, and the other part would rather have jumped out of the window than have to suffer it. The door opened, and Stephanie nonchalantly sauntered in, casually holding a brown paper bag of takeout with a beaming smile. She looked as if she was going on a hot date judging by the floral summer dress she was wearing, and she was no longer using the melodramatic neck brace I saw her in on the news that day. We made eye contact, and rather perplexingly, she just warmly smiled in my direction. Everything about her made my skin crawl.

"Hey, you!" she beamed at Nathaniel as she amorously kissed him on the lips.

"Hi," Nathaniel started, "I can explain, Olivia was only here because Aurora was—"

"Missing again. I know," she smiled back.

"I was just leaving, actually," I dryly announced.

"So soon? Please, take a seat," she chirpily offered.

"What? No, I'm fine, thank you."

"I told you to take a fucking seat, Olivia," she sinisterly ordered.

"Stephanie, nothing was going on, I swear," Nath added.

"Shush," Stephanie said to him with her finger on her lips, "I'm speaking to her."

"Let's cut the bullshit. If it makes you feel any better, I hate myself for hitting you the other night. So, I'm sorry, okay?" I firmly stated.

"Oh, Olivia, that didn't sound very sincere at all! What do you think, Nath? Should I accept her crappy apology?"

"Can we just talk about this later?" Nath wearily pleaded.

"No!" she scornfully shouted. "I want to hear her give me a genuine apology, or neither of us is leaving this room."

"Get over yourself," I remarked.

"Go on then. How long has this been going on?" she antagonistically asked.

"What are you talking about?" Nath meekly requested.

"You and her. The day she got back? A few days later?"

"Nothing's going on, you mad bitch," I interrupted.

"Quiet, darling. The adults are speaking."

"Nothing is going on. I swear," Nath repeated.

"Likely story. So why is she visiting you at work and looking all flustered when I came in?"

"Like I said, Aurora was missing, and she came by to tell me she found her."

"Does she not have a phone?" she mockingly questioned.

"Yes," Nath defeatedly responded.

"I tell you what, Nath," she began as she took out a sandwich from the bag, "if you tell her that it's over between you two, she should leave you alone, and there's no chance you will ever get back together, I'll forget all about this."

"You are demented," I uttered under my breath.

"Nath?" she expectantly prompted.

"I…" Nath stuttered.

"Nathaniel?" she sternly warned.

"No."

I sniggeringly tried to conceal the victorious grin emerging across my face, but it was far too powerful to quell.

"What?" she gasped.

"No, I won't say that. What's more, we should push back the wedding until this whole mess is sorted out. It isn't the right time."

"Are you seriously picking her over me?" she bellowed.

"You've been constantly whispering in my ear since Olivia came back, and I just need some time to fucking think for myself! I understand you feel threatened, but stop trying to control my every waking moment for once."

"Cut ties with her right now, or I'm walking out of here, and I'm never coming back," Stephanie warned.

"I told you, Nath, she's a sociopath," I interjected.

"And you!" he exclaimed as he pointed at me. "Don't think I don't know what you're trying to do by coming here. I know you want to pick up where we left off, but it isn't as simple as that, clearly."

"Come on, Nath, let's go home and talk about this," Stephanie persuasively swooned as she delicately twirled her hair with a single finger.

"Jesus. I think I'm going to be sick," I perkily announced.

"You know what?" he began with a single cynical laugh, "work it out between you two because you're as bad as each other if you ask me."

Nath then proceeded to storm out of the studio and slam the door behind him, leaving me alone in a frantic attempt to disguise the smug satisfaction plainly imprinted on my face. His dumbfounded fiancée, who was gripping her sandwich so hard that the filling had started to spill from the sides, was literally shaking with rage, and I wondered if she had seen what I did in Nath's eyes when he defied her. The dynamic had changed; the tables had turned in my favour, and suddenly, I didn't feel so downtrodden about the whole mess. I leaned over and grabbed the second sandwich from the bag, and as I unwrapped it, Stephanie contemptuously stared at me with pure venom as I took a boorish bite. I remember thinking it was ironic that I witnessed the start of their relationship; it was only fitting that I would see the end.

"Well," I began between obnoxious chews, "this is awkward."

24

THE VISITOR

OLIVIA – 2020

It only took me six torturous years to finally realise it, but my life was actually pretty good. Ever since my defiant eyes were opened, I began following the rules to the letter, and Benjamin began treating me fairly in return. Even the perpetual monotony of the place had faded, and instead of obsessing over escape or hatching schemes, I spent all day doing what I loved most: writing. In the past year alone, I handwrote dozens of manuscripts, and although I wasn't sure if anybody would ever read them, the stacks of literature on the racking were a pleasure to behold and made my heart swell with pride. I did leave the odd few chapters sitting in the airlock in the hope that Benjamin might care to read them, but he never mentioned them.

To feel closer to my estranged fiancé, I had also taken to sketching, and although I couldn't measure up to him, I was enjoying that, too. Nath always told me that if I practised, I would get better, and with nothing but endless time on my hands, my artistic progress was evident throughout all the doodles that I had used to crudely decorate my cell. I only ever drew him or Aurora, as it was my way of keeping their memory alive, and as cooky as it sounds, it was nice to have some familiar company.

Obeying my captor's decrees had other perks, too. I was just putting the final touches on my latest sketch, with the sweet fragrance of autumnal pine wafting through the bunker because Benjamin started to allow me to have the door open for fifteen minutes every day. The aromas had inspired me, and I was trying to recreate the memory of a hike that I took with Nathaniel and Aurora before I was taken. We had impulsively gone for a beautiful stroll beginning at South Grove trailhead, and I remembered it as the epitome of what my family life used to be like. To her horror, Aurora had her first wobbly tooth that day, and on the winding trail, she lost her footing, which knocked it out. Nath and I were worried she would be distraught, but instead, she was entirely proud of herself. Just as I was shading in the gap between my daughter's teeth, my overzealous hand slipped, and the lead of the pencil tore through the paper.

"Fucking hell," I grumbled.

"What's the matter, Olivia?" Benjamin gently asked over the intercom.

"I've ripped the paper by accident. This one was perfect."

"You can always draw another," he softly reassured.

"Maybe tomorrow," I uttered as I began to tidy the sprawling art supplies away.

"Good. Are you ready for today's broadcast?" he asked.

"Oh, yes, please!" I enthused as I pulled a chair over to the television.

"You better brace yourself. This is a big one, and I'm sure you're just going to love it!" he heartily gushed.

"Is it Aurora? She hasn't brought a boyfriend home, has she? Did she get her prom dress?"

"No, it's better than that. Did you save the bag of popcorn from the food drop when I asked you?"

"Yes, I think so," I contemplated.

"Grab a bowl."

I dutifully rose from my chair, poured the popped kernels into a plastic bowl, and submissively took my seat again. I realised that, given my circumstances, it was a privilege to watch them and in no way a punishment. At first, my perception of these little presentations was that it was psychological torture, but after six years of watching them, it was more akin to catching up on your favourite soap opera. In my head, I had instinctually disconnected the beloved characters on the screen from the living members of my family, and each week, I patiently waited for the next instalment.

"Ladies and gentlemen, quiet please, and remain seated for our feature presentation!" he dramatically announced.

"Benjamin, that gave me the chills!" I excitedly effused.

I shuffled in my chair to get comfortable and grabbed a fistful of popcorn as the television slowly came to life. I had gotten used to the shaky, long-lensed footage that he showed me, and usually, it was just video taken from outside our home, but this episode began on Main Street. Although it wasn't entirely clear, I could still spot businesses there that existed before I was taken, and I strained my eyes to make out the name of the restaurant the footage featured.

"Is that *Amore al dente* in town?" I asked.

"No. Regrettably, it got taken over a while back."

"That's a shame. I loved that place. The fettuccine alfredo was out of this world," I remarked.

"Shush, keep watching, you're going to miss it."

The camera made its way across the road and zoomed in through the window to a table at the back of the restaurant. The smile on my face widened when I spotted Aurora happily tucking into a massive pizza without hesitation and Nathaniel jovially swirling his spaghetti with his fork. They were both uncontrollably laughing and joking in between bites, and it warmed the cockles of my heart to see them enjoying themselves. I leaned in to get a better look at them and grabbed another helping of the sweetened popcorn on my lap.

"They look so happy," I tearfully mused.

"They are."

"This place looks fancy. Are they celebrating something?" I asked in a whisper.

"Just watch," Benjamin dryly instructed.

Nathaniel spotted someone walking towards him off the frame, placed his fork down, and shot them a beaming grin. Aurora briefly looked up at them before devotedly continuing to devour the remains of the pizza still in front of her. I was left thinking who it might be for a few moments, and I tilted my head as if it would somehow allow me to see around the corner of the video. Unexpectedly, a slender blonde woman seated herself at the table and twirled her hair with a single finger as Nathaniel warmly spoke to her across it.

It was a date.

The smile started to fade from my face when I realised what I was watching, and as the television abruptly turned itself off, leaving me staring back at the reflection in the glass, I suddenly wasn't hungry for popcorn anymore.

"So, he's moved on," I meekly announced.

"He has, and oh boy, what a true stunner she is! Aren't they just so cute together?" Benjamin exclaimed.

"I'm happy for him," I firmly stated.

"You should be! He finally has some help with that troublesome daughter of yours, and his new flame is certainly an upgrade, don't you think?"

"Like I said, I'm happy for him," I agitatedly repeated.

"Are you really, though?"

"Of course. Why wouldn't I be?" I lied as I readjusted my posture and insincerely regained my smile.

"I wasn't sure if you were ready to see this, but I'm so pleased you are taking the moral high ground on this, I really am," he said almost proudly.

"He's well within his rights. I've chosen a new life here, and it's only fair he can do the same."

"That's a fantastic outlook, Liv. Tell me, do you want to see more?"

I paused for a moment.

"Sure," I uttered with false sincerity.

"Well then, you might want to hold onto that positive mental attitude for this next clip," he ominously suggested.

The television fired up once again, and it began with the footage I was most used to: amateurish videography of our house. The camera creepily hovered through our side gate, slowly made its way around the house and pushed the lens up against the window of our old bedroom. The shot had fortuitously just been lined up in time to catch a glimpse of the same exquisite woman as before leaving the en suite bathroom, dressed in nothing but striking black lingerie.

As the stranger pounced on an excited Nathaniel, who was breathlessly waiting on the bed, it didn't take a fortune-teller to know what I was about to see. She whipped the duvet cover from the bed, exposing his naked body, and jumped on top of it as she passionately dragged her long, black fingernails from his neck and down his chest. When she passionately lunged at him, and I could see the back of her head bobbing from side to side as she stuck her tongue down his throat, I turned my head away. I could already feel the handful of popcorn nauseatingly travelling back up into my throat, and I couldn't bear to witness a second more.

"Oh, Olivia, is this upsetting you? I promise you that it wasn't my intention," Benjamin empathetically asked.

"No, I'm not upset. I just don't want to watch that happen, thank you," I sobbed quietly.

"Maybe you can hear it."

Benjamin remotely turned the volume up on the television, and for the first time in six years, I heard the familiar sound of Nathaniel's voice.

"You look incredible," he heatedly babbled.

"Nath, I can't tell you how long I've wanted to do this," the woman sultrily explained.

"Turn it off, please," I uttered.

"What was that? Speak up, I didn't hear you," Benjamin tauntingly asked as he turned the volume up higher.

"Turn it off," I firmly said.

"One more time?" he teased.

"Turn it off!" I screamed as I put my hands over my ears.

The television immediately turned off, and I gingerly removed my hands from my ears. I could hear Benjamin's stifled laughter through the intercom as I woefully looked up at the camera that was still pointing directly at me.

"Everyone who looks at a woman with lustful intent has already committed adultery with her in his heart," he recited.

"How long has it been going on?" I asked.

"About six months," he laughed.

"Who is she?"

"None of your concern."

Truthfully, I didn't know how to feel about it. I told myself that I had accepted the predicament that I was in, but that being said, that acceptance was only palatable because I thought my family were waiting for me on the other side of it. What Benjamin had just laughingly subjected me to was needlessly cruel, and for the first time in a while, I began to question his motives once again. It started small, a glimmer of scepticism, which quickly snowballed into full-blown distrust, and suddenly, I saw the past year for what it was: another disturbing game. He wasn't my guardian angel but a fallen one, and he had ground me down until I was this pathetic and malleable creature, only existing for his twisted amusement.

As the embarrassment of my wilful obedience in the past year had left an increasingly sour taste in my mouth, I was driven by the dire need for retribution and vengeance, and I rebelliously tossed the bowl on the floor. As the contents spilt out onto the concrete, it ominously rolled towards the entrance and then struck the open door with a metallic clang. Benjamin must have seen the bulb light up in my head and remained uncharacteristically silent as I slowly turned back to the CCTV camera trained on my face.

"Now, now, Olivia. Don't do anything rash," he said with a tut.

"I could just walk out of here right now, and you wouldn't be able to stop me," I uttered.

"Think about how far you've come. You would be throwing all that away."

"You got in my head and *made* me into this person. I didn't choose it. Or any of this," I frantically explained.

"Your family have moved on. What's even left for you out there? Nothing, that's what," he disdainfully stated.

"They moved on whilst you had me doing arts and fucking crafts in this dungeon you've built, and I'm done."

I stood up, slowly walked towards the door, and carefully placed my foot on its threshold as I took a deep breath. I timidly turned around to face the camera, raised my trembling hand, and aggressively extended my middle finger.

"Imagine what your life in here will be like if you fail. Do you think you've had it bad already? I will make it my life's work to make you miserable," he menacingly threatened.

"Fuck you, Benjamin," I bitterly spat.

I took my first faltering step towards freedom and then leapt through both doors as quickly as I could. Ahead of me was a set of dusty concrete steps, and I took them two at a time as I battled the urge to return with every stride. I reached the top that was shrouded in shadows and took a cursory final glance down at my old home before I continued around the corner and to freedom.

Yeah, I didn't get far.

Out of the darkness, a steel rod emerged, the tip stuck into my chest. I heard a click, and every single one of my muscles painfully spasmed all at once. With an abrupt yelp, I instantly dropped to my hands and knees to instinctively crawl back down the steps and into the false safety of the bunker. It stung me again, followed by the swift heel of a boot to my ribs, and I uncontrollably rolled down the concrete stairs in agony. A split second later, I crashed at the bottom in an anguished heap, and as I turned my head to groggily look up the steps at the source, I came face to face with the masked figure that held me there. It was all a trap, and Benjamin had been patiently waiting outside the entire time for me to fall for it.

As I frantically scrambled to get back inside, I was being pummelled from all angles. First, a few sharp kicks to the ribs, interspersed with the cattle prod being stuck between my shoulder blades. Then, a gloved fist carelessly grabbed my hair, slammed my face into the cold ground and dragged me in circles before I managed to break free. By the time I somehow made it inside, I felt like I had been thrown down those stairs a hundred times or more, and I desperately crawled underneath the table to meekly protect myself from the never-ending onslaught.

"I'm sorry, okay?" I shouted.

"You aren't. But you're going to be," the figure taunted.

As much as the attack physically hurt, the thought of being confined in here for the rest of my miserable life was what pained me the most, and I knew I would never physically best this man looming over me. As misguided as it was, I decided not to let him know that I was absolutely terrified, so instead, I elected to goad him further to stupidly take some victory in it.

"Oh shit, is that your actual voice?" I teased facetiously, "I always thought it was just distorted because of the intercom."

"Do you ever stop talking?" he boomed.

"Christ, I bet you got bullied in school."

"Shut your mouth," he warned.

"Little browbeaten Benny never got over what the other mean kids said to him, and now he locks up women to make him feel better. Boo-hoo!"

In an unsurmountable rage, Benjamin angrily launched the table protecting me into the corner of the room, scattering the drawings I had left there in the air, and they drifted towards the floor.

It was the first time I had got a good look at him. He was dressed all in black, baggy clothes, with a hood over his head and a modified ski-mask that obscured all of his facial features, even his eyes. I stared directly into the sunken pits where his eyes should be, desperately trying to exude unwavering bravery and defiant determination as he used the prod he was holding to peel back the top of my overalls slightly. I felt the chill of the metal prongs making direct contact with my skin just below my collarbone, and I saw his trigger finger twitch slightly.

"Sleep tight," he whispered, "don't let the bed bugs bite."

He joylessly mashed the trigger down, and I violently convulsed on the floor in agony. He paused for a second, but when I let out a gasp, he put all his weight behind it and squeezed the button again. Then again. And again. He continued without relenting until all of my uncontrollable limbs where pinned by themselves onto the floor, and I was forced to sleep staring at the open door I failed to exit through.

25

THE RETURN

OLIVIA – 2024

That sandwich was the most scrumptious and satisfying meal I had ever had in my entire life. Before gleefully leaving Nathaniel's studio, it was plain to see that Stephanie had already erupted in an irrepressible fury. She frantically set about scouring the drawers for something sharp, and when she eventually came across a box cutter, she began slashing all his paintings in a self-inflicted jealous rage. I decided it was safer not to be there when she ran out of canvases to slice. Much to my enjoyment, she was finally showing her true colours once again, and I committed to memory the delightful look on Nath's face when his opinion of her unexpectedly took a dark and suspicious turn.

I took on the chin what Nathaniel had said about me because I sensed the tide was finally turning in my favour, and it would only be a matter of time before Stephanie was exposed as the psychotic nut she undeniably was. She thought she was calling all the shots, but her violent reaction in Nath's studio told me that she was losing her mind even further, and in her current unhinged state, she was bound to make a misstep. I just had to wait.

My phone started buzzing in my pocket, and I hoped it was Nathaniel, with some lame apology for what he said, but it was Alex returning my earlier call instead.

"Hello?" I answered.

"Did you find her, then?" Alex asked.

"Aurora? Yeah. Smoking it up at the skatepark with her crummy mates like a little reprobate. She gave me an earful, so I ended up leaving her to her own devices there."

"She can be tough, sometimes."

"I suppose it's nice to see that at least something from me rubbed off on her. I am worried about her, though."

"It's only a bit of pot. I never said it, but Nathaniel did overreact about it."

"Not the pot, just how she was with me. It was night and day compared to when we picked her up at the rehab centre."

"Teenagers and their hormones, eh?"

"Actually, speaking of raging hormones, I just had an encounter with Stephanie at Nath's studio."

"What happened? Are you okay?" he said with concern.

"Nothing much, and I'm fine. Quite smug, in fact. She all but flat-out accused us of having an affair and ordered Nath to cut all ties with me. It was quite the performance."

"Christ. What did he say to that?"

"He roundly said no, pretty much called her a nutter, and stormed off," I said with a smile.

"That's good. Do you think he is ready to hear what we have to say yet? Or he needs more time?"

"No, we still need something concrete."

"Okay, I trust your judgement," he said matter-of-factly.

"I remembered something interesting about the day I found out Nathaniel had moved on."

"What about it?"

"Benjamin showed me footage of it happening. It was essentially a porn movie with Stephanie and Nathaniel playing the leads."

"That's sick."

"I know, but it got me thinking that if Stephanie was the star of the show, who was behind the camera?"

"Are you implying she's no longer responsible for the kidnapping?" he sternly questioned.

"No, I'm convinced she was involved. But at the very least, she has an accomplice. There's no way she constantly kept an eye on me and lived her life at the same time. There had to be someone giving her a helping hand."

"That makes sense. I'm actually at the sheriff's office now, so I can run it by Daniels. I've been trying to talk him into reopening Nicole's case."

"Were you successful?"

"Not sure," he started with a sigh, "he was pushing back quite a bit. I did have an idea, but Daniels thought I was mad, and I'm not sure about it either," he anxiously admitted.

"Spit it out, Alex."

"Do you think you are ready to return to the bunker? Have you psyched yourself up for that?"

"What?" I fearfully asked.

"Bear with me. If you saw the place again, it might trigger a memory of something you might have forgotten. The human mind can repress things, especially something so traumatic."

"Yeah, I don't think I want to go back there."

"Okay!" he began, "it was just an idea, and I thought as much. I wanted to go alone, but Daniels wouldn't let me because there isn't a scrap of evidence the two cases are linked."

"Why the hell would you want to go there?"

"I just want to see where Nicole died."

"Of course. Shit, I'm sorry, Alex."

"Over the years, I've spent countless hours at the roadside where I thought she had crashed, wondering what took place that fateful day. It feels strange knowing that it happened somewhere else entirely."

I inhaled deeply when I heard the profound sadness in Alex's voice. He had done so much for me when he had no obligation to, and I wanted to repay his kindness with some of my own, even if it meant returning to that pit of misery unwillingly.

"You know what, Alex, if you are intent on going there, I'll go there with you."

"Are you sure?"

"Yes. You're right; it might trigger something that will help us find out who did this to both of us. I can't deny you that opportunity."

"Who? So, you aren't sure about Stephanie anymore?"

"I don't know, mate. Aurora is pretty certain it wasn't her, and so is Nath, so it's shaken my confidence a little bit. I mean, there's no denying she is a world-class, psychotic monster, but I might be barking up the wrong tree."

"We'll just go where the evidence takes us," Alex stated.

"See, you're already sounding like a detective," I quipped.

"I'm still outside the station. Do you want us to meet here, or shall I come round and pick you up?"

"No need, I'm only a minute away."

"I'll see you shortly, then," he said as he hung up the phone.

When I turned the corner, I saw Alex and Daniels not engaged in conversation but frostily standing beside Alex's car, which was parked outside the sheriff's office. I gave them an awkward wave as I approached, and when the sheriff noticed my presence, he clapped his hands together and pointed at me.

"Good afternoon, Olivia," Daniels said.

"Are we all set for our little field trip?" I asked.

"Yes?" he confusedly replied.

"She has a tendency to crack little jokes when she's nervous. You'll get used to it," Alex knowingly smirked.

"Is that your professional opinion? Because, if so, that's privileged information," I sarcastically pointed out.

"It is. Hop in, and I'll drive us. Daniel's is going to lead the way."

After climbing into the car, we began driving in convoy with Sheriff Daniel's cruiser ahead of us. Alex was right; I did make jokes when I was nervous, but anxiety was quickly evolving into dread the closer we got back to that deplorable place. That was the first time I had left Hammerdale since I escaped, and as I tried to get my head around what I had agreed to, I realised I had already gone beyond the point of no return.

"I can see the look in your eyes, Liv. Are you absolutely sure about this?" Alex reassured.

"Yes. If I stopped doing something when I felt uncomfortable, I wouldn't ever get out of bed," I remarked.

"Again, with the jokes! Just breathe, relax, and know that I can put a stop to this whenever you feel uncomfortable."

"Okay, I'll try. I mean, obviously, I'm safe, right? It's not as if they are going to come back with Daniels there, anyway."

"Exactly. It's perfectly safe."

"Did Daniels mention the investigation? Do they have any leads yet?"

"Not even a partial print or a strand of hair in sight. Not even yours. Apparently, it's the cleanest crime scene he's ever been to."

"Great, so he's invited us on this little fishing expedition because he's clutching at straws?"

"Unfortunately, it seems that way."

My legs began to bounce up and down beyond my control.

"She's going to get away with it, isn't she?" I uttered.

"No, we just need to keep the pressure on," he reassured.

"She will have finished slashing all Nath's paintings to ribbons by now and must be looking for her next victim."

"She slashed what?"

"When I left her, she was madly swiping at all the canvases with a box cutter. I don't fully comprehend how Nath can witness her behaving like that and still refuse to be on my side, pointing the finger at her, too. She must be even worse behind closed doors if you ask me."

"Nath already knows too well what my view of her is. He barely mentions her to me anymore to avoid the inevitable lecture."

We slowly cruised around a right-hand bend, and there it was: the clearing I emerged from that night. In the cold light of day, it looked different somehow, but to me, it had still retained all of its menace. As I thought about where that meandering path led, my heart accelerated to a rate that was perilously uncomfortable, so I loosely gripped my chest as the anxiety continued to build. Daniels parked up in front of the taped cordon, got out of his car before we arrived, and Alex carefully parked behind him. When he turned the engine off, he looked at me searchingly, and I remained staring at the footwell to avoid his gaze.

"You don't have to do this, you know," he said as he softly put his hand on my arm.

"No, I need to if we are going to prove anything, and I want to help you."

"Remember, just say the word, and I'll pull you straight out of there."

"Okay, thanks, Alex."

We both slowly exited the vehicle and cautiously followed Daniels underneath the weathered police tape and down the beaten trail towards the very birthplace of my worst nightmare. My hands were clammy with cold sweat and dithering as I walked, and when Alex noticed them, he reassuringly held onto one to steady my nerves. To be clear, I wasn't worried I was in any physical danger;

I was more terrified about what vile memories would come rushing back when I stepped foot in that haunting place and whether I would be able to stop them coming after the floodgates were opened. The memories I had retained were harrowing in themselves, and I was reluctant to go digging for anything sinister enough for me to repress them. If it didn't derail the investigation and leave Alex without justice, I would have gladly left them buried.

After a few minutes of walking in silence, we reached the hatch. I wondered how many pairs of ignorant walking boots had trodden on it or marched past it over the years, with their owners not having the faintest idea I was horrifyingly trapped in a prison beneath their feet. The hatch stuck out like a sore thumb once the wild, overgrown fauna was stripped back by law enforcement, and it was clearly visible even from a distance.

Daniels was the first to climb down the ladder and immediately turned his torch on when his boots hit solid ground so as to light the way for the rest of the party. I hesitantly followed next, and the sheriff helped me down as my knees wobbled on every rung. Alex was the last to descend, and once he joined us, we all walked down the concrete steps towards the place I called home for ten years.

"If you don't mind, can I have a minute alone in there before we begin? I want to see the place where Nicole lost her life." Alex solemnly asked.

"Absolutely not. I have to accompany you both, or we don't go in there at all," Daniels insisted.

"Sheriff, his wife died," I gently argued.

"Sorry, but it's protocol."

"Then this whole thing was a waste of time. Repressed memory exercises mean recreating the scene around the victim, so it isn't going to work with you in there with us," Alex explained.

"Is it guaranteed to work?" Daniels defeatedly asked.

"No, but it's worth a shot," Alex said.

"Please, sheriff, we need to do this. Otherwise, the investigation will be dead in the water."

"Okay, fine," Daniels uncertainly began with a deep sigh, "two minutes."

Alex smiled at me and gave the sheriff an acknowledging nod before tentatively walking through the steel doors. The resulting screeching sound when they opened made me wince, and I was left outside with Daniels, uncomfortably staring at each other in sombre silence, before he noticed my discomfort and broke it.

"How are you feeling?" he asked.

"Not good," I shakily responded.

"Yeah, it can't be easy coming back here."

"I didn't know you were a therapist, too," I sarcastically remarked.

"This exercise really is a Hail Mary; the perpetrator was meticulous and hasn't left us anything to go on."

"Alex told me you didn't find any fingerprints, or anything else for that matter. Don't you think that's strange? That they managed to clean it up so quickly?" I asked in a cautious whisper.

"We just go where the evidence leads us," Daniels quietly replied.

"Uh-huh," I responded with a half-smile.

"There's still nothing pointing to Stephanie having anything to do with all this. We will have to cast the net wider if we don't come up with something soon. The county is bound to be on my ass if we don't have a suspect soon enough."

"I was just talking to Alex about it. Although I'm certain she had something to do with this, I don't think she could have done this on her own. She must've had help."

"Hey, how long has he been in there?" Daniels distractedly asked.

"It can't have been longer than a minute."

"Come on," Daniels said as he knocked on the door with his torch, "time's up."

Alex sheepishly walked around the heavy door again with a sniffle and tears in his eyes, and we both stared at him, trying to gauge what state he was in. He didn't look particularly upset or hysterical, just broodingly sombre, and silently stood between us as he dried the tears with his sleeve.

"Are you okay, Alex?" I gently asked.

"Yeah, I think so," he sniffled.

"We can come back another day; we don't have to do this now," I suggested.

"No. I need to find the person who did this to her. To both of you," he firmly insisted.

"Come on then!" I said as I took his hand and led him back beyond the doors with Daniels in tow.

It was eerie. Anything that wasn't bolted down had been removed by my kidnapper to evade capture. The ever-watchful eye was still proudly mounted on the wall, and so was the intercom that carried his voice. He had even gone as far as to diligently fill in each of the five-hundred-and-twenty indentations I had made on the wall, and it was almost as if I never existed there. Was he trying to convince everyone that it never happened? Or was he preparing for another occupant?

"Sheriff, if you wouldn't mind," Alex politely said.

"Five minutes and not a second longer. I'll go and make some calls. Don't make me regret this," Daniels announced.

"Thanks," I mumbled.

Daniels quietly left the room, and I pulled down my old bed and perched on the end of it.

"This feels really weird," I expressed.

"I want you to close your eyes," Alex breathily said.

"Okay," I muttered as I closed them.

Suddenly, Alex hit some kind of tuning fork, which produced a loud, high-pitched sound that resounded through the air. I could feel my heart thumping in my chest, and I had already begun to sweat profusely.

"Are you okay to continue?" Alex lightly said.

"Yes," I dismissed with a deep breath.

"I want you to think about the worst day you had in here."

I remained silent and nodded in response.

"Imagine how you felt. Recreate the room around you exactly how it was. What did it smell like?"

"Musty," I stuttered.

"Can you hear anything?"

"The fan overhead and the camera whirring."

"Good. Was it hot or cold in here?" he asked as he paced around the room.

"Sweltering. My neck was wet through," I uttered.

"Good. So you're sweating because it was so hot, and then you—"

"No, because I was sick," I interrupted.

"You got sick?"

"Yes," I muttered.

"So, what were you doing?"

"Looking for something to eat and laying down, mostly."

"Okay, lay back on the bed."

Reluctantly, I slowly lowered myself back onto the steel I was sitting on with my eyes still closed, and I began to shake as I was guided by Alex deeper into my imagination.

"What did Benjamin say to you that day?" he asked.

"I can't remember. I was out of it," I replied.

"Try."

"Some mad biblical passage about medicine and dried-up bones."

"Ahh," he said, "very good. Just relax."

Alex didn't speak for a while, but I could hear his shoes gently tapping the concrete floor as he moved around. After a few seconds, the taps grew louder, and I heard the door begin to move. When the rusty hinges began to screech, panic immediately gripped me, and I opened my eyes to see him shutting me in. I immediately got on my feet and ran over to the door, and even though the door didn't lock anymore, he was holding it shut from the other side.

"Alex, this isn't funny! Let me out!" I screamed.

"A joyful heart is good medicine, but a crushed spirit dries up the bones," a distorted voice said from behind me.

As I turned around to locate the source of the sound, the lights started flickering violently, to the point where I could barely see. I had my arms outstretched, trying to find the corner of the bed to anchor myself again, when I heard the sound of heavy breathing bouncing off the walls.

"Remember," the voice ordered.

"Alex, please open the door!" I pleaded.

"Remember!" the voice shrieked.

I became hysterical. The combination of the rapidly flashing lights and my erratic heart rate forced me to cower in the corner. I held my legs between my arms, belligerently rocking and quietly sobbing as I silently begged for it all to stop. Pins and needles started prickling their way up and down my neck as I began sweating even more copiously, and I clutched my chest as the shooting pains darted across it. My breathing was so fast that I felt like I was barely taking any air in, and I gripped my head as hard as I could just to remind myself that I was still alive.

"Calm down," the voice boomed, "and remember."

"It's not real, it's not real," I repeated to myself.

I tried to calm myself down by determinedly taking long breaths in through my nose and out through my mouth, and my heart rate finally began to slow down. I pictured Nathaniel standing in front of the chapel with his comically short tie and Aurora dancing in the carpark with flowers in her hair. There was a look of excitement and happiness on their faces as they dotingly stared back at me. The warmth of the mental image allowed me to regain some composure, and suddenly, unwanted memories came flooding back. They were heavily fragmented at first, but when I concentrated, I started to make sense of them, and more and more details started to unveil themselves.

I remembered something specific, and as I cautiously opened my eyes in between the flashes, I spotted it reflecting the light. The key to proving everything was still stuck beneath the bed, begging to be removed, and I shakily crawled over to it to peel it away with my fingernail. In the bursts of light, I saw the words written on it, and all semblance of doom quickly dissolved after my discovery.

"You can stop Alex. It worked. I've got it," I shouted.

26

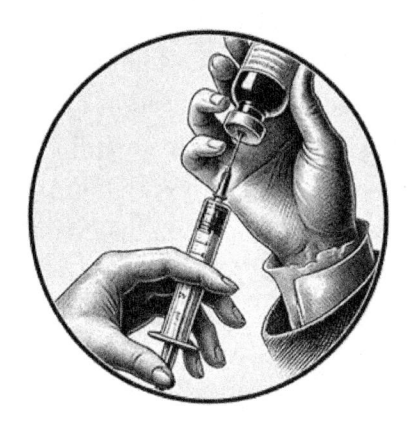

THE NEEDLE

OLIVIA – 2021

I'll be blunt; that year was utter hell. Benjamin had long since abandoned the psychological warfare, and instead, he seemed as if his only intention was to take me to the very brink of death, only to pull me back at the last possible moment. The dwindling supply runs became increasingly scarce, and I would often run out of drinking water days before the next lot arrived. Everything I received had to be carefully rationed, but without knowing when the next meal would come, I ended up barely eating a scrap. He continuously pushed the boundaries each time, providing me with slightly less, just to sinisterly observe how little he could offer me but still keep me breathing.

I was so hungry, but I would be damned if I let him see even a glimpse of it. However, that day, I broke my self-imposed rule. I had my entire head in the small cupboard, where I kept the food like a starved animal, in a desperate search for enough stale crumbs to form together into a single bite. Predictably, food dominated my every waking thought, and the constant forage for stray morsels quickly became a necessary obsession. I had been regressed to a primal existence, so much so that I would have happily speared a wandering rat and cooked that if the opportunity presented itself. My umpteenth search for sustenance was vexingly fruitless, and I reluctantly retreated to my bed to collapse in a starving heap, desperately trying to preserve what little energy I had left in me.

"I need to eat," I groaned to myself.

It should come as no surprise that I lost a tremendous amount of weight in a relatively short period of time. I was constantly lightheaded, having to grip onto something solid for dear life as I pottered around the bunker during the daytime, while at nighttime, I could barely sleep through the crippling stomach cramps. My issued jumpsuit that used to cling to my skin was baggy and ill-fitting and did little to insulate the clicking rattle of my bones scraping together as I moved around in what little space I had.

Despite all those trials, I was pleased that I had finally snapped out of the sickening trance he had placed me in, and all it took to bring me back to reality was a cattle prod to the chest and a few suspected cracked ribs. Once the spell was well and truly broken, I felt ludicrous for ever thinking his intentions were noble, and I understood that I was an unwilling plaything for his twisted amusement: nothing more.

The remorseless hunger diverted my attention from my endless captivity a lot of the time, and my irrational self actually welcomed the distraction. If I had been well fed, I might have had the brain capacity to worry about what Nathaniel was doing whilst my splintering fingernails were scraping around in the dirt for crumbs, so there was one tragic benefit. Then again, even if I inexplicably escaped that very second, I was so gaunt and sickly that he wouldn't even have recognised me if he had seen me, and I certainly couldn't hold a candle to his new conquest in the morbid state I was in. He had inevitably moved on, and I fervidly intended to do the same, but contemplating my relationship when my very life hung in the balance seemed trifling.

Oh, God, I could murder a trifle.

Nath hadn't even heard of a trifle when I met him, especially in its British iteration, and I always tried to make one every Sunday. It was one of the only traditions that I willingly took from my mother after she died, and even through all her shortcomings, one thing had to be admitted: she made a mean dessert. I closed my eyes as I reminisced about the perfectly ripe summer strawberries delicately placed atop silky whipped cream, and my mouth began to water as I imagined plunging a spoon through it, delving beneath the creamy set custard and into the decadently sweet sponge below.

Just as I envisioned bringing the overloaded spoon to my cracked lips, I lost my balance on the edge of the bed and fell to the floor with a crash. My stick-thin arms were too perilously weak to cushion my fall, so I ended up face-first in the dust. The lingering particles immediately caught the back of my throat, and I began to uncontrollably splutter and writhe on the floor as I struggled to push myself back up on my feet. The hacking cough that I had developed in the past few weeks was only getting worse, and as I violently choked into my hand, I noticed a little trail of blood running through the thick, nauseating mucus.

"Wow. You look like shit, Olivia," Benjamin announced.

I intended to scathingly tell him to go fuck himself, but I barely mouthed the first syllable when the incessant wheezing resumed, and I produced even more blood into my shaking palm.

"I think I'm sick," I hoarsely uttered.

"You think?" he sarcastically replied.

"There's blood in this. I'm seriously ill."

"Have you been taking the vitamins I give you?"

"Yes, but they clearly aren't working."

"A joyful heart is good medicine, but a crushed spirit dries up the bones," he solemnly recited.

"Enough with the fucking Bible. I need some antibiotics and some real food. And water."

"Quite the shopping list. Anything else?" he laughed.

"I'm serious; I'm going to fucking die in here."

He paused for a moment.

"So?" he taunted.

As I was struck down with yet another coughing fit, I precariously hung onto the bed and shakily made my way over to the sink to fill an empty bottle from the tap. I knew that I shouldn't drink the tepid water from there because it would make me sicker, but I was desperate for even a drop to moisten my throat. The corroded tap violently screeched as I turned it as quickly as I could, and the pipes began to ominously rattle, only for it to produce about six drops of disgusting brown liquid before it ran dry.

"Oh, sorry, the water is off," Benjamin stated.

"I need water, now!" I shouted as I threw the bottle at the CCTV camera.

"Now, now. You're like a stroppy teenager, worse than Aurora, even. You can wait until tomorrow. I'm busy."

"No, I can't wait," I screamed as I started kicking the air lock door as hard as I could.

"Being angry will only make it worse," he warned.

He was right, and I immediately regretted my misguided outburst. The sudden eruption of physical activity made me dangerously breathless, and I was fighting for every gasp of air as I again fell backwards onto the sooty concrete. My head impacted the stone, allowing the dizziness to take hold of me. My heart began to slow, my whistling chest became fatigued, and I stared up at the flickering lights above, thinking it was the end before I slipped under.

"Olivia?" he worriedly asked.

It's impossible to say how long I was out, but when I frantically awoke with a harrowing gasp, I was being carelessly dragged from the floor and onto the bed. Delirious and sweating profusely, I had no idea what was happening, and for a split second, I thought it was Nathaniel carrying me. It was only when I heard Benjamin's laboured breaths being distorted by his voice-box that I realised where I was.

"I told you I was sick," I feverishly babbled.

"He heals the broken-hearted and binds up their wounds," he joyfully recited as he hoisted me on the bed.

"Just let me out of here, please," I wearily argued.

"Shut up and stay still," he instructed.

"Look at me. You've won, and you've already taken everything from me. Let me go."

"And lose my favourite plaything? You just need a shot of antibiotics, and you'll be fine. Stop being so melodramatic."

I watched Benjamin produce a sheathed syringe and a small glass vial from his pocket. He slowly drew the liquid into the needle and tapped it before placing both of them on the side. I began to struggle in futility when he tried turning me around on my stomach, but in my weakened state, he effortlessly spun me around and pinned me to the mattress with one arm. As his hand slid down to my left buttock, I madly flailed my arms about as much as I could to shake him off, but it was to no avail. In the struggle, I must have caught the empty vial that was resting on the side, and it pinged on the floor as it rolled beneath the bed and just into my eyeline.

"Last warning. Stay still, or this needle is going in your neck," he menacingly commanded.

Even though I was still incredibly confused, I somehow had the presence of mind to covertly pick up the small glass container, and I began hurriedly peeling off the label with my thinning thumb nail. Just as he plunged the needle into my backside against my will, I managed to free part of it from the glass and stuck it on the underside of the bed in an effort to conceal it. He removed the needle, and I went limp as he unpackaged another vial behind my back.

"One more," he mumbled.

"More antibiotics?" I slurred.

He remained frighteningly silent, and I let out a drained yelp when I felt the second needle pierce my skin. The light headedness was immediately intensified tenfold, so much so that I nearly rolled off the bed when he struggled to turn me around on my back again. I was groggily clutching the vial still in my hand, and he forcibly took it from me as my eyes started to grow heavy again.

"I'll take that," he said as he placed the vial in his pocket.

"What did you stick me with?" I woozily asked.

"Just a little something to help you sleep and to forget this ever happened. I just can't stand your constant coughing."

"I hate you," I whispered.

"Sleep tight; don't let the bedbugs bite," he whispered as he stroked my hair with his gloved hand, and I begrudgingly conked out.

27

THE LAW

OLIVIA – 2024

Alex quickly unblocked the door and apologetically burst into the room with his arms raised after his dramatic memory experiment to find me standing in the middle of the bunker with a beaming grin. He sheepishly approached me, clearly expecting me to clock him on the nose, but in my excitement, I ran into his arms, grabbed both of his cheeks and victoriously kissed him on the lips instead. If he had let me in on his risky gambit, I would have flatly refused to even go back there, but it had worked spectacularly. The perplexed smile on his face grew wider, and we shared a strangely intimate moment before Daniels unexpectedly barged into the room.

Whilst firmly gripping his holstered firearm, the sheriff immediately pinned Alex directly against the concrete wall by his neck and got so close to him that Alex could feel the heat from his breath. Alex was clearly flummoxed by the surprisingly sudden act of aggression, and I quickly slipped the prescription label from the vial into my pocket whilst they were both distracted. The fury in the sheriff's eyes told me if I wasn't standing there, he would have put a bullet in Alex's skull without a moment's hesitation, and I realised that we had a very different problem to contend with. Alex didn't know it yet, but the man responsible for everything, including the death of his bride, was standing between us and freedom.

"Sheriff, calm down, please, it's fine," I pleaded.

"What the hell is going on in here? I heard screaming," Daniels breathlessly interrogated.

"It's repressed memory therapy. Maybe I got a little carried away, but she consented to it, right, Olivia?" Alex desperately explained.

"Is that true, Olivia?" Daniels shouted over to me.

"Yes," I shakily nodded.

"Did it work?" he asked.

"No, sorry," I lied with feigned sincerity.

Daniels let out a sigh of reprieve as he released the grip he had on his pistol, and to my relief, he reluctantly let go of Alex too. Alex immediately slid to the floor to catch his breath, and I silently urged him with my eyes not to provoke the sheriff further so we could get out of that place alive.

"This wasn't what we agreed to. It sounded barbaric," Daniels menacingly said.

"Sorry, I thought we would get something. I just want to get the bastard who did this to my wife," Alex admitted.

"Come on, both of you. This has gone too far, and we need to go now," Daniels ordered.

I didn't need telling twice. I grabbed Alex's arm as we quickly made our way up the ladder to the hatch, and then we walked back to the cars in a strained reserve, totally transfixed on Daniel's firearm. I tried to accurately convey my false disappointment in not finding anything, and I knew that even the slightest misstep would spur him to react volatilely. The sheriff shot a contemptuous headshake in our direction as he stood by his cruiser in silence, with every fibre of my being urging him to get inside and just drive away. After a moment of tension, he got in his vehicle with a tut and started the engine, leaving Alex and me at the roadside.

"Olivia, I'm so sorry I did that to you. It was incredibly unprofessional. I was just desperate for you to remember something," Alex announced with evident shame.

"Er… I did," I said with an anxious smile.

"I thought you said—"

"I know what I said. Here," I said as I stealthily handed him the label.

"What's this?"

"I got a nasty chest infection and nearly died. Benjamin had to give me a shot of penicillin, but I was too ill to inject myself, so he came and did the honours. He dropped the bottle that it came in, and that label was attached."

"Matthew… Daniels?"

"Uh-huh," I knowingly nodded.

"Daniels as in… Sheriff Daniels?" he whispered.

"One and the same."

"How is that even possible?" Alex gasped.

"I have no idea, but there's no denying his involvement after finding this. That snake was interfering with the investigation since day one."

"It explains why no evidence had been found."

"Exactly. He got rid of it," I replied.

"What do we do now?"

Daniels menacingly revved his engine as he continued to look contemptuously at us in his rearview mirror, clearly waiting for us to clear out, and we received his threat loud and clear. Instinctively, without a further word, we climbed into Alex's vehicle, and he immediately locked the doors. After the sheriff was satisfied that we were leaving, he circled back towards Hammerdale, and we began to cautiously follow him.

"Stick on him," I suggested.

"Olivia, this is getting dangerous now. He's armed to the teeth," Alex said.

"Just follow him. We need to know where he's going."

It didn't take long for us all to get back to Hammerdale in convoy, and Daniels pulled into the station as expected. He walked inside the front door, and we parked down the street to closely survey his movements. Alex was shaking like a leaf, but I was far too engrossed in the mystery of it all to feel the fear. I just desperately wanted it to reach a conclusion.

"I can't believe we didn't see this before. There's no way that Stephanie pulled everything off on her own," I mused.

"So, what do you think happened? Stephanie planned it all, and Daniels did the heavy lifting?" Alex theorised.

"Uh-huh," I nodded.

"Why would he do that?"

"She paid him off? He's fucking her? Does the reason even matter? We have him bang to rights now."

"I suppose not."

Our stakeout only lasted a few minutes when an unmarked car slowly pulled out onto the road, and we almost disregarded it until I realised it was Daniels in the driver's seat. Alex quickly gave chase again, and the off-duty sheriff continued through Hammerdale to get on the I-5 freeway. When I saw the signs for Sacramento overhead, my wild theories began making perfect sense, and I started to laugh when it all fell into place.

"Sacramento," I chuckled, "he's running back to his master like a lap dog to tell her what's just happened."

"He must be meeting her at her office," Alex huffed.

"We are going to get them both," I excitedly announced.

We continued following him on the freeway for almost an hour until he turned off into downtown Sacramento. He looked incredibly sketchy when he parked on the road beside Southside Park and then warily continued on foot with his head on a swivel. Not wanting to alert him to our presence, we parked a few blocks behind him and cautiously followed him through the winding paths at a safe distance. He stopped at the benches beside the small lake that was there and took a seat, not taking down his guard even for one second. We halted in the shadows of the trees that grew there, hid behind some foliage, and diligently interrogated his every move.

"This is actually quite fun," I whispered.

"You have a grim sense of fun. That man over there did horrendous things to you," Alex reminded.

"Yeah, but I'm enjoying watching it all unravel before our very eyes."

After a few minutes, it wasn't a surprise to either of us when we spotted Stephanie confidently sauntering through the park towards him, dressed in a hot-pink miniskirt and a strappy crop top. Suddenly at ease, Daniels casually rose to his feet when they converged, and she gave him a nauseatingly amorous kiss as he shamelessly slid his hand up the back of her skirt. I didn't know whether to laugh or cry, and I turned to Alex, who was rummaging around in his pockets for something, to gauge his reaction.

"What are you doing?" I asked.

"I'm taking some pictures," Alex distractedly said.

"Oh, they are guilty as sin. It's no wonder why he never entertained the idea of her being responsible. He's fucking the main suspect."

"I wonder what Nath will say," Alex sullenly said.

"He will kick that bitch to the curb, and then she is going straight to jail."

Thankfully, they stopped playing tonsil tennis, and Daniels suddenly became animated as he began telling Stephanie a story. Even without hearing what was being said, I could tell that he was reenacting the scene that unfolded at the bunker a few hours earlier, and for the first time since this began, Stephanie actually looked anxious about it.

"What do you think he is telling her?" Alex asked.

"He's explaining what happened to us at the bunker, but he has no idea what I found."

"She looks really pissed."

"She does indeed!" I smiled.

"Where do we go from here? Do we call the FBI or something? We can't go into the sheriff's office with that label; he'll just make it disappear."

"I'm British, and I haven't got the first idea of how any of this works. I'm just feeling quite vindicated and thankful that I'm not going insane like everybody said."

Without warning, Alex began creeping closer to them, and I tried to hold him back, but he dismissively shook off my grasp without a word. He cautiously made his way around the bushes we were hiding behind and covertly began approaching them with his camera phone aimed at them in his hand.

"What the hell are you doing?" I sternly whispered.

"I need to get closer; the pictures are all blurry," Alex breathily replied.

"No, come back! We can't risk being seen. Whatever shots you have will have to do."

Alex ignored my frantic request and quickly got out of whispering range. As he got about halfway between me and them, he knelt down to take a final picture when a car backfired behind me, which got Stephanie's attention. She immediately saw Alex and I hiding in the shrubbery, frenziedly saying something to Daniels as she pointed at us, and he challengingly turned around, exposing the pistol stuffed in his waistband.

Alex understood the peril and immediately got up to start running back towards me, with the athletic sheriff hot on his tail. I took flight too and began sprinting back to the car, getting there first, and testily yanked the door handle as I impatiently waited for Alex to notice me waiting by his car and unlock it so I could escape in it. Finally, the vehicle beeped as Alex's key fob got within range, and I retreated inside. I immediately started searching the compartments in case Alex kept a firearm of his own, but they were only filled with papers.

Alex had a slight head start on Daniels, but the sheriff was much faster than he was and continued to narrow the gap. I leaned over to open the driver's side door before Alex arrived, and he jumped inside, frantically turned the key in the ignition, and hastily reversed out of the space just in the nick of time. Daniels planted his feet on the ground as we began to peel down the road, pointing the pistol at us, and managed to fire a few rounds, which impacted the rear of the vehicle with a flurry of harrowing thuds.

"Wow," Alex breathlessly gasped.

"You could have got yourself fucking killed," I scorned.

"There's still time, he's right behind us."

I frenziedly whipped my head around to look behind us and spotted Daniels furiously drifting around a corner whilst manically flashing his lights. Alex was clearly flustered, incredibly out of his element, and wildly swaying on the road as he struggled to maintain control of the vehicle. The enraged sheriff was within touching distance, and I could see his gritted teeth through his windshield as Alex took a sharp left, then a right, and got straight back on the freeway towards home.

"Give me your phone," I ordered.

"Who are you calling?" Alex said as he madly turned the steering wheel to avoid cars in his path.

"Nathaniel."

Between wild course corrections, Alex carelessly threw me his phone, and I quickly dialled the number. The line rang as Alex recklessly swerved through the early evening traffic, and I desperately tried to hang on to the phone as I was jostled around in the passenger seat. I could barely hear the dialling tone over the symphony of screeching tyres and blaring horns surrounding us, and I pressed the phone as tightly to my ear as I could.

"Afternoon, Al, what's up?" Nath answered.

"Don't hang up," I abruptly said.

"Olivia? What's going on? Where's Alex?"

"Driving like a lunatic beside me. Sheriff Daniels is trying to ram us off the road."

"What? Why?" Nath frantically questioned.

"We've just caught him with Stephanie."

"Caught?"

"They were in on it together. He's been hiding the evidence; that's why they said none had been found."

"Olivia… I thought we went over this. I don't know what you're trying to do, but—"

"For fuck's sake. Hang on," I interrupted.

I quickly took the phone from my ear and hastily sent Nathaniel the pictures Alex had just taken.

"Check your messages," I frantically said.

"What am I looking at here?" he bemusedly said.

"It's *Officer Friendly* with his hand up your psycho fiancée's skirt. We've just been back to the bunker to get more evidence, and he's immediately gone running to Stephanie to tell her all about it."

"What the fuck?" Nathaniel distraughtly muttered.

"Exactly, do you believe me now?"

"How could she do that to me?" he hysterically asked.

"My heart bleeds, it really does, but like I said, he's trying to kill us. We could do with a little help here and pronto."

"Okay. Sorry. What do you need me to do?"

"Ring the FBI or someone. We're going to lead him to the sheriff's office. Try to have someone waiting there for us when we arrive."

"Okay. Where's Stephanie?"

I awkwardly turned back around in the seat to get a better look at Daniels' vehicle in pursuit, but I couldn't spot Stephanie in there.

"I think he left her in Sacramento."

"It's Friday," he sighed.

"So what?"

"Every Friday, Aurora gets the bus up there after school, and they do a bit of shopping."

"What are you telling me, Nath?"

"She might have Aurora there with her," Nath defeatedly admitted

Without a further word, I hung up the phone and immediately began calling Aurora. I dialled her on repeat on both of our phones, but to my dismay, she didn't answer either. Nathaniel was probably racked with guilt and doing the same after he foolishly allowed Stephanie to take her there in the first place under the guise of a frivolous shopping trip.

"Stephanie's got Aurora, and she's not answering the phone," I anxiously announced.

"One problem at a time," Alex distractedly said as he ducked and dived through the traffic.

"That psychotic bitch knows that we know, and she's got my fucking daughter." I frantically stated.

"We can deal with that when we are back in Hammerdale in about thirty minutes. Did Nath make the call to the FBI?"

"Yeah, I think so," I muttered.

"Did he?" he firmly repeated louder.

"Yes!" I shouted.

"We need them waiting for us there when we arrive."

We arrived back in Hammerdale, and Main Street was eerily quiet as we ripped through it at full speed, with the mad sheriff still in unyielding pursuit. With no other choice, Alex sharply turned into the sheriff's office car park and slammed on the brakes as we slid sideways to a complete halt. Daniels echoed the manoeuvre, blocking the exit with his vehicle, and immediately sprang out of his car whilst aiming his pistol directly at us.

"Get out of the car," he shouted.

Alex and I both looked at each other as we held our hands up in surrender and slowly exited the car.

"Think about this," Alex shouted, "you can't kill us here right outside the office! Your life and career will be over."

"You mean putting down two murder suspects like dogs in the street? Hell, they'll pin a medal to my chest," Daniels laughed.

"Murder suspects?" I demandingly shouted.

"Oh, poor Nicole," the sheriff mused, "murdered because she found out about your affair. Then, racked by guilt, the once-doting husband throws his crazed mistress into a bomb shelter to keep her quiet. That's what we in the biz call two birds with one stone."

"It shows how much you actually investigated it, none of that made any fucking sense. No one will believe you," I mumbled.

"Believe me? There will be evidence, so they won't have to. Now, get on your knees," Daniels ordered.

Alex and I fearfully glanced at each other and defeatedly knelt down with our hands still in the air. The sheriff started slowly moving towards us, the gun still trained on us, stopping close enough to get a guaranteed headshot.

"Before you pull the trigger, just tell me why," I pleaded.

"Why what?" he bemusedly asked.

"Why did you do all this?"

"Because I love her, and you're trying to frame her," he tearfully smiled.

"She doesn't love you. She's fucking using you, open your eyes," I defiantly remarked.

"She isn't like you think she is. You've got her all wrong. And she does love me. She was about to leave Nathaniel before you complicated things with your wild accusations."

"I've known her a lot longer than you. She's a parasite."

"I'll put a bullet in your skull. Let's see how talkative you are then," he agitatedly said.

"After all the years of torture, the threats are getting pretty thin, buddy. You aren't going to do shit," I taunted as I dropped my hands down.

"Olivia!" Alex whispered.

"Keep your hands up, or I'll smoke you. D'you hear?" the sheriff instructed as he firmed the grip on his pistol.

"No," I firmly said as I stood up and began casually pacing around him.

"Get back on your knees. Now. Final warning."

"No! I've come too far for my story to end like this. You and Stephanie are going to pay for what you've done even if it fucking kills me," I shouted.

The standoff was interrupted by the sound of helicopter blades whirring overhead, and as we all raised our heads to locate the source, a searchlight beamed down, which blinded us both.

"Finally, the cavalry is here," I chirpily announced.

As I turned back to look at Daniels, I heard an ear-shattering single gunshot, and he slowly lowered his weapon with the smoke around him still illuminated by the bright light dazzling me from above. I frantically patted myself down to check for possible wounds until Daniels collapsed to the floor in a heap, and blood started oozing from his chest. I frenziedly turned to see Alex breathlessly on the floor with his smouldering pistol still pointed at the sheriff.

"Drop your weapons," a voice from the chopper ordered.

28

THE SEARCH

OLIVIA — 2024

Alex and I were both witheringly perched on the back step of an open ambulance, wrapped in a foil blanket each, silently watching as the FBI agents quickly erected a tent around Daniels' lifeless body. I reservedly glanced at Alex, who had a thousand-yard stare in his eyes, and the blankets between us rustled as I reassuringly placed my hand on his knee. He had saved my life, along with his own, and if he hadn't acted when he did, it would have been me bleeding out in that tent rather than the man jointly responsible for all this.

I always had misgivings about Stephanie, and she was the obvious conclusion, but I never expected Daniels, of all people, to be embroiled in the terrifying ordeal I was put through for ten eternal years. He staged a truly prolific performance, starting from the very first moment I staggered into the sheriff's office after my escape. Although I had found him mostly incompetent, I never for one-second thought he was even remotely capable of the heinous acts he had committed in Stephanie's thrall. He had placed so many lives in danger to preserve his affair with her, and I wondered if, in his last moments, he had even regretted any of it. I kept picturing the self-assured expression on his face when he told me that she loved him, and it mirrored Nathaniel's whenever I had a bad word to say about her.

I spotted Nathaniel arrive agitatedly at the edge of the cordon after elbowing his way through the massing crowd. He wildly pointed over to us, and the agents begrudgingly let him through. He had a brief conversation with one of them beside the sheriff's open car as they were pulling boxes out of the trunk, and then he hastily ran over to speak to us.

"What happened? Are you both okay?" Nathaniel feverishly asked as he briefly put his arm around me.

"Alex saved us. The sheriff was going to execute us in cold blood right here and then frame us for everything," I numbly explained.

"You shot him, Alex? I thought it was the FBI," he gasped.

Alex remained emotionlessly silent, still locked in an unyielding stare at the men concealing the sheriff's corpse. I nudged him lightly to try and elicit a response from him, but it barely broke his trance even momentarily. Judging by the way he nearly sprinted out of his office with his pistol to go and shoot Stephanie when I had convinced him of her guilt, I thought he would have been less racked with remorse. The sheriff did murder his wife, after all.

"Alex, you are a fucking hero, mate. You mustn't think otherwise for a second," I said insistently.

Alex just sighed under his breath.

"I've just seen them pulling all sorts out of Daniel's trunk. There was such a mountain of files and papers that the FBI will be sorting through it for weeks. He even had the rock that had been thrown through my patio doors."

"It *was* Stephanie, you know. Daniels almost admitted it before he caught that bullet. He was her puppet. She had him firmly wrapped around her little finger, just like you."

"Not anymore," he uttered.

"So, you finally see it?"

"I do. I think I was just lying to myself. Why would she do that to you? To us? That's the only thing I can't get my head around."

"She's psychotic. Jealousy does strange things to people. The only way she was ever going to win you over was to put me in the ground, so that's what she did."

It was the first time that I had called Stephanie a psychopath in front of Nathaniel, which didn't immediately put him on the defensive. Instead, a reflective acceptance washed over his face, and I knew that he had finally begun to understand the ultimate truth. He winced slightly, and with a huff, he sat next to me on the edge of the ambulance and took out his phone.

"I still can't get hold of Aurora; she isn't returning any of my calls. She normally sends me at least a text to let me know she's okay."

"Stephanie has her."

"She wouldn't hurt her."

"Are you sure about that?"

"I'm not sure about anything anymore," he mumbled.

"What are we going to do?"

"I just spoke to an officer over there. The FBI has already contacted their field office, so they're already on the lookout for both of them. They'll find her, Liv, and we can finally put all this shit to bed."

"Let's just focus on finding our daughter first. We can have a proper talk later."

"Miss Lakewell," a voice to the side of me boomed.

"Yes?" I responded as I turned around.

A big and burly agent was standing beside the ambulance, suited and booted, with a notepad poised to take notes on the conversation we were about to have. I could tell that he meant business just by the determination in his eyes, and in the hour that they had been there, he had uncovered far more of the truth than *Officer Friendly* ever did.

"I'm Agent Frank Aldrich, and I'm leading the investigation into what happened to you all. Have you been brought up to speed yet?"

"No, have you found my daughter yet?" I urgently questioned.

"Not yet, but we are closing in. Rest assured that the search is underway, but we need to discuss the treasure trove of evidence the cadaver over there had stashed in his car."

"What about it?"

"Well, we've only had a chance to flick through the paperwork that was left there, but it seems all of it is pointing to Stephanie, who you've already named. It turns out that the sheriff was wilfully concealing the evidence and derailing the investigation from within. He sent all the samples off; he just never filed the results from the lab. There were multiple fibres and hair samples found in the bunker from Miss Ward, you, and a third source that we have yet to determine, but that's likely to be Daniels. There was also some handwriting analysis done, along with some fingerprint samples taken from a note that was thrown through a window in your home."

"What about the label I just gave you?"

"We still have to do some checks on that, but it certainly appears genuine. At first glance, it seems Daniels got a prescription for himself and administered it to you, but the pharmacy that had dispensed it is closed at the moment."

I let out a sigh of relief and untensed my shoulders. Someone was finally taking me seriously, and the agent's steely resolve gave me the confidence that I needed to know they would make short work of finding Aurora.

"So, it's over then. It was them."

"Yes, it does look that way," he stated before turning to Nathaniel, "Mr Anderson, we need to take your phone and any information you have pertaining to Miss Ward. We have agents at your house too, and I assume you won't object to that search, even without a court order?"

"No, of course not," Nathaniel distractedly uttered as he handed his phone over.

"And sir? Mr Green?" Frank said to Alex.

"Alex?" I nudged.

"Yes?" Alex twitchily responded.

"I overheard what Olivia just told you, and I want to repeat it: you're a hero. We were watching from the whirly, and if you didn't do what was necessary, we wouldn't be having this conversation."

"Thanks," Alex grumbled.

"What about Alex's fiancée? She was another victim of theirs," I reminded.

"Daniels also had some files on that case in his possession, but at first glance, we didn't understand the link. We'll now proceed and investigate it all as one offence. On behalf of law enforcement, I'd like to apologise for the chaotic way this case has been handled so far. If the bureau had been informed you had been found, we would have taken control of it straight away. Under normal circumstances, you would have been referred to a mandatory physical and mental evaluation as soon as you were found. Afterwards, a caseworker would have been assigned to help you transition back to your normal life. Regrettably, none of that happened, which is what I find most disgusting. Unbeknownst to us, Daniels was a rotten apple who intentionally mishandled this case from the outset with a view to concealing his involvement, and I will make it my priority that all those responsible are brought to justice."

"Thank you, officer," I warmly said.

"Keep your phone on. We'll be in touch the second we find Aurora," Frank said before walking back to the rest of the agents.

"What do we do now?" Nath anxiously asked.

"Maybe we should head back to Sacramento to see if we can find her," I announced.

"Someone needs to stay here in case Aurora comes home; she can't come back to a house full of agents."

"I'll stay," Alex shakily offered.

"Al, mate, you should go home and get some rest. You've been through a hell of a lot," Nath suggested.

"No, I need to help, but I'm in no fit state to come with you. I'll go to yours. You two head up there and see if you can find her."

"The FBI has probably checked it out already, but I have keys to Stephanie's office. We should start there."

In a sudden burst of energy, I shook the blanket from my shoulders as I eagerly stood up and began briskly pacing on the spot. We were so close to uncovering the whole truth that I could almost taste it, and I couldn't just sit there knowing that Stephanie was still out there roaming freely with my daughter in her possession.

"Come on then. Look lively!" I ordered as I clapped.

Nathaniel wearily rose to his feet and started following me towards the edge of the FBI cordon. The agents there lifted the tape just high enough for us to crouch underneath, and we pushed through the gaggle of nosey onlookers until we reached Nath's parked car down the street. As soon as we got inside, there was already an awkward atmosphere between us, and after a few seconds, it became too thick to ignore. Nathaniel sighed as he turned to me with a guilt-ridden expression on his face, and I agitatedly tapped the dash.

"Olivia, I just—" he started.

"We haven't got time for this. We can talk on the road," I firmly urged.

"No, wait. I just wanted to say I'm sorry that I didn't believe you earlier."

"*Finally*," I whispered to myself.

"You've been through hell and back, and I should have trusted you the instant you said it. If I had, we wouldn't be in this mess right now."

"Nath, I understand, honestly. It's no use blaming yourself. I did go a little mad myself."

"You've always been a *little* mad, anyway," he softly teased.

"Exactly, now that we've had this fucking heart-to-heart with each other, can we just go?"

"Yes," he said as he started the engine.

Just as he was about to embark, I nearly jumped out of my skin when someone started banging on the glass beside me, and Nath slammed on the brakes so we could see who it was. I barely recognised her at first, as it had been over a decade since I last saw my best friend Stacey, but I was overcome with joy when I realised that, against my wishes, she had flown out to visit me. I immediately jumped out of the car, and she pinned me against it with the tightest hug I had ever been given.

"Olivia! I've missed you!" she hysterically declared.

"I've missed you too, but please let go," I pleaded as I slowly patted her back.

"Sorry," she started as she finally released me with tears streaming down her face. "What the hell has happened here? Are you all okay?" she frantically asked.

"There's no time to explain. Just get in. We can use all the help we can get," I said.

29

THE JUDGEMENT

OLIVIA – 2024

It's amazing how easily you can boil down ten years of brutal torment and unheard-of wickedness to an anecdote lasting less than an hour. I told Stacey the entire tale on the way to Sacramento, during which hearing the words leaving my mouth so matter-of-factly and witnessing Stacey's initial reaction to them made me realise how horrific my account actually was. Stacey, who has been tempered by family life in the last decade, balled her eyes out throughout my monologue, almost leaping into the front of the car to console me, and Nathaniel had his moments too, as he silently drove us to conclude this rotten mess. I didn't shed a single tear because, in many ways, I was over it, and I just held firmly onto my resolve to find my daughter, to make sure that the woman responsible paid dearly for her vile transgressions.

"So, it was her this entire time? Nath, seriously, how could you not see it?" Stacey angrily asked.

"I'll be asking myself that for the rest of my life," he pensively uttered as he shook his head.

"It wasn't all his fault, Stace. She's a master manipulator, but we finally have her backed into a corner," I said.

"Oh, I'm going to smash her face in when we catch her. She messed with the wrong family," Stacey threatened.

"Get in line," I dryly replied.

Nath caught our attention by indicating and gently applying the brakes as he pointed to a block of offices a few hundred metres away.

"We're here; her office is just over there on the left. It looks like the FBI beat us to the punch," Nath announced as he pulled up on the curb.

We all jumped out of the car, and Nath hesitantly walked over to the door of '*Sacramento Smiles*' to inspect the flimsy yellow notice that had been nailed to the door. Stacey and I hung back slightly, and I looked at the offices on the floors above to see if there were any signs of life. It was an impressive-looking building, and if I hadn't known a sociopath was running the joint, I could well have been attracted as a client. Directly above the glass frontage, there was a huge glitzy sign featuring a heavily edited picture of Stephanie with a gleaming white smile, and her eyes inexplicably followed us around the pavement as we paced.

"It says it's an active crime scene, and we aren't allowed to go in. It's just got a number on for Agent Aldrich," Nath blusteringly said.

"I don't give a shit. They might have missed something that will lead us to them," I replied.

"Just stop being a wimp for a minute and crack the door open, Nath," Stacey tauntingly added.

"Fine," he said as he produced the keys and unlocked the door, "but it's on your heads."

We all walked inside, and the alarm started beeping until Nath tapped the code into the control panel, and it ceased. He turned on the lights, which illuminated the pristine waiting room we found ourselves in. Stephanie's sickening arrogance knew no bounds. The entire room was plastered with colourful posters featuring her sickening grin beside promotional offers for cosmetic dentistry. Stacey gripped one of them and pettily ripped it off the wall, which made chortle with delight.

"She's a real vain bitch, isn't she?" Stacey whispered.

"You don't know the half of it," I remarked.

"If it wasn't for all the plastic injected into her face, she would look a right goblin."

"Hello?" I sarcastically said as I pointed to myself.

"Don't be stupid, Liv. You know you are beautiful."

"Thanks, mate," I smiled.

"Ladies?" Nath said as he quietly beckoned us behind reception.

He led us up the bland stairs behind it and to Stephanie's corner office at the end of the dimly lit hallway. Nath cautiously made his way inside, clearly terrified that the enraged owner would jump out at him like some kind of beast as soon as he entered, but it was safe, and he casually switched the lights on.

Even considering that the FBI had clearly ransacked the place prior to our arrival, it was remarkably clean and tidy. Sterile, even. The only thing in there that would set it apart from any other professional office was the trivial collection of framed photographs sitting atop the desk. Stacey saw me looking at them and placed them face down as we immediately started rifling through the drawers and shelves, looking for something that the FBI might have missed. Nath looked shell-shocked and just aimlessly stood there, numbly watching us as we ravenously tore it apart.

"Nath?" I prompted.

"Sorry, I'm just struggling a bit. This feels quite surreal. A few weeks ago, we were picking wedding venues, and now this," he shakily admitted.

"Just make yourself useful and try to guess the password for her computer or something," I suggested.

"I wouldn't know where to start."

"Well, you were going to fucking marry her, so I'm guessing you knew something about her that isn't total bullshit. Just try something."

"Like what?" he asked with a shrug.

"Her birthday? Childhood pets? The usual." I listed.

"Hey, try the name of her favourite serial killer; that's sure to get you in," Stacey teasingly added.

Nath half-heartedly sat down at the desk and started furiously tapping the keyboard with a single finger until he tossed it to one side with a flummoxed sigh. He groaned as he got down on his hands and knees to check the computer underneath and let out a single incredulous laugh.

"Of course," he uttered.

"What is it?" I asked.

"The FBI must've taken the actual computer; they've just left everything else."

"Great," I sarcastically mumbled, "so look through something else, then. Do I have to tell you to do everything?"

"Honestly, Liv, what are we doing here? If the FBI has already gone over this place with a fine-tooth comb, then what exactly are you hoping to find? A treasure-island-style map showing us exactly where she's taken our daughter?"

"Don't take that tone with me, bucko. To begin with, it's your fault we're in this mess," I chastised.

"Excuse me?"

"You heard me," I mumbled.

"You've made your fair share of mistakes too, Olivia."

"You really don't want to go tit-for-tat with me because you will definitely lose."

"Can you just set aside your crippling jealousy for a second and use your brain so we can actually find our daughter?"

"Jealous?" I mockingly laughed. "Are you kidding me right now? Jealous of what, exactly? Your psychotic plastic-princess?"

Nath silently discarded the files he was idly flicking through back onto the desk and turned his back on me.

"Are you telling me you've walked into this place before and not spotted a single red flag?"

"No," he mumbled.

"This whole building is basically a shrine to her own superiority complex! You must have known how vapid and self-absorbed she was, or did the big silicone tits make you forget?" I berated.

Stacey slammed a book on the floor in frustration and got up to stand between us.

"Oh my God! Enough!" Stacey shouted.

"You're pathetic," I mouthed at Nathaniel.

"You kids obviously need a few minutes alone to hash this out, so I'm going to leave you alone and search downstairs for a while."

"I'm fine," I sternly muttered.

"Liv, I'm telling you this as your best friend. You need to quit being such a bitch, curb the obvious envy, and start working together. Otherwise, we're wasting our time here."

"Well said, Stacey," Nath meekly murmured.

"Nath, I didn't say she was wrong, did I?" Stacey scathingly asked.

Like two naughty schoolchildren, we were aghast at Stacey's words, and I felt like I had been well and truly outed. As I sheepishly glanced at Nathaniel, who was just staring at his own shoes in guilt, I realised that my best friend's speech was steeped in truth but not totally accurate. In London, I accepted that Nath wasn't to blame for bringing Stephanie into our lives in the first instance, and he wasn't to know he was being stalked by a crazed fiend. I even forgave him for willingly inviting her into our family in my absence after everything she had done. Then he asked her to marry him, and I hadn't even mentioned that either. What I was really sore about was the resolute way he defended her innocence to the hilt, even when he could see how fervently sure I was, and the fact that he supported her so passionately that I actually started to question my own wavering sanity. I knew first-hand how manipulative and devious she was, yet part of me still expected Nathaniel to see through that. My bitterness was getting in the way of the truth, and Stacey was right. I needed to let it go before it ate away at me from the inside out.

"You're right. Give us five, please," Nath said.

I remained silent as Stacey left the room and quietly shut the door behind her. Nathaniel lifted his head up from his shoes and stared at me for a few seconds before letting out a deep exhale.

"You asked me back in the studio if I still loved you," he sullenly uttered.

"I did," I tearfully mumbled.

"I *never* stopped loving you," he firmly stated as he walked closer to me. "Not even for a second," he added.

"Me neither."

"It would be so easy for me to tell you that I never loved Stephanie, but I honestly did. In spite of all her bad qualities – even though it was all an act – she helped me through some really grim times. Aurora too. I'm just struggling to separate the woman I knew from the monster she has become, you know?"

"Okay. I get it. I never blamed you for moving on; I was gone for years. I just wanted you to believe me."

"I thought about you every single day you were missing, and I never gave up hope that you would return. And I did believe you. I just didn't want to."

"Why didn't you say all this earlier?"

"Liv, it was complicated, and I was clearly lying to myself. I was just hoping that everything would sort itself out, but we haven't even had five minutes to process what's happened, let alone have a heart-to-heart."

I perched on the side of the desk, raised my head to the ceiling, closed my eyes, and exhaled a huge sigh. Nathaniel took a few steps closer to me and tucked some hair behind my ear.

"What are we going to do? Everything's a fucking mess," I groaned in frustration.

"We are going to find Aurora, put Stephanie behind bars, and all move very far away from here," he determinedly said.

It was everything I wanted to hear. I dropped my head down and moved closer to Nathaniel as my trembling hand found him, and he delicately pulled me in. Just as his lips drew closer to mine, we both felt my phone vibrate between us, and I pulled away slightly.

"No, just ignore it for a second," he whispered.

"I can't. It could be Agent Aldrich," I uttered.

I tentatively backed off from him and pulled my phone out to find a message from an unknown number waiting.

> *Judges 21:23. No FBI, or else. X*

"What the fuck?" I perplexedly said under my breath.

"What is it? Have they found her?" Nath asked.

"No. I have no idea what this means," I replied as I showed him the screen.

"Is that a place and a time? Do you think it's Steph?"

"Wait a second," I said as I started frantically rifling through the books that Stacey had thrown to the floor in her search before picking up the Bible I had seen discarded amongst them. I quickly searched through the contents page to find the Book of Judges, and as I flicked through to the section I was looking for, I noticed the passage was already highlighted in fluorescent pink ink.

"So, the sons of the tribe of Benjamin did as instructed and took wives according to their number from the dancers whom they carried away. Then they went and returned unto their inheritance, repaired the cities, and dwelt in them," I read out loud.

"What does it mean?" Nath asked.

"She has her. They're at the bunker."

30

THE WHITE FLAG

OLIVIA – 2024

Like passing ships in the night; as we were speeding back up the freeway towards Sacramento to search Stephanie's office, she was on the other side of the road, dragging my daughter against her will to the very worst place on Earth. After deciphering her tauntingly cryptic text message, we immediately began barrelling back down to Hammerdale and directly to the place where all this began. The thought of my daughter even breathing the air in that grimy place filled me with fury, and once I got my hands on Stephanie, I wouldn't be able to stop myself from killing her.

"If she's hurt her—" I began to ponder out loud.

"No," Nath interrupted, "we've established she's crazy, but she would never hurt Aurora, I'm sure of that."

"We don't know what she is capable of," I remarked.

"Give Alex a call, he's closer, after all," he suggested.

"I've tried him, and it keeps going to voicemail."

"What about Agent Aldrich?"

"Didn't you read the message? She said no FBI. If we show up with a dozen suits in tow, God knows how she will react," I worriedly said.

"We need to call *someone*; we're still thirty minutes out."

"It's clearly a trap because she wouldn't have told us where she is otherwise."

"She doesn't know about me, though," Stacey interjected from the back seat.

"No offence, Stace, but what are you going to do?" I asked.

"None taken. I can hang back in case something goes wrong. She doesn't even know who I am. And for the record, I have a mean right hook."

My phone started ringing on my lap, and I quickly saw it was Agent Aldrich calling me. I almost immediately answered it until I realised that I had to keep the liaison we were speeding to a secret.

"Shit," I said under my breath.

"Who is it?" Nath asked.

"Aldrich."

"Answer it."

"Oh, God. I don't know what to do! Shall I tell him about the text or not?"

"No, I think you are right. We don't know what frame of mind she is in," Nath defeatedly said.

I shakily answered the phone, tentatively put it to my ear, and took a deep breath.

"Hello?" I said.

"Miss Lakewell, this is Frank Aldrich," he sternly responded.

"What can I do you for?" I gawkily replied.

"I've just had a report from the agents surveilling Miss Ward's office in Sacramento that you and Nathaniel were seen entering the premises with an unknown woman. Why were you there?"

"We were looking for our daughter."

"You need to leave this to us, Olivia. Stephanie could have come back, seen your vehicle, and thought better of it. Your interference will hinder the investigation and prolong finding Aurora."

"I'm sorry, we didn't know what else to do."

"Go home, lock the doors, and call me the instant you see Stephanie or your daughter."

"That's where we are going now," I lied.

"Did you even learn anything?" he asked with a sigh.

"No, it appears your agents were very thorough."

"Go home, Olivia. We'll call you the instant we find something, but you needn't get involved," he instructed.

"Okay, we will. I promise," I said as I hung up the phone with a sigh.

Nathaniel shot me a sideways glance before returning his attention to the road.

"Well, it's done. We have to deal with the psychopath on our own," I nervously announced.

"I hope that wasn't a mistake," Nath mumbled.

"Me too."

"Hey, Nath, you don't have guns in here, do you?" Stacey asked from the back seat.

"No. Not all Americans are gun-obsessed," he replied.

"Alex has a pistol? We could swing by his to collect it," I suggested.

"No, we aren't taking a gun. For a start, the FBI confiscated it at the sheriff's office."

"So, what are we going to do? She's quite clearly leading us into a trap, and we are just wilfully walking into it. Also, she clearly doesn't have the same hangups about guns as you," I anxiously said.

"We'll just have to play it by ear," he mustered.

"Fucking hell, Nath. This isn't deciding where we are going for dinner. She's a cold-blooded killer," I scorned.

"I'm going to talk to her," he gulped.

"You?"

"Yes. She did all this to be with me, right? So, she isn't going to hurt me. That's my theory, anyway."

"She might if she thinks we're getting back together."

"Then we'll keep that part quiet."

"Wait, you guys are getting back together? When did that happen?" Stacey gasped.

"We had a good chat at the office," I uttered.

"Christ. I only left you in that room for five minutes," she remarked with a touch of sarcasm.

We came off the freeway and continued driving through Hammerdale towards the path to the bunker. Once we arrived, we spotted Stephanie's predictably hot-pink convertible parked up beside the road with the engine still running. Nathaniel cautiously parked up behind it and tried to peer through the windshield to see if Stephanie was still in the vehicle. When he was satisfied that she wasn't, he took the key out of the ignition and leaned back in his seat with a weary huff.

"How much phone battery do you have?" I asked Stacey.

"About twenty-five per cent," she replied.

"I'll call you before we walk in there. Keep an ear out, and if it sounds like things are going tits up, ring Aldrich."

"Will do. Be careful."

"We will. You ready, Nath?"

"Ready as I'll ever be," he shakily replied.

Nath and I determinedly got out of the car, leaving Stacey at the roadside, and we made our way down the muddy trail towards the hatch of the bunker. That night was particularly eerie, as a thick mist had descended and was swirling amongst the trees we walked through. Every inscrutable rustling within the foliage we jumpily treated with mutual fear, and we were both expecting a maniac to pounce out of it on us at a moment's notice. As we got closer to the bunker, the fog thickened even further, to the point where we almost had to grope our way through it with our hands outstretched to see even a few metres ahead of us.

"I don't like this," Nathaniel whispered.

"Me neither. I can barely see the tip of my nose," I uttered.

"Do you think she is waiting for us in there?"

"Uh-huh," I nodded.

"Like I said, she wouldn't hurt me. She might just want to talk."

"I can tell you with total conviction that she doesn't give two hoots about hurting me, so she'll probably just shoot me on sight."

"Then why are you doing this?" he asked.

"Aurora," I mumbled.

We arrived at the hatch, and I stopped a few paces away from it. Bizarrely, it was almost welcoming, as it had been left open for us, with the warm lights on inside. Every thought racing through my mind told me that it was a trap, and it was likely that I would never walk out of there ever again. Nonetheless, the thought of Aurora being trapped there was enough for me to ignore my instincts, and I took out my phone to call Stacey. I heard her answer, and without a word, I placed it back in my pocket.

"Whatever happens, Aurora needs to walk out of there," I whispered.

"All three of us are walking out of there," Nath quietly assured.

"I'm serious, Nath. If shit starts to hit the fan, just grab her and get the hell out of there."

I placed my shaking foot on the top rung of the filthy ladder and began making my way down into the depths as it creaked under my weight. When my feet were firmly on the ground, I paused for a moment as I waited for Nathaniel to join me, and then we both peered down the concrete steps to the closed steel door at the bottom. We started creeping down the steps one at a time, trying to hold onto the element of surprise, but when we started hearing Aurora's pained screams from inside, we instinctually sprinted the rest of the way and slammed into the closed door.

The door was incredibly stiff but luckily unlocked, so between us, we managed to frenziedly pull it open. Gripped by the panic, I kicked the next door open that was left ajar, and it flew open, exposing Aurora in the centre of the room, wearing the same jumpsuit I did and tied to the very same rickety chair I sat on for ten torturous years. She must have heard us come inside and started screaming incessantly through the bag that had been left over her head, and as we both raced over to her to remove it and untie her bounds, she realised that it was us and began to cry hysterically.

"Mum? Dad? Is that you?" she screamingly sobbed.

"We're here, sweetie, you're safe," I assured.

"Where's Stephanie?" she asked.

"We don't know. Did she bring you here?" Nath replied.

"I met her at the office, and I must have fallen asleep or something because when I woke up, I was tied to this chair. I was so scared, Dad," she wept.

"I know you were, honey, and I'm so sorry this has happened to you," Nathaniel said as he tried to undo the knots behind her.

"Mum, I'm sorry for what I said at the skatepark. I didn't mean it. I was just being horrible to you," she sniffled.

"Baby, you don't have to apologise for a damn thing. I'm just glad you're safe, and I'm never letting you out of my sight again," I explained.

"Come on, we need to get out of here before she shows up," Nath frantically stated as he got the last knot undone.

Once she was free, Nathaniel carefully lifted Aurora out of the chair, and we began slowly making our way out of the bunker. Barely had my foot crossed the threshold of the first door when I heard the ominous whirring of the CCTV camera moving behind me, which made me stop dead in my tracks. I slowly turned around to confront it, and the familiar foreboding noise of the intercom connecting made Nathaniel and Aurora stop a few metres ahead of me.

"I always told you that you were a fucking coward," I provokingly reminded. "Who even does that to a child?"

"You know what your problem is, Olivia? You talk too much, and you never listen," the voice boomed.

"Maybe I could understand you better without that pathetic child's toy you are intent on using to hide your voice."

The voice laughed.

"You will seek me and find me when you seek me with all your heart," the voice recited before it disconnected.

"What the fuck does that mean?" Nathaniel asked.

As I spun my head back around to reply to him, I saw some mad scrawling on the back of Aurora's jumpsuit. As I got closer, I realised that it was a set of coordinates and a crudely drawn crucifix.

"What's that?" Nathaniel asked.

"A white flag," I laughed.

31

THE LETTER

OLIVIA — 2024

Stephanie's insatiable flair for the dramatic had left her without any leverage, whether it was intentional or not. I was surrounded by everyone I ever cared about in my life, and she had given me an open invitation to find her with no possible repercussions. Maybe she thought that I would be stupid enough to accept her bidding alone, in some misguided attempt to deliver justice by my own hands, but for the first time since this began, I had the advantage, and I planned to arrive at those coordinates with the full weight of the FBI behind me.

Aurora was a weeping wreck after what had happened, still delirious from whatever narcotic Stephanie had used to knock her out, and constantly apologising to Nathaniel and I for going missing. We tried to console her the best we could, but with the menace interminably looming, we would have to leave her again to make sure it was extinguished for good. Once we arrived back at the roadside, and she was safely seated in Stephanie's ridiculous vehicle with Stacey at the wheel, I took out my phone and called Aldrich back.

"Olivia?" he answered.

"I'm sending you some coordinates. You need to send some agents there immediately, we have her cornered," I said matter-of-factly.

"You have who cornered, exactly?"

"Stephanie – Miss Ward."

"I told you not to get involved in the—"

"Just be there. Nath and I are on our way there now, and we could do with some backup," I instructed as I hung up the phone and sent the coordinates.

"I bet that felt good," Stacey remarked.

"Mum, you can't seriously be planning to confront her? What if she takes you away again? Or hurts you both?" Aurora anxiously said.

"Don't worry about us. Dad is coming, so he'll protect me if it comes to that."

"Yeah, right," Stacey muttered from the driver's seat.

"Hey!" Nath shrugged, "I'm standing right here."

"Stacey is going to take you back home. You're both going to lock the door and stay there until this is over," I sternly ordered.

"Okay, just promise me you're both coming back," Aurora tearfully said.

"I promise. I love you, sweetheart."

I stepped back from the vehicle, and Stacey quickly pulled out onto the road with Aurora on the back seat, not taking her eyes off us. Nathaniel and I waved as we diligently watched them begin their journey back to Hammerdale and disappear into the distance. We both returned to his vehicle, and I carefully inputted the coordinates into the navigation app on my phone. The location was only a few minutes' drive away from us, and under my direction, we started further away from home.

"What do you think she has planned? I'm not going to lie: I'm shitting myself here," Nathaniel awkwardly mumbled.

"I don't know if she has any tricks left up her sleeve, and to be honest, it doesn't even matter anymore. Once the FBI is done with her, there will be enough evidence to put her away until the day she dies," I pensively mused.

"It's incredible; all of this was just to win my affection and take me from you. She's insane."

"You know I hate saying I told you so."

"Look, I know I keep repeating it, but I'm sorry for—"

"Wait," I interrupted, "park up here."

"We are here already?"

"Apparently. She was within spitting distance the entire time."

We drove as close as we could to the blip on the map, and Nathaniel parked the car once again. We both got out and started following my phone through the winding trail back into the forest. The beaten path was far narrower than its counterpart back to my bunker, more precarious, and obviously far less travelled. We fought with all the sprawling branches that were rudely encroaching onto the zigzagging trail as we passed, until we reached an unexpected clearing with an identical hatch concealed by overgrown ivy. The corroded padlock had been discarded beside it, and Nathaniel slowly lifted the hatch as I tore the ivy to one side, exposing a set of rusted ladders underneath it.

"Well, I'm getting déjà vu," I dryly said.

"There's two of these hellholes?" Nath exclaimed.

"It appears that way."

"Liv, I don't like this. We should wait for the FBI. We literally have no idea what we are walking into," he worriedly said.

"They'll be a few minutes behind us, and I want to hear what that bitch has to say before they get here," I dismissed as I started climbing down.

We both made our way down the ladders and although it was lit far dimmer than the bunker that I had been held captive in, I could see it was in a far worse state of repair. The walls glistened in the light and almost appeared as if they were excreting a slimy green substance thanks to the mildew that was left unchecked. The floor was littered with stray cigarette ends and debris that rolled into the deep cracks between each step. Those unfamiliar concrete steps seemed to spiral into the earth forever, but at the very bottom of them sat a rusty steel door that was an exact duplicate of the one I stared at for a decade. We crept over to it, futilely putting our ears to the door, hoping to hear what was going on inside. It was deathly silent.

"Are you sure you are up for this?" I whispered.

"Yes," he mouthed.

I slowly turned the handle, and the door violently screeched as it opened, exposing a dark room, only illuminated by the dozen active CCTV screens mounted above a messy desk that was directly facing us. As we tentatively approached the desk, all the screens malfunctioned slightly and flashed brightly, outlining the unmistakable silhouette of Stephanie sitting at the desk facing the screens. We were both instantly rooted to the ground in fear of what we had just seen, and as we guardedly waited for her to turn around, I grabbed Nathaniel's hand by my side tightly. Did she not hear us come in? Was this part of the plan? I could feel Nathaniel's rapid heartbeat through his fingertips, and I squeezed his hand before breaking the silence.

"Quit the theatrics and get on with it," I shouted.

She didn't move a muscle.

"Stephanie, just stay calm. We just want to talk. No one else has to get hurt," Nathaniel softly said.

After a few tense seconds of silence, we confusedly looked at each other and began creeping further until we were almost within touching distance. I felt my shoe lose traction slightly on the floor, and only after looking down to see what I had stepped in did I notice the lake of blood surrounding Stephanie. I cautiously lifted my shoe out of the crimson puddle and flicked on the light switch I had spotted on the wall. As the dull hum and pop of the fluorescent lighting above started to illuminate, we had a full, unfiltered view of the grim tableau that Stephanie had left for us.

She had taken her own life.

As twisted as it was, my first thought was that it was ironic that she had chosen to slit her wrists because that was my exact same plan, too. Somehow, she had managed to remain gruesomely propped up in the chair, with all the colour drained from her face and a veritable cornucopia of blood-tainted evidence piled on the desk in front of her. I rolled back my sleeve slightly to place two fingers on her neck to check for a pulse. She was still lukewarm but long gone. I slowly turned to Nathaniel and grimly shook my head to signify she was dead, and he gasped as he recoiled in shock towards the entrance.

"I think I'm going to be sick," Nathaniel gasped.

"See, I told you that you were a coward," I gently whispered to her.

"What the fuck happened here?"

"She's killed herself, Nath."

"Why? She would never do that."

"She knew the net was closing in on her, and committing suicide was the only thing she could do to keep control."

"Jesus!" he exclaimed.

"Honestly, I'm sorry. I know you had feelings for her."

Nathaniel came over and reached out to touch her hair slightly before thinking better of it. He was clearly hysterical, pacing the space with his head in his hands and repeating something indiscernible under his breath. I held my arms out to comfort him, and he dismissed them to continue walking around in circles.

I turned around, and as I disdainfully looked at the scene before us, I realised that place was Stephanie's macabre trophy cabinet. Amongst the items was Aurora's unsent birthday card that I traded my dignity for, a crudely cut fabric patch from the shirts of each of the men who had tried saving me, and a vile collection of naked polaroids that were taken of me when I was unconscious. That freak had even sliced a lock of my hair without my knowledge, and it was taped to one of the monitors along with a bundle of Nicole's. The screens were frozen on various images from my time in the bunker, which served as a final insulting reminder sent by my captor from beyond the grave.

Nath seemed to psyche himself up in the corner of the room with deep breathing before he came back to look at me. He could barely look at Stephanie's body and instead tried to focus on all the items surrounding her.

"You don't have to do this, Nath. The FBI will be here shortly. They can sort through all this," I suggested.

"I'm fine," he bitterly mumbled.

"Nath, honestly—" I started.

"I said I'm fine," he repeated. "Is that you?" he bemusedly asked as he pointed to the screens.

"Yes, and please don't look at them," I grumbled in embarrassment.

"Why are you naked on these?"

"Benjamin – I mean Stephanie – made me."

"You're smiling on this one. Why?" Nath pointed out.

"I can't remember," I mustered.

"You are smiling on quite a few of them, actually."

"I was filmed twenty-four-seven for ten years, so she had a lot of footage to pick from."

"Huh," Nath grunted as he picked up a letter left on the keyboard that was addressed to him, "it's for me."

My heart sank as he slowly opened the envelope and read the contents in silence. I could see a whole palette of emotions painting his face as he made it through each paragraph before he angrily discarded it back onto the keyboard. His tearful eyes met mine, and he coughed slightly to clear his throat.

"Is this true?" he heatedly asked.

"What?"

"The letter."

"Well, I don't know, I haven't read it, Nath," I said mockingly.

He smiled slightly at my scornful jibe before taking a deep breath and putting his hand over his mouth. The tears started flooding down his cheeks, and he wafted the air in front of his face as he averted his eyes from mine.

"What did it say?" I softly asked.

"I need to get out of here," he agitatedly announced as he took one final glance at the screens above and then calmly walked out of the room.

"Nath?" I shouted after him.

When I heard the sound of his boots banging against each rung of the ladder as he climbed it, I realised that he wasn't coming back. I picked up the incriminating letter, which had somehow escaped the deluge of blood surrounding it, and I began to read.

Nathaniel,

I don't have much time, so I'll cut to the chase. What Olivia accused me of is the truth: I'm the one responsible for her kidnapping.

This will hurt, and I hope it does, but I don't think I ever loved you. When you so callously rejected me twenty years ago, you quickly turned into an obsession for me, and I have since lived my life trying to convince myself that I was worthy. Your spiteful indifference to my feelings has turned me into the sour woman I am today, and I now realise that the desperate measures I was forced to stoop to are entirely your fault.

Back in high school, I only ever wanted your affection, and I would have done anything to get it. Nonetheless, that hopeful young girl doesn't exist anymore. She was pumped so full of silicone and plastic that she didn't even recognise her own reflection and was mortally poisoned by the bitterness and shame of your constant rejection. I had to do things in the name of our supposed love, *terrible* things, and the first thing you do when you see your sallow ex-fiancée is try to rekindle what you had, like we were *nothing*.

Seeing as how Daniels hasn't returned my calls, I assume that he has been arrested or worse, and by now, you will have heard about my affair with him. Even though it made me sick to my stomach, your actions forced me to trade sexual favours with Daniels to protect what we had. He is no more than an opportunist pervert who uses women like objects, and God's judgment is coming for him.

I have nothing else to lose, so you know that you can implicitly trust what I am about to tell you. Olivia is no angel; she's been lying to you from the start.

It didn't take her long to start a consenting sexual relationship with Daniels herself, and she would even often pose totally naked in front of the camera like the whore she is to entice him to visit her. He would sickeningly take photographs of his relations with her, and this control room is littered with sordid images of their liaisons.

I may have set the plan in motion to take her, but Daniels made it his own. I see now that what I did was inherently wrong and that I should have just moved on, but I needed to prove to myself that I was worthy of your love. Although all of this could have been avoided long ago by being polite to me, as a parting gift, I absolve you of the guilt.

I'm going now. I'll save a seat for you all down here.

Stephanie.

32

THE GOODNIGHT

OLIVIA – 2024

I could already hear the low droning of the agents descending on the hatch when I was sullenly climbing the disintegrated ladders, and as I slowly emerged above ground, I was immediately cuffed and calmly escorted away from the hatch. I didn't put up a fight because I fully accepted the consequences of my actions willingly.

As the unknown agent was pushing me back through the woods, I couldn't help but be in awe of what I had just witnessed. I really had to hand it to Stephanie; she was backed into a corner, she reacted, and in the end, she played an absolute blinder. The only people who could prove the letter was nothing but flagrant lies were already dead. Nathaniel's emotions were so erratic that he would have believed literally anything she could have written on those pages. Stephanie's final words had irreparably ruined my relationship forever, and as soon as I finished reading it, I already knew that. She had taken the coward's way out, leaving me a final 'fuck you' from the grave, and there was no denying that she vacated this mortal coil victorious.

I reflectively looked down at the ground as we walked, laughing to myself about her offering to save us all a seat in hell. It was quite the biting witticism for her to end on, and I couldn't help but applaud her creativity in her final moments. I should have felt relieved that she was finally gone. However, in many ways, she was still as alive as ever. Granted, the danger around us had been extinguished, but we were all still ensnared by the web of lies she had carefully crafted over two decades.

More than anything, I was just disappointed. I wanted to witness the agents physically slap the cuffs on her, hear those sweet words while she was read her rights, and be the last grinning face she saw when all sense of freedom was stripped of her for the rest of her wretched existence. She knew what the ending to this long-drawn-out story would be, probably from the beginning, and like everything else, she took the satisfaction of ensuring it concluded without me. Psychopaths like her thrive on controlling their victims, and taking that power away is like confiscating a child's favourite toy. Come hell or high water, they will do absolutely anything to get it back.

I barely noticed the fleet of vehicles parked up at the roadside until even more of them arrived, and I was taken to a large trailer that served as a mobile operations centre. As I was led up behind it, I could see Agent Aldrich seated inside, and the disappointment in his face when he glanced at me was intense.

"Sir, we've located Miss Lakewell," the agent holding me said.

"Thanks, Steve. You can uncuff her," Aldrich instructed.

"So, I'm not in trouble?" I asked.

"You should be. Evidence tampering and interference of an active investigation are both very serious offences. Although, after considering your emotional state after what happened to you, I can let it slide, but you need to bear in mind that you won't get another free pass."

"I appreciate it," I mumbled.

"Be under no illusions; what you did by going in there alone was incredibly reckless, but fortunately for you, there are no federal laws prohibiting stupidity."

"That's good. Otherwise, they'd have thrown away the key a long time ago, wouldn't they?" I dryly joked.

"Uh-huh," Aldrich nodded as my obvious gag drifted above his balding head, "what did you learn in there?"

"Stephanie's dead, with a written confession sitting in front of her and a whole host of other items that prove beyond a doubt what she did."

"We have agents in there now collecting evidence. We will return to you for a statement in the morning, but for now, your involvement in this case is over. One of the agents will drive you home."

"Thank you," I said as I turned away before immediately turning back. "Hey, you didn't see Nathaniel come through here, did you?"

"Mr Anderson? No, he must have left before we arrived. Please let him know we will need to speak to him, too. I still have his phone."

"I will," I softly replied as an agent came to collect me.

For hopefully the final time, I was being driven away from the bunker with a stranger in the driver's seat, and it was every bit as harrowing as the first. In a way, I felt like I had lost even more since my escape because I managed to take a small taste of what my life could be like if I had somehow succeeded in repairing it. Nathaniel was painfully out of reach again, but this time by his own choice, and I had run out of words to convince him otherwise. I was just mentally drained, and if it wasn't for the grimacing agent driving me, I felt like I could have nodded off there and then.

At my request, the agent dropped me off at Alex's house instead. The night had already been far too long to extend it further by having a blazing row with Nathaniel. I had accepted he would need time to come to terms with what had happened to him, and I knew that the common denominator for every shitty thing that happened in his life was me, so for once, I took the moral high ground and gave him the space he needed.

As I knocked on Alex's door, it creaked open slightly, so I just ambled inside. I could hear the soft rock music coming from his office, and I gingerly crept down the hallway to place my ear against the door. As I slowly entered, I saw Alex, clearly half-cut judging by the bottle of whiskey beside him, silently pawing through a photo album on his lap by candlelight. He didn't notice me enter, and I sheepishly sat next to him on the sofa.

"Hey," I whispered.

"Oh, hi," he slurred.

"Been doing some drinking there, buddy?" I asked.

"A little," he hiccupped.

"Come on, sharing is caring," I remarked as I held my hand out for the bottle.

He obliged, and I drank from it deeply. As the amber liquid burned my throat on its way down, I realised that I hadn't touched a drop for over ten years.

"What happened to you?" I softly asked.

"I *killed* him. I put a bullet in his chest without thinking twice about it," he drunkenly explained.

"Believe me, after what I've learned, he fucking deserved it," I said as I passed back the bottle.

"I just always thought it was an accident with Nicole. You show up to tell me otherwise, and within a few days, the man responsible is dead," he said between swigs before returning it to me.

"Stephanie's dead too."

"What?" he gasped.

"Topped herself. She couldn't stand to be arrested and left Nathaniel a suicide note filled to the brim with all kinds of bullshit about me."

"Did he believe it?" he asked.

"Yep," I said with a glug.

"I'm sorry, Liv," he said as he gently put his hand on my knee and took the bottle with his other hand.

"Me too," I pensively replied.

"As your therapist, I order you to drink," he jibed as he swished the bottle in my face.

"Yessir," I saluted as I welcomed the bottle back.

I tried to readjust my posture, but the sudden influx of hard alcohol coupled with my sheer exhaustion had left me feeling quite tipsy, so I slumped back into the plush sofa. I looked smilingly over Alex's shoulder at the photographs featuring him and Nicole on a cherished foreign holiday. He saw me peeking, handed me the album, and I studied each picture carefully.

"You guys looked happy," I remarked.

"We were," he uttered.

"Isn't it weird how one sick woman's actions can send shockwaves through so many lives?"

"Did Stephanie mention Nicole in her letter?"

"No, sorry," I admitted.

"I thought as much. She never cared about anyone else other than herself.

"I'll drink to that," I said with another nip.

I looked up from the album and saw the warm candlelight dancing across Nathaniel's painting, which was hung on the wall. I could feel the intense emotion building within me, and Alex must have spotted it too, because he took the album and the bottle from me, placing his hand back on my knee.

"Listen, Olivia—" he started.

"Shush," I gently interrupted, "just look at it."

He leaned back, and as we both just looked at the canvas, silently taking different meanings from it, the song playing in the background built into a dramatic crescendo.

"What do you see?" I asked.

"Regret," he responded, "you?"

"Myself," I mumbled.

When I first saw that painting hung in his office, I saw the unbridled fury and unfathomable sadness behind every drop of paint, and I was shown the parts of myself that I had lost. I didn't know if it was the bourbon talking, but that canvas may as well have been a mirror. I could see a heap of emotions all bleeding into one another, the lines between guilt and innocence blurred, and the bleakness of the future coating all sense of hope. I was left a numb husk, trying to make sense of what was going on in my own mind and wondering if I would ever see the old painting ever again.

After a few minutes of silently contemplating the image before us, Alex's hand slowly started drifting up my thigh. I thought nothing of it at first and didn't even tilt my head to look, but his delicate strokes quickly evolved into a grip, and as he squeezed, I found myself wanting him to continue. I saw him turn to me in the corner of my eye as his hand reached the top of my jeans, slid underneath my top, and carefully made its way across my stomach.

I succumbed to the touch and turned to him. Both of us still had tears in our eyes, and we instinctually leaned in for an impassioned kiss. As we tenderly began to undress each other, we shared a brief moment of intense eye contact, by which we seemed to form an unspoken agreement that we were both going to be thinking about someone else. I obviously desired Nathaniel's hands gliding across my body and his lips pressing into mine after he whispered sweet nothings into my ears. Alex was clearly imagining his darling Nicole, desperate to spend just one more passionate night with her after she was so brutally taken away from him at the height of their love. Both of us had lost so much, our very souls shattered beyond all understanding, and it felt so therapeutically liberating to finally let go of everything, leaving our bodies to explore each other without a single thought for the consequences.

When it was over, I didn't feel any semblance of regret, shame, or anything for that matter. I simply existed in the moment and could barely form an opinion on what we had just done. Alex was the first to stand as he wearily held his head, and I looked at him with an empathetic half-smile as he tried to pick out his clothes from the messy pile sitting in his office.

"Well, that was unexpected," he laughed.

"You can say that again," I remarked as I searched for my underwear.

"Listen, I don't think we did something wrong, but I'd rather you didn't mention this to Nathaniel," he awkwardly explained.

"Likewise. Although to be honest, I don't think he'd give a shit."

Alex gawkily smiled, holding the rest of his clothes as he desperately tried to think of something to say.

"By the way, with everything that's been going on, I haven't had a chance to sort out the guest room."

"I'll just crash here."

"Are you sure? I mean, you can just sleep in my bed. I promise I won't snatch the covers."

"Honestly, I'm fine here," I smiled.

"Okay then, well, I'm going to head up. I think I'm going to have the hangover from hell in the morning."

"Yeah, me too. My head is mashed."

"If you need anything, just give me a shout."

"I will. Good night, Alex."

Alex leaned down to give me a kiss on the forehead, and as he stroked my hair, he said something in my ear that instantly sobered me up and made all the hairs on my neck promptly stand on end.

"Sleep tight," he whispered, "don't let the bedbugs bite."

33

THE LOVE

OLIVIA – 2024

I could feel my racing heart violently beating as high up as my throat, and my barely clothed body was immediately besieged by a vast army of goosebumps. Alex seemed to have creepily noticed it when he stroked my arm good night, and without giving me an explanation, he turned round and left the room. As soon as he was out of the door, I started hyperventilating with my quaking hands over my mouth to try and mute the noise. I couldn't explain what I had just heard, but oddly enough, there was something unmistakable in the cadence of his voice that led me to believe with unwavering certainty that I had heard him say that exact phrase before. His footsteps were coming closer, so I desperately tried to catch my breath and calm down before he entered the room again. I turned my head slightly towards the door as he came in carrying a blanket, so I mustered the best smile I could manage given the circumstances. Like a hunter wrapping his kill, he tightly shrouded me in the blanket to the point where I could barely move and gave me a light kiss on the forehead.

"Is that better?" he softly asked.

"Uh-huh. Much better. Thank you so much," I gushed in a frantic attempt to conceal my abject terror.

"If you need anything else, I'll be upstairs," he said.

"I'm sure I'll be fine. Thanks, though. Good night," I wildly stammered.

"Is everything okay, Olivia? You're still shaking," he asked matter-of-factly.

"Just a little cold. Not to worry, I'll soon warm up."

"Okay, good night, then," he said as he turned off the light on his way out.

I remained paralysed on the sofa, thinking about every encounter I had with both Alex and Benjamin over the years, trying to remember anything that would allow me to disregard what I heard in his voice as sheer coincidence. Nonetheless, I couldn't ignore the screaming voice within me urging me to run away from there or the deadening shame I felt for just sleeping with the man I suddenly realised could be the monster that held me in captivity for an endless decade of torture and humiliation. I heard mattress springs being depressed upstairs, so in the dark, I quietly but hastily put on my clothes that were lying strewn on the floor, tiptoed to the office door, and slowly turned the handle to make a quiet exit.

It wouldn't budge.

My worst fears were confirmed: I was locked up in there. I stealthily moved around the room, diligently checking every window for a possible means of escape, but each of the panes sat behind inch-thick steel bars. I frantically ran over to his desk, hoping to find the pistol he kept in it, but the drawer had been gallingly emptied out. I furiously patted down my jeans to try and locate my phone, but as I didn't have it on me, I got down on my hands and knees to search for it underneath the furniture, thinking that I might have dropped it earlier. It was then that I noticed a slight imperfection on the wooden flooring beneath a rug. Curiosity got the better of me, so I slowly peeled back the corner, exposing an access hatch hidden under the coffee table. I silently lifted the table, removed the rug as quietly as possible, and looked down on the hatch with some trepidation, dreading and anticipating what it could be hiding. With a deep breath, I firmly grasped the handle that was enclosed in the timber and pulled it open.

Underneath was a set of concrete steps leading down into the pitch black. After tentatively going down a few of them, my forehead struck a bulb dangling from the ceiling, which was glimmering in what little light made it down there, and I pulled the cord beside it. Suddenly, the staircase was flooded with light, and at the bottom of it, I spotted an armoured steel door. I descended the steps to try the handle but found it locked. I noticed a small, illuminated keypad beside it, and with bated breath, I tried the first combination that sprang to mind.

"1234," I whispered to myself.

The keypad beeped and flashed red.

"All the zeroes," I uttered.

It flashed again.

"Hmm," I mused to myself, "2123."

The keypad turned green. I heard the door unlock with a loud clunk, and I pulled it open. Although it was clearly a different place, Alex had gone to extreme lengths to recreate my bunker as perfectly as he could. The shower, bed, and kitchenette were identical, and they were even installed in the same places. He had even gone as far as to recreate every single line I had etched on the concrete wall as if he had copied it directly from a photograph.

It was his plan all along. Alex, for reasons unknown, had condemned me to the bunker many years ago, and since my escape, he had shepherded me towards this very moment and to place me back in his thrall. My head throbbed with pain while trying to make sense of it all. Was Stephanie even involved? Or was she just a convenient scapegoat, given her past transgressions? Did the death of his fiancée snap something inside of him? Or had he always been like this? Was Daniels innocent and just got caught in the crossfire between two sociopaths trying to outdo each other while pursuing their twisted thrills?

As I tried to unravel the string of questions strangling my mind from within, I heard a thud behind me and, quick as a flash, whipped my head around to locate the source. The only thing that seemed out of place was a large floor-to-ceiling cupboard comprised of steel that he had placed there instead of the rusted racking that was in mine. Curiosity got the better of me, so I edged closer to peer inside, and as soon as I opened it, Nathaniel fell out in a groggy heap. It was plain to see he had been beaten up, handcuffed and gagged, and I violently shook him to wake him up.

"Nathaniel! Wake up!" I shouted.

"What the hell is happening? Where am I? I have a splitting headache," he groggily questioned.

"Underneath Alex's house, he's played us all like a fiddle."

"Oh, God, I remember. He jumped me when I got back home. Is Aurora okay?"

"I have no idea. She was with Stacey, remember?"

"We need to get out of here."

"I don't think that's a viable option. He's built this place underneath his study, and he's locked the door."

"Where is he now?"

"Upstairs."

"I don't have my phone on me. Do you have yours?"

"No, he must have taken it without me realising."

Nathaniel readjusted his posture the best he could, and I helped him prop up against the wall beside the cupboard he had been abandoned in. He sighed and, in frustration, banged his head twice against the concrete with his eyes closed.

"I'm so stupid. How did I not see this coming?" he asked himself out of desperation.

"It's not your fault, Nath. Listen, I'll try and find something to get those cuffs off you," I animatedly said.

"There's no point," he dismissively stated.

"Nath? We need to find a way to get out of here. God knows what he has planned for both of us."

"Olivia, just sit down for a moment," he softly instructed.

"Nath, no, we need to—"

"Please," he gently asked.

Against my better judgement, I decided to comply with his request only because of the truly haunting expression spanning his face.

"That day you were kidnapped was truly the worst day of my life. I loved you more than you could ever know, and you just vanished into thin air in the blink of an eye," he tearfully explained.

I remained silent.

"I couldn't bring myself to believe it at first. I kept thinking there was some kind of mistake, or it was even some kind of misguided prank. But it was when you still didn't show up a few days later that I started to think the worst."

"Nath, honestly, I think we should—"

"Just listen," he interjected.

I sullenly nodded.

"It shattered me, and when I had to explain to our little girl that her mummy wasn't coming home, it broke her heart too. For years, we lived our lives in wait, praying every single day that you would come home, and even when the missing posters started disappearing and the police stopped looking, we still had faith and lived each passing day in the desperate hope of finding you."

"I can't begin to imagine the loneliness you must have felt."

"Alex was there, right beside me, supporting me like any best friend would. We spent hours combing the woodland, looking for any trace of you. He printed the flyers and even tided me over with money when I was too miserable to work. He would pick Aurora up from school when I was too depressed to get out of bed and make us all dinner when I was too drunk to cook. Christ, he even shut down his construction company to qualify as a grief counsellor; he said he didn't do it for me, but deep down, I knew that he did."

"I'm sorry, Nath," I whispered.

"There's more. I was at my lowest of lows when I reconnected with Stephanie. I was so lonely, and Alex kept telling me to move on, so I did. When he found out about her, he changed."

"What do you mean, changed?"

"He was angry. Absolutely livid. He seemed to think I owed him something for all those years he supported and offered me a shoulder to cry on. Alex and Stephanie were constantly at each other's throats, but I thought that after twenty years, he would have got over what happened."

"Got over what?"

"You have to believe me," he started hysterically, "I never thought he would go this far, not even for a second."

"Nath, what are you talking—"

"I just thought it was just an innocent crush," he pensively interrupted.

"Stop. What are you talking about?"

"Alex is in love with me, okay? He always has been," he abruptly admitted.

34

THE NIGHTMARE

OLIVIA – 2024

Nathaniel's admission gave me more questions than answers. I leaned back on my hands to try and make sense of it all, and he was breathlessly staring into my very soul, trying to gauge how I was going to react.

"Sorry, what?" I mustered.

"It happened a few weeks after we met. One night, we got really plastered and ended up fooling around. I barely remembered it the day after, and I tried my best to laugh it off, but our intimacy that night must have awoken something in him so much that he became obsessed over me."

"Why didn't you tell me?"

"I was embarrassed," he announced defeatedly. "When he showed up after our first date in London, I thought I had managed to get through to him after he convinced me that he just wanted to stay friends. It didn't take him long before he started to incessantly ring me whenever he knew we were together."

"I always thought that person was Stephanie in the shadows and constantly pestering you with phone calls. In fact, you did tell me it was her at the time."

"No," he began defeatedly, "it was Alex all along. I just lied because it was much easier to explain it away with Stephanie."

"Where does she come into this?"

"She has always liked me since high school, and Alex has always despised her, so we never went beyond being friends. Don't get me wrong, she was always a little kooky, and as her letter said, I think she just saw me as a challenge more than anything else."

"Nath, she was more than a little crazy. Alex told me about the time she dressed up in my old clothes and dyed her hair. It's the behaviour of a sociopath."

"Stephanie? What?" he confusedly asked. "That was Alex," he added matter-of-factly.

"What? He dressed up as me?"

"He said it was to cheer me up," he muttered.

"Fucking hell, Nath. Why didn't you just cut him off?"

"After you moved over here, I spoke to him about that weird housewarming gift he left us. He promised the weirdness would stop, and for some time, it did. When you went missing, he was my old friend again, and since I had already lost you, I couldn't afford to lose anybody else."

"So, Stephanie was innocent, and he's pinned the whole thing on her?"

Before Nathaniel could reply, we both heard the sound of ominous clapping behind us at the entrance. I turned around to see Benjamin standing there in his black clothes and mask until he took it off, and Alex emerged from underneath. I had never seen the crazed look in his eyes before, and I instinctually shuffled closer to Nathaniel.

"If it isn't the lovebirds all cosied up in my basement," Alex merrily enthused.

"You fucking stay away from us, you psychopath," I uttered.

"I'm not going to hurt either of you. Not yet, anyway. I heard Nathaniel's monologue from upstairs, and I just couldn't bear not being able to correct the inaccuracies."

"Why did you do all this? You were supposed to be my friend, and you pinned the whole thing on Stephanie. Why?" Nathaniel wearily asked.

"Oh, my sweet summer child. Stephanie wasn't innocent! She was the one who convinced me to do all this shit in the first place."

"You're lying," I remarked.

"Look at me! I'm unmasked, and you're both helplessly sitting in my basement torture chamber. Do I strike you as somebody who needs to hide anything anymore?"

"Why did Stephanie kill herself, then?" I asked.

"Kill herself? What on earth gave you that idea? I did that, and believe me, she deserved—"

"She left a note, Alex," I interrupted.

"Duh, it didn't take much ingenuity to write her suicide note, and I barely had to touch the rest of the scene at all."

"Why would you do that to her?"

"I never liked her, and she broke the terms of our agreement!" he flamboyantly explained.

"What agreement are you talking about?" Nath interjected.

"I tried splitting you two lovebirds up, but against all odds, you stayed together. I realised I needed a woman's touch, and lucky for me, that's when Stephanie came to me with her idea."

"Her idea?" Nathaniel asked.

"She wanted to work together. Stephanie never wanted you, Nath. She just wanted to see your relationship break after you rejected her. She agreed to split you both up, and I would be there to pick up the pieces."

"You're sick," Nathaniel mumbled.

"It didn't work, though. All of our meek attempts ended in failure. When you stupidly got Olivia pregnant and proposed on a whim, we realised we needed to do something drastic. It took years, but between us, we finally built the bunker."

"You both built it?" I muttered.

"Yes. Well, I did the heavy lifting. Her majesty didn't want to break a nail. Stephanie agonised over when to take you, but it was her twisted idea to do it on your wedding day. It only took an old rag and a squirt of chemicals to knock you out. The rest is history."

"Which one of you demented perverts was behind the camera? You? Or her?" I heatedly asked.

"Does it really matter?"

"I suppose not," I muttered under my breath.

"I have to say, it was like looking after a baby. You required round-the-clock attention, and in the end, we had to split the time we both had to keep you from burning the place down or starving to death. It was after the time Nathaniel finally caved into Stephanie that I took over, because she wasn't interested in you anymore."

"What about Nicole? You fucking killed her like she was an animal sold to a slaughterhouse."

"Ahh, I actually feel bad about that one."

"That *one*? She was a person with hopes and dreams, and you suffocated her like she was nothing."

"Well, I needed to do something to convince Nath I had moved on, so I proposed to Nicole out of sheer stupidity. She was smarter than she appeared to be, so it didn't take her very long to stumble on my hobby, and as you can imagine, it was hard to explain away. After I asphyxiated her with some gas Stephanie used in her dental surgery, and it didn't take much to stage the accident by pushing her flaming car off the edge of North Ridge."

"She *adored* you. It was plain to see in her eyes on every photograph!" I shouted.

Alex wryly shrugged.

"Hey, don't worry! She didn't die in vain! The footage I collected was a very compelling reason for you to behave yourself. It was shortly afterwards that Stephanie decided to back out of our deal, so poor Nicole was no longer needed."

"Why did Stephanie backtrack on the deal?" Nath asked.

"She got bored and decided Olivia's suffering wasn't enough for her tastes. She convinced me she was going to use her feminine wiles to make you fall for her, then dump you like a piece of trash so I could become the shoulder for you to cry on afterwards. But predictably, she fell for you again."

"Then what did you do?" I asked.

"Well, I let you out, of course. You didn't think you escaped on your own, did you? Aww," he said with feigned sincerity.

"Why?" I demanded.

"You were meant to be a good girl, put a stop to Nathaniel's relationship, and then you'd disappear again. But the sap beside you decided he was in love with you again."

"I bet Stephanie didn't like that," I remarked.

"Not one bit, actually. That's when she begged the sheriff to keep everything under wraps and me at bay. It's amazing how men react when a fit blonde with big tits flashes a smile at them. Isn't that right, Nath?"

"Fuck off," Nath hissed furiously.

"So, let me get this straight, Daniels wasn't actually involved? She just used him to cover it up?" I asked.

"No. The moron thought Stephanie was in love with him. She thought that I didn't know that the sheriff was her pathetic backup plan if our agreement went awry. She had been sleeping with him for years."

"He stuck me with the antibiotics. It was his name on the prescription."

"It was an emergency, so Stephanie lifted it from his apartment. Ironically, he probably had it to treat an infection that whore gave to him. How stupid of her to think that I wouldn't notice the name on it when I came into the bunker to give it to you."

"That was you?" I gasped.

"See, I'm not all bad! You would have died without my help."

"You are deranged," Nathaniel added.

"I did all this to protect you, you ungrateful fuck! I'm the only one who ever understood you! Stephanie was cheating on you, and Olivia never loved you; I don't understand how you can't see what we have!" he shouted.

"It was just a drunken mistake two decades ago. It might have left you thinking you love me, but you really don't," Nathaniel scathingly uttered.

"After that amazing night together, a light bulb went on in my head. I always knew I was different, and you helped me finally realise why. I bore my soul to you that night, and the day after, you just gave me the brush-off like I was trash. For years on end, I've looked after and cared for you and your fucking daughter! You owe me an explanation, Nath."

"I don't owe you shit! You caused everything."

"What about when I found out that Stephanie had kidnapped Aurora? I saved her. Your daughter is totally innocent in all this, and she's already been through so much just so you could see the truth."

"What do you want? My thanks? You are ridiculous!"

"Admit to me that you love me!" he squealed.

Nathaniel and I looked at each other fearfully, both of us knowing that his old friend had turned totally insane without our notice. We shakily turned back to Alex, who was clearly wallowing in the twisted splendour of his tale but infuriated by Nath's defiance to respond to his clear threat.

"What happens now?" Nathaniel shakily asked.

"She knows," Alex whispered.

"Because we aren't getting out of here," I softly said.

"Okay, she doesn't know!" he heartily laughed as he pulled out his pistol. "That bitch is definitely getting out of here. She won't be breathing, mind you, but I'm sure you will forgive me, Nath, especially after you spend a few years down here. You see, I made a mistake ten years ago."

"What mistake?" I gently asked.

"We took the wrong person," he replied as he pointed the gun at me.

I closed my eyes, and as I took a deep breath, I saw that everything seemed to be happening in slow motion. First, I heard the click of the trigger being depressed and then the pop of the gunpowder igniting. What felt like a lifetime later, I heard the bullet strike the concrete behind us and even felt the dust as it impacted the wall. Thinking he had missed, I opened my eyes, and I saw Nathaniel, still almost floating in the air after he threw himself in the line of fire. Time started to pass normally again, and he struck the floor like a ton of bricks, with the blood already streaming from his shoulder.

"Look what you made me do!" Alex angrily shrieked.

He frantically rushed over to remove Nathaniel, who was on top of me but hadn't noticed I managed to grip the handle of a frying pan that was kept underneath the stove. I wildly swung it as hard as I possibly could, and it smacked him directly in the side of his head, sending him careering into the corner of the room. Without wasting time, I dragged Nathaniel to his feet and walked him out of the room before I slammed the bunker door behind me. I watched the keypad turn from green to red, and I heard immediate banging from the other side.

"No!" Alex roared. "I'm the only one who ever loved him!"

The raucous, manic banging intensified as I desperately began to help Nathaniel up the stairs, and he deliriously groaned with every step as the blood ran down his legs and onto the stone below. Alex had left his study door unlocked, and we busted through it, running straight through to the front door to find Stacey standing outside looking perplexed.

"Jesus Christ! Do any of you Yanks ever answer the door? I've been out here ages," she said before noticing what was happening in front of her.

"Where's Aurora?" I feverishly shouted.

"In the car, what's happening?"

I looked past Stacey to see Aurora standing up in the passenger seat, trying to see what was going on. The panic that was gripping me slowly started to ease off, and I realised what I needed to do.

"Can you get Nathaniel to a hospital and ring Aldrich on the way? I have something to do," I asked.

"What?" Nath wearily asked.

"I need to speak to him, and don't try to stop me," I matter-of-factly announced.

"Olivia, wait," he mumbled.

"What is it?"

"I love you," he whispered.

"I love you, too."

"Come on, let's get you patched up before you bleed out," Stacey said.

I watched them walk over to the car and get inside before I rushed back into Alex's house and made my way down to the bunker door. I took a deep breath, then melodically tapped on the steel with my knuckles.

"Are you listening?" I softly asked.

"Yes," he uttered in a huff.

"You took away ten years of my life. You stole a decade of watching my daughter grow up. You robbed me of both my dignity and sanity. You ripped my daughter's innocence away from her and destroyed the love of my life. There isn't a single conceivable punishment that could possibly make up for the evil you've done."

"What are you going to do about that?" Alex mumbled.

"I was going to slam that door behind you and watch you rot in there like you did to me. I wanted to plague your every waking thought until the intense guilt was so powerful that you took that pistol you are holding, pressed it against your temple, and wilfully pulled the trigger."

"You know you haven't got it in you, don't you, Olivia?" he mocked.

I manically laughed as I rhythmically slammed my hands against the door.

"You're right because I'm not like you. I've just seen my daughter outside, and when I looked into her eyes, everything became crystal clear."

"What?" he asked fearfully.

"I'm going to make it my mission to ensure that you are locked away for the rest of your worthless life and rot in prison. You're going to be shitting in a bucket for the rest of your miserable existence, and I will be free, living my best life, loving and being loved."

Alex remained silent.

"Do you still have the pistol?"

"Yes," he mumbled.

"The FBI are on their way. You have a few minutes if you want to take the coward's way out."

I intended to leave on that note, but I couldn't help myself.

"Sleep tight," I whispered, "don't let the bedbugs bite."

As I turned around and slowly sauntered up the steps with a deep sense of relief and satisfaction, the FBI vehicles had already started arriving. The red and blue lights danced down the polished concrete of the steps, and the armed agents pushed past me as I reached the top.

"The combination is 2123, boys," I shouted.

With a nod, the lead agent tapped in the number, and I saw Alex on his knees, with the pistol hysterically lodged into his mouth but clearly too chickenshit to pull the trigger. They quickly wrestled it off him, and I savoured every emotion on his face as they pinned him to the ground and forcefully put the handcuffs on him. Before I walked out of that house for good, I waited for him to make eye contact with me through the mass of agents swarming around him, and once he did, I smirked and gave him a taunting wave.

The nightmare was finally over.

EPILOGUE

AURORA – 2025

London was okay. I mean, the weather was shit, all my friends were back in California, but I agreed when Mum and Dad said we needed a fresh start. To my parents' delight, I decided to kick the weed and finally follow in Dad's footsteps by enrolling in art school. Mom wanted to keep me close after everything that happened, so I chose not to fly the nest and live at home so we could get to know each other again. We both thought forming a bond would be a struggle, but to be honest, it was much easier than we anticipated as it came naturally. It turns out that even though we were separated for more than half my life, we were far more alike than we first realised.

Even though we moved five thousand miles away, I packed my lingering nicotine addiction with me, and I was just about to light a secret cigarette when Mom came out of the church doors, catching me red-handed.

"Mom, it's nothing. It's a special occasion!" I pre-emptively argued.

"Can I bum a ciggy?" Mom asked with a cheeky smile.

"*Bum a ciggy?* What does that even mean?" I laughed.

"Jesus, fine. May you, perchance, have a spare cigarette you could gladly furnish me with?" she said in a posh voice.

"Much better," I replied as I handed her one.

"This is weird, isn't it? Dad and I getting married, I mean," she asked.

"It's long overdue if you ask me."

"Yeah, you're right," she pensively replied with a smile in between drags.

"How's Dad? Is he a jabbering wreck yet?"

"No idea. It's bad luck seeing the bride before a wedding; I'm not making that mistake again."

"Shall I go and check on him?"

"Not yet. Keep me company for a while."

We both sat down on the church steps and gleefully nodded at the passersby, who sent congratulatory smiles our way as we finished our cigarettes. Mom stubbed hers out on the steps before it was finished and lovingly put her arm around me, pulling me in tightly.

"I love you, Aurora," she beamed.

"I love you too, Mom," I smiled.

"I can't believe we finally made it here. It was touch and go there for a while.

"Are you worried he might come back for you and Dad if he ever broke out of prison?" I asked.

"Who?"

"Uncle Alex."

"It's just Alex," she firmly corrected.

"Sorry, force of habit."

"I doubt it, as he is locked in a maximum-security prison for life. I still think about him from time to time, though, and what he did to us, but don't you worry, love, because he won't hurt us anymore."

"That's reassuring to know."

"Do you still think about Stephanie?" she asked.

"Sometimes. I miss the good parts, but I have to remind myself that all of it was a pack of lies."

"I'm sure it wasn't all lies."

We both heard a car backfiring down the street, and as we stared down it, we saw the hot-pink convertible speeding towards us. Mom let out an incredulous laugh as it approached, and it was only when it parked directly in front of the church that I realised it was Auntie Stacey.

"Stacey, you've got to be fucking kidding me," Mom jovially chastised.

"What?" Stacey shouted from the car window.

"Well, for one, you are massively late, and two, what the hell is this car?"

"One, I had to drop the kids off at Mum's, and two, I loved it so much that I decided to get one when we got back."

"Unbelievable," Mum mused.

"Hi, Aurora," Stacey grinned as she strutted out of the car.

"Hello, Auntie Stacey. I love your dress," I beamed.

"Thank you, darling," Stacey said with a little twirl.

"Sweetheart, can you go in and check if Dad's not having a panic attack? I need to have a catch-up with this reprobate," Mum asked.

"Sure," I replied as I skipped through the church doors.

The churches in England were so old and weird that the musty smell turned my stomach the minute I walked inside to see how Dad was faring. I was expecting him to be standing by the altar, but instead, he was standing directly in the lobby, and I nearly bumped straight into him, knocking him clean off his feet.

"Dad, shouldn't you be waiting inside?" I asked.

"Do I look okay?" he calmly asked.

"You look fine, Dad. Very presentable," I mustered.

"How's Mum? Is she a bundle of nerves?"

"Not really, she's just outside with Auntie Stacey."

"That's good."

"Are you nervous?"

"No, why?" he confusedly asked.

"No reason. Are you ready?" I smiled.

"I was born ready," he joked.

"I'll go and get her, then."

"We'll both go," he grinned.

"You can't see the bride before the wedding. It's bad luck!" I sternly gasped.

"Honey, we've had enough bad luck to last ten lifetimes. Come on, let's go get her," he said before pushing the doors open.

We joyously sauntered out of the church doors to find Mom and Stacey enjoying another cigarette together. Mom tried desperately to discard it before Dad saw her, but he had already witnessed it, which prompted a knowing smile on his face.

"Mom?" I sternly prompted.

"Oops!" she mischievously replied.

"I hope you brought some gum," Dad warned.

"Why, are you planning on kissing me?" Mom swooned.

"Maybe," he flirtatiously replied.

"Guys, gross!" I exclaimed.

"I thought it was bad luck to see the bride before the wedding?" Mom asked provokingly.

"What can I say? I'm unconventional," Dad declared.

Dad merrily walked over to Mom, tenderly placed both of his hands on her cheeks, and pulled her in for a kiss, which elicited an excitable whoop from Stacey. The last time they tried to get married, it was the single most traumatic thing that ever happened to me. Despite it all, with every day that we drifted further away from that engulfing darkness, I witnessed my parents fall in love all over again, and the old wounds started to heal. I could feel our family becoming the truly wonderful thing they always envisioned it to be.

Their undying love had endured unspeakable things, and no one could be blamed for thinking it was doomed to fail. As corny as it sounds, I felt infinitely privileged to witness it unfold, and I was eternally grateful that, in the end, everything thankfully returned to how it should have been.

Just as we were all about to walk into the church, a large white van screeched to a halt on the other side of the road. We all turned around, and a small, weather-beaten delivery driver hopped out, holding a crudely wrapped package.

"You must be Olivia Lakewell?" he hesitantly reckoned.

"I am," Mom announced with some trepidation.

"I have a package for you," he said as he handed her the package before getting back in the van and driving away.

"Mom, what is it?" I asked bemusedly.

She gawped down at the package and nervously tore through the brown paper. Inside, there was a filthy wedding dress that had been painstakingly bundled up in blood-red string with a note attached. On seeing the contents, Dad covered his mouth and recoiled in horror as Mom unfolded the piece of paper with trembling hands. In a matter of seconds, Mom's expression went from slight bewilderment to total terror as she read the note to herself in silence. Suddenly, the blushing bride lost all colour on her face and became white as a sheet. She frantically started swivelling her head left and right as though she was straining her eyes to zero in on someone watching us unbidden from afar.

"What does it say, Mom?" I trepidatiously asked.

Mom stared at me blankly and took a deep breath before calmly walking over to a nearby trashcan to stuff the whole contents of the package into it.

"Nothing," she replied, tearfully forcing a smile. "Are you ready to get married, husband?" she abruptly asked with a chirpy grin.

"Ready as I'll ever be," he said with a knowing nod.

"Well, *fuck*, here we go!" she excitedly announced as we all made our way into the church.

PHILIP ANTHONY SMITH

HUNGRY FOR MORE?

Did you know that you can get a free digital copy of my debut psychological thriller, "Run For Your Life," on my website? All you need to read it is a mobile phone, tablet, or even an Amazon Kindle if you're feeling fancy!

Visit **philipanthonysmith.com** for more information!

MORE FROM THE AUTHOR

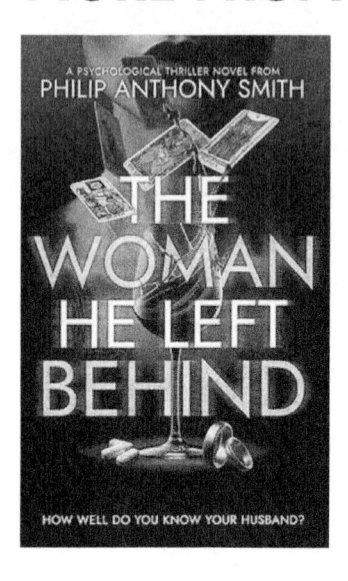

ACKNOWLEDGEMENTS

When I first got the sudden, uncontrollable urge to write a book, I never thought I would finish it, and I never dreamed that anyone would actually read the thing! Then again, here you are, skimming the acknowledgements page of my fourth novel. My first acknowledgement is to *you,* the reader who made it this far. You are the reason authors do what they do, and I sincerely hope that you enjoyed the ride! If you truly enjoyed this book and you have five minutes to spare, I would love to read a review from you on the platform of your choice. Don't forget to tag me in your post if it's on social media!

To Lindsey, my amazing wife, how you put up with my insufferable book musings is beyond me, and I'm incredibly lucky to have someone like you to share my life with.

To my good friend, Domingo Alvarez, once again, your discerning eye and voracious desire for perfection have made this novel immeasurably better. Your devotion and command of the English language are second to none, and I thank you for spending your precious time unstintingly improving my humble book.

THE FORGOTTEN BRIDE

Last but certainly not least is the long list of incredible bookstagrammers who, against the clock, managed to read this book before its release and post their review. I really mean this when I say it: if I didn't have your support, I probably wouldn't have carried on writing, and I'm eternally grateful for it.

Alexandra @maxi.mumbooks
Amy @mooreads_
Anna @annamulreads
Ben @bookstarreviews_
Bethanie @bethanies_bookshelf
Caroline @caz.readz
Charlotte @booksandacrochethook
Crystal @welcome.tomy.library
Darcy @darcyinthepages
Denise @Domestic Thrillers Readers Book Club
Emma @emma.reads.thrillers.22
Emma @empalmer09
Gail @gales.tales70
Holly @_fortheloveofbooksx
Jacqueline @the_scorpio_reader
Jen @jen.lifeinbooks
Joanne @joebella_p_reads
Julie @julielovesbooksandpugs
Julie @juliereadzintherockies
Karen @Lovetoread2023
Katie @katies_cosy_reading_corner

PHILIP ANTHONY SMITH

Kelly @little.shropshire.reader
Lisa @lisas_library91
Lou @Lollysbooknook
Rachael @rachaelsreads
Rebekah @bookish_beks
Sakura @sakura_lostinbooks
Sally @sally_stone63
Sam @sams.book.space
Sarah @reading_happy18
Sarah @sarahisreadingagain
Shellie @yorkshire.bookworm
Vanessa @vdkeck
Zoe @northyorkshirereader

Printed in Great Britain
by Amazon